Triads & Turbulence

ONCE UPON A TIME IN
NORTHEASTERN CHINA

Volume 1

By

Kong Ergou

Translated by Stacy Mosher

rinchen
寶仁
典欽
books

ISBN: 978-981-11-8492-5 (paperback)

Rinchen Books 仁欽寶典
15 Phillip Street #08–00
Tan Ean Kiam Building Singapore 048694
Tel : (65)–65323160
Fax : (65)–65323161
Email : rinchenbooks@gmail.com

Cover Illustration by cheriefox

Table of Contents

Translator's Note

Kong Ergou's novel is a depiction of a specific time and place: northern China in the last half of the 1980s. These were the prime years of Deng Xiaoping's Reform and Opening policy, when China was opening to the outside world and individuals were breaking off from the collective and finding a new place in Chinese society. Although inconvenient for a Chinese author to mention, these were also the years when popular discontent with corruption and yearnings for democracy gradually led to mass protests culminating in the violent official crackdown in June 1989, which sent China off in a new direction.

In depicting this milieu, Kong Ergou's novel includes frequent references to popular culture. Writing twenty years after the events in this book, the narrator Ergou reflects the eventual influence of Hong Kong culture on urban mainland China, mainly through comic books, the martial arts 武侠 (*wuxia*) novels of Louis Cha 金庸 (writing as Jin Yong) and the movies and television series based on them – TV series like *The Bund* 上海滩, set in Shanghai's gang world in the 1920s, and gangster films by directors like John Woo 吴宇森, all depicting a romanticized version of the underworld, past and present. Japanese culture imprinted itself on a generation of Chinese youth through electronic games and *manga* depicting the traditions of *samurai* and *ronin*. The protagonists of this book, however, still live in a world of strict film embargoes and without access even to television and video tapes, much less to the eventually ubiquitous video compact disc (VCD) and DVD players and pirated films from Hong Kong and further afield. Their cultural influences are pop songs, pulp *kungfu* novels and the occasional *kungfu* movie, as well as classical novels like *The Water Margin* 水浒传 and traditional tales of ghosts and fox fairies.

I believe that readers can enjoy this novel without understanding all these cultural references, so I've chosen to let them stand without the annoyance of footnotes or elaboration that would be as counterproductive as a drawn-out explanation of the punchline to a joke. Rather, I've used English versions of names and titles that can be looked up on Google, Wikipedia, or imdb.com by readers who desire a deeper understanding of the popular culture of this period.

Finally, for readers who are fond of "old media" and who wish to better understand the traditional roots of China's modern underworld, I recommend *The Chinese Knight-Errant*, by James J. Y. Liu (Routledge & Kegan Paul Ltd, 1967), which is sadly out of print. Its passage on "Knights-errant and Mohists" (pp. 10-12) is echoed at the end of this novel:

> The knights-errant and the Mohists, the followers of Mo Tzu 墨子, whose life span fell between 479 and 381 B.C. and who preached universal love, obviously had much in common. Indeed, it has been suggested by Professor Feng Yu-lan that the Mohists originated from the knights-errant. His theory may be summarized as

follows. After the collapse of aristocratic government about the time of Confucius (551-479 B.C.), a new class of professional men came into being, known as the *shih* 士. At first this word simply meant any man of special talent or skill, and such men were kept by the aristocracy. After they lost their employment, they became what we may call free lances. Those who specialized in ritual, music and education were the 'scholars' (*ju*), of whom Confucius was one, and their moral code developed into Confucianism (*Ju-chia,* literally, 'scholasticism'). Those who specialized in warfare were the knights 侠 (*hsia*), and their moral code developed into Mohism 墨派. Both were inspired by an altruistic spirit and a strong sense of justice, and both acted on a universalistic principle, as against the Confucian principle of degrees of love and duty. Both belittled wealth and shared what they had. Both were absolutely truthful and trustworthy.

On the other hand, there are considerable differences between the two…The Mohists led an austere and disciplined life; the knights-errant were often free and easy. The Mohists were a highly-organized body of men, whose leader had the authority of life and death over the members; the knights-errant were only loosely associated on a voluntary basis. The Mohists, though they helped weak states in self-defense, were against fighting in principle; the knights were always ready for a fight. Basically, the Mohists were concerned with political and social equity, but the knights-errant were only concerned with personal justice.

Preface

Exploring Society and Human Nature

I once read an essay by an Englishman entitled "China, Land of a Thousand Identical Cities," a sentiment I heartily endorse. Most of China's cities were rebuilt from the post-war rubble under the historical circumstances and policies of New China, and have followed similar patterns of development. This development process has typically involved the growth of criminal gangs, which, like their host cities, share many similarities. It's safe to assume that criminal gangs – like Tangshan's notorious Cleaver Squad – emerged in most of these one thousand identical cities in the 1980s, along with hooligan bands consisting largely of the sons of employees of massive state-owned factories. The 1990s saw the emergence of many "debt collection agencies" of dubious background.

I grew up in a city in northern China with a population of less than one million, and worked my way into the hard-won comfort of a white-collar existence in Shanghai. I was never involved in the criminal underworld, but an old family friend has been my hometown's generally-acknowledged "Big

Brother" for 20 years, and I personally witnessed much of his tumultuous rise in the gang world.

I haven't written this book with the intention of luring readers into a life of crime; I'm sure that eighty percent of the people who finish this book will vow never to have anything to do with the criminal underworld, and I hope that some who are currently involved in the underworld, perhaps even some "big brothers", will scale back their violence after reading it. This novel may turn out to be very long, perhaps as many as a million words. Although it focuses on the hooligans and criminal underworld in my hometown over the past twenty-odd years, I hope readers will see more in it than this. I hope they will see what has happened and what has changed in our country and our society over the past two decades, and how our spiritual and material existence has been transformed.

The things I'm exploring are society and human nature.

While visiting this book's protagonist during Spring Festival last year, I came across a photo album that could be called a living encyclopedia of the underworld. It stirred up many feelings in me. Two things were consistent in all of the photos: this Big Brother always sat in the center, and everyone in the photos wore dazzling smiles. Three things changed as the album progressed. The people in the photos were different from year to year, with some in prison, on the run, recovering in a hospital, or permanently disabled. I found that the further into the album I flipped, the more complicated the expressions in their eyes became, even though they wore the same cheerful smiles. From polyester Mao jackets to woolen versions and then to white ones, and from white shirts and crimson ties to black suits and black ties, they became increasingly fastidious about their attire. The album presented an evolutionary history of the Chinese male wardrobe.

I knew most of the people in the album and what had become of them. Seeing some of them made me weep, while others aroused my pity and still others my disgust. That's when I decided to write this book.

I plan to write this novel in four parts covering the past twenty-odd years. The present volume covers events before the 1990s, because I feel that back then, hoodlums had a kind of purity and chivalry; they fought each other out of a sense of honor and justice rather than for fame and wealth. The second volume covers events from 1990 to 1996, because I feel that at this point, the world-views of many gangsters shifted toward crass materialism. The third part covers events from 1997 to 2000, when gangs acquired the qualities of genuine organized crime syndicates. The fourth part covers events from 2000 to the present.

The text that follows will be narrated through the eyes of several young people of the 1980s. The story involves joy and sorrow, coming together and breaking apart. Because, in the end, aren't these the things that constitute our lives?

In the story that follows, Ergou is me, and I am Ergou.

Prologue

A Boy's Unnatural Death

This prologue relates a story that is only loosely related to the novel that follows, in honor of a classmate who passed away twelve years ago.

On Christmas Day 2007, when Ergou was on his way to Times Square on Huaihai Road to have dinner with some friends, he saw a five-story purple Christmas tree at the entrance to the square. His heart quaked in recognition. More than ten years earlier, a classmate – a simple, decent boy – had given Ergou a greeting card imprinted with the image of an identical Christmas tree. Soon after, he had met with an unhappy fate. Ergou had kept that card all these years.

Back then, Ergou was in eighth grade. He was a member of his class's study committee and the English class monitor. Eighth grade had just begun when a new student with a very odd surname was transferred in. The other students didn't know how to pronounce his surname, and even the teachers were unfamiliar with it, so they just called him by his given name, Guanghui. Guanghui had just moved to the city from a rural village. His father worked on a construction site and his mother earned money at home knitting sweaters. Guanghui was an only child, and at seventeen was older than the rest of his class by two or three years. His parents had gone through a lot to get him into an urban middle school.

Guanghui was a simple and honest boy, guileless and eager to help others. He resembled the boy Runtu in Lu Xun's story "My Old Home." Because he had just arrived from the countryside, his clothing was shabby and worn. He studied hard at school, but never really excelled, and his English was so poor that nobody understood him. The head teacher had him share a desk with the girl whose English was the best, and who had previously been Ergou's desk mate. The girl despised Guanghui's shabby appearance and refused to talk with him, hardly even sparing him a glance, so whenever he had a question, Guanghui usually turned around and asked Ergou. When Ergou was small, his parents had taken him to stay with his grandmother in the countryside, so he had nothing against Guanghui. In fact, he thought he was great, and was happy to answer his questions.

Over time, Ergou and Guanghui became good friends, and Ergou often gave Guanghui a ride on his bicycle to and from school. Guanghui couldn't afford a bike of his own. Back then, in 1994 and 1995, bicycles were a luxury. Ergou's family was rather comfortably off, and his parents had bought him a "racing bike" with different speeds when he reached seventh grade. Ergou still remembers that bicycle; it was red and cost 1,100 *kuai*, and was the first "racing bike" owned by anyone in his middle school.

Guanghui and Ergou's homes lay in the same direction, so Ergou could take Guanghui part of the way. Since other classmates looked down on Guanghui, he felt deeply indebted to Ergou. When he learned that Ergou's parents were too busy to make breakfast, he started bringing Ergou one of his mother's home-made sesame pancakes every morning. Ergou still remembers the taste of Guanghui's mother's delicious pancakes – soft and spongy inside with a crispy exterior.

The incident related here occurred the winter after Guanghui arrived at Ergou's school.

Physical education class in winter usually consisted of free activities, and the most popular sport at the time was badminton. On that particular day, a girl student hit the shuttlecock onto the eaves of the sports equipment shed outside the school. The shed was about eight feet high, and none of the students was tall enough to climb onto it. At that time, the school had only one shuttlecock, so everyone was anxious to retrieve it.

Guanghui came forward in his usual helpful way and said, "Let me try."

The other students became excited. Someone offered to boost Guanghui up on his shoulders, but Guanghui smiled and said it was unnecessary. We watched as Guanghui backed up a dozen paces, then with a running leap landed his foot on the window sill, propelling himself upward until his left hand grasped the wide ledge beneath the roof of the shed. With a burst of strength, he reached his right hand onto the roof and then swung himself high enough for his left hand to knock the shuttlecock off the roof. He then reversed the process to land safe and sound on the ground.

What a display! He had done all of this with such effortless agility that his classmates could only look on in mute wonder. It was like watching a masked marauder in the movies. His classmates were amazed, as was the section head for that grade, Mr. Wang, and Ergou's head teacher and English teacher, Ms. Feng, who were passing by at the time.

"What was that?" said Section Head Wang in a tone of voice that could have been admiring or critical.

Assuming the latter, Ms. Feng shouted, "That's very dangerous! Don't go up there again! If you do, I'll call your parents. I never knew you were such a rascal."

Bowing his head, Guanghui said, "I won't do it again, Ms. Feng."

Nodding, Ms. Feng and Section Head Wang walked off.

Not five minutes after they left, another classmate, Han Qian, hit the shuttlecock back onto the roof of the equipment room. There was still a quarter of an hour of Phys Ed left. Han Qian wanted to keep playing badminton, but he couldn't get onto the roof. Short and stout, Han was a good student, but he had an overbearing attitude because his cousin, Han Bing, was the middle school's top dog.

Han Qian smiled at Guanghui and said, "Help me get the shuttlecock down, will you?"

"Ms. Feng doesn't want me going up there," Guanghui said. "You heard what she said."

"Don't worry," said Han Qian. "She's gone."

"I'm not going up there. If I do, I'll get in trouble," said Guanghui.

Ergou knew that Guanghui treasured his hard-won opportunity to study in an urban school, and feared getting in trouble with the teachers more than anything.

"Damn it, are you going up there or not?" demanded Han Qian, who had always looked down on Guanghui.

"No, I'm not!" said Guanghui.

"If you don't, I'll whip you!" said Han Qian, enraged.

"Go ahead. I still won't," said Guanghui.

He had barely finished speaking when Han Qian charged at him and punched him in the face. Guanghui was too well-behaved to hit back.

"Are you going up there or not?" demanded Han Qian, even more aggressively when he saw that Guanghui wouldn't fight back.

"Why did you hit me?" Guanghui cried. "I'm not going up!"

Han Qian aimed a kick at Guanghui, but Guanghui ducked and at the same time reached out and flung Han Qian's leg backward, sending him tumbling. There was snow on the ground that day, making Han Qian's fall even more awkward. The other students hooted with laughter.

His rage fueled by embarrassment, Han Qian leapt up and began tussling with Guanghui, who by now was also provoked. The two began raining blows on each other. Most of the class just looked on. Whenever someone intervened, it was usually on Han Qian's side. Ergou tried to pull them apart, but the two boys were battling too fiercely.

Just then, Ms. Feng rushed over and bellowed, "Stop fighting!"

All of the middle school students feared their teachers. As soon as they heard the head teacher yell, the two boys stopped fighting.

At this point it was clear that even with others helping him, Han Qian had come off worse. His nose was smashed and blood covered his face, while Guanghui seemed barely to have been touched.

"Both of you! Come to my office!" cried Ms. Feng.

Guanghui and Han Qian followed her, heads bowed.

Phys Ed class ended ten minutes later. As the English class monitor, Ergou went to Ms. Feng's office to collect the homework. As soon as he entered the office, he saw Guanghui sitting alone; Han Qian had been sent to the school clinic for his nosebleed.

"Guanghui, why were you fighting?" Ms. Feng started out.

"Han Qian hit me!"

"He hit you? Why you and not someone else?" Ms. Feng demanded.

Inarticulate at the best of times, Guanghui was speechless in the face of Ms. Feng's shrewish fulmination.

In his three years at middle school, Ergou had heard this teacher "settle a case" on countless occasions. "Why did he hit you and not someone else" seemed to be her classic, most plausible and most unanswerable question. In the eleven years that Ergou spent in elementary school, middle school, and high school, he encountered many thoroughly unreasonable teachers like Ms. Feng.

If she had sincerely listened to Guanghui's explanation instead of treating him the same as Han Qian, the subsequent events might never have occurred.

That afternoon, after the kangaroo court in Ms. Feng's office, Han Qian muttered to Guanghui, "Just you wait!"

After school, Ergou gave Guanghui a ride home as always. Around 200 yards from the school, they were surrounded by Han Qian and several others, including Han Qian's cousin Han Bing, whom Han Qian had obviously called in to avenge him.

"Go away, Ergou," said Han Qian. "This is nothing to do with you."

But Ergou tried to smooth things over.

"Are you planning to beat up Guanghui?" he asked. "He's your classmate. Why do you want to beat him?"

"Stay out of it, Ergou," barked Han Qian. "I need to set him straight."

"Well, I'm here, and you're both my classmates. Neither of you is going to do any hitting," Ergou said.

Ergou knew that while Han Qian might try to bully Guanghui, he would never try it on Ergou. Although Ergou was a well-behaved fellow who never got into fights, everyone knew that his closest childhood friend was Zhao Xiaobo – the nephew of a top gangster, Zhao Hongbing, and a well-known hoodlum. Zhao Hongbing had been like a father to Ergou, and the two were very close. Neither Han Qian nor Han Bing would even think of laying a finger on Ergou.

Even still, Han Qian clearly had no intention of listening.

"Get lost, Ergou. I'm going to whip him, no matter what!"

Han Bing moved first, pulling Guanghui off the bicycle. Then, he and the others pounced on him, punching and kicking at his head. They were wearing the army boots that were all the rage at the time, and their kicks landed hard.

In a panic, Ergou threw down his bike and tried to break up the fight, but there were at least three people beating on Guanghui. Ergou found it impossible to pull them off.

Just then, seven or eight schoolmates were passing by. They dropped their bikes and ran over to break things up. Some were girls. When Han Qian and the others saw them join in, they were too ashamed to keep going. They let up on Guanghui.

Guanghui, his face covered with blood, launched himself like a tiger at Han Bing; his fist made contact and knocked out Han Bing's front tooth. This simple and honest country boy had finally been driven into a fury. His own rage inflamed by pain, Han Bing reached out and yanked Guanghui's hair. By then, Ergou and the other students were standing in front of Guanghui, shielding him.

"If you want to hit him, you'll have to hit me," Ergou said. "Do you want me to have Xiaobo come and reason with you? If you think Xiaobo isn't good enough, I'll have Hongbing come instead!"

Ergou rarely mentioned his relationship with these ne'er-do-wells, but the other students knew that Zhao Xiaobo often came to the school looking for Ergou, and that Zhao Hongbing had fetched Ergou from school in his car several times.

"This isn't over," Han Bing muttered, stalking off with Han Qian and the others.

Guanghui didn't want to go straight home and have his family see he'd been beaten, so he stopped at Ergou's home to wash up.

"Han Qian and those guys went too far," Ergou said. "Why did they have to beat you up?"

"I think they'll come for me again," said Guanghui anxiously.

"They won't. But if they do, I'll take Zhao Xiaobo over to talk to Han Bing. That'll be the end of it."

Ergou didn't take the matter too seriously, and this became the greatest regret of his life. If he'd gone to see Zhao Xiaobo or Zhao Hongbing that night, the subsequent events would never have happened.

It wasn't out of laziness that Ergou didn't go. It was because, first, he didn't believe Han Bing would retaliate. When he'd said, "This isn't over," Ergou thought it was just bluster.

Second, although Zhao Xiaobo had been his best pal since childhood and was his father's godson, Ergou avoided having too much contact with people like him. Not least, Zhao Xiaobo was ruthless and heavy-handed; if he were brought into this, it would end with Han Bing being beaten to a pulp. Then Han Bing would report it to the school, and Ergou would be disciplined. Ergou had a mortal fear of getting into trouble.

Early the next day after the fight, Ergou noticed that Guanghui was carrying a fruit knife. It had a yellow handle and a very long, sharp blade that gleamed in the sunlight. Guanghui had stuck it into his belt.

"Why are you bringing a knife to school?" Ergou felt compelled to ask after second period, as the class went out for morning exercises.

"For self-defense," said Guanghui with his usual honest smile.

"Are you crazy?" Ergou said. "Stick it in your book bag, quick!"

"I fibbed to my parents and asked for five *kuai*," said Guanghui. "I bought this knife for 2.60, and got this for you." He handed Ergou a huge greeting card.

In those days, most greeting cards were very small, but this one was letter size. On it was printed a large, purple Christmas tree. Unlike ordinary greeting cards, this one was sprinkled with glittery stars. It was clearly top quality. Ergou had received maybe twenty cards in his life, and this was by far the grandest. He knew it must have cost at least 2 *kuai*. Usually Guanghui was reluctant to spend even 10 cents on cotton candy, and for him to spend so much on a card moved Ergou very much. To this day, Ergou remembers what was written in it: "As long as swans may soar, may you reach the heights with them."

"Thank you, Guanghui," he said.

"Don't mention it."

"Go ahead. I'm on duty in the classroom today, so I'm not going out for exercise."

"Lucky you. Okay, see you later."

These were the last words Guanghui ever spoke to Ergou.

He didn't go out for exercise, so he didn't see exactly what happened. An eyewitness described it to him: After the morning exercises finished, Han Bing and his classmates went over to Guanghui. They hauled him behind the school building and beat him up. While he was being beaten, Guanghui pulled out his yellow-handled fruit knife. With his hair pulled so his head was bent down toward his waist, Guanghui couldn't see who was in front of him. He just slashed out in a frenzy. The person he stabbed was Han Bing. He stabbed him six times, and each stroke was deadly. The others who had ganged up on Guanghui scattered in every direction.

Afterward, the school police took Guanghui away. Twenty minutes later, the news came back that Han Bing had died in hospital. Ergou's deepest impression was of Han Bing's mother – a middle-aged woman, whose graying hair made her look much older. Her anguished keening echoed in Ergou's ears. "Give me back my son!" she screamed, her cracked and calloused hands grabbing the collar of Ms. Feng's shirt as she ran into the room.

"You boy was killed by a student, not by me," said Ms. Feng, shrewish as ever.

"Give me back my son!" howled Han Bing's mother, who by then was out of her senses and hoarse from repeating those words.

"If you don't let go, I'm calling the school guards!" said Ms. Feng in a towering rage.

"Give – me – back – my – son!" Too weak to even cry out any more, Han Bing's mother was frozen in place.

"Let go, I tell you!" Ms. Feng tore away the hands that gripped her collar and stalked out of the room. Han Bing's mother lay on the podium sobbing until some girls went over and helped her out of the room.

When Han Bing's mother entered the classroom, Ergou recognized her as the old lady who sold melon seeds in front of the Railway Workers' Cultural Palace. He had always thought she must be at least fifty years old, and had never guessed she had a son who was only fifteen. He later learned that Han Bing's father had died young. As his mother was basically uneducated, she could only eke out a living from her little stall in front of the Cultural Palace, selling melon seeds for 30 or 50 cents to pay for Han Bing's schoolbooks. Han Bing had been all she had to live for. Now he was dead.

After that, Ergou no longer saw Han Bing's mother plying her trade. It was not until the Dragon Boat Festival three years later, when he was in his last year of high school and was riding his bicycle to the East Wind Movie Theater, that he once again saw the woman sitting on the roadside. Her hair white and matted, her face wrinkled; she looked very old and frail. Her hand clutched a wooden stick from which hung folded paper gourds. It was customary in these parts to hang these colorful gourds in the windows of homes as good luck charms during the Dragon Boat Festival.

"How much are these, Auntie?" Ergou asked, stopping his bike.

"One *kuai* each," said Han Bing's mother, eyes lowered.

"I'll buy them all." Ergou took out the ten *kuai* his mother had given him for lunch and bought the seven paper gourds.

"Son, here's your change," said Han Bing's mother, handing him three *kuai* with a faint smile on her lips.

Ergou took the gourds and got back on his bike, his heart heavy. Of course, Han Bing had been wrong to pick on Guanghui, but did he deserve to lose his life? Was it really worth dying in the prime of his youth over such a trifling matter? And what about Guanghui? This country boy with the goofy smile had become a murderer before the age of sixteen. Seven months later he'd been beaten to death by his fellow prisoners. He had outlived Han Bing by only seven months, likewise paying for this incident with his life.

The world was funny that way. Some hooligans spent the first half of their lives beating and killing and were still hale and hearty at fifty years old, while others died in their very first fight.

Two young lives had withered and fallen like blossoms. One became known among the students as the biggest hooligan in the hundred-year history of the school, the "notorious" Guanghui. That simple, honest boy who had always said, "Ergou, would you like a pancake? My mom made it."

Ergou's heart ached as he wept.

But what does this incident mean? That those who deserve to die live on, and those who don't deserve it die young. Can this be fate? When someone does something wrong, often those who suffer the most for it are their parents or others who loved them. And people who are good, or who were once good, are often perceived by others as irredeemable scoundrels. When people go bad, other apparently upstanding people should bear some of the blame.

In the story that follows, we'll meet some veteran soldiers who fought bloody battles, protecting their country's territory and the safety of its people on the mountainous Laoshan frontline on China's southern border, spending their youth in damp air-raid shelters, mustering their courage against the thundering cannon fire of the Vietnamese. Then, years after being demobilized, they turned their striking knives and double-barreled shotguns on the countrymen they'd risked their lives to protect. Just like Guanghui.

Part One

Demobilized

CHAPTER 1

Zhao Hongbing and His Comrades-in-arms

SHORTLY BEFORE SPRING FESTIVAL IN 1985, Kong Ergou came to the end of his three-year education by peasants in his grandmother's village, and boarded a Jeep that took him back to the city. The first real events of his life could be said to have started that day.

It was only years later that he realized his rural exile was the result of the substandard living quarters assigned by his father's work unit. Drafty in winter and leaking rain all summer, the quarters were unsuitable for raising a child. So, as soon as Ergou was weaned, he was sent to the countryside to live with his grandma. In 1985, the factory allocated new housing to workers of departmental grade or above, providing each of these seven families with a two-story stand-alone unit within the factory compound. Ergou's father was promoted just in time to be allocated one of these units, and he immediately sent for his son. It was a neighbor in this compound who exposed Ergou to the kind of violence that dutiful individuals like himself would normally never hear of, or even imagine.

The first person Ergou met on his return to the city was Mr. Zhao. After winding through the city's streets, the Jeep finally stopped outside a row of two-story houses. Ergou's father opened the first door to the courtyard, and then went eagerly to open the second door to the house. However, it was stuck. Perspiration streamed down his face as he tried to force it.

The weather was cold. Missing his grandma, Ergou began to cry. He had just started sniveling when he heard a thundering voice from the neighboring courtyard: "Xiao Kong! What's going on?" Ergou had never heard such bellowing. More than twenty years later he still recalls it as the manliest voice he ever heard. It startled him out of his weeping just as his father replied, "Director Zhao! The door is jammed."

More noise from the neighboring courtyard – the sound of laughter. Even his laughter was impressive.

"Let me have a look."

Through the outer door came a man in his fifties wearing a dark blue woolen Mao jacket. His back was ramrod straight, and his resolute face was unlined but for a deep crease running down each side of his mouth. His eyes gleamed with vigor and were crowned with the thick, black eyebrows of a man of character. Without saying anything to Ergou's father, the old man walked straight over to the boy and grabbed him by the cheek, roaring, "Keep crying, bawl calf!" There was not a trace of a smile on his face, and his words hit home. Dumbstruck by the man's sternness, Ergou didn't dare utter another whimper.

While Ergou grew up to be a conscientious, cautious, and decent fellow, he was a very naughty child, prone to howling. One weekend two or three years later, when he was at his mother's office watching television with some other children, one of his mother's colleagues switched the channel from *Captain Kitty*. Ergou was distraught, and howled, "I WANT CAPTAIN KITTY!" Everyone in the office quaked at the sound. In the years that followed, children who had been watching television with Ergou that day often threatened their parents by saying, "Watch out, or I'll yell like Ergou!" The only reason Ergou stopped howling that day was that his mother whispered, "Mr. Zhao is here." At that, the boy fell silent and minded his manners.

Back at the entrance to the house, the old man took the key from Ergou's father and twisted it a couple of times with no result. Knitting his eyebrows wordlessly, he turned and left. Five minutes later he returned with a pencil, a jackknife, and a piece of paper. He began whittling the pencil with the jackknife, creating a little pile of lead filings on the piece of paper. He then picked up the paper, folded it into a funnel, and slowly poured some of the filings into the key hole. Then he picked up the key again and turned it lightly. The door opened.

"There you go!" the older man said with a hearty laugh. "It just needed some lubrication."

"Director Zhao, please come in," said Ergou's father.

They went into the house. Ergou's mother put the kettle on while the boy went exploring. Everything in the house was new to Ergou, and he made several circuits of the upstairs and downstairs areas. It was the first time he'd seen a house that was two stories tall, and the first time he'd seen an electric light.

"I hear Hongbing has been demobilized and is coming home," said Ergou's father.

"That's right," the older man chuckled.

"I hear he was awarded a medal in the war."

"Yes, he did well enough just to come back alive."

"It's been years since we've seen Hongbing," said Ergou's father. "I look forward to having a good chat with him over Spring Festival."

Mr. Zhao turned to leave. "I've held you up long enough. It's time for me to go."

He headed for the door before Ergou's father could urge him to stay.

Before he left, he paused and said, "Xiao Kong, now that you're all together again and we're neighbors, come over for dinner at the Lunar New Year."

It sounded like an order as much as an invitation.

Ergou's father didn't bother to demur. "Alright. We'll be there."

During this brief conversation, Ergou was impressed by the older man's humor, straightforwardness, and commanding presence. Mr. Zhao remained the object of his deepest admiration until the day he died.

Ergou later learned that Mr. Zhao had been transferred to head up the Municipal Organization Department, and would take up his new post after the Spring Festival. Before that, he'd been the head of Ergou's father's work unit, and Ergou's father had been his secretary since graduating from college. The work unit employed many people who had gone to college before the Cultural Revolution disrupted the education system. Among them, Director Zhao held Ergou's father in highest regard. The two men were more like father and son than merely colleagues.

The Hongbing they spoke of was Mr. Zhao's second son, who had just returned from living up to his patriotic name,

"Red Soldier," as a military scout on the Laoshan battlefront. Hongbing had three elder sisters and an elder brother, and their strict upbringing had ensured that they were all law-abiding citizens. Their mother had died during the Cultural Revolution due to her controversial political background. Director Zhao had never remarried. Whenever something bothered him, he spoke to the portrait of his dead wife; the two had clearly been devoted to each other. The older Zhao siblings had already settled elsewhere in the city, leaving only Hongbing and his father in the small two-story house.

Ergou saw Zhao Hongbing the very next day when he went out early in his gloves and cotton army cap to sweep away the snow. Technically, each household was responsible for sweeping the snow in front of their own quarters, but Zhao Hongbing did all seven houses, leaving his own for last. His work was meticulous; the snow piles in front of each house were uniform and evenly spaced. When Hongbing saw Ergou's father take the boy out on his bicycle, he stopped for a moment and set aside his broom, calling out:

"Brother Kong!"

He dashed over to Ergou's father and gave him a bear hug, nearly tipping over the bicycle. Taking off one glove, he pinched Ergou's cheek and asked:

"What's your name?"

When the boy told him, Hongbing laughed and said, "That's a great name."

Ergou studied Zhao Hongbing carefully and noticed large eyes, a high-bridged nose, and the same thick, distinguished eyebrows as his father's. He looked like a handsomer version of the elder Mr. Zhao. His face was slim rather than square – a movie star's face, with the kind of hero's brow that seemed to vanish in China's young men after the 1980s. Ergou liked the look of him, and wanted to be his friend.

"You've filled out, Hongbing," Ergou's father remarked.

"You too, around the middle!"

"Seems you've been through a lot over the last few years."

Zhao Hongbing stood to attention and threw a salute. "Serving the people!"

Ergou and his father laughed.

"I'm taking Ergou to have his hair cut before New Year. If we get there early, we won't have to wait in line. I'll catch up with you when we get back."

"All right," Hongbing said good-naturedly.

As Ergou and his father rode off on the bicycle, Hongbing called after them, "Brother Kong, my dad says you're all coming over for New Year's dinner! We're looking forward to it!"

"Us too!" Ergou's father called back.

The handsome, jovial Zhao Hongbing left a very good impression on Ergou that day; there had been no vigorous young men like him in the production brigade where Ergou's grandmother lived, nor in the rest of the village.

On the afternoon of New Year's Eve, Ergou's family went to Director Zhao's house for dinner. The place was bustling with excitement. Apart from Hongbing, all of Mr. Zhao's children were married. Most of their children had been born around 1980, making them about the same age as Ergou. Ergou forgot how much he missed his grandma as he played with Mr. Zhao's grandchildren downstairs while the grown-ups took their places at the table. As the core member of the family, old Mr. Zhao took the innermost seat, with his children and Ergou's parents in a lively circle around him. The usually taciturn Mr. Zhao was especially cheery and talkative. Accustomed to the role of leader, he cleared his throat to speak a few words before dinner. His children fell silent, laying their chopsticks on the table. The little ones settled down as well.

Mr. Zhao said, "Our city has had an abundant harvest this year. Since the third plenum of the Eleventh Central Committee, living standards have improved. The farmers will live well this year. We have much to celebrate!"

Later, Ergou realized that once a family feast exceeded six people, Mr. Zhao turned it into a "Party Congress"; the old revolutionary never changed his ways.

After his opening remarks, Mr. Zhao paused and said, "The good news for our family is that Hongbing has been honorably discharged. Let's drink a toast to him. Hongbing, you're now old enough to drink at home. But you mustn't drink too much, apart from on New Year."

Everyone raised their glasses and drank down the fiery Wuliangye liquor. The mood grew even warmer. It didn't take long for some of the adults to feel tipsy.

Soon it was time for the children to eat. Having just arrived from the countryside, Ergou didn't know the rules. Sitting at his mother's side, he reached for a pastry. Before he could grab it, there was a cracking sound, and he felt a dash of pain across his knuckles. Mr. Zhao had given him a sharp rap with his chopsticks.

From then on, Ergou understood that he had to eat with chopsticks rather than using his hands, especially when so many people were present. He developed the habit of never putting anything in his mouth without chopsticks. At college, his classmates laughed at him for eating steamed buns with chopsticks instead of grabbing them with his fingers. When he started working, his colleagues ridiculed him for asking the waiter for chopsticks when he ate crayfish. Old Mr. Zhao probably never anticipated the lasting effect of his punishment.

As everyone drank and the mood livened, tongues loosened. Zhao Hongbing was something of a lightweight. Soon he was thoroughly drunk, and began to ramble about fighting the Vietnamese, gesticulating wildly as he spoke.

That's when both Ergou and his father noticed that three of the fingers on Hongbing's right hand were missing the top two joints. The skin over the stumps was well-healed, indicating an old injury.

"Hongbing!" Ergou's father said with surprise. "Your hand..."

Hongbing shrugged. "It was crushed by a rock in a battle."

The mood immediately fell. Zhao Hongbing hated it when people mentioned his injury. During the winter, he wore thick gloves when he went out. Indoors, he kept his hand rolled into a fist to conceal the missing portions of his fingers. He often kept his right hand in his pocket. Although he'd lost his fingers five months earlier, he still found it hard to accept his disability and was too proud to let others see it.

This handsome young man had become known in the city for his talents and kindness by the time he was sixteen or seventeen. He was good at basketball and ping-pong. Coming from a senior cadre household (the elder Mr. Zhao was the director of a provincial deputy department) made him even more popular with girls. Following his demobilization, the rigors of military service lent him a heroic air that made him even more irresistible to women. And yet, he was rendered semi-disabled at the age of twenty-two.

It was Hongbing's pride and his shame over his missing fingers that sparked the tragedy of his subsequent years.

At a New Year's gathering after Ergou was grown, Hongbing told him that he regretted the path he had taken.

Ergou said, "You know, it was your character and your situation after discharge that set you on this road."

Hongbing said, "It could have been different."

"How?"

"If my medical treatment had been a little better, or if the doctors had tried a little harder, they wouldn't have had to amputate my fingers."

Ergou couldn't think of anything to say.

That Lunar New Year's Eve was twenty years after their first New Year's feast together. As before, snowflakes floated outside the window. In those twenty years, Ergou had grown from a callow boy who was just beginning to notice things into a capable young man, while Zhao Hongbing had transformed from a decorated soldier into one of the city's most notorious gang leaders. That day, Ergou was about the same age as Zhao Hongbing had been at their first meeting. The difference was, Ergou at twenty-two was full of hope and promise, while Zhao Hongbing had been filled with despair over his missing fingers.

That year, Zhao Hongbing introduced Ergou to three comrades-in-arms who had been discharged with him – Feisi, Xiaoji, and Lisi. They hadn't fought in the same unit, but they'd been at high school together. They'd joined the army at the same time and enlisted in the same army group. Because the urban enlistment quota was limited, these young men felt a strong connection with each other, even though they'd served in different army units.

Lisi and Zhao Hongbing had both been army scouts, while Feisi and Xiaoji had been artillerymen. All four had fought in the major skirmish at Laoshan in April 1984.

Feisi was tall and powerfully built – a full six feet tall. While far from handsome, he had a manly air. Loud and brimming with energy, he came across as a sincere and honest man. Following his discharge, he'd been assigned a job as a driver for the Industry and Commerce Department, and had started working just before Spring Festival.

Lisi had become an odd-job man for the municipal government. He was thin and dark-complexioned with a high-ridged nose and a slightly hunched back. Hooded eyes gave him the drowsy look of an opium addict, and he was always yawning. Lisi said little, but when he did speak, he got straight to the point.

Xiaoji had been assigned work in a small town about twenty miles from the city. However, he'd declined it and instead opened a recycling stall not far from Zhao Hongbing's home. He took in mainly scrap metal, along with antiques and spare parts stolen from factory machinery. He had a shifty smile that implied he always was up to something.

Although Ergou had begun associating with the four of them at an early age, he only ever knew them by their nicknames. It was only years later, when he saw their verdicts posted outside the courthouse, that he learned their proper names.

Just as the first falling leaf signals autumn, that Spring Festival dinner gave Ergou a glimpse of what was in store for these young men.

Feisi and Xiaoji were the first to arrive at Hongbing's home to pay their respects on the first day of the Lunar New Year. The elder Mr. Zhao had set off early in the morning to exchange greetings at the municipal guesthouse, and Hongbing was left home alone. Back in the 1980s, leisure activities were limited, so during Spring Festival, young people liked to set off fireworks for entertainment. Ergou's city welcomed the God of Wealth with firecrackers first thing in the morning. When Feisi, Xiaoji, and Lisi arrived at Hongbing's home that morning, they put on a real show for the compound's residents.

Feisi had a special method for setting off fireworks, known as the "double-bang". Usually people would place the rocket on the ground, light the fuse, and then run away. But in Ergou's city, the custom had always been more daring, with adults and children holding the fireworks in their hands, pointing them upward and lighting the fuse. The first explosion would send the rocket shooting into the sky, where it would then explode a second time. While dangerous, it only caused a problem if the second explosion occurred too close to the ground.

Feisi achieved his "double-bang" by grasping the rocket firmly in his right hand and pointing it upward, lighting the fuse with this left hand. When the firework exploded for the first time in his hand, he didn't let it go. He held it until about two seconds before it was about to explode. Then, he threw it like a hand grenade, so it went off just fifteen feet in the air with a massive bang. No one dared watch, but Feisi laughed his head off; he seemed to need that jolt of danger. As a former artilleryman, he had nothing to fear from fireworks. Ergou's father gave him a terse appraisal, calling him a "draft animal".

Feisi's method put his daring and unruliness to best effect, while Xiaoji's method demonstrated his violent tendencies. At that time, Hongbing's family owned a German shepherd, which attracted Xiaoji's interest the moment he walked in the door. Hongbing said, "Tie on some firecrackers," and Xiaoji jumped up and attached a string of five hundred firecrackers to the dog's tail. Before the dog knew what was happening, Xiaoji lit the firecrackers. They went off with an extraordinary racket, scaring the dog witless. It began to bark madly, and went running pell-mell around the courtyard. It bolted in a panic up onto the enclosing wall and then onto the roof, where it continued to run about madly. No matter what it did, the poor creature couldn't escape the firecrackers tied to its tail. It circled the roof two or three times before they finally stopped exploding. Even then, the dog was terrified; its legs were trembling. The incident, along with Xiaoji's wild laughter, remained deeply etched in Ergou's memory.

It was just as this time that the elder Mr. Zhao came home from paying his New Year's respects. Opening the door, he was greeted with the sight of his beloved dog running around on the roof with a string of firecrackers tied to its tail. Filled with rage, he walked over to Xiaoji and gave him a kicking. Ergou was impressed that Mr. Zhao knew exactly who had set off the firecrackers. He clearly had the full measure of his son's friends.

It was only Lisi who didn't do anything with firecrackers that day. Ergou initially thought it was because the young man was kinder and less of a trickster than the others, but within five days his impression had completely changed.

On the sixth day of the Lunar New Year, Zhao Hongbing took Ergou and his nephew Zhao Xiaobo to spend some time at Lisi's work unit. It was a local custom for rural folk troupes to dance with pipes and drums in the street, and then go to each work unit to pay their New Year's respects – a pretext for asking for money. That year, five or six groups came with their hands out, and it grew tedious after a while.

Lisi was responsible for handing out the money to the song-and-dance troupes, but he had no patience for this petty extortion. Even though his work unit leader had given him money, he didn't want to give it out. Instead, he took out a bucket used for storing carbon paper, which was about three feet deep and a foot in diameter. Using this as the core, he pasted layer after layer of brown wrapping paper around it until its proportions were about the same as those of a double-bang firecracker. Then, he wrapped it in red paper left over from writing New Year's scrolls. At the bottom, he drilled a hole and threaded a fuse made of brown wrapping paper. This produced the biggest double-banger in human history, but it was fake and would never make a sound.

This prop played a crucial role in Lisi's plot. At around eleven o'clock that morning, just as he had finished making it, a song-and-dance troupe arrived in the courtyard of the municipal government office building and began to perform. It was clear that they had no intention of leaving until someone came out with money. What they got instead was an extra-large double-banger.

Lisi came charging out of the office building, clutching it like the hero Wang Cheng with his Bangalore torpedo in the movie *Heroic Sons and Daughters.* This was at the start of the Reform and Opening period, when all kinds of new things were appearing every day; when the dance troupe saw the gigantic double-banger, they eyed it curiously as they continued to perform.

To their surprise, Lisi wove among them and planted the double-banger in the middle of the troupe. He then drew out the fuse and made as if to light it with the cigarette dangling from his lip. The members of the dance troupe began shrieking in terror and running in every direction. They were all on stilts, making it much harder for them to run. Some tumbled to the ground while others rushed out of the courtyard. Lisi continued to brandish the double-banger, bending over it with his sleepy eyes and sly smile, making as if to light it. His performance was so convincing that the entire troupe fled from the courtyard. They stood at the gate, hands covering their ears, looking in with terror. Not a single person dared to go back. Lisi's tactic proved effective. The troupe received no money from the municipal government that day, nor did any of the others.

With so much spare time on their hands, discharged soldiers like Hongbing, Feisi, Lisi, and Xiaoji were guaranteed to cause trouble. Even so, Ergou never imagined that these young men would engage in so many shocking crimes, becoming underworld gang leaders with turfs of their own.

CHAPTER 2

Never Insult a Soldier

NOT LONG AFTER SPRING FESTIVAL, Zhao Hongbing was assigned a job. The Zhaos and Ergou's parents were thrilled at the news; only Ergou and Hongbing's nephew, Zhao Xiaobo, were disgruntled by the fact that Zhao Hongbing would now only be free on weekends to take them out firing slingshots and building snow castles. Zhao Hongbing was a keen shot, felling at least one out of every three sparrows he aimed at with his crude weapon. Anyone who has used a slingshot knows how impressive this is, because some birds that are hit manage to fly off, and even some that are knocked down revive and fly away; only those that are hit in the head never fly again. Ergou fooled around with slingshots for nine years and broke countless windows without felling a single sparrow.

Zhao Hongbing was assigned a job in the office of a bank. This office was responsible for receiving guests and arranging events for the bank's leaders. It was a "fat job", with plenty of opportunities for bribes and kickbacks. Zhao Hongbing was bright-eyed, well-dressed, and refined, with none of the ruffian air that years on the battlefield can impart. The bank's president could tell at a glance that Hongbing would enhance the bank's image. Nobody could have imagined what actually transpired.

The incident Zhao Hongbing encountered would be considered nothing nowadays; anyone going to the Discipline Inspection Commission or the Anti-Corruption Bureau reporting that So-and-so was corrupt under these circumstances would be regarded as a lunatic. Zhao Hongbing was this kind of "lunatic."

The office where Hongbing worked regularly received guests from other banks, and Hongbing soon grew fed up. These guests were supposedly "inspectors", but all they really came for was to gorge themselves. Turning their noses up at roast chicken, they insisted on fashionable foods like deep fried pork tenderloin or sweet-and-sour fish, and only drank top-drawer liquors like Maotai or Wuliangye. They would arrive in the morning to carry out their inspections, eat and drink themselves into a stupor at lunchtime, and then spend the afternoon sleeping it off on the sofas in the bank's reception office. Once night fell, they were ready for another bacchanal. A dozen dishes would be set before them, and they'd leave ninety percent of it to be thrown into the trash.

Zhao Hongbing was crazy enough to find this intolerable. His heart ached at the criminal waste of state-funded food. So he began to think: *how long ago was it that I enlisted? Back then, lots of people considered even rice a luxury, and now our country has become so rich that platters of meat can be tossed in the bin. And one visiting leader has to be accompanied by an entourage of a dozen lackeys?* This young lunatic, born under the Red Flag and raised at the dawn of the nation, may not have realized that China had prospered so much during the years when he was serving his country. What he witnessed was not the result of prosperity but of corruption.

At noon on Hongbing's twelfth day on the job, another provincial leader came down for a meeting. Within half an hour he was gorging himself on mountains of food and oceans of liquor. The feasting continued for three hours before they returned to the office. The head of the reception office, Mr. Li, was Hongbing's direct supervisor, and by the time they returned, he could hardly see straight. Hongbing, as a staffer, had kept them company without overindulging. Of course, that's what Hongbing said, but Ergou knew Hongbing well enough to be sure he also drank too much that day. Hongbing was the kind of man who drank either nothing or too much; in the twenty years Ergou had known him, there had never been an exception to this rule. No one knew what his drinking capacity was; some said 15 ounces, some said a pint, some said a quart. He seldom drank with outsiders, but when he did, it was rice liquor – a pint to a quart or more, and always too much.

This self-described sober "lunatic" staggered into the office that afternoon to find his boss, Mr. Li, on the phone. Back then, telephone lines were still routed through a switchboard, and the caller had to instruct the switchboard operator which number to dial. Zhao Hongbing heard Li tell the operator to connect him to the city's guesthouse, and his first thought was, *we just finished eating, and now he's arranging for us to spend the evening wasting even more of our country's money and food?* Mustering Dutch courage, Hongbing reached out and hung up the phone.

With a gust of liquored breath, Li laughed and said, "Xiao Zhao, don't be angry. I'm just reserving a table for the leader tonight."

Hongbing said, "I'm not going along with this. We just

left so much food behind at lunch and you're planning to eat again tonight?"

Li said, "Sure. Why not? What else are we going to do?"

"How can you waste state funds like that?"

Li realized from Hongbing's tone of voice that he wasn't joking. He said, "Xiao Zhao, didn't you go out drinking with us at lunchtime? Wasn't that a waste of the state's money?"

Tongue-tied for a moment, Hongbing said, "I went at lunchtime, but I'm not going next time."

"That's up to you, but don't interfere with my phone call." Losing patience, Li pushed his hand away.

This infuriated Zhao Hongbing, who employed his prodigious vocal chords to yell, "You're just a bunch of moths and maggots!" His use of the plural included the bank's president in his insult.

"Fuck you! Where do you get off criticizing others?" said Li, who was no nice guy himself.

"Did we bleed on the Laoshan front to protect parasites like you?"

"Lousy soldier boy. Do you really think a few days in the army gives you the right to lecture me? Who needs your fucking protection?"

"No one insults a soldier!"

"You cripple! If it weren't for your father..."

Those were the last words Li would speak for the next two weeks, because they were followed by a roar that shook the building, and then a crashing sound.

At the hospital, the doctor asked Li's colleague, "What kind of heavy object hit his chest hard enough to break so many ribs?"

"He was beaten."

"How many people did it take to do this to him?"

"One."

"What did he beat him with?"

"He kicked him."

"How many times?"

"Just once."

"Who was this person that kicked him?"

On hearing the answer, the doctor reportedly stood there gaping. He had never treated such a serious kicking injury before. When the police called to follow up, he maintained that several assailants must have been involved. It was impossible to attribute so much damage to a single blow. The doctor couldn't know that Zhao Hongbing used that kick to vent his shock and indignation at society, his shame over his missing fingers, his resentment of his boss's shamelessness, and his panicked disillusionment.

Twelve years later, when Ergou was in his third year of high school, the man Hongbing declared a "maggot" was brought to justice. When Ergou hurried to a public trial after school, he saw a notice posted off to the side: "While serving as the vice-president of the Bank of Industry and Commerce, Li XX embezzled XX million *yuan* in public funds for gambling. The Court of First Instance has sentenced him to eleven years in prison."

Back at home, Ergou reported this jubilantly to Zhao Hongbing, who by then was the leader of an underworld gang. To his surprise, Hongbing was indifferent. "Ergou, he's just one maggot. You have to remember, that day I said, 'You bunch of maggots.'"

It was true. A single maggot could be brought to justice, but how long would it take to deal with an entire maggot-ridden country? That's when Ergou understood that Zhao Hongbing had not been aiming his kick at just one man.

For fourteen years after this incident, Zhao Hongbing never again publicly referred to his military service. At least, Ergou never heard him mention it. Even at gatherings of his old comrades-in-arms, while everyone else was recalling their experiences in the army, Hongbing kept silent.

It was not until the summer of 1999, when Ergou was in college in another city and had come home to visit his family, that he heard one of his high school classmates tell what he considered as a joke. Even though this happened eight years ago, Ergou still remembers every word his old classmate said:

"Ergou, did you go to the protest?"

It was soon after NATO's bombing of the Chinese Embassy in Belgrade, and China was still roiling with protests.

"Yes! I yelled myself hoarse."

"We went too, but it was ridiculous."

"Bombing our embassy was a serious matter. What's ridiculous about it?"

"Most of the people at the protest were local college students, but do you know who was marching at the front and yelling the loudest, and who kept marching all day after others dropped out?"

"Who?"

"Hongbing! You know, Big Brother Hongbing! He was out in front with Feisi and bunch of other gangsters carrying a banner. They seemed to be enjoying themselves; they marched from the south side of the city to the north, then to the western waterfront and on to the cotton mill. All the punks and lowlifes standing along the road joined in when they saw Hongbing, and by the end of the day there must have been two hundred of them with dyed hair or shaved heads, tattoos, shirtless and in flip-flops – all kinds! By lunchtime we reached the school, and us students dropped out to hit the canteen. That bunch of hoodlums Hongbing led were tough all right, marching half a day without even stopping for a drink of water. Hongbing told the students he'd been a soldier and so had Feisi and Xiaoji. They'd fought in the war, and now that the country was in trouble, if they were needed, they'd go back into the army and not be afraid to die. It was fucking hilarious! That bunch of middle-aged gangsters thinking they could go back into the army! Who would want them?! If China had to depend on riffraff like that, we'd be finished! Some of my classmates said, 'Who knew gangsters can be patriots, too?' Ergou, why do you think they were making such asses of themselves? What do you think they were getting at? Why don't they just try committing fewer crimes or chopping up a few less people?"

"You're full of shit. Shut up. You don't know what you're talking about."

"Ergou, what's the matter? Why are you talking like that?"

"Piss off!"

Zhao Hongbing clearly hadn't forgotten that he'd once been a "lousy soldier boy".

CHAPTER 3

Gangland Aristocracy

Ergou was unfailingly polite, but the reason he'd told his old classmate to "piss off" was that he hadn't detected the slightest indignation over the American bombing of the Chinese Embassy in Yugoslavia, or even a thread of sympathy for the three countrymen who had lost their lives in a foreign land. In his classmate's animated narrative he couldn't detect the slightest grief over the incident. Why was such a person even protesting in the first place? He must have just wanted to join the fun.

Six years later, in 2005, on the Yan'an East Road overpass near Shanghai's People's Square, Ergou was heading home after working the night shift when he saw a group of students with cheeky grins on their faces carrying banners calling for a boycott of Japanese products. Seeing the emptiness of the eyes in those agitated faces yelling slogans as if China had conquered the world, Ergou couldn't share their excitement. He found the whole scene unspeakably depressing.

Ergou pulled the boy aside who was grinning the most and shouting the loudest and asked, "What is this protest about? Is it because some Japanese politician has gone to pay homage at the Yasukuni Shrine again, or what?" The student hemmed and hawed for a while, unable to answer the question. Ergou's heart sank. He was sure there were many patriotic and well-meaning students among the protesters, and he respected them. However, he heartily despised those who carried a Chinese flag and joined protests just for the fun of it, as if it were a carnival.

Zhao Hongbing had been ridiculed for protesting because he was a hoodlum – an underworld gang leader who had been in and out of prison several times. Ergou was certain that Hongbing, who had experience the flames of war and lost three fingers in battle, was every bit as patriotic as any of these protesters. But once a person was labeled a gangster. Even patriotism had become a joke.

Zhao Hongbing spent half a month squatting in a prison sweatbox for beating his office manager. As for Li, he returned to work after three months of bed rest, and was considerably less arrogant.

Zhao Hongbing came out of the sweatbox a different person – silent and unfathomable. With his father's influence, he could have gone back to work at the bank, but he didn't, no matter how hard his sisters urged him. He spent more than a month lying around, taking occasional strolls outside. Mr. Zhao held back from criticizing his son. Although strict, he was also a reasonable man; he knew that in principle his son had been right, and that the kicking had been an act of foolish impetuosity triggered by being called a cripple.

In fact, Zhao Hongbing thought a lot about what to do after losing his job. He considered joining Xiaoji in running his recycling stall, or taking out a contract for a tour bus, or running a general store. He thought of practically every job worth considering, but never considered joining the underworld.

Ergou's parents, taking Zhao Hongbing's side out of friendship and a sense of justice, proposed some ideas to him. Ergou's dad was friends with the head of a state-owned hotel near the train station, as well as with the official over him. He pushed Hongbing to take on the contract for the hotel in early 1987. After considerable negotiation, the matter was finally settled, and the new sense of direction made Zhao Hongbing noticeably cheerier.

Two or three months later, on a warm spring day, Zhao Hongbing was on his way to buy a spoke for his brother-in-law's bicycle. He was riding his own bike with Ergou sitting in front and his nephew Xiaobo in back, when a voice behind them called out, "Hongbing! Hongbing!"

Turning to look, Zhao Hongbing grinned with surprise. "Zhang Yue!"

Zhang Yue climbed off his bike.

"Hongbing, when were you discharged? Why haven't you come to see me?"

"I don't want to talk about it. How about you? Have you graduated?"

"Yes, I've been assigned a job at the Grain Bureau," Zhang Yue said.

"How did you get back here so fast? Doesn't it take four years to graduate? I thought you were still at school, that's why I didn't look you up."

"I just went for professional training and graduated in three years," laughed Zhang Yue.

The two of them stood before each other, hands clasped, never guessing that this handshake would change both their fates.

As the two reminisced, Ergou learned they'd been best

friends in high school. Zhang Yue was a slim, pale, refined-looking fellow – well-spoken and cultivated. There was a shrewd look in his large eyes, and he had the long, slender fingers of a pianist. Months later Ergou learned that Zhang Yue's bookish and gentle appearance was deceiving; once his mind was set, ten oxen couldn't hold him back.

Ergou also subsequently learned that Zhang Yue was the scion of an "underworld aristocracy." Back in the 1930s and 1940s, Zhang Yue's grandfather was a famous brigand known as Zhen Dongyang, or "Quell Japan". With a hundred followers, he had swept through the region's cities to "resist Japan and save the nation". They looted and pillaged, killing any Jap devil they saw and robbing any landlord or bandit they came across, in utter disregard of law and order. During their crime spree, they meted out special treatment to the Japanese, whose heads they would hang in public places. At that time, Ergou's locality was part of what was then called Manchukuo – a puppet state under Japanese rule. Every town was guarded by several Japanese soldiers, but never more than ten, and they were no match for a hundred ferocious local bandits. The "Jap devils" genuinely feared the appropriately named Zhen Dongyang, whose nomadic lifestyle made him impossible to capture.

Ergou heard of one exploit in which Zhen Dongyang attacked a puppet police station to free two of his gang members who had been arrested a month before. After entering the police compound, he stood in the doorway and bellowed, "I am Zhen Dongyang. Release my brothers now or I'll burn down your police station!"

Only three policemen were on duty at the time, and they grabbed their guns and rushed out. Seeing Zhen Dongyang taunting them at the entrance of the compound, they moved to arrest him. Zhen Dongyang had thought his name alone would be enough to intimidate the policemen, but it turned out they were braver than that. Zhen Dongyang was carrying two Mauser pistols (known for good reason as "box cannons"), and he fired a warning shot to keep the policemen at bay. There were no televisions back then, otherwise Zhen Dongyang might have known that warning shots should always be fired in the air and not at the ground. Whether because he'd drunk too much or because the gun barrel was off kilter, Zhen Dongyang managed to shoot himself in the foot. Amazed at their luck at having the notorious Zhen Dongyang cripple himself on their watch, the policemen shouted, "Get him!" and charged forward.

Seething with pain, Zhen Dongyang vented his wrath by firing at the policemen. Following an exchange of a dozen or so rounds, two policemen were dead and the third badly wounded, while Zhen Dongyang suffered no further injury.

People say that during the shoot-out, the policemen were shooting and dodging bullets at the same time, while Zhen Dongyang didn't move anything but his trigger fingers. This is the kind of ruthlessness required of a bandit leader. The man who held his ground came off without a scratch, while those who ducked and dodged ended up dead or wounded. If that isn't the stuff of legend, what is? After the gunfight, Zhen Dongyang calmly freed his two gang brothers and they swaggered off.

A genuine resistance fighter would have packed it in after the "Jap devils" surrendered, but with no more enemies to maraud against, Zhen Dongyang turned his attention to landlords. Later on, people praised him as a Robin Hood who killed the rich and helped the poor. That's not how Ergou's father saw it, though. He said, "Zhen killed the rich because the poor had nothing for him to steal. He helped the poor by tossing a few coins at the people his gang lodged with while they were on the run. All he cared about was money. Don't believe what they say about his noble spirit."

Zhen Dongyang became so legendary that no one could catch him – neither the "Jap devils", the puppet regime, nor the Nationalist government. However, in 1947 he fell into the hands of the Chinese People's Liberation Army. Soon after that, he found himself kneeling by a roiling river, waiting to be executed with several other bandits. Just before the bullet could penetrate his skull, he leaped into the river, and no one knows if he lived or died. His body was never found. He was never seen again.

When Zhen Dongyang escaped that bullet, he probably never dreamed that his grandson would fall before a gun more than forty years later. This grandson was Zhang Yue. People have exaggerated the virtues of Zhen Dongyang's son, saying he was benevolent and just, rational and not at all barbaric. But when Red Guards ransacked his home in 1966, they learned that while Zhen Dongyang's son was righteous, he was even more of a wild man than Zhen Dongyang.

Since Zhang Yue's grandfather had been a bandit, his family was naturally targeted during the Cultural Revolution. Early one morning, a dozen or so Red Guards burst into the courtyard, preparing to ransack the Zhang home. But before they could proceed, Zhang Yue's father dashed out. According to one of the Red Guards who invaded the home – a female cousin of Zhao Hongbing's – they saw a rail-thin man rushing at them with a shoulder pole in his hands. He was naked except for red briefs, which failed to conceal the impressive object between his legs. Many of the female Red Guards had never seen that appendage before, and they turned away shrieking. Apparently, Zhang Yue's father had just gotten out of bed and still had his morning erection. Ergou was in awe of his cleverness – dashing out almost naked, he robbed his opponents of half their strength by disarming the girl Red Guards.

"What are you doing! We're here to search your house!" yelled the Guards.

"Go fuck your mothers, you little shits! Come one step closer and I'll waste you!" hollered Zhang Yue's father.

Having ransacked a multitude of homes without encountering the least resistance, the Red Guards never expected to land in this briar patch. "Get him!" cried the leader of the group, unfastening his belt buckle to use as a whip. Zhang Yue's father remained composed and simply swung the shoulder pole he was carrying. *Bang*! The metal belt buckle slammed against Zhang Yue's father's head. At the same moment, his pole struck the Red Guard's head, and the boy dropped to the ground. Roaring like a tiger and covered with blood, Zhang Yue's father charged through the narrow courtyard swinging his pole at the other Red Guards, who hadn't had a chance to loosen their own belts. The Red Guards howled in pain as he rained blows on them, but he didn't strike a single one of the girls. That belt buckle to the head was the only injury Zhang Yue's father suffered.

"Get the fuck out of here!" he yelled.

"Just you wait," said the Red Guard leader woozily as the others carried him off.

An hour later, more than a hundred Red Guards on

bicycles whirled aggressively into the *hutong* where Zhang Yue's family lived, every hand carrying some kind of weapon and not a girl among them.

Zhang Yue's father was waiting for them on the roof of the gate house at the entrance to the courtyard. He was still wearing only his red briefs, but his time he was carrying a hatchet. Behind him stood his eldest son, the fourteen-year-old Zhang Fei, also carrying a hatchet but dressed more appropriately than his father. It seems that the older generation was more open in those days. Or maybe Zhang Yue's father, by then in his fifties, was wearing special clothes to ward off bad luck in his "threshold year" in the lunar calendar. Why else would a grown man have been running around in red skimpies? Everyone in the city over fifty years old knows of this battle. The army of Red Guards ground to a halt, having failed to anticipate that the elder and younger Zhangs would be waiting for them.

"You sons of bitches. What are you doing back here?" Zhang Yue's father called down from the roof.

"We're going to search your house!" This Red Guard leader was older and more authoritative. As he spoke, he unbuckled his belt, and the Guards behind him dismounted from their bikes and raised the scrap iron, table legs, and cleavers they were carrying.

"Motherfuckers!" The elder and younger Zhang leaped down from the roof, landing less than a yard from the Red Guards, who at this point noticed that Zhang Yue's father was barefoot.

"Step aside!" yelled the Red Guard leader.

Zhang Yue's father didn't reply, but said to his son, "That's a nice army belt he has there. Go grab it for me."

Zhang Fei whipped his hatchet at the Red Guard leader, who cried out and dropped his belt to the ground. Zhang Fei picked it up. The Red Guards were dumbstruck. More than a hundred of them had come to ransack this house, but they had become the underdogs, their leader disarmed in the blink of an eye. Half a minute passed, and no one moved a muscle. "Get them, Son!" roared Zhang Yue's father.

The elder and young Zhang plowed through the Red Guards without meeting the slightest resistance. Thoroughly unmanned by this unexpected reception, the Red Guards scrambled through the narrow *hutong* like rats in a trap. None of them dared fight back, overwhelmed as they were by the vehemence and ferocity of the Zhangs' attack.

In a matter of minutes, all that was left in the *hutong* was a pile of abandoned scrap metal and table legs and Zhang Yue's brother and father, completely unharmed. The rising sun sent down a beam of light that warmed the skeletal frame of Zhang Yue's father in his red briefs. Clearly, his self-respect and the sanctity of his home meant more to him than life itself.

According to an incomplete reckoning after the event, more than forty Red Guards were injured in varying degrees, but none lost their lives. From then on, the number of ransackings and public denunciations in the city decreased considerably, and some said it was because of the Zhang family's ambush. In that absurd era, perhaps it was only genuine warriors who could ward off Red Guard militants dazzled by a revolution they never understood.

CHAPTER 4

The National Day Lantern Show

AFTER THEIR CHANCE ENCOUNTER, ZHANG Yue and Zhao Hongbing arranged to meet again.

In 1986, all of the city's kindergartens were being reestablished, so Ergou hadn't been able to go to school since coming home. Once the kindergartens reopened in early 1987, Ergou went straight to the upper level, and within half a year was promoted to the "Red Education Class," as preschool was then called. The upshot was that Ergou's first year back in the city wasn't spent with pretty young kindergarten teachers but rather with a group of young hooligans. Busy with work, and lacking family in the city to turn to, Ergou's parents entrusted him to Zhao Hongbing. Zhao was unemployed, and was also looking after his nephew Xiaobo, likewise deprived of a kindergarten. "You're already minding one kid, and the two of them will entertain each other," Ergou's mother reasoned.

Babysitting was Zhao Hongbing's main duty from early 1986 to 1987, even though it eventually became just a sideline. Hongbing actually liked it. He treated it as an enjoyable hobby, as did his friends. At one point, the provincial government transferred Ergou's father out of the city to handle a census while Ergou's mother was sent to manage a laboratory in another city for a nationwide land survey, so neither parent was at home. Ergou ate and slept at the elder Mr. Zhao's home during that time, and became virtually part of the family.

A week after the encounter in the street, Zhang Yue came over to Zhao Hongbing's home with his neighbor, Sun Dawei. Tall and stout, with clear, pale skin and hair parted far off to the side, Sun was a jobless vagrant. His chattiness had earned him the nickname Big Mouth Sun, but he was clearly intimidated by Zhang Yue, who could shut him up with a single glance.

Ergou remembers that Sun Dawei brought a guitar with him that day, and Zhao Hongbing instantly fell in love with it. Hongbing had a natural talent for music and could master any instrument in a month. Over the next ten years or so he made Ergou and Xiaobo his apprentices. Neither boy liked music, and they especially disliked the guitar, but Hongbing forced them to learn regardless. They were limited to instruments that could be strummed, because that's all Hongbing's maimed right hand could manage.

That guitar brought Zhao Hongbing closer to Sun Dawei, as he borrowed it for a week and then came back to borrow it again the day after returning it. After a few months, Zhao Hongbing finally asked his elder sisters for money to buy his own guitar, but by then, Zhao Hongbing, Sun Dawei and Zhang Yue were spending nearly every weekend together.

Through Zhao Hongbing, Sun Dawei and Zhang Yue became acquainted with Hongbing's old war buddies, Feisi, Xiaoji, and Lisi. The six of them were always upstairs in old

Mr. Zhao's home, talking and messing around. Sometimes they pulled enough money together to go out for drinks. After three or four months, they became a closely-knit crew. Sun Dawei's chattiness, Xiaoji's impish tricks, Zhao Hongbing's steadiness, Zhang Yue's erudition, Feisi's practicality, and Lisi's sincerity all left a favorable impression on Ergou.

In September 1986, another of Zhao Hongbing's old army buddies came to visit from Beijing. Hongbing asked his father for 200 *yuan* to host dinner at the city's prime establishment, the Purple Moon. Ten people came. Apart from Zhao Hongbing, his three comrades-in-arms and Zhang Yue and Sun Dawei, Zhang Yue brought along another neighbor, Li Wu, and then there was Hongbing's Beijing war buddy as well as Ergou and Xiaobo.

Zhao Hongbing's Beijing war buddy was very thin, but solid, with a high-bridged nose, large eyes, ramrod-straight back, and the irreverent air of a typical Beijing "player".

Zhang Yue's neighbor Li Wu sported the permed hair, bell-bottomed trousers, and white leather shoes that were all the rage in the 1980s. Most local people who dressed like that were petty hoodlums, and Li Wu was no exception.

The dinner conversation focused largely on the war exploits of the former soldiers, which fascinated those who had never served in the army. Most of the guys became more exuberant as they drank and talked, but some dissolved into melancholy. Eventually everyone was thoroughly drunk except for Ergou and Xiaobo, who continued gobbling down the sautéed beef.

Sun Dawei proposed that the eight of them become sworn brothers, and in a surge of emotion the other seven agreed and knelt on the spot to swear their eternal allegiance. Zhao

Hongbing was the eldest of the group, followed by Xiaoji, then Zhang Yue, Feisi, Sun Dawei, Li Wu, Hongbing's Beijing war buddy, and last of all Lisi. Becoming sworn brothers was all the fashion in the 1980s.

This casual dinner changed the fates of all eight men, and gave birth to this city's most notorious and enduring underworld gang.

This loosely-knit group had no "Big Brother" in the genuine sense; it was just a group of friends. Zhao Hongbing eventually came to be regarded as the leader of the gang because he was steady, cool-headed, and clear-thinking, seldom taking the initiative to make trouble, and his gang brothers were willing to listen to him. But he was not the final or absolute authority within the group.

These young men rose to fame together, but the loose structure of their gang allowed each to attract his own followers and develop his own "career". After becoming famous, they remained in close contact and helped one another, but they weren't substantially involved in each other's businesses.

Of course, on the night that they became sworn brothers, none of them imagined that they would eventually evolve into a hooligan gang.

On that day, they used the camera Zhao Hongbing's Beijing friend had brought with him to take a black-and-white photo. Xiaobo pressed the shutter, and the picture came out tilted. This photo, with Zhao Hongbing seated in the middle, was the first to be taken of the group.

Zhao Hongbing's Beijing war buddy stayed with him for half a month. The two of them were very close, having been best friends in the army. Everyone called him "Little Beijing".

On October 1st 1986, the newly sworn brothers decided

to go together to the city square to watch the National Day lantern festival. Little Beijing was going home the next day, so they'd all had a drink together before going to the square, and were animated but not drunk. Taking Ergou and Xiaobo with them, they went to see the lanterns at around seven o'clock. Back in the early 1980s, National Day was a major holiday. Most work units set off firecrackers, and lanterns were displayed at two venues: the sports ground in front of the Sports Committee offices, and Red Flag Park. Hongbing and the others went to the sports ground, which was closer to home.

October 1st was the first day of the three-day lantern display. Nearly everyone in the city turned out, with old people, women, children, and bands of students in a crush that inevitably resulted in a certain amount of bumping and shoving.

"Hey, asshole! You stepped on my foot! Do you need glasses?" an ugly, long-haired youth shouted at Zhao Hongbing.

"Sorry... I didn't mean to," said Hongbing politely.

"Watch what you're doing next time, asshole!" said the long-haired fellow, but when he saw that Hongbing was a decent guy, he left it at that and turned to go.

"Mind your mouth and cut the foul language!" Little Beijing scolded in his thick accent.

"What's it to you?" said the long-haired guy, turning back to them aggressively.

"What's this? Do you want to fight? Is your hair long enough? Do you have enough teeth for me to knock out..."

Little Beijing kept on like this in a very entertaining fashion with at least a dozen more questions that Ergou couldn't possible remember, never stopping for a breath or repeating himself. To Ergou's young mind, Little Beijing's rebukes reached a plane he could never hope to attain – a verbal Mount

Everest. More than ten years later, at college, Ergou carelessly bumped his bicycle into a middle-aged Beijing woman and learned that Little Beijing was not the sole progenitor of this talent. But that's another story.

Infuriated, the long-haired youth sent a fist flying. Little Beijing had not been an army scout for nothing. His hands were as skilled as his mouth. He grabbed the wrist of the long-haired youth and gave it a twist while tripping him with his foot. The fellow went sprawling to the ground, where Little Beijing gave him a kick in the head for good measure.

Xiaoji and Feisi joined in. Apparently discharged soldiers share a love for brawling. But Zhao Hongbing didn't raise a hand. With Little Beijing, Feisi, and Xiaoji involved, three against one was enough.

By then the youth had covered his face with his hands and was yelling, "Tiger! Tiger! Help! I'm being beaten!"

Ergou saw the faces of everyone but Little Beijing freeze at the mention of that name. Everyone knew that Tiger was a major hoodlum over at the eastside woolen mill. He had a gang of dozens of brothers, most of them kids of the mill's employees who had grown up together. Living out in the suburbs, they only came to the city in packs of thirty or forty. The nationwide "Strike Hard" anti-crime campaign of 1983 was recent enough that the most of the city's most notorious gangsters were still in prison, and the only gangs that dared bother Tiger's boys were Railway's gang at the southern train station and Rascal Zhang's gang. These gangs were always rumbling and trying to gain the upper hand.

Bystanders scattered as a couple of dozen guys rushed over, all wearing the same hairstyle as the youth on the ground. Leading them was Tiger. Ergou clearly remembers that

Tiger's hair was long and permed, giving him an androgynous look. Twenty years later, while home for the Spring Festival, Ergou saw Tiger at a distance. The old guy was in a wheelchair, waiting for the traffic signal to change. He still had his long, permed hair – an obvious tribute to his glory days two decades earlier.

"Motherfucker! Who's beating up my brother?" roared Tiger, brandishing a combat knife. Several guys behind him also pulled out combat knives and striking blades, but the rest didn't seem to be armed.

"Me," said Zhao Hongbing, grinning at him. For discharged soldiers, facing a bunch of guys with knives was child's play.

"Do you know who I am?" Tiger demanded belligerently.

"Yeah," said Little Beijing in a small voice with his head lowered, pretending to be cowed. That clearly pleased Tiger until Little Beijing burst out, "We know you're a dumb shit with long hair!"

Laughter exploded among the bystanders. Boiling with anger, Tiger thrust his knife at Little Beijing, and what followed was the fiercest fight Ergou had ever seen.

Before Little Beijing could move, Feisi leaped out from behind Zhao Hongbing. With lightning speed he grabbed the blade of Tiger's knife with his bare hand. The knife blade! Blood dripped from Feisi's hand, but it didn't seem to bother him. With a burst of strength he snapped the knife in two. He held it in his hand, and all Tiger had left was the handle.

Tiger was stunned. In all his years wielding a knife, he'd never had someone grab the blade. Feisi thrust it at Tiger's head while Little Beijing sent a kick to his chin. Tiger's burly form went crashing to the ground.

Startled, the gangsters behind Tiger rushed forward, knives drawn against Zhao Hongbing, Feisi, and Little Beijing at the front of their group. The two gangs began tangling, both sides skilled fighters. Zhao Hongbing's group consisted mostly of trained soldiers, while their hooligan opponents had dominated the eastern suburb for years. One side had eight men and the other more than twenty – six or seven of them armed with knives.

Apart from Sun Dawei, Zhao Hongbing's group seemed not the least bit intimidated, and targeted the men wielding knives. Ergou retains several fragmentary memories of this battle:

The best fighters were Zhao Hongbing and Little Beijing; anyone who came near either of them ended up on the ground. Watching them was like watching a *kungfu* movie where the good guy knocks down the bad guy like a piece of wood, while the good guy doesn't even get touched. By the time the fight ended, Zhao Hongbing had a combat knife in his hand, and Little Beijing held a striking blade.

The fiercest fighters were Zhang Yue, Xiaoji, and Li Wu. They seemed less skillful and drew a lot of blood. While Zhao Hongbing and Little Beijing looked like stars in a *kungfu* movie, the other three were street brawlers fighting to the death.

Feisi chased after someone at the beginning of the brawl and disappeared.

Lisi was also an army scout and a powerful if less flashy fighter. Few of those he hit got up again, and he usually only needed to hit them once.

Sun Dawei was felled by a stab to the leg, but the beating stopped. Strangely, the person who feared knives most was the only one to be stabbed. Since Zhao Hongbing's group had three skilled fighters and another three who were fearless, they overcame their opponents in about five minutes. Tiger's gang began fleeing pell-mell, and Hongbing's guys didn't pursue them.

This fight had been very satisfying. Even though Sun Dawei had been injured, and Li Wu and Xiaoji had been knocked around, it was a clear victory for Zhao Hongbing and his friends. Sending the gangsters packing before the eyes of a multitude did them much more credit. The eight young fellows were jubilant.

After the fight, Zhao Hongbing took Sun Dawei and Feisi to the hospital to have their wounds dressed. Ergou and Xiaobo were escorted home by Zhang Yue and Lisi. They had no apparent injuries, and would not get a scolding from Mr. Zhao.

They never guessed that a much more violent fight awaited them. Ergou went home to bed, but woke up in less than an hour to the sight of six blood-soaked men before his bleary eyes. From their conversation, Ergou learned what had happened.

After going to the hospital, Feisi and Sun Dawei were able to get their wounds dressed quickly. As they and Zhao Hongbing left the emergency room, they encountered Tiger's gang, whose seriously injured members had also come to the city's No. 3 People's Hospital to have their wounds treated. Fate having brought the two gangs together again, they immediately began fighting in the narrow hospital corridor becoming. Zhao Hongbing and his friends were at a disadvantage because another dozen or so had joined the rest of Tiger's gang at the hospital, making them thirty-odd against six. Hongbing's gang was trapped in the hospital corridor and could only fight their way out.

Li Wu reportedly made the first move by hurling a fist at Tiger. Tiger struck back and knocked him down. Li Wu as pinned to the ground by trampling feet. Zhao Hongbing lunged forward, but the narrow space restricted his fighting skills. Hongbing and the others quickly realized that if they remained trapped inside the corridor, they were dead men. Hongbing had already taken several blows, but he was strong enough to stop himself being knocked down.

At this chaotic juncture, someone managed to break through the encirclement and change their fates. It was Little Beijing.

When the fight broke out, Little Beijing and Feisi were at the entrance of the emergency room, and they ran inside and grabbed two flower-patterned metal thermos flasks filled with boiled water. Feisi also grabbed a metal stand used for IV infusions.

Little Beijing ran out of the emergency room hurling the thermos flasks like hand grenades against the wall, one on each side. The shattered flasks sent boiling water flying, and the fighters uttered blood-curdling shrieks. Of course, Zhao Hongbing and Sun Dawei were also scalded. Taking advantage of the chaos, Feisi began jabbing Tiger with the IV stand. As Tiger backed off, the men behind him dispersed. Zhao Hongbing grabbed the opportunity to pull Li Wu to his feet, and they fought the rest of their way out of the hospital, with Little Beijing bringing up the rear as the others ran toward the exit. Everyone knew enough of Little Beijing's skill to feel certain that he would not be captured as long as he had room to maneuver.

Outside the hospital, the five of them kept running a considerable distance. When they saw that no one was following, they realized Little Beijing had been left behind. Zhao Hongbing turned back for him, but retreated at the sight of police officers arriving and arresting Tiger and his gang. Soon after that, Little Beijing caught up with them, laughing his head off.

It turned out that Little Beijing had kept fighting as he backed out of the hospital. Noticing a 24-hour funeral parlor across the street, he went inside. Bolting the iron door behind him, he jumped out the rear window and made a clean getaway. Meanwhile, Tiger and the others were arrested while trying to break down the funeral parlor's door.

On reaching home, they found that while five of the six of them were bleeding, their injuries weren't serious. The one uninjured person was Little Beijing. He was also covered with blood, but none of it was his.

The elder Mr. Zhao wasn't home at the time, so the eight guys held an informal "rumble summing-up meeting". Maybe this was a habit they'd acquired in the army. They always had to do it after any major event, good or bad. No one took minutes, but otherwise it looked like the real thing.

Zhao Hongbing directed the meeting, and the other seven chimed in eagerly. The meeting started out by accurately forecasting that this would not be their last fight, and that Tiger and his gang were sure to seek revenge once they were released. They also summarized the successes and failures in this battle. Ergou recalls the following successes:

Feisi was a brave and aggressive fighter, breaking the combat knife with his bare hand and crushing the morale of the opposition. He had the courage needed for battle (Zhang Yue's words).

Little Beijing employed the tactic of catching bandits by first catching the ringleader. By kicking Tiger to the ground, he beheaded the dragon (Xiaoji's words).

Xiaoji, Lisi and the others were brave and fierce before a formidable foe (mutual adulation on all sides).

By going one against ten in the hospital corridor, Zhao Hongbing gave Little Beijing time to grab the thermos flasks.

Little Beijing had the laudable ability to improvise and make creative use of whatever weapons were at hand. Lisi's use of the IV stand was also innovative (Sun Dawei's words).

As for the failings:

Sun Dawei was out of shape, and his fighting skills were mediocre, leading him to be knocked down right away. His combat readiness was deficient, and in the next gang fight he would have to be armed.

Feisi's fighting was organized but undisciplined. By getting excited and chasing someone, he risked becoming isolated. He would have to stay with the group next time there was a fight.

Zhang Yue's moves and tricks were too simple and easy to anticipate. He needed to diversify next time.

Li Wu was too impetuous, resulting in his being knocked down in the hospital corridor. If it had been Zhao Hongbing who struck first, he would certainly not have been knocked down.

The final conclusion could be summarized in four sentences: in the next fight, they would have to be completely united, with no one breaking formation. They needed to develop the brave and aggressive spirit they'd demonstrated at the sports ground. They needed to hone their fighting skills, and they should try to carry weapons whenever they went out.

Next time they fought, they needed to make full use whatever materials were at hand.

Ergou felt that the main reason this gang eventually became unbeatable was that they were good at drawing summaries and conclusions, and at criticism and self-criticism. Afterwards, Zhao Hongbing presented the captured combat knife to Xiaoji and the striking blade to Zhang Yue.

CHAPTER 5

The Battle at the No. 6 High School

GOING BACK A BIT, ZHAO Hongbing and others held this "rumble summing-up meeting" not in anticipation of fighting with others, but rather to prepare for Tiger's revenge. Tiger's gang was famous for constant altercations; right after the 1983 "Strike Hard" campaign, they'd begun "jabbing" their way to the top in the eastern suburb. Due to their superior numbers, they'd never known defeat. This time in the city they'd lost an enormous amount of face, so they could be counted on to wreak revenge.

During the summing-up meeting, the wounded Sun Dawei repeatedly suggested peace talks with Tiger's gang, but the others overruled him.

"They lost the fight, and some of their guys ended up at the police station. There's no way they'll talk peace," Li Wu said. An unemployed vagrant from a market town, he was a born lowlife. He'd already been streetwise before joining the group, although he hadn't made any kind of a name for himself.

"Dawei, a guy should do his best to stay out of trouble, but when trouble arrives, he can't back away from it," Feisi said. His hand was still seeping blood.

"What it comes down to is that some were meant to make it home and they did. We only live once, so why live in fear?" Zhao Hongbing always spoke calmly and courteously and never seemed to get upset, no matter what happened.

Streetwise readers will have observed that a group that manages always to come out on top in street fights must include the following kinds of people:

- Someone who likes to stir things up. Whenever such people join a gang, that gang will get into more fights because this kind of person likes making trouble. Zhao Hongbing's gang had three such people: Little Beijing, Zhang Yue, and Feisi. Little Beijing had a smart mouth, and Zhang Yue and Feisi were quick-tempered. For example, while they were at the square viewing the lanterns, if Little Beijing hadn't goaded the long-haired youth, Zhao Hongbing would have let it pass; Little Beijing's presence turned the situation into a melee.
- Someone who likes to strike the first blow. Taking the initiative brings an advantage in terms of momentum and tactics, and those forced to react tend to lose the fight. It could be said that in Zhao Hongbing's gang, everyone but Hongbing and Sun Dawei liked to make the first move.
- A person who fights fearlessly, regardless of the odds. It could be said that everyone in the gang except Sun Dawei had this kind of fearlessness. Zhao Hongbing, Zhang Yue, and Little Beijing in particular would stand

their ground unflinchingly in the face of a thousand troops and horses. Ergou remembers back in high school watching a Hong Kong movie called *Wise Guy*. Toward the end, the protagonist Chan Ho-nam says, "Do we need to outnumber them?" In an instant, hundreds of guys rush out from every side, and his opponents are so scared that they surrender. In fact, a real tough guy doesn't care how many people there are – the tougher the odds, the more fired up he gets. But very few people are like that.

- Someone who has actual combat experience. Someone who has training in martial arts reacts faster, and his strength and accuracy are greater than the average person. In countless brawls following their demobilization, Zhao Hongbing, Lisi, and Little Beijing almost never had anyone grab their hair, collars, or wrists, and this was due to their outstanding fighting skills. Also, while always holding back in a fight, they'd been trained in the army to kill with the first blow.
- Someone who can negotiate. In the 1980s, local hoodlums were seldom content with one fight, and they also rarely called the police. Under normal circumstances, they would fight three to five times or even more, until one side had been beaten into submission, and then they would negotiate a truce. The outcome of such peace talks was usually that the losing side would pay medical expenses, and the member of the losing gang who had started the trouble would get smacked around. After that, everyone could be friends. In Zhao Hongbing's gang, the negotiator was Sun Dawei; it was a favorite activity of his, especially when representing the winning side.

Although they'd had this big fight with Tiger's gang, three of Zhao Hongbing's crew had proper jobs, which put them at a disadvantage to Tiger's unemployed hoodlums. From then on, when they went out at night it was almost always in a group out of fear of revenge from Tiger. They also avoided the east side of town, where Tiger's gang could jump them.

The only person who went out on his own was Sun Dawei, because he was chasing a girl at the No. 6 High School. Where pursuing girls was concerned, Ergou felt there are several grades of technique; Sun Dawei's ways and methods fell into the lowest possible class. Sun was neighbors with this girl, and he claimed to have started liking her when he was only six or seven years old. This had been going on for more than ten years, and the girl had rejected him at least a dozen times.

Ergou no longer remembers what that girl looked like, even though she once gave him a hug. He only remembers that when the gang was at the train station seeing Little Beijing off after National Day, Little Beijing said to Sun Dawei, "Dawei, did a mule kick you in the head? Why are you so stuck on Pigsy's Aunt?"

"I like Pigsy's Aunt and anyone else in Pigsy's family," smirked Sun Dawei.

The girl Sun Dawei was pursuing was a good student. Dawei waited for her outside the school every afternoon, rain or shine, even though she seldom spoke to him. Not long after National Day, he found another way to approach her. It turned out that this girl's mother had been admitted to the hospital with a case of appendicitis, and Dawei discovered her there while having his bandages changed after the fight. Thinking this would be an excellent opportunity to gain his prospective mother-in-law's approval, Sun Dawei took her a basket of fruit and canned goods. This woman had known Sun Dawei since he was a little boy and had nothing against his sweet-talking, but the girl herself was irritated and hurried Dawei off, saying he was disturbing her mother's rest.

Sun Dawei's sly side came out: "I'll leave if you want, but tonight after your evening study session, you have to come to the school athletic field to hear me play the guitar."

"As long as you leave now, I'll promise you anything," said the girl, who just wanted to be rid of him.

Back then, Ergou hadn't yet formed his worldview, and he naively believed that Sun Dawei's method was effective – if you were thick-skinned enough, you could catch a girl. Several months after this incident, when the kindergartens were reopened, Ergou became acquainted with a classmate surnamed Zhang, who was the prettiest little girl in the entire kindergarten. Absorbing the lesson of Sun Dawei's success, Ergou pursued her shamelessly.

He clearly remembers one day in the kindergarten, the teacher arranged the little green chairs in a circle, and had each child say what they hoped for their future. When the little girl Zhang stood up and said she hoped to be a nurse, her piece of playdough fell to the ground. Ergou saw it and reached under her chair to get it for her, just as she finished answering. She bent down to pick it up but it was gone.

"Ergou, give me my playdough," she said, looking pitifully at him.

"Zhang XX, I love you," said Ergou, looking amorously at her.

The little girl didn't seem to know what the word "love" meant, and ignored Ergou's avowal.

"What are you on about?" she said. "Hurry and give back my playdough!"

"I'll give it back if you say you love me," said Ergou, mimicking Sun Dawei.

"Wah!" The little girl sat down, bawling her eyes out.

One can well imagine what followed. The incident caused a sensation throughout the kindergarten. A thousand students and their parents heard about it, and Ergou was made to stand in the corner for three days. From then on, his name became a synonym for puppy love among the teachers and parents. No one hears of the good you do, but your mistakes are reported far and wide. This incident followed Ergou right through primary school, middle school, and high school, and was constantly brought up to humiliate him. Worse yet, this girl attended the same school as Ergou right through high school. Every time they saw each other, they both blushed. This incident cast a lasting shadow over Ergou's life. Over the next twenty years, he never dared tell any girl he loved her, no matter how deeply he felt about her.

As for Sun Dawei, he was ecstatic at finally getting the girl to agree to meet him, and boasted about it to the whole gang. He brought Zhao Hongbing and the others in a grand procession to the athletic field of the No. 6 High School to hold a joint "guitar concert". Back in the 1980s, there wasn't much to do in the evening, and young people liked to hang out together. So, when the seven young guys went to the athletic field that night, they brought Ergou and Xiaobo along.

The No. 6 High School was notable for having a road separating its athletic field from the classroom buildings. The athletic field had spacious bleachers and there were hardly any people around.

After the evening study session ended, the girl Sun Dawei was pursuing did in fact turn up. She brought along her desk mate, a very pretty girl named Gao Huan. Ergou thought Gao Huan must be an angel from heaven. Later when he saw the actress Cecilia Cheung in the Hong Kong film *The King of Comedy*, he reckoned that she could have been Gao Huan's twin sister.

Several of the gang started strumming their guitars and singing, and they were pretty loud. With his beloved at his side, Sun Dawei didn't hold anything back. The truth was, he didn't play nearly as well as Ergou. He seemed always to be off-beat, and his chord changes were ragged. Lisi, sitting at the top of the bleachers, made a better show of it. He had brought his harmonica, and he played it with a pure and rather mournful melodiousness that contrasted starkly with his drowsy appearance. In the twenty years that followed, Ergou never heard anyone play the harmonica as well as Lisi. Of course, it's likely that no one even plays the harmonica anymore. The punks of the 1980s were different from the petty hoodlums of today, who only know how to hang around nightclubs. In the old days, most punks could play some kind of musical instrument.

Across from the bleachers another group was also singing. Besides guitars, they had someone playing a bamboo flute. Since they were only about a hundred yards apart, and everything was quiet around them, the two groups tried to drown each other out. As the music became louder, tempers flared, and they began insulting each other.

"Hey, asshole! Quiet down!"

"Fuck you! Come over and make me!" Zhang Yue yelled. With girls around, especially one as pretty as Gao Huan, Zhang Yue's temper became even harder to control.

There was no answer from the others. In the darkness, all that could be seen was a dozen or so guys walking toward them.

"Get down here!" the other group yelled at Zhao Hongbing's gang as they arrived at the base of the bleachers.

"Ha! Who's afraid of you!" Zhao Hongbing handed his guitar to Gao Huan and strode down the bleachers with his friends while Gao Huan, Ergou, Xiaobo and Sun Dawei's girl stayed on the bleachers.

The two groups faced off, and someone said, "Which of you shouted for us to come over just now?" It was impossible in the darkness to see who spoke, but the voice was steady and powerful.

"It was me," laughed Zhao Hongbing.

"What's your name?" said the other man in an ordinary tone of voice, as if this were just a normal conversation rather than the prelude to a fight.

"Zhao. Hong. Bing." He pronounced each syllable with a pause in between.

"Oh, I know you! My younger brother was in school with you. My name is Railway." The other man's tone was still polite.

When that name was spoken, everyone on Zhao Hongbing's side felt their hearts sink as they thought: *What bad luck! It's been less than a month since we offended Tiger from the eastern suburb, and that's not even over yet. Now we've come up against another God of the Plague – Railway – and he's at least as ferocious as Tiger.*

Railway was a notorious hoodlum in the 1980s. He was not a local, and had always lived along the railway, hence his nickname. His father was in the military, and his mother was a performer in a song-and-dance troupe, renowned throughout the city for her beauty and musical talent. The Party organization had arranged for Railway's lovely, gentle mother to marry his father – a coarse and ugly man. Railway had inherited his mother's musical talent, and it was said that he was especially good at the bamboo flute. He had also inherited his father's propensity for violence and cruelty.

Railway's gang members had been friends since childhood, and had made their way to adult life through the school system for dependents of railway workers. Railway had led that band of boys since elementary school. Once they graduated, the youths were provided with jobs on the railway or continued to follow Railway into the underworld. In the early 1980s, hoodlums were restricted to a fairly narrow domain mainly involving theft, and Railway's gang lived off their own turf. Since they were well known to the all the railway employees, from stewards to railroad police, this provided them with easy pickings. Railway's gang had two special traits: the first was their relative wealth, and the second was their tendency to dress well, in particular their overcoats and shoes, which they usually managed to "pick up by mistake" while working the trains. Fighting was just a hobby for them, but when they fought, it was with a particularly ruthless cruelty and refusal to admit defeat, and their numbers and cohesion made them especially formidable.

"Brother Railway! Of course I've heard of you!" Zhao Hongbing copied his courteous tone.

"Brother, the voice I heard yelling at us just now didn't sound like yours. Tell me who it was, and I won't involve you." Railway still spoke as politely, as if this were just an ordinary conversation.

"What happens if I don't tell you, Brother Railway?" Hongbing asked with a smile.

In the subsequent "rumble summing-up meeting," everyone expressed admiration for Zhao Hongbing's special ability to remain cool and collected, no matter how ferocious his opponent or fearful the occasion; he always managed to be a cut above the rest. This temperament had much to do with his family background and his military experience. He had been brought up to fear no one, and his military experience had taught him a similar boldness in any situation. This disposition gave him a natural advantage, as well as bolstering the courage of the brothers behind him.

"Just tell me. I won't do anything but knock a couple of his teeth out," said Railway, his tone as pleasant as ever.

"Hey Zhao! Show you know what's good for you, or we'll whip your cocky ass as well!" came a clearly less restrained voice from behind Railway.

A fight was inevitable.

Then, to everyone's surprise, there came a percussive sound, followed by cries of pain from among Railway's men. Zhao Hongbing looked around, but no one near him had made a move. Puzzled, he looked again and realized that Feisi and Xiaoji had at some point edged away to a pile of brick fragments ten or so yards from him, and were now chucking brick pieces at Railway's men with all their might. Both of them were artillerymen, so their arms were particularly strong. It looked like the previous "rumble summing-up meeting" had been effective in pressing home the lesson of making use of the materials at hand. Their military formation was also similar to that used in the PLA, with the scouts in front and the artillery lobbing munitions to provide cover. The two artillerymen seemed to be maintaining the PLA's proud tradition of ruthlessness and accuracy as well; every brick hit its mark, and they kept them coming in rapid succession.

Railway's gang also showed their competence. Once they saw their opponents making a move, they quickly regrouped.

Leading the way was the man behind Railway who had yelled at Zhao Hongbing. He had just rushed forward when he felt the cold metal of a striking blade pressed against his neck. It was Zhang Yue, holding the blade that Little Beijing had snatched from Tiger's gang. Again, the conclusion of the "rumble summing-up meeting" – to never go out unarmed – had yielded good results.

"One step closer and I slit his throat!" hollered Zhang Yue.

"Don't be hasty, brother. Let him go." There was a note of anxiety in Railway's voice now as he motioned for those behind him to stay back.

"Motherfucker! You wanted to knock my teeth out, did you? You'll feel my knife today!" Zhang Yue was venting the anger he'd been holding back.

"Okay, brother, if you want to give me a jab, go ahead. Do it here," said Railway, stretching his head toward Zhang Yue. He was sure this kid wouldn't have the nerve to actually stab someone, especially a man of Railway's stature. It was a display of reckless daring that he would come to regret, and one he might never have ventured had he known who Zhang Yue's grandfather was, and who his father and elder brother were.

"Fuck your mother!" yelled Zhang Yue, releasing the punk in his grip and thrusting his striking blade at Railway. Railway instinctively turned his face, and the knife sliced into his right cheek.

This thrust of the knife immediately unmanned Railway, who now knew the strength behind that thrust and that if he didn't escape it he was a dead man. Although Railway's gang normally used knives in fights, they seldom used striking blades, and their jabs were always aimed at thighs and arms. They had never encountered a desperado like Zhang Yue who aimed for the neck.

Zhang Yue didn't leave it at that. He thrust his blade a second time, only to be stopped by Zhao Hongbing, who grabbed Zhang Yue's arm while at the same time aiming a kick at Railway, connecting with his kneecap and sending him sprawling.

With Railway down, Hongbing and Lisi lunged at the men standing behind him. They had learned from last time when Li Wu had been knocked down while leading the charge; this time it was the most skillful fighters, Zhao Hongbing and Lisi, who led the assault. Railway's men were stripped of the advantage of their number, and those within range of Zhang Yue's blade scattered in all directions.

Rising to his feet clutching his jaw in his hands, Railway yelled indistinctly, "Stop fighting, damn it! Enough!" Railway could turn up the volume when he wanted to. Zhao Hongbing's guys had also had enough, and they stopped.

"Zhao Hongbing, tomorrow night at eight o'clock I'll have a grave waiting for you at the top of Nanshan Hill." Railway was bearing the pain as best he could, but with his hands covering his face, his words were muffled. There was a gaping wound where the striking blade had slashed him.

"Better save that grave for yourself," laughed Zhao Hongbing. "I'll come for you when the time is right." He wasn't even breathing hard.

Ergou knew there was nothing scary about Zhao Hongbing and his gang, but the two girls in the bleachers were petrified. Ergou sensed Gao Huan beside him, clutching her arms and shivering from either fright or cold. The girls knew that Sun Dawei was disreputable, but they'd never guessed he was friends with desperados like these, and they'd never witnessed such a violent brawl.

Back in the 1980s, hoodlums were always fighting over matters of face and to show who was boss; it was all so simple then. The reference to Nanshan Hill was just gangster speak for a meeting, borrowed from China's ancient tradition of knight-errantry.

Ergou realized that Zhao Hongbing wasn't afraid because he could tell Railway didn't have the nerve to kill.

Early the next day, after Mr. Zhao had gone off to work, the gang met at Hongbing's home for a "rumble summing-up and Nanshan Hill mobilization meeting". The first to join the meeting were the jobless vagrants Xiaoji and Li Wu. Zhang Yue and the others arrived in the afternoon after finishing work. The meeting harshly criticized Zhang Yue's impetuous violence, while greatly praising Xiaoji and Feisi for their flexible use of available resources. The core issue of the meeting was how to deal with Railway's gang that evening.

"Railway's already been scared stiff by Zhang Yue," Lisi said.

"Railway doesn't have the guts to kill, but he has the guts to hurt someone badly," said Zhao Hongbing, deep in thought.

"All of us have to be armed tonight," Zhang Yue said.

"If we get word out about the meet-up with Railway, they won't dare go overboard," Sun Dawei said.

"As long as they don't go for the kill, we're bound to win," said Feisi.

"Let's try to talk it out with them. Any problem can be solved through negotiation," Sun Dawei said.

"Enough talk, let's get our weapons ready." With those words from Zhao Hongbing, the group dispersed.

Northern China is cold at the end of October. On the desolate peak of Nanshan Hill, the wind rustling through the withered underbrush created an even bleaker atmosphere.

Zhao Hongbing and his guys arrived fifteen minutes early, each carrying at least one knife. Lisi's weapon stood out: he had sawed a steel heating pipe into a sharp point so it could be used to both hit and stab; he called it a prong. Usually the weakest fighter, Sun Dawei had brought the most advanced weapon – a shotgun. No one knew where he'd gotten it, but from then on, Dawei was never without this weapon until he exchanged it for a double-barreled shotgun two years later.

There was no one else on the mountain, and no sign of the grave Railway had mentioned.

Zhang Yue climbed onto the first step of the Memorial to the People's Heroes, his hand gripping his striking blade as he yelled into the frigid air, "Railway, you motherfucker! Where are you? I'm going to take another slice of you tonight!"

His voice rang over the expanse of the hill, but there was no reply.

The autumn night was unusually cold, especially in this city on the plains. By eight-fifteen, there was still no sign of Railway and his crew, and Zhao Hongbing and his brothers were shivering in the cold. Just then, a boy who looked like a high school student appeared on the hilltop.

"I'm Railway's neighbor," said the boy. He wouldn't have been able to see Zhao Hongbing and the others clearly in the darkness, but he must have sensed their ferocity, because his voice shook a little.

"Okay, so where's Railway?" said Zhao Hongbing, his voice as calm and gentle as always.

"He's in the hospital," the boy quavered. "He got stabbed in the face and his lower jaw is broken. They've had to bind it up and sew his mouth shut, so he can't talk and he hasn't eaten since yesterday. He can't come tonight."

"Oh, if he can't make it, that's fine. We'll leave it for another time," said Hongbing. "In any case, I know where to find him."

Ergou had to admire Zhao Hongbing's nerve. Although he didn't go with them to Nanshan Hill, he listened in on their meeting and knew that Hongbing hadn't actually wanted to fight, and had only gone to Nanshan Hill to save face. When his opponent failed to show, this gave him a way out, yet he didn't immediately back down but said he'd settle accounts with Railway later.

"I have a note for you from Railway," said the boy, handing Hongbing a piece of paper.

"Okay, you go on now. Or maybe we should all go down together," said Hongbing.

"That's all right. I'll go first," said the boy, and quickly put a good distance between himself and what he regarded as a band of fiends.

On the note were written the words "Honor demands vengeance." This phrase was fashionable at the time, but it was hard to see Railway as someone with a sense of honor.

"Zhang Yue scared off Railway and his bunch with his knife," said Zhao Hongbing. "They won't be giving us any more trouble."

Subsequent events showed that once again, Zhao Hongbing was absolutely right. From then on, Railway seldom showed his face in the city, and seldom fought; he'd lost face in more ways than one. But he adhered to underworld etiquette and never reported the matter to the police. When one person falls, another rises in his place, and the story quickly spread through the "underworld" – how Zhao Hongbing and his gang had overcome their numerical disadvantage and had then arrived first on the mountaintop, with Railway a no-show. I put "underworld" in quotation marks because in the 1980s, it was as Ge You said in the movie *Bigshot's Funeral* – "There is no underworld in China."

The criminals and ruffians of the early 1980s had mostly been wiped out in the 1983 nationwide "Strike Hard" campaign. The new generation of hooligans consisted mainly of young guys from the residential quarters of the massive factories – really, just shiftless punks with no particular fighting skills. All this changed when people like Zhao Hongbing and his friends came to the fore.

This was the first time Railway had suffered such a brutal defeat, and his followers were disgraced along with him. They all feared death, and were especially afraid of Zhang Yue – that devil incarnate who seemed hell-bent on murder. Zhao Hongbing's gang became famous through that one fight and through Zhang Yue's deadly knife. Railway's gang of petty thieves and pickpockets had been shooting stars in the underworld firmament, but they were never a match for Zhao Hongbing and his band, however great their number.

Large numbers are good for nothing but bullying the weak and throwing weight around. But Zhao Hongbing and his gang picked on the strong and on those who had made their name as hoodlums. This was the road they continued to follow, and it proved to be a shortcut to promotion within the gangland world.

Fifteen years later, Railway had become a big boss in the railway restaurant and entertainment industry when he ran into Zhao Hongbing on a business occasion. The two of them laughed and shook hands and put their enmity behind them. After they'd downed a few drinks and their eyes were blurred and their ears burning, they began talking of the past.

"Hongbing, I'd really like to know who it was who stabbed me back then. It was too dark for me to see him then, and to this day I still don't know who it was."

"Why do you want to know?"

"I'm forty years old now, and I've never been a bullshitter, but that time I was really scared. He was going to kill me."

"Do you want revenge?"

"No. As you know, I've focused on business since then."

"Even if you want revenge, you'll never get it."

"Why's that?"

"He went to prison year before last, and last spring he was executed. It was Zhang Yue."

"Really! I actually wanted to thank him."

"Why?"

"If it hadn't been for him, I might have stayed a punk the rest of my life. When he stabbed me, I realized I wasn't cut out for the underworld – I didn't have the guts."

The way Ergou sees it, the phrase "a blessing in disguise" can apply to anyone or anything.

Railway lacked the heart of a killer, but that doesn't mean no other gangsters had that kind of nerve. One who did was Tiger.

CHAPTER 6

Revenge of the Eastside Gang

ERGOU FOUND THAT AFTER COMING down from Nanshan Hill that day, Zhao Hongbing began paying attention to his personal appearance. Every day he stood in front of the armoire mirror at home and used home-made tweezers to pull out the whiskers scattered on his face. He had always been clean-cut but never vain, so what was going on? Hongbing also kept trying on his father's dark blue woolen Mao suit and frowning at himself in the mirror. Finally he dug out a fountain pen that his sister had given him when he enlisted. After sticking it in the right breast pocket of the Mao jacket, he gave a nod of satisfaction.

A few months later Ergou learned that Zhao Hongbing had fallen for the enchantress he'd encountered on the athletic field of the No. 6 High School that night – Gao Huan. However, Hongbing wasn't as thick-skinned as Sun Dawei, and was embarrassed to admit that he wanted to see Gao Huan again. Sun Dawei solved the problem by somehow managing to talk his paramour into meeting him at the school and hearing him play the guitar again. Upon learning that Gao Huan would also be there, Zhao Hongbing started practicing his guitar day in and day out.

The first song Zhao Hongbing practiced was "Come Together, Young Friends". He played it so often that for years afterward, hearing that song made Ergou run off with a gut ache, because Zhao Hongbing always insisted that Ergou or Xiaobo sing along as he hummed.

Dissatisfied with his progress, Hongbing asked Sun Dawei to bring his tape recorder and practice with him. Sun Dawei had always been a trend-setter in loafer circles, and almost everyone in the city knew about his single-deck tape recorder.

Sun Dawei hopped on Zhang Yue's brand new Flying Pigeon bicycle with his battery-powered tape recorder hanging from the handlebars. The tape recorder was always set on its highest volume and always played just two songs: the theme tune to the Shanghai gangster epic *The Bund*, and the title music of the TV series about the famous *kungfu* fighter Chen Zhen. Ergou can't remember the name of that second song, but the lyrics went something like, "Smart guy, this is your home, its elegant courtyard...splattered with blood." Sun Dawei wore an old quilted army jacket he'd gotten from Feisi, and carried his battered guitar on his back. Behind him was the Zhao family's German shepherd. This portly music-lover spent the better part of each day whizzing around the city's streets on his bicycle, becoming a familiar figure to everyone from old folk to toddlers. Sun Dawei's Flying Pigeon bicycle and single-deck tape recorder were a bigger deal back then than a motorcycle was a decade later, and his get-up quickly caught on with other young people who were "awaiting employment". The Flying Pigeon bicycle, German shepherd, tape deck, quilted army jacket, and guitar became all the rage. By 1987, the streets were full of Sun Dawei imitators.

When Sun Dawei and Li Wu arrived at Zhao Hongbing's

home, Hongbing was wearing his father's Mao suit and looking at himself in the mirror. Sun Dawei implored him, "Brother, don't look in the mirror or it'll break!"

"Knock it off. Did you bring the tape for 'Nights on the Naval Port?'

Just then there was an urgent pounding on the door. "Ergou, go open it." Tired of always being ordered around by Sun Dawei, Ergou reluctantly obeyed. In the doorway stood a man covered in blood. Ergou was no coward, but he cried out in fear before calming down enough to recognize Xiaoji, his army coat drenched in blood.

"Ershu!" (Meaning "second uncle", which is what Ergou always called Zhao Hongbing.) "Uncle Li, come quick! Uncle Ji's been hurt!" Ergou wailed as Zhao Hongbing and the others ran over.

"Who did this?" demanded Hongbing, eyes blazing.

"Get him to the hospital!" cried Sun Dawei.

"It was Tiger, that motherfucker!" groaned Xiaoji angrily.

Sun Dawei ran out and stopped a man pulling a donkey cart. They took Xiaoji to the hospital. He had been stabbed seven times in the chest and belly, and the doctors considered it a miracle that he was still alive. Somehow not a single stab had struck a vital organ.

It turned out that Xiaoji had been taking in scrap at his recycling stall when the man he'd fought with at the sports ground on National Day came to sell some steel tubes he'd just stolen. He didn't recognize the man, but the man recognized him, and later on, Tiger and his gang arrived, stabbed Xiaoji and sauntered off. Xiaoji's recycling stall was only sixty yards or so from the Zhao home, but thinking he was a dead man, he just lay there. After a few minutes, he realized he might survive after all. Fearing his enemies' return, he dragged himself to Zhao Hongbing's home.

By eight o'clock that night, all of Hongbing's gang had heard the news and arrived at the hospital. There Hongbing held another meeting. Unlike the last two times, he called for revenge, and they had to take the initiative. "We'll raid Tiger's home at night. Who knows where he lives?" Hongbing spoke of the raid as calmly as if planning a courtesy visit.

"I don't know, but I can ask around," said Sun Dawei.

"What he did to Xiaoji we'll do to him tonight," said Feisi, who was Xiaoji's closest friend.

"Dawei, you find out his address. The rest of us will get our tools together."

Around 9pm, everyone had gathered downstairs at the hospital with their weapons of choice, but Sun Dawei hadn't yet found out Tiger's address.

"We'll just have to look until we find him," said Zhao Hongbing.

"Get in!" said Feisi, opening the door of his work unit's white van.

They drove straight to the residential quarters of the woolen mill in the eastern suburb, and the first person they encountered was able to tell them exactly where Tiger lived. Tiger was clearly very well known in the area.

His home had a metal door and no doorbell. Feisi went up and pounded thunderously it.

"Who's there?" came Tiger's voice.

"Your granddad!" Feisi replied.

There was no sound from inside. Feisi kept hammering on the door. After about five minutes, there was the clank of a bolt being drawn, but the door didn't open. Feisi kicked the door open but then froze in place with the cold double barrel of a shotgun aimed at his head.

"You want to stay alive?" One of Tiger's gang brothers was holding the gun, and at least a dozen others were inside; it looked like Tiger had been expecting them.

"Shoot me if you have the balls!" sneered Feisi.

"Don't think I wouldn't dare," said Tiger's brother.

"Shoot, then! Go on, shoot!" yelled Feisi.

Just at that moment, Zhao Hongbing landed a kick on the gunman's wrist. The gun blasted into the air. Hongbing grabbed it, only to find another shotgun aimed at his head. This one was held by Tiger.

"Move and you're dead," growled Tiger.

"Would you dare?" asked Hongbing. He didn't move, and his speech was as calm as ever.

"What's your name?" Tiger asked.

"Zhao. Hong. Bing." Hongbing always spoke his name very deliberately, whatever the circumstances.

"Oh, so you're Zhao Hongbing!" said Tiger. A true son of the soil, he couldn't even give Hongbing's name the proper Mandarin pronunciation.

At that point a third shotgun appeared and pointed at Lisi's head. "Brothers, hand me a chopper," said Tiger. "If anyone fights back, I'll hack them all to death!"

Streetwise readers will be aware that chopping is used for intimidation rather than killing. If anyone is said to have been chopped to death, they either got chopped too many times or dropped dead after reaching home. Chopping is meant to shock and awe.

After a few blows of the knife, Zhao Hongbing and his friend turned and left, their flesh wounds nothing compared with the blow to their spirits. The bravado they'd gained from defeating Railway and his gang had been vanquished by Tiger. It was their first defeat since appearing on the scene, and a crushing one at that. They'd gone out on a raid only to be sent packing; the proud and ambitious Zhao Hongbing had gotten carried away, and he was sunk in silence. His father's dark blue woolen Mao jacket was ruined. There was no way he could wear it to see Gao Huan.

Back they went to the hospital, this time to have their own wounds dressed. Because the elder Mr. Zhao was away, Ergou went with them to the hospital. Dressed for the cold in padded jackets and leather coats, they had suffered only flesh wounds. Sun Dawei had escaped without a scratch thanks to his heavy army jacket.

Ergou read from their silence that they'd lost this time. Unlike their other fights, they didn't hold a meeting after this one.

"It isn't over yet," said Zhao Hongbing, breaking his silence with unusual vehemence.

"There has to be a way to catch Tiger off guard!" Feisi said.

"Who knew that fucking Tiger would have so many guns," Sun Dawei said.

"A gun is just a hunk of metal before it's fired," Zhao Hongbing said. "But once it's fired, the person holding it gets the courage to kill. After I kicked his wrist and the gun went off, someone was sure to open fire. Otherwise, all their guns would have been scrap metal."

That night, Zhao Hongbing and Sun Dawei stayed at the hospital with Xiaoji. Li Wu, who had been more severely injured, remained under observation, and Zhao Hongbing asked Zhang Yue to stay with him. Ergou understood why Hongbing kept Zhang Yue at the hospital – given his nerve and temperament, Zhang Yue would have gone back for Tiger that night.

Hongbing told Lisi and Feisi o go home so they could relieve him and Sun Dawei in the morning. He never guessed it would be two months before he saw them again.

The truth was that Feisi and Lisi were just as daring and hot-tempered as Zhang Yue, especially after being humiliated. Instead of going home, they drove straight back to Tiger's home at the woolen mill residential quarters. Lisi was carrying the sharpened pipe he liked to use, and Feisi was carrying a boning knife.

If Zhang Yue had gone after Tiger, he would have banged on the door and charged in at risk of his life. Lisi and Feisi did things differently, lying in wait behind a woodpile outside Tiger's home. Waiting to catch Tiger off guard was the difference between an army scout like Lisi and a desperado like Zhang Yue. When the time came for them to make their move, their hands were frozen stiff.

That night was especially clear. Faint starlight glimmered down on the two army vets shivering behind the woodpile as they smoked one cigarette after another while keeping their eyes glued to Tiger's door.

"After we take care of Tiger, what should we do?" Feisi whispered.

"Take off," Lisi replied.

"Will we have to spend the rest of our lives on the run? What about our families?" Rough as Feisi was, he was a filial son who was always worrying about his elderly parents.

"Maybe not our whole lives," said Lisi. "If the cops catch us."

"So then ..." Feisi probably never considered the possibility of ending up in prison.

"So you're just going to take being chopped?" Lisi said. "Don't you want to trash Tiger?"

"Easy. We'll trash him for sure," Feisi said.

He later explained that Lisi had fired him up enough to go ahead with it.

Around four in the morning, when the sky was still dark, Tiger came out of his house with about fifteen others. Failing to notice two pairs of wolf-like eyes watching them from the entrance of the lane, they sauntered out to celebrate their victory at the nearby Noodles and Ribs restaurant, which always opened first thing in the morning. Seeing their number, Feisi and Lisi held back. About an hour and a half later, Tiger returned with just one other guy – the man who had first pushed the gun out of the door the night before. They later found out that this was Tiger's own brother, known as Little Tiger.

By the time Tiger and Little Tiger reached the entrance of the lane, dawn was just breaking. They had obviously been drinking, and staggered woozily past the woodpile without noticing Feisi and Lisi. As Tiger and Little Tiger went to open their door, the two men who had spent five hours in the freezing cold crept up behind them and stabbed Little Tiger. Feisi then hacked at Tiger's hand and leg. The doctors were subsequently able to reattach the tendons of Tiger's hand, but he never walked normally again. Ten years later, someone else smashed Tiger's kneecaps, and he spent the rest of his life in a wheelchair.

Lisi and Feisi went straight to the railway station and caught the next train south.

Part Two

Love

CHAPTER 7

Opposites Attract

"Last night I dreamed of Tiger running around with a knife in his hand, looking for Lisi. It scared me to death!" This was the first thing Sun Dawei said to Zhao Hongbing when he regained consciousness in the hospital.

It was the first inkling the others had of Sun Dawei's uncanny premonitions. One month later, Little Tiger set out with a dozen others, his arm wrapped in bandages, knife in hand, roaming the city in search of Lisi and Feisi. When he couldn't find them, he started looking for Zhao Hongbing. Although Sun Dawei had dreamed of Tiger instead of Little Tiger, he was right about the weapon and the target.

Meanwhile, Lisi and Feisi had pulled together a hundred *kuai* or so and skipped town. With plenty of friendships forged in battle, they looked in on old war buddies as they headed south, drinking their way all the way down to Guangdong Province and then west to Sichuan, and from there north to Beijing. Warmly received wherever they went, they feasted daily on mountains of fish and meat and rivers of liquor. By the time they made their way back to the northeast, they were ruddy with health and rotund with overindulgence, the trials of their friends back home all but forgotten. When Zhang Yue met the beaming fugitives at the train station, he gave each of them a kick in the ass for the ferocious fighting that had occurred while they were AWOL.

The day after Lisi and Feisi trashed Tiger, Zhao Hongbing heard that the bedbound Tiger had proclaimed he would kill Feisi sooner or later. Hongbing didn't expect a man like Tiger to accept defeat without some kind of payback. He believed him capable of murder, but he didn't think he would actually kill Feisi.

"I really hope Tiger comes for me after he recovers," said Zhao Hongbing with a laugh.

"Why's that?" Sun Dawei asked.

"We still owe him for that night outside his place," said Zhao Hongbing and Zhang Yue almost simultaneously.

"Didn't Feisi and Lisi already pay him back?" Sun Dawei asked.

"I still need to set him straight!" said Zhang Yue.

Within that group, Zhang Yue only took orders from Zhao Hongbing, and only Hongbing could keep him in line. Zhang Yue was cocky to begin with, and being better educated made him even more arrogant, but he had always admired Zhao Hongbing. Hongbing was steady, clear-thinking and followed the code. Rather than being the kind who bullied the weak and cowered before the powerful, he was a natural-born leader. In high school his grades had been as good as Zhang Yue's, and Zhang Yue had always looked up to him.

Even so, it would have been very odd for the impetuous descendent of a bandit to remain under the thumb of the steady Zhao Hongbing. Hoodlums have their own lineage, after all. Zhang Yue eventually became the first in the gang to strike out on his own. From the late 1980s until the mid-1990s he was involved in many major incidents that sent shockwaves through the city, his reputation overtaking that of Zhao Hongbing. But whenever someone said to him, "Zhang Yue, you're the undisputed gang boss of this city," Zhang Yue replied, "No way. Hongbing is my big brother." Whenever Zhang Yue got in over his head, he always went to discuss things with Zhao Hongbing, or asked Hongbing to step forward and resolve the matter for him.

Although Zhao Hongbing avoided the limelight to the point of being shy, but he still quickly made a name for himself. In the year since his demobilization, he'd fought only twice. However, it was with the city's two most notorious gangs, and victory had fueled his meteoric rise in local gangland circles. As if this weren't enough, he soon performed another deed of such reckless bravery that even women and children learned of it; he fell in love.

Just a few days after Feisi and Lisi skipped town, Sun Dawei arrived for his scheduled guitar concert at the No. 6 High School. Even Xiaoji, who was still getting daily IV drips, hobbled over. It goes without saying that Zhao Hongbing was there as well.

Early Sunday morning, Zhao Hongbing took Ergou on his bike to his elder brother's home. Using the pretext of picking up Xiaobo, Hongbing actually wanted to borrow his brother's woolen Mao suit. So far, he'd managed to hide the other ruined suit from his father, but it still left him with nothing to wear to see Gao Huan that night. The recollection that his brother had a similar suit brought him to his door at the crack of dawn.

While Zhao Hongbing was a steady and reasonable fellow, his brother – Zhao Hongjun – was notoriously ill-tempered. He was a mid-ranking cadre at the glassworks in the city's northern suburb, where people referred to him as Wildman Zhao. Normally, Wildman Zhao was just like everyone else, but when he went crazy, he really earned his name. Ergou's mother had been Wildman Zhao's high school classmate, and she said that one time he'd gotten into a fight with another student during class and had jumped on desks chasing the other student around, knocking over tables left and right. When he finally caught the other boy and started beating him, a teacher had tried to intervene, and he'd smacked her around as well. That's when Wildman acquired his nickname. Maturity had brought his behavior under control, however, and he seldom went crazy any more. Whenever Ergou's mother saw him, she would jokingly say to him, "What's up, Wildman Zhao?", and Zhao Hongjun would scratch his head with embarrassment over his youthful antics. Zhao Xiaobo eventually turned out just like his father, but he took things further and became a notorious hoodlum.

"Hongbing, can't you let a guy get some sleep?" Wildman Zhao roared from inside. "Keep knocking and I'll come out and thump you!"

"Brother, open up!" Zhao Hongbing yelled, continuing to pound on the door. "I'm here for Xiaobo!"

"Why so early? Hongbing, I'll do anything if you'll just stop pounding!" Wildman Zhao was almost pleading. Who wanted to climb out from under his nice warm quilt on a northeastern winter morning?

"Brother, there's something else. Please let me in!" Hongbing said, continuing to pound. His desire to look presentable in the eyes of his beloved was making Hongbing obnoxious.

"I give up," sighed his brother.

About three minutes later, Wildman Zhao opened the door and cuffed Hongbing in the head. Hongbing led Ergou in with a sheepish grin.

"So what is it you want? Spill it!" said Wildman Zhao, still fuming.

"I – I want to borrow your Mao suit," Hongbing said with obvious embarrassment.

"You want my Mao suit? Why? Are you visiting a prospective bride?" his brother asked.

"Well, something like that," said Hongbing, blushing.

"Ha! You little devil! Go get it from the closet. I'm going back to bed." Wildman Zhao turned back to his bedroom.

Ergou could see Hongbing's excitement at borrowing the suit. Grabbing the half-sleeping Xiaobo, he took the boys home to try it on. On the way, Hongbing kept humming happily to himself, "Come together, young friends . . . " At home he stood in front of the mirror again, checking himself out. Copying Sun Dawei, Ergou said, "Hey! You'll break the mirror!"

Zhao Hongbing, Ergou, and Xiaobo arrived at the No. 6 High School with the guitar at ten o'clock that morning, and found everyone waiting for them as they entered the classroom. Apart from Zhao Hongbing, there was Zhang Yue, Sun Dawei, Li Wu, and the bandaged Xiaoji. On the girls' side there was Sun Dawei's 'girlfriend', Gao Huan, and another student named Li Yang – eight in all, plus the two little boys. Since it was Sunday, they had the classroom all to themselves. Among the eight, Zhao Hongbing was the handsomest, and he was especially well dressed that day. Among the girls, Gao Huan was the prettiest. Ergou still remembers her wearing a yellow turtle-neck sweater, with her hair in two long braids like Feng Chengcheng in *The Bund* – young and enchanting.

The most thick-skinned among them, Sun Dawei got up and launched into the theme songs from *Legend of the Condor Heroes* and *Fearless*. He wasn't much of a singer, being off-pitch and enunciating poorly. When he finished everyone booed.

"Quick, tell all the farmers to close up their pigsties, or Sun Dawei's howling will start a stampede!" said Sun's heart-throb sarcastically.

"Never fear!" said Sun Dawei, always ready with a come-back. "My howling will draw the hunters from Nanshan Hill, so there's nothing to worry about."

"Let's hear Zhao Hongbing now," said Sun Dawei's 'girlfriend'.

Hongbing started strumming and singing "Come Together, Young Friends". Since the tune was lively and cheerful, everyone started singing along. Ergou noticed that Gao Huan watched Hongbing with her chin in her hand. When he finished, she clapped vigorously. Ergou, only six years old but perceptive of others' feelings, decided then and there that it had been worth Zhao Hongbing's trouble to borrow the Mao suit and practice his guitar: Gao Huan was in love with him.

Everyone urged Hongbing to continue, so he started "Nights on the Naval Port". This was normally for a female voice, so everyone suggested that Hongbing play guitar while Gao Huan sang. Gao Huan had a lovely voice – clear, resonant, and tender. As she sang, she looked at Zhao Hongbing. Their eyes met in mutual understanding.

The final, romantic strains of the song lingered in the classroom, its occupants too spellbound to clap. In that innocent time, fewer worldly concerns complicated relationships between men and women; the right song could win a woman's heart and bind her to a man forever. Although the two of them were to face many trials and spend nearly ten years apart, their feelings never descended into resentment or regret. They remained true to each other forever.

Just at that moment, the classroom door opened and a youth strode in. He was tall and imposing, looking a lot like Ray Lui playing Ting Lik in *The Bund*. He had come to the classroom to pick up his books just in time for the 'concert.' "Gao Huan, who's this?" he asked.

"They're friends of mine," Gao Huan replied. "They came to play some music."

"Hi there!" said the youth urbanely to Zhao Hongbing and the others.

"Hi!" Zhao Hongbing replied with a smile.

The young man didn't linger after picking up his books. He left the classroom after the exchange of greetings. His name was Yan Chunqiu, and he was the son of the local Public Security Bureau's political commissar. Everyone knew he had a crush on Gao Huan. Zhao Hongbing and the others didn't realize it at the time, but this refined young man would be a thorn in their sides over the next twenty years.

After the guitar concert, Zhao Hongbing and Gao Huan were pretty much a couple. It turned out that Gao Huan had fallen for Zhao Hongbing the first time she saw him on the athletic field. His exchange with Railway before the fight had convinced her that apart from being handsome, Hongbing was steady, rational, and manly – someone she could depend on all her life. She had come to Sun Dawei's guitar concert in hopes of seeing Hongbing again, and had made a point of looking her best for him.

Why would a girl like Gao Huan, clever and beautiful, fall for an unemployed street brawler like Zhao Hongbing? Ergou could never figure it out until one day a friend observed, "A lady longs to be a brigand chief's wife." Thinking about this, Ergou concluded that a leader of mountain outlaws would be a man among men, and therefore irresistible to women. It was the law of opposites attracting; a clever, refined, and gentle girl would form a mutual attraction with a rough, strong outlaw leader. Women always believe they can change a man, and a woman of special abilities will rise to the challenge of turning an outlaw chieftain into an upstanding citizen. Because a lady longs to be a brigand chief's wife, Gao Huan fell in love with Zhao Hongbing, and would love him as long as she lived.

CHAPTER 8

Encounter at the Hospital

ERGOU DISAGREES WITH MENCIUS'S VIEW that men are born good, preferring the concept of original sin. However, as a person grows up under the instruction of his parents and teachers, the perversity of human nature gradually decreases depending on his upbringing and environment.

Many ruthless and violent people become a danger to society simply because they aren't brought up properly, and Tiger and Little Tiger were classic examples. Little Tiger was just as brutal as Tiger, if not more so.

Ergou heard of an incident that was referred to as "Little Tiger kills the ox". Little Tiger's family lived in the eastern suburb in an urban-rural continuum. This area included not only huge factories like woolen mills and breweries, but also a scattering of farming households. Some of these farming families still raised plow oxen. However, by the 1980s, as agricultural mechanization made oxen less important, some households began to kill off their cattle.

At the time, Little Tiger was not yet fifteen. He was still in middle school. Passing the home of a peasant family, he saw a lot of people standing around and ran over to join the action.

It turned out that a farmer was planning to kill his faithful old ox with a pig-butchering knife about an inch and a half wide and one foot long. The ox had been tied beneath a tree in front of the courtyard, but the burly, middle-aged farmer hadn't been able to complete the task. Before a hood could be slipped over its head, the ox realized that the man under whom it had toiled for more than a decade was about to kill it. It knelt silently on the ground, its big, limpid eyes brimming with tears. All of those standing around were moved, and the peasant's eyes were red; he couldn't bring himself to kill his old partner. Most of the bystanders advised the farmer not to kill the ox. From the time this village had been founded, plow oxen had been allowed to die a natural death. The peasant relented and prepared to release the beast from its tether.

Little Tiger found this a total bore. He'd come to see an ox slaughtered, and now he was being deprived of the pleasure. Little Tiger was acquainted with the peasant. Pretending to be helpful, he trotted over and said, "Uncle, give me your knife, and I'll kill your ox for you." The peasant saw the teenaged boy standing before him and doubtfully handed him the knife. Little Tiger wasted no words. He ran over to the ox, grabbed one of its stubby horns, and stabbed it in the neck. The ox didn't die with the first jab, so Little Tiger kept on stabbing it a dozen more times until the old creature finally expired.

By the time Lisi stabbed him, Little Tiger was twenty years old, and had helped Tiger rise in the eastern suburb. The two brothers were devils incarnate, beating others outside and each other at home. Three or four days before being tuned up by Zhao Hongbing's gang, Tiger had torn off half of Little Tiger's ear during a fight. Zhao Hongbing and his gang were probably the only people willing to take on these demons in 1986.

Three or four days after the guitar concert at the No. 6 High School, Little Tiger, who was not as badly injured as his brother, arrived in the city with his arm in a bandage. He was accompanied by a dozen other guys. They roamed the streets daily, looking for Lisi and Feisi. Little Tiger always had a knife with him, wrapped in newspaper. It was the pig butchering knife he'd used to kill the ox. Although renowned in the eastern suburb, Little Tiger and his crew had few acquaintances in the city. They knew that one of the gang members who had come to Tiger's home was named Zhao Hongbing, and that another ran a metal recycling stall near Red Flag Park. When Little Tiger went to Xiaoji's recycling stall, it was closed. Xiaoji was still in the hospital. So, he turned his attention to Zhao Hongbing instead.

Little Tiger's thinking was very simple: he was going to find whoever had hurt him. The people he really hated weren't Zhao Hongbing or Xiaoji, but rather Lisi and Feisi. All he wanted from Zhao Hongbing was to learn the names of the guys who had attacked him and his brother.

Apparently Little Tiger learned who Zhao Hongbing was and where he lived. He also found out that Hongbing's father was a member of the Party's municipal standing committee, and head of its organization department. He was willing to take on Zhao Hongbing in the street, but he didn't want to go looking for trouble at the home of a senior Party official.

Feisi and Tiger and Lisi and Little Tiger were destined to be enemies. They fought for more than ten years, up until the end of the 1990s, when Tiger became permanently crippled and Little Tiger ended up dead in the street. The only person who managed to interrupt their feuding was Zhao Hongbing. If the demonic Little Tiger was intimidated by anyone on this earth, it was Zhao Hongbing.

New Year's Day was fast approaching. Tiger and his gang still hadn't located Feisi and Lisi through their aimless roaming, so they decided to grab Zhao Hongbing. Since their objective was mainly to question Hongbing, they didn't bring their striking knives and shotguns. By noon they were hungry. They stopped for lunch at a big dumpling restaurant with more than thirty tables. At this restaurant, Little Tiger encountered another old enemy, Rascal Zhang.

They say Little Tiger spotted Rascal Zhang the minute he walked in the door. Baring his teeth in a smile he said, "Rascal, buy me a drink!"

Little Tiger's eastside hoodlums and Rascal Zhang's gang of punks had frequently come to blows in the past. By the summer of 1986, Rascal's gang had been forced to admit defeat, sealing a truce through a feast.

"Little Tiger, are you short on cash?" Rascal Zhang asked with a malevolent smile.

"I have plenty of cash, but you're still buying me a drink," said Little Tiger in a nasty tone of voice.

"All right, young friend. Have a seat and let your big brother treat you," said Rascal, not wanting to stir up trouble again over a meal. The past was the past. Regardless of all the fighting, they were grudging allies now. Rascal Zhang had six or seven guys with him, while Little Tiger had a dozen. They took two tables and sat down to eat.

When they first started drinking, the mood was friendly, with everyone laughing and clinking glasses. However, after they'd downed a few rounds, their rowdy natures resurfaced. Little Tiger became garrulous.

"Rascal, I've come to town looking for someone. See my arm?" Little Tiger said, his temper rising.

"I hear it was Zhao Hongbing and his gang. I saw you a few days ago roaming the streets. When I asked Wei Dong what you were up to, he said you were looking for Zhao Hongbing."

"Do you know him?" Little Tiger asked.

"I know of him," Rascal Zhang said. "He's the one who jabbed that moron Railway."

"They stabbed Railway, too?" Little Tiger asked.

"Haven't you noticed that Railway doesn't come to town anymore?" Rascal Zhang said. "They had to wire his jaw together. Zhao Hongbing's gang are a bunch of bad-asses."

"Actually, it wasn't Zhao Hongbing who wounded me and my brother," Little Tiger said. "It was two other guys in his crew."

"You and your brother are total losers, getting dropped in the doorway of your own crib!" said Rascal Zhang. The liquor had made him reckless.

"What the fuck are you saying, Rascal? They snuck up on us from behind!" Little Tiger looked like he was about to lose control.

"Fuck, man. Of course you're losers. Two against two, and having the shit kicked out of you," said Rascal Zhang even more caustically.

"You fucking asshole! If we hadn't made our truce – watch your fucking mouth from now on!" Little Tiger stood up and motioned for his guys to follow.

"Who are you mouthing off at?" said Rascal Zhang, not so easily intimidated.

"Boss, you can add the cost of your plates and dishes to Rascal Zhang's bill!" said Little Tiger to the restaurant owner, flipping the table over as he spoke.

"Fuck your mother, Little Tiger!" yelled Rascal Zhang.

Although he'd admitted defeat to Tiger and Little Tiger before, he was still a gang leader and up for a fight.

The two gangs began punching at each other and flipping over tables as the other customers fled in terror. Men who not long ago had been drinking together with their arms around each other's necks had suddenly been transformed into deadly enemies.

Little Tiger was clearly drunk. Before he could unwrap his knife, Rascal Zhang had snatched it away. His bandaged arm made him clumsy. Rascal squeezed it until Little Tiger collapsed to the floor in pain, where Rascal aimed several fierce kicks at him. One of Little Tiger's gang pulled out a bayonet and jabbed it into Rascal Zhang's leg. As Rascal fell to the floor in agony he grabbed a flower pot and smashed it into Little Tiger's head. At that point, the restaurant's cooks ran out with rolling pins and cleavers to help Rascal Zhang. Although Rascal's gang had been unarmed to start with, the support of the cooks quickly gave them the advantage.

After two or three minutes of fighting, the restaurant's elderly wait staff started pulling the men apart. Even hooligans are only human, and when old ladies in their fifties and sixties began urging them to stop, they didn't have the heart to continue. Three of the guys on Rascal Zhang's side had been stabbed in the arm. On the other side, Little Tiger had suffered the blow from the flower pot, and another man had been slammed in the back of the head with one of the cooks' rolling pins. This man was unconscious, so Little Tiger and the others carried him out of the restaurant, cursing and swearing. They grabbed a taxi to the No. 3 People's Hospital. That was where Xiaoji was being treated. Zhao Hongbing was filling out the forms to have Xiaoji discharged just as Little Tiger and the others were fighting at the dumpling restaurant. That city had more than twenty hospitals, large and small. How all those gangsters ended up at the No. 3 Hospital is anyone's guess.

The punk hit with the rolling pin was in pretty bad shape, and was still unconscious when they arrived at the hospital. Little Tiger and the others took him to the emergency ward. They came out just in time to see a woman in her thirties at the entrance to the elevator, pointing at Zhao Hongbing and scolding him as Hongbing listened with his head bowed. Beside him stood a beautiful girl. Zhao Hongbing recognized Little Tiger, but Little Tiger didn't recognize him.

Zhao Hongbing was being scolded because he and Gao Huan had just "seen a ghost". Gao Huan had met up with Hongbing after skipping class that afternoon on the pretext of going out to buy colored paper and melon seeds for the school's upcoming New Year's party. This was their first date. Hongbing's original plan was to get Xiaoji checked out of the hospital and then take Gao Huan to see the circus performing at the East Wind Theater. Hongbing had arranged for Gao Huan to meet him at 1:30 on the third floor of the hospital's inpatient department, but Gao Huan didn't realize the hospital had two separate blocks. The front block housed various specialty clinics and the operating room, and the rear block provided inpatient services. She went looking for Hongbing on the third floor of the front block.

After waiting a long time with no sign of Gao Huan, Zhao Hongbing realized she may have gone to the wrong block. He hurried to the operating theater on the third floor and spotted her, waiting with an anxious look on her face as soon as he exited the elevator.

"I'm sorry I'm late," Hongbing said, puffing with exertion. "I thought you'd know where to go."

"That's all right, it was my mistake," Gao Huan said charitably. "I got mixed up with the directions,"

"Let's go get Xiaoji," Hongbing said.

Just then, the elevator doors opened. Several white-gowned doctors rushed toward the operating room with a gurney carrying a woman in her thirties wearing a red coat. The woman had been in a car accident, and her face was an unrecognizable mass of blood. She looked unlikely to survive.

"Has she stopped breathing?" The doctors were talking to each other as they pushed the gurney. "Mm…She might be dead."

Gao Huan squealed in horror at the woman's appalling condition.

Hongbing comforted her, pressing the elevator button. "It's all right. Let's go downstairs."

An elevator arrived quickly from the fourth floor. Gao Huan, eager to leave this scene of horror, rushed in as soon as the door opened. Hongbing followed close behind. In order to transport gurneys and other emergency equipment, the hospital elevator was larger than most. Once inside, Gao Huan and Hongbing were horrified to discover the dying woman they'd just seen, huddling in the far back corner with her face turned away. Terrified at the sight of her spectral form, they tried to back out of the elevator, but the doors had already closed, and they were trapped inside.

Gao Huan, screamed and leaped into Hongbing's arms. It was the first time he'd ever held a woman. Zhao Hongbing was braver than most, and while Gao Huan continued to scream, he held her with one arm while kicking at the ghost.

"Ugh!" cried the red-clad specter with surprise and pain.

Seeing the effectiveness of his assault, Hongbing released Gao Huan and aimed another kick at the ghost. The first had been a dry run, but this was the real thing. The crouching fiend collapsed to the floor. "Why are you kicking me?" it wailed.

Zhao Hongbing then spoke words that Gao Huan continued to tease him about for years to come:

"You think being a demon makes you so tough?" he yelled. "After I die, I'll be a fucking demon, too, so don't think being a fucking demon is enough to scare me!"

"You're the demon! What do you think you're doing, beating me up?" The ghost was ready to expire from Hongbing's ferocious kicks.

"So now you're pretending to be human!" roared Hongbing, preparing another kick.

"Hongbing, I think she really is a human," said Gao Huan, who had regained her senses and was holding Hongbing back. Hongbing also began thinking more clearly and realized that there had been a distinctly unghoulish solidity to what he'd kicked. The elevator doors opened, and Zhao Hongbing and Gao Huan dashed out.

"You little bastard! What are you doing beating me! Stop right there!" The 'ghost', who was actually a woman in her thirties wearing a red coat, struggled to her feet and stumbled after them.

"I'm really sorry. I thought you were a demon," said Hongbing, realizing to his enormous embarrassment and shame that she was simply wearing the same kind of coat as the woman who'd been in the accident.

"You're the demon! You're going with me to the police, and then you're going to pay my medical bills!"

This episode was a fine example of the perils of mistaken identity.

"I'm really sorry. If I injured you just now, I'll take full responsibility," Hongbing said gently. Hongbing's virtue was that he was a real gentleman.

But the woman wasn't about to let him off so easily. She continued to berate him, using the ripest local vulgarities. Hongbing knew he deserved every word, and could only hang his head in shame. Gao Huan, who was just a young girl after all, dissolved into silent weeping.

As onlookers gathered, Hongbing blushed deeper, unable to vent his growing frustration. He happened to raise his head just in time to catch sight of Little Tiger, his head bloodied.

It seemed another fight was inevitable.

CHAPTER 9

Outnumbered

ZHAO HONGBING LOOKED AT LITTLE Tiger, and Little Tiger looked at Zhao Hongbing.

Four eyes met – Hongbing's large, shrewd, and intelligent; Little Tiger's pig-like, ignorant, and crafty. Hongbing's memory was stronger, and he immediately realized that the man standing before him with blood running down his face was the one who had pointed a shotgun at Feisi's head that night at Tiger's house. For his part, Little Tiger felt there was something familiar about the good-looking young fellow in front of him, but he couldn't place him as the man he'd been roaming the streets trying to find.

"I'll deal with this lady," Hongbing said to Gao Huan. "You go on to the theater. I'll meet you there in about twenty minutes. Go on." The truth was that Hongbing would rather lie to get Gao Huan out of the way than having her see him beat up Little Tiger. Gao Huan, for her part, was more than happy to leave.

"Wait here," Hongbing told the woman in the red coat. "I'll deal with your problem in a minute." He then strode over to Little Tiger.

"Brother, do you know Tiger?" Hongbing asked, suppressing his anger with a smile. Zhao Hongbing didn't like to start trouble, but at the moment two things were infuriating him: one was the sight of the man who had humiliated him at Tiger's home, and the other was the tongue-lashing he'd had to mutely accept from the shrewish woman. He was not the kind of man who would beat a woman. In any case, he'd been in the wrong when he kicked her, so the best he could do was vent his fury on Little Tiger.

"Tiger's my big brother," said Little Tiger. "Who are you?"

Hongbing could see he still hadn't recognized him, probably because their last encounter had been in the middle of the night. Little Tiger was also in bad shape at that moment. His head was bloodied from having a flower pot smashed against it, and blood dripped from the shoulder wound inflicted by Lisi's sharpened pipe. Plus, he was covered with soil and gave off an unmistakable odor of beef and onion soup. Hongbing answered Little Tiger's question in the same deliberate fashion as he had that night in Tiger's doorway:

"Zhao. Hong. Bing."

"Motherfucker! I've been looking all over for you!" said Little Tiger. However, he didn't attack Zhao Hongbing, because Rascal Zhang had snatched the butcher knife he'd been carrying. All his gang brothers were waiting for him at the entrance to the emergency room.

"Hah, and you have the nerve to curse me?" Zhao Hongbing had been well brought-up and seldom used foul language. His encounter with the 'ghost' in the elevator had been an exception brought on by the unusual circumstances.

"Curse you? I'm going to beat you up!" said Little Tiger, lunging at him.

Zhao Hongbing had been hoping Little Tiger would take the initiative. There was cleverness in this. If the police were called in, the man who attacked first would be blamed for the fight, while the skills Hongbing had acquired as an army scout assured him of victory even if his opponent made the first move. Failing to recognize Zhao Hongbing was one thing, but how could Little Tiger have forgotten how Hongbing had kicked his wrist and sent the shotgun flying from his hand? It was obvious that a kick of such speed and accuracy indicated to an opponent that a hooligan like himself could not hope to take on unarmed. As Little Tiger's fist came at him, Zhao Hongbing stepped back slightly, shot out his left hand, and grabbed Little Tiger's fist. Then he sent his right fist solidly into Little Tiger's arm while kicking him hard on the kneecap. Little Tiger tumbled to the floor.

These were Zhao Hongbing's favorite moves. He invariably grabbed his opponent's fist, twisted his wrist, and kicked him in a joint. He seldom punched people, but extended his left hand to grab some part of his opponent's body and then kicked hard at a knee or ankle to send him tumbling. Ergou later discovered that Little Beijing's technique was identical to Zhao Hongbing's, except that he used his right hand for grabbing; Hongbing had switched to his left hand after his right hand was injured. Hongbing's other method of delivering a blow to his opponent's arm after grabbing his wrist was one that Ergou later saw Jet Li used in the movie *Fearless.*

Once Little Tiger landed on the ground, Zhao Hongbing started kicking him. Little Tiger rolled around the floor. Every time he tried to get up, Hongbing kicked him again.

By then, Little Tiger's gang brothers had noticed that he

was under attack, and they rushed over – there were three or four of them. The leader lunged at Zhao Hongbing with a bayonet, but Hongbing dodged it by stepping backwards. Once again, the fight was in a hospital corridor. Hongbing retreated as he fought, his arm cut by the bayonet.

Zhao Hongbing still had fate on his side. At this point, Xiaoji appeared behind Little Tiger's gang with a thermos flask in his left hand, which he hurled at the head of the man with the bayonet. Scalded by the boiling water, the knife-wielding punk screamed in pain and shut his eyes. Hongbing took the opportunity to aim a kick at his opponent's hand, sending the bayonet sailing through the air. Darting forward, he grabbed the bayonet and made as if to stab Little Tiger, who bolted with the others. Xiaoji stood aside to let them back into the emergency room.

It turned out that Xiaoji had lost patience waiting for Hongbing in the inpatient department, and had come down to look for him. He arrived just in time to see Hongbing battling Little Tiger and his gang. Seeing a thermos flask placed at the entrance of the pediatrics department to his right, he had remembered their last fight in the hospital, and had used Little Beijing's method to free Hongbing from his encirclement.

Although Zhao Hongbing had grabbed the bayonet and looked like he was about to attack Little Tiger, it was only posturing. His intention was payback rather than serious injury. Zhao Hongbing chased them as far as the emergency room. Xiaoji yanked a six-foot hunk of wood off a hospital bench and followed close at his heels. Upon reaching the emergency room, Hongbing and Xiaoji waited at the entrance. The doorway was very narrow, allowing only two people to pass through at a time. By standing in the doorway, Hongbing could effectively prevent a group exit and force his opponents to fight him one-on-one. In this case he would be hard to beat, even if he weren't armed with a bayonet. On the other hand, if he ran into the emergency room, or outside to the corridor, he could easily become trapped. Hongbing was too smart for that.

Xiaoji and Zhao Hongbing teamed up to hold their position at the entrance, like the PLA captain Gu Zidi staunchly defending his position at Wen River in the movie *Assembly*. Neither advanced nor retreated a single step. With Xiaoji holding the longest weapon, coupled with Zhao Hongbing's lethal feet, the thirteen-member opposition suffered a solid loss. Xiaoji brandished his wooden plank energetically; their opponents couldn't prize it away from him.

Army veterans accustomed to holding "rumble summing-up meetings" obviously had an incomparable tactical advantage over a bunch of rural hooligans, and the two of them thoroughly bested their thirteen opponents. After tangling for about three minutes, Little Tiger's gang couldn't take it anymore. In all their years of fighting, they'd never seen two men fight against thirteen, nor had they seen a fighter as good as Zhao Hongbing or such excellent coordination and strategic partnership. They slammed shut the door to the emergency room and locked it, apparently unable to put up further resistance.

"You, Zhao! Have you had enough?" Little Tiger had been beaten into submission; even though Zhao Hongbing hadn't aimed to kill, he'd inflicted heavy damage, and Little Tiger was in extreme pain from head to toe after being kicked around.

"You're a dead man!" Zhao Hongbing threatened. He then backed up a few steps and aimed a flying kick at the emergency room door. The door was unexpectedly hollow and flimsy, however. Instead of kicking it open, Zhao Hongbing sent his foot straight through it. He hastily pulled his foot back, only to have his heavy shoe drop off inside the emergency room.

"Give back my shoe and I won't beat you up any more today," said Zhao Hongbing, having pretty much vented his anger by now.

"Don't bullshit me!" said a voice inside. "As soon as I open the door you'll fucking attack me again."

"When I say I won't attack you, I won't," Hongbing said. "But of course if you want to keep going, I'll be happy to keep you company."

"That's enough for today! We have a guy in the hospital, so we'll settle with you another day," Little Tiger said.

"If you want to settle things, let's get it over with now. Open up and we'll keep going," said Zhao Hongbing, hopping around on one foot in the corridor.

"All right, no more fighting. Here's your shoe." The door opened a crack, and Zhao Hongbing's shoe was tossed out, after which the door slammed shut again.

Zhao Hongbing put his shoe back on. He and Xiaoji were about to leave the hospital when they encountered the "ghost in the red coat" at the hospital entrance. Zhao Hongbing said very sincerely, "Sister, there's nothing to say but that I was wrong. If you need medical treatment, I'll cover the cost. But you shouldn't have yelled at me that way."

"It was a misunderstanding, brother. I'm fine and I don't need hospital treatment, so you run along." Waspy as the woman had been just a short time before, she was scared out of her wits after watching the fight.

Zhao Hongbing went on to the East Wind Theater to watch the circus with Gao Huan. He asked Xiaoji to tell Zhang Yue, Sun Dawei, and Li Wu to come to the Ten Thousand Cranes restaurant to celebrate his becoming a proprietor. After the New Year, Zhao Hongbing would take over operating the three-story guesthouse next to the train station.

By the time Hongbing took Gao Huan back to school, night had fallen. When Hongbing arrived at Ten Thousand Cranes, he found Xiaoji, Sun Dawei, and Zhang Yue waiting there along with Ergou and Xiaobo. The greedy scamps never missed out on a feast if they could help it. Only Li Wu was missing.

The four of them had a small-scale "third rumble summing-up meeting", with Zhao Hongbing presiding as usual. Everyone spoke up energetically. The meeting unequivocally pointed out three missteps in the most recent gang fights, as well as five items requiring attention.

The first misstep underestimating the enemy, resulting in the crushing defeat outside of Tiger's home. "From the strategic standpoint, we need to despise the enemy, but from the tactical standpoint, we need to take him seriously," Zhao Hongbing said.

The second misstep was inadequate information channels, resulting in ignorance of the tendencies and strength of the opposition. No one in Zhao Hongbing's gang was aware that Tiger's guys were roaming the streets looking for Hongbing. "Never go into a fight unprepared!" Xiaoji said.

The third misstep was that Feisi and Lisi were too rash. Taking the risk of attacking the enemy on his own doorstep had resulted in them having to skip town, and previous experience had already shown the error of such a tactic. "The supreme art of war is to subdue the enemy without fighting," observed the more educated Zhang Yue, quoting Sun Tzu.

The five items requiring attention (largely summarized by Zhao Hongbing) were as follows:

It was essential to be armed at all times as a precaution against Little Tiger's vengeance.

The striking blade that Zhang Yue carried was too dangerous and lethal. Given Zhang Yue's rash tendencies, he should exchange weapons with Xiaoji.

No one should go out alone at night, for fear of running into Tiger's gang.

Xiaoji should keep running his recycling stall, but he had to have someone working with him in case Tiger's guys mounted another surprise attack. Since Li Wu and Sun Dawei were still "awaiting employment," so it made sense for them to do their waiting at Xiaoji's stall.

They needed to track what the enemy was doing at all times. They should gather more information about Tiger and his gang, and also be on the alert against Railway, who would be discharged from the hospital soon.

As the meeting was about to end, Li Wu rushed in saying, "Little Tiger and the others got arrested. They'll probably be put away for at least a year and a half."

"Who's Little Tiger?" Zhao Hongbing asked.

"That's the guy you tussled with this afternoon. Tiger's younger brother," Li Wu said.

"Why were they arrested? For fighting with us?" Xiaoji asked.

"No, for fighting with Rascal Zhang," Li Wu said.

It turned out that when Little Tiger and his gang left the dumpling restaurant with a man down, Rascal Zhang figured they must be going to the hospital, so he rounded up a dozen men and went after them. Right after Zhao Hongbing and Xiaoji left the hospital, Rascal and his hooligans had arrived for what gangsters refer to as a "last hit". Having just taken a beating from Zhao Hongbing, Little Tiger opened the emergency room door to see Rascal Zhang and his gang, who charged right in. During the melee, Little Tiger was stabbed along with three others, and he seriously wounded one of Rascal's guys with his combat knife.

That's when the police arrived and fired their weapons to end the fighting. All the gangsters were rounded up and taken to the police station. The police had actually been called while Zhao Hongbing was fighting Little Tiger, but when they arrived, they arrested Rascal's as well.

Ergou observed that in confronting the same gang at the same location, Rascal's large gang suffered an injury while Zhao Hongbing and Xiaoji didn't get so much as a scratch, indicating the obvious superiority of Hongbing and Xiaoji's intelligence and tactics compared with other hoodlums. Rascal Zhang's band of punks just barreled in without rhyme or reason, their brawny ferocity failing to compensate for their lack of brains. Meanwhile, Zhao Hongbing and Xiaoji had overcome the numeric superiority of their opponents by taking the lay of the land into account. IQ is always the crucial hardware in any realm, trade, or era.

"Little Tiger was really out of luck," Zhao Hongbing laughed. "By the time I saw him, he was already beaten half senseless, I gave him another thrashing, and then he gets stabbed by Rascal Zhang. It's a wonder he's still alive! But enough of that," he added. "Let's have a drink!"

With that, the curtain dropped on the third "rumble summing-up meeting".

What Zhao Hongbing and the others didn't realize was that their own run of bad luck wasn't over yet.

CHAPTER 10

Zhang Yue, the Man and His Deeds

NOT LONG AFTER THE FIGHT with Little Tiger at the No. 3 Hospital, at around six o'clock in the evening of December 31st 1986, the elder Mr. Zhao was out of town for a meeting when Sun Dawei, Xiaoji, and Li Wu gathered in Zhao Hongbing's bedroom on the second floor of the house.

Once classes ended at the No. 6 High School for the New Year's holiday, lights were kept on all night in the classroom building so students could continue playing poker and Chinese chess after their New Year's parties ended. Zhao Hongbing had told Gao Huan that he would come over to play poker after midnight. Sun Dawei, always thinking of his 'girlfriend', wanted to go along, and Xiaoji, Li Wu, and Zhang Yue raised enough of a fuss that Hongbing felt obliged to take them as well. Zhang Yue was still in the countryside collecting grain tax, so the others sat around chatting while waiting for his return. Zhao Hongbing listened to the others while contentedly strumming his guitar, apparently planning to take it to the No. 6 High School.

"Hongbing, when you get there, play chess and not poker," Sun Dawei said with mock seriousness.

"Why shouldn't I play poker?" Hongbing asked.

"Look at your hand! If you play cards with Gao Huan's classmates, they're sure to think, 'Why would a beautiful girl like Gao Huan be going out with a cripple?'" said Sun Dawei, looking solicitous.

Zhao Hongbing stopped strumming as he contemplated this problem. "Hm, I can just use my left hand to play chess, and if no one else plays, I'll just hang out." He took Sun Dawei's ribbing seriously and wanted to spare Gao Huan any embarrassment.

Just then there was a knock at the door. The Zhaos' German shepherd didn't bark, so everyone knew it must be Zhang Yue. If it were anyone else, the dog would bark. Whenever Zhang Yue appeared, it would slink trembling into its kennel and refuse to come out. That's because one day in November 1986, when Zhang Yue came to Zhao Hongbing's home, the dog lunged at him, barking ferociously and trying to bite him. Infuriated, Zhang Yue grabbed a shovel propped next to the courtyard flower patch and smashed it against the dog's head. Used to being treated with great dignity by the elder Mr. Zhao, the dog immediately leaped up again and bit Zhang Yue. The clothes Zhang Yue was wearing that day were too thick for the dog's teeth to penetrate, and he struck the dog again with the shovel. This time the dog turned and ran off, but Zhang Yue wouldn't let it go. He kept chasing the dog around the courtyard and hitting it until it finally slipped into its kennel. Zhang Yue continued to stand at the entrance and jabbed the shovel inside as the dog howled in pain.

Zhang Yue's battle with the dog was witnessed by Zhao

Hongbing and Lisi, who had not yet skipped town at that point. "Who do you think is tougher, the dog or Zhang Yue?" Hongbing asked Lisi.

"Zhang Yue for sure. The dog is only half wolf, but Zhang Yue is the real thing," Lisi said. Ergou felt Lisi's appraisal was spot on.

"Let's not get in the way if Zhang Yue tries kill the dog today," Zhao Hongbing said. He hated that dog, because whenever Mr. Zhao was away, he had to take care of it, and any real man would resent that. He always hoped for the animal's death, and considered Zhang Yue's actions a kind of payback.

"That dog isn't going to die easily if the shovel hardly hurt him," said Lisi regretfully.

"It's over now. The dog is in his kennel and the door is too small. If it was bigger, Zhang Yue could squeeze in and engage in hand-to-hand battle with it," said Hongbing, regretting that he hadn't made the door larger.

Ergou believes it was always Zhao Hongbing who best understood Zhang Yue. Once Zhang Yue's blood was boiling, anyone or anything that offended him – man or animal – took their life into their hands. Zhang Yue's defining characteristic was his disregard for consequences. If the door to the dog kennel had been any larger, Zhang Yue would have squeezed in and fought the German shepherd.

"Fuck! Do you see what Zhang Yue is doing?" Lisi cried out. When Zhang Yue saw that he couldn't get at the dog through the door, he began tearing down the kennel.

"Zhang Yue, stop it! I'll be the one who has to fix that when my dad gets back!" Zhao Hongbing had finally had enough. Once he spoke, Zhang Yue had to stop. It's a mystery why that wild man always obeyed Zhao Hongbing.

From that day onward, the sight of Zhang Yue made the dog tremble with fear, and hearing him at the door sent it running for its kennel.

On December 31st when Ergou ran down to open the door for Zhang Yue, he found him in a towering rage. Lifting Ergou up onto his shoulder, Zhang Yue walked upstairs without a word. When they reached the second floor, Ergou noticed scratches all over Zhang Yue's face and neck.

"Zhang Yue, who have you been raping to get scratched up like that?" hooted Sun Dawei.

"I'm the one who got fucking raped," said Zhang Yue angrily.

"Who raped you, Uncle Zhang?" Ergou asked, not knowing what rape was, and thinking it just meant a hard beating.

"Some lousy old battle-axe," Zhang Yue said.

It turned out that when Zhang Yue went to a village that day, the village head received him by slaughtering a chicken and inviting him to lunch at the Party committee office. Zhang Yue had just sat down when a village loafer named Chen Yi, who spent most of his time drifting aimlessly, appeared. Seeing that the village head was treating Zhang Yue to lunch, Chen Yi invited himself to sit down on the heated *kang* and prepared to eat.

"Who's he?" Zhang Yue asked the village head.

"Hey, Chen Yi. This leader from the city is asking who you are." The village heads referred to even county-level cadres as "leaders", not to mention city cadres like Zhang Yue.

"My name is Chen Yi, and I'm thirty-two years old. You got a problem, brother?" said Chen Yi, showing his hooligan side.

"Why are you eating with us?" demanded Zhang Yue, becoming irritated.

"Why shouldn't I? This is my village, not yours." Chen Yi was obviously unaware that the man before him was the devil incarnate.

"Get out and I won't beat your fucking ass," said Zhang Yue.

"You'll beat me? I've been around and seen everything. I'll fucking flatten you," Chen Yi said.

"Fuck your mother!" roared Zhang Yue, springing up from the *kang* and aiming a kick at Chen Yi's head that sent him sprawling to the floor.

Before Chen Yi could react, Zhang Yue grabbed a fire-tong (present in every northern village home for stirring the coals in the stove) and swung it. Covering his head with his arms, Chen Yi leaped to his feet and ran out the door with Zhang Yue chasing after him. Both men were barefoot.

Chen Yi kept saying, "I'm going to fucking flatten you!" but Zhang Yue retorted, "Try that after I've beaten you to death!" The two of them ran barefoot in the snow for about five hundred yards. Eventually, having failed to catch Chen Yi, Zhang Yue returned to the village Party committee office.

"Leader, are you...?" The village head had never received a leader as ferocious as Zhang Yue.

"If my granddad were here, he'd have shot him dead," said Zhang Yue, still fuming as he climbed back on the *kang*.

"Your grandfather was..."

"My grandfather was called Zhen Dongyang," Zhang Yue said.

"Oh..." Back when that village head was still in swaddling clothes, his parents had probably threatened him by saying "Zhen Dongyang is coming."

The village head and Zhang Yue continued their meal. After they'd had a few drinks, they noticed quite a few people gathering outside. They were led by a ferocious-looking woman in her thirties, and carried sickles, axes, pickaxes, and other farming implements.

"Give me my man's shoes or you won't be going back to the city tonight!" yelled the woman.

"Who's that stupid old battle-axe?" Zhang Yue asked the village head.

"That's Chen Yi's wife," the village head stammered. He feared Zhang Yue was finished, and that he'd end up taking the blame. The village head underestimated Zhang Yue, however; Zhen Dongyang fully deserved his reputation, and his direct descendent was cut from the same cloth.

"We'll see who goes home tonight!" said Zhang Yue, putting on his own shoes and walking to the door with Chen Yi's. "Here's your man's shoes," he said as he stepped outside.

"Give them to me, motherfucker!" said the foul-mouthed woman.

Zhang Yue later claimed that he intended to give the shoes to her, but when she started cursing him, it got his dander up. He flung the shoes into the Party committee's well. "Fuck you, bitch!"

When the woman saw what Zhang Yue had done, she lunged at him and began clawing his face before he even knew what was happening. Even more enraged, he shoved the woman to the ground and began kicking her. He was not as gentlemanly as Zhao Hongbing, and if he was willing to fight a dog, he hesitated even less to fight this woman.

Seeing Zhang Yue knock down the woman, the other villagers charged at him while the woman grabbed a sickle and joined them. Zhang Yue turned tail and ran. He wasn't fleeing, however. He'd noticed a pitchfork next to the Party committee office door, and with that in hand he turned on his pursuers. As previously noted, Zhang Yue fought to kill, and this was no exception. He lunged at the woman with the pitchfork. She was so petrified with fear that she couldn't dodge it. Luckily for her, the young fellow next to her warded Zhang off with a hoe. Even so, one prong of the fork jabbed the woman in the arm. Zhang Yue tried to jab her again, but the old village head grabbed him from behind in what Zhang Yue described as a "python's grip".

"Son, don't do it," the village head said to Zhang Yue. Then to the others he said, "Friends, don't attack him. Do you know who he is? He's Zhen Dongyang's grandson! Zhen Dongyang!"

The village head had served for years as head of the local militia, and he carried some weight. When the villagers heard Zhen's name they backed down. It seemed that even forty years after his disappearance, Zhen Dongyang still enjoyed some influence.

"Why mention my grandfather? I'll kill anyone who attacks me!" Zhang Yue felt he could deal with these villagers in his own right. After returning to the Party committee office, Zhang Yue took his time eating the rest of the chicken. Then he swaggered out of the building and made a circuit of the village empty-handed, no one daring to get in his way, before boarding the next bus back to the city. That is how Zhang Yue arrived at Zhao Hongbing's home with his face and neck scratched up.

"Zhang Yue, you're really something, standing your ground all alone in the village!" Everyone was doubled over with laughter.

"You guys go ahead and laugh. If I ever see that old bag again, she'll get more than scratches from me," Zhang Yue scowled, which only made the others laugh harder.

That was Zhang Yue: from the outside clean-cut, refined, and even attractive, but with the blood of a wild beast pumping through his veins. He had a bandit's lineage but had studied hard. Both he and his elder brother, Zhang Fei, had gone to college and gained sterling reputations. Before Zhang Yue became an underworld gang leader, the family seemed to prove the fallacy of the Cultural Revolution slogan: "the son of a reactionary was bound to be a scoundrel".

Given his disadvantaged and impoverished childhood, Zhang Yue craved respect even more than most people; he devoted the same rabid energy to fighting as he had to studying and working. "Do your best at everything you do," was Zhang Yue's motto. It's a pity he applied his energy in the wrong place.

Before Zhang Yue was executed in the late 1990s, Zhao Hongbing went to visit him, and the two had the following conversation:

"You have to take responsibility for the situation you're in, Zhang Yue. Don't think about it too much. Just go in peace."

"Hongbing, you've given me a lot of advice over the past ten years or so. I always said I agreed but never went along with it, and now I really regret it."

"Don't be sorry. Whatever anyone says, you lived large here in our city for more than ten years. The name Zhang Yue always gets a thumbs-up."

"Hongbing, you've known me since high school. I always hated bandits and gangsters. I grew up in poverty because of my family background. All I really wanted was to make something of myself so my sons and grandsons could live with their heads held high."

"In spite of your death sentence, your crimes weren't all

that horrific, so don't blame yourself. From now on, your son will be my son, so put your mind at rest, brother."

"Thanks, Hongbing. But I'm not finished. Ever since I became a real underworld gang leader, I've blamed myself constantly but I could never find a way out. I never saw anything glorious in being a triad Big Brother. I'm ashamed to be called that."

"Ha! That's what they call me now, and don't I live well enough?" Hongbing said.

"Once you're on this boat, there's no turning back. I never found my way out, but today I'll finally be free," Zhang Yue continued, ignoring him.

"You're free," Hongbing agreed. "Go in peace."

Zhang Yue sighed. A smile of genuine happiness lit up his pale, drawn face.

CHAPTER 11

'Tis Better to Give than to Receive

TEN-THIRTY FINALLY ARRIVED. DRESSED FOR the occasion and impatient with waiting, the five young men leaped at Zhao Hongbing's order and set off for the No. 6 High School. They took Ergou and Xiaobo along since they were too young to stay home alone.

After entering the appointed classroom, Zhao Hongbing and the others saw fewer than twenty students still there. Apart from Gao Huan, Sun Dawei's heartthrob, and Li Yang, the remaining students were boys. They were sitting in small groups playing poker.

Hongbing didn't join them. He sat by the window conversing softly with Gao Huan. Li Wu and Xiaoji played chess but were bored out of their minds and already regretted coming. Sun Dawei sat next to his 'girlfriend' watching a poker game while keeping up a constant patter. Zhang Yue was playing Chinese checkers with Li Yang, obviously smitten. It was clear why he'd wanted to come.

"Zhang Yue, what happened to your face?" Li Yang asked with a giggle.

"Oh... we have a cat at home," Zhang Yue said.

"Wow – that must be a really big cat!" Li Yang teased, seeing as anyone could that the scratches were human.

"Yeah, an old cat. Almost thirty years old and weighing ten pounds." Flushing and blanching with embarrassment, Zhang Yue mumbled the first thing that came to mind – as if anyone had ever heard of a thirty-year-old cat.

"Wow, thirty years old! Male or female?" Li Yang asked with an enchanting smile.

"Uh, female," Zhang Yue stammered.

"No wonder! She's obviously possessed!" Li Yang had by now laughed herself to tears. "Ha! I won, Zhang Yue!" she said, jumping his last checker piece. The garrulous Li Yang, while less beautiful than Gao Huan, was still very attractive.

Meanwhile, Zhang Hongbing and Gao Huan seemed to have forgotten all the noisy young people around them. They were gazing dreamily out at the stars as they continued the kind of small talk that anyone else would find meaningless.

"Which star is me?" Gao Huan asked.

"That one," said Zhao Hongbing.

"Which one?"

"That one. The brightest one!"

"Which is the brightest one? And which one is you?"

"That one."

"Which one?"

"The same one as yours."

"Haha..."

Just then, Zhao Hongbing felt a sharp pain at the back of his head. He crumpled in a dead faint. When he came to, he was on the ice-cold cement floor with several policemen standing around him. On his left, Xiaoji squatted with his hands covering his head. Gao Huan was weeping next to him. Zhang Yue, Sun Dawei, and Li Wu had disappeared. A crowd of onlookers had gathered outside the classroom.

Zhao Hongbing struggled to his feet, but a burning pain at the back of his head made him pass out again. This time he regained consciousness in the office of the campus police, and less than ten minutes later, he and Xiaoji were taken to the municipal police station.

Ergou witnessed the entire proceedings: the man who hit Zhao Hongbing was Yan Chunqiu – the young man who was in love with Gao Huan, and the son of the public security political commissar.

Yan Chunqiu had been drinking with half a dozen other boys in the classroom next door when Zhao Hongbing arrived. When he came back in, he found Zhao Hongbing and Gao Huan mooning by the window. His anger fueled by liquor, Yan Chunqiu silently returned to the neighboring classroom and told the other boys, "Some punk is chatting up Gao Huan. I'm going to trash him!"

"Who is it? Bring him in here and we'll cut him up!" said the others, likewise emboldened by drink.

"There are five or six of them, so we should have our tools ready," Yan Chunqiu said.

"We'll drive them out of the school!"

Ten minutes later, the youths burst into the classroom carrying stool legs and bricks. Engrossed in his game, Zhang Yue didn't see them coming, and neither did Ergou and Xiaobo, immersed in their checkers.

Yan Chunqiu came up behind Zhao Hongbing and

slammed a brick against his head. Hongbing, caught entirely unawares, fell to the ground. Yan Chunqiu wanted to keep attacking him, but Gao Huan threw herself on Hongbing's prone body and cried, "If you want to hit him, you'll have to kill me first!"

By then, Zhang Yue had realized that Hongbing was being attacked. He grabbed the stool he was sitting on and hurled it at Yan Chunqiu. Yan thrust his arm out to protect himself, sending the stool crashing into Gao Huan. As he threw the stool, Zhang Yue charged bare-handed at Yan Chunqiu, grabbing his hair and kicking him in the head. Behind him, Xiaoji, Sun Dawei, and Li Wu each grabbed a wooden stool and leaped to Zhang Yue's defense. The two sides began an all-out war.

Zhang Yue suffered several blows to the head with stool legs and brick fragments. However, he maintained his death grip on Yan Chunqiu's hair and continued to kick his head and body, in one of his deadly rages. Sun Dawei fought with unusual ferocity this time, perhaps because his 'girlfriend' was watching. He used his stool to parry several of the blows aimed at Zhang Yue. Stronger fighters, Xiaoji and Li Wu wielded their stools energetically until they were reduced to a stool leg in Xiaoji's hands; Li Wu held only a bench board embedded with nails. At the outset, the students were fueled by alcohol, but their energy soon failed them. They were only up to bullying weaker classmates, and were no match for street hoodlums who spent their days brawling. One by one, the students ran off with Sun Dawei and Li Wu in hot pursuit while Xiaoji joined Zhang Yue in fighting Yan Chunqiu.

"You motherfuckers think you can get away with this? Do you know who my dad is?" said Yan Chunqiu, keeping up his tough façade.

"Who gives a fuck! We're going to beat the shit out of you!" Zhang Yue roared as he kept on kicking.

"Just stop! I'll pay you! My family has plenty of money!" begged Yan Chunqiu, realizing his threats were useless.

"Who wants your shitty money?" yelled Xiaoji as he rained blows on Yan Chunqiu's head with his stool leg.

"Xiaoji, you take care of him. I'm going after those two punks who hit me with the stool legs," said Zhang Yue, giving Yan Chunqiu a last kick before running out of the classroom.

Xiaoji was about to lay into Yan Chunqiu with his stool leg when he was grabbed by several of the card-playing students. Yan Chunqiu was still rolling on the floor, felled by Zhang Yue's merciless beating. By then the campus police had learned what was going on. When they arrived, Xiaoji was cornered.

"Chunqiu, who did this to you?" demanded one of the older policemen.

"They beat me up, Uncle Li," Yan Chunqiu wailed.

Ergou had always felt this fellow was spineless, attacking a guy from behind. Now he was blaming others for the fight he had started. What kind of fellow blubbered like that when he was almost twenty years old?

"Don't cry, Chunqiu. Just tell me who hit you," the policeman said. The campus police were part of the municipal force, and were under the supervision of the municipal public security bureau where Yan Chunqiu's father worked.

"It was them!" said Yan Chunqiu, pointing at Xiaoji and the unconscious Zhao Hongbing, even though it was Zhang Yue, now long gone, who had beaten him.

"Squat down!" barked one of the policemen, whacking Xiaoji on the head. Xiaoji covered his head with his arms and squatted on the floor."

"Quit playing dead!" said another, kicking Zhao Hongbing. Hongbing came to for a moment and then passed out again.

The policemen carried Zhao Hongbing to their office along with Xiaoji, who tried to escape several times without success. The policemen dashed a bucket of cold water over Zhao Hongbing's head, and he finally regained consciousness. Soon after, he and Xiaoji were bundled into a van and taken to the municipal public security bureau.

Back in the classroom, Xiaobo and Ergou were still speechless with shock. When she learned that Hongbing had been taken to the police station, Gao Huan went there with the two boys, and they waited together in the first floor reception area. There was no heating in the buildings then, and the reception area was bitterly cold.

Inside, Zhao Hongbing was being interrogated.

"Name?"

"Zhao Hongbing."

"Age?"

"Twenty-three."

"Your name sounds familiar. Why did you start the fight?"

"I didn't start it. Someone attacked me!"

"Why were you causing trouble at the No. 6 High School? You're not a student there!"

"I wasn't causing trouble. I just went there for the party."

"Why would someone like you be partying at a high school? Tell me why you started the fight!"

"I told you! I was the one who was attacked!"

"Okay, let's say I believe you. Tell me who attacked you."

"... I don't know. By the time I came to, I was in the campus police office."

"You don't know? Why would anyone attack you?"

"I don't know! I was just chatting with a friend and I was attacked."

"Ha! So you claim not to know anything! Let me tell you, even if you didn't hit anyone, your friends did, so tell me their names."

"Xiaoji. You brought him here with me, didn't you?"

"Who else?"

"That's all."

"That's all? If you stick with that, I won't believe anything else you tell me, either. Witnesses at the scene said there were five of you but three ran off. Who were the other three?"

"I didn't know them."

"You didn't know them? Then why did you come to the school together?" The policeman had underestimated Zhao Hongbing. A war veteran wouldn't confess so easily. Countless PLA soldiers had spent years lobbing grenades at the Laoshan frontline, but only a handful were taken prisoner by the Vietnamese. Even if the police put Zhao Hongbing on the torture rack and poured chili water down his throat, he wouldn't confess.

"I really don't know them. I just ran into them on the street. They asked where we were going, and I said we were going to play poker at the No. 6 High School, so they came along." Hongbing couldn't think of a better story on the spur of the moment.

"You seem to make friends easily! Can you go out and find a few more friends to fight with you?"

"Sure. Let me go, and I'll find some!"

"Smartass! Are you forgetting where you are?" demanded a young police officer angrily.

At that moment, an older policeman who looked like a

senior officer came in. When he saw Zhao Hongbing being interrogated, he was taken aback. "Hey! Isn't that Hongbing? Are you back from the war?"

"Yes, Uncle Yan. I've been back for a year. Someone attacked me, but they've arrested me instead of my attacker. I'm being interrogated." Zhao Hongbing was used to attacking others, and he was indignant at being attacked himself.

"Oh..." The senior police officer was Yan Chunqiu's father. He'd heard that his son had been beaten and had come in to see who had done it. Zhao Hongbing didn't know Yan Chunqiu, but Commissar Yan was a veteran cadre who was friendly with Hongbing's father. He had come to Hongbing's home a number of times to play chess.

"Hongbing, how did you come to be attacked?" Commissar Yan asked.

"I was chatting with a friend when someone – I don't know who – came up behind me and cracked me on the head..." When he heard Zhao Hongbing's story, Commissar Yan realized that his son had tried to attack someone and had come out the worse for it.

"Are you all right?"

"It still hurts. I think I should go to the hospital. See, it's still bleeding."

"This is Director Zhao's son. I've known him since he was a boy. Let him go to the hospital. If there's more we can get back to him later," Commissar Yan told the younger police officer.

The name "Director Zhao" startled the young police officer, who quickly said, "Of course we'll release him."

In fact, Zhao Hongbing seldom made use of his father's position and never lorded it over others. Gao Huan dated him for several months before learning who his father was.

Commissar Yan was a veteran revolutionary and very upright. Although he loved his son, he was rational. Even if the young man before him had not been Zhao Hongbing, once he understood what had happened, he would have let him go, although perhaps with more procedural bother.

After returning home, Commissar Yan gave his son a smacking, which made Yan Chunqiu hate Zhao Hongbing even more.

Hongbing had been lucky to encounter an honest police officer like Commissar Yan. Xiaoji was less fortunate; given that he'd been seen hitting someone and refused to name Zhang Yue and the others, the police worked him over. He left the station with a bloody nose and black eye.

As they emerged from the police station, Zhao Hongbing and Xiaoji found Gao Huan, Ergou, and Xiaobo shivering in the reception area, and Gao Huan began weeping uncontrollably.

"Silly girl! If we hadn't come out, you'd have frozen to death here!" said Zhao Hongbing. He took off his quilted army coat and wrapped it around Gao Huan, who was wearing only a thin down jacket.

"I don't care. I wanted to wait for you," sobbed Gao Huan with what could have been weeping or laughter.

"Crazy girl!" Zhao Hongbing said. They'd known each other barely a month and had only met a few times, but they already acted as though they were committed for life. Only someone in love would understand.

"Who attacked me?" Zhao Hongbing asked Gao Huan, sensing that it had something to do with her.

"My classmate. His name is Yan Chunqiu," said Gao Huan softly.

"Yan Chunqiu? Isn't he Commissar Yan's son?" Everything was becoming clear now.

"Yes. How do you know?"

"Oh, no reason. Why did he attack me?" Hongbing asked.

"Uh… because it seems… he's in love with me," Gao Huan said with great effort.

"I thought it must be something like that," Hongbing said.

"Hongbing, will you promise me something?"

"I'll promise whatever you want."

"When you teach Yan Chunqiu a lesson, please go easy on him. I'm afraid you'll get in trouble – and his father is the political commissar.

"Don't worry. I won't beat him up."

This surprised Gao Huan. She was sure Hongbing would go after Yan Chunqiu as soon as he was released. Xiaoji jumped in: "Fuck, man. He just about killed you and you're not going to do anything?"

"This is a conflict that can be reconciled. He's just a kid. I'm not going to beat him up."

"You didn't hesitate to go after Tiger," Xiaoji pointed out.

"Our conflict with Tiger can't be reconciled. He's a ruffian and a class enemy," said Zhao Hongbing with a joking reference to political rhetoric. "Besides that, Gao Huan has to keep studying with Yan Chunqiu in school for another half a year. If her boyfriend beats up her classmate, how can she show her face?" he added.

"Hongbing, you're the best!" said Gao Huan. She understood that Zhao Hongbing would always put her first. That remained the case for the next twenty years. By then they had reached Gao Huan's home. She reached out and touched Hongbing's head. "Does it still hurt?"

Even her light touch hurt so much that Zhao Hongbing nearly passed out again. "Ow! Now it does…"

"It's all my fault," said Gao Huan tearfully.

"It's nothing. Go inside. We have to go."

On the way back to Hongbing's house, Xiaoji was still steaming.

"Hongbing, you were fucking useless today! If you're not going to take care of that punk, me and Zhang Yue will!"

"Forget it. I lost the battle but won the war."

"You won? How do you figure that out?"

"I won Gao Huan's heart, and that's what counts."

"*What?*"

"The Song statesman Su Dongpo once wrote something like, 'Being courageous is more than pulling out your sword and fighting. The truly courageous man is unafraid when faced with sudden danger, and is not moved to wrath when unfairly accused.'"

"What the hell are you trying to say?"

"Yan Chunqiu is just a mediocrity. Girls like a man who's really courageous, who thinks things out and waits for the right opportunity. I'm that kind of man." Even though he'd been attacked, Zhao Hongbing was in a particularly good mood and more voluble than usual. He knew that Gao Huan had fallen madly in love with him.

"You have a pretty high opinion of yourself!" Xiaoji chided with a laugh.

"You asked," Hongbing grinned.

Yan Chunqiu seemed to have won the advantage by knocking Zhao Hongbing out, but for the next twenty years, Gao Huan never spoke another word to him.

Less than five years later, the municipal public security

bureau used the "public security college recruitment" program to select a recent graduate of a certain college whose performance had been outstanding. This student became the first to rise to deputy commander of the crime squad without graduating from the police academy. While serving on the crime squad, this police officer made a point of creating difficulties for Zhao Hongbing and Zhang Yue. He was none other than Yan Chunqiu – the student Zhang Yue had reduced to a sobbing and quivering mess. No one would have guessed that this rash young man would eventually become a wily public security officer.

CHAPTER 12

Little Beijing on War, Zen and Mao Zedong Thought

AFTER THE NEW YEAR, ZHAO Hongbing took over management of the state-owned hotel by the train station. He was a stickler for cleanliness, and he found the hotel filthy. There were footprints all over the walls, and the bedding looked like it had never been washed. He decided to close the hotel for refurbishment, mainly whitewashing the walls and painting the heat ducts. Because the paint fumes would take time to disperse, Hongbing decided to formally reopen the hotel after the Spring Festival.

Mr. Zhao said, "Those disreputable friends of yours are always hanging around our house. Not one of them seems to have a proper job. You should get them to help you with the painting and repairs. One of them can stay here to look after the boys, and you can all come back here for dinner as long as you don't drink too much."

Zhao Hongbing's father knew nothing about the fights Hongbing had gotten into since National Day. He thought his son was just hanging around with the other guys out of boredom, never guessing how much trouble they'd gotten into or that two of them had had to skip town. Zhang Yue had a job to go to, and Xiaoji was still running his recycling stall, but Sun Dawei and Li Wu were free. Zhao Hongbing had no choice but to bring them in, since there was no arguing with Mr. Zhao.

Li Wu immediately said, "This will be a cinch! A few little brothers have started hanging with me recently. They can work for you while we supervise them."

"You have little brothers?" asked Hongbing in surprise.

It turned out that Li Wu had been a petty hoodlum before knowing Zhao Hongbing, but he hadn't done anything to make a name for himself. After ganging up with Zhao Hongbing and the others to battle Tiger and Railway, he'd gained something of a reputation; some teenaged boys had started hanging around with him and treating him like their hero. These young punks spent most of their time stealing, mainly bicycles and copper and iron parts from the state-owned factories, which they disposed of through Xiaoji's recycling stall.

There was nothing impressive about Li Wu's "little brothers", but he was still the first in the group to attract a band of followers. Zhao Hongbing had always felt there was something not quite right about Li Wu. It was only out of respect for Zhang Yue that he'd included Li Wu in the sworn brotherhood the night they'd gone drinking together. He didn't like associating with him any more than necessary. Even so, Li Wu had always shown him the greatest possible respect and had acquitted himself well enough when they fought, so Zhao Hongbing let him stick around.

"Don't these little brothers of yours have to go to school?" Hongbing asked.

"They pretty much dropped out after middle school and

they don't have real jobs," Li Wu said. "They're just loafing around. Let them come over and help out."

"All right, but they need to behave themselves. I don't want them stealing stuff around the hotel," said Hongbing, who had no time for petty thieves.

"You think they'd dare steal from you?" laughed Li Wu.

"I said stealing *around* the hotel," Hongbing said. "If people hear thieves are hanging out at my hotel, no one will want to stay there."

"Got it!"

To this day, Ergou still finds some of Zhao Hongbing's behavior fascinating. He yearned to engage in public service. If a neighbor's heater or bicycle broke, he just needed to give a yell outside Hongbing's home. Hongbing would be down in a flash, never asking for any kind of payment, no matter how much work was involved. In the depths of winter, when bicycle repairmen had all been driven inside by the cold, Hongbing would spend half an hour in sub-zero temperatures fixing flat tires, slowed down by his crippled hand.

At home, however, Hongbing was extraordinarily lazy. On countless occasions, Ergou saw him refuse to do even the simplest task, like feeding the dog, until his father started shaking the feather duster at him. He treated the hotel the same way. If it had been someone else's, he would have rushed over to help. But because it was his own, he couldn't be bothered. He left it to a bunch of petty thieves whom he despised.

The work began a few days after the New Year. Sun Dawei stayed home looking after the boys, while Li Wu and Zhao Hongbing went to the worksite to oversee operations. Apparently Hongbing showed a natural talent for engineering and renovation work, and even professionals were impressed by his painting work. This talent didn't go to waste; twenty years later, he was one of the city's top property developers, and his projects were renowned for their attractive exteriors and solid construction.

Sun Dawei's cooking skills were reflected in Zhang Yue referring to him as "chief eunuch of the imperial kitchen". He was also good at looking after the boys, keeping them spellbound with his renditions of tales from *Journey to the West.* It was only after Ergou learned to read that he began to suspect that Sun Dawei hadn't actually read *Journey to the West*; although the Tang monk Xuanzang experienced countless trials, he didn't actually encounter eighty-one harpies, as Sun Dawei claimed. Who knows where he came up with that number?

One morning shortly before Spring Festival, when the renovation work was largely completed and only the cleaning was left, Sun Dawei arrived very early at Zhao Hongbing's home and told him, "Last night I dreamed that Little Beijing was drinking and shooting the bull with us. I guess I really miss him." This was the second time Ergou knew of Sun Dawei having a prophetic dream.

"Little Beijing called me a few days ago. He told me that our old company commander was badly wounded, and he went to visit him," Hongbing said. "He still doesn't have a real job. He just runs around all the time."

The renovation work finished that afternoon. Just as Hongbing and the others were getting ready to go home and celebrate with lots of food and liquor, Zhang Yue strode in with a big grin on his face. "Lisi and Feisi are coming back tomorrow, according to Big Mouth Sun," he said.

"They still remember where home is?" said Zhao Hongbing grudgingly.

"Yeah, they're with Little Beijing. They ended up there after roaming around the country for a while. They called me at home and asked if there was a warrant out for their arrest, and when they heard there wasn't, they decided to come home for the Spring Festival. They're probably already on the train and will get here around noon tomorrow."

"How do you know?"

"Dawei's at home cooking and can't get away, so he called and asked me to come and tell you when I got off work."

"Those guys ... They managed to disappear when we were fighting and working, and now they show up after the hard part's done. I wonder if their old work units will take them back," Hongbing said, somewhat worried for them.

"Not likely! They took off for two months without even giving notice. What work unit wants people like that? I heard they were sacked right away. All they have to do is sign the papers and they'll be proper jobless vagrants." Getting a real job was no easy matter back then, and Zhang Yue became irritated at the very mention of those two.

"All right. Tomorrow is Lunar New Year's Eve, so you should be off work. You and Li Wu go to the train station to meet them, and Dawei and I will reserve a table at Ten Thousand Cranes to welcome them back. We'll have Li Wu's gang come, too, since they've been working so hard these last few days," Hongbing said with a grin.

The next day, Zhao Hongbing and Sun Dawei went early to Ten Thousand Cranes and reserved a separate room with a table large enough to seat fifteen people. "Dawei, you dreamed of Little Beijing, so why is it Lisi and Feisi who are coming this time?" Hongbing asked.

"I might have remembered it wrong after I woke up, but my dream wouldn't have been wrong!" Sun Dawei said.

Just then, the door to the room opened, and standing in the doorway were Lisi and Feisi, fat and rosy, with Little Beijing right behind them.

"Hongbing! Dawei! We've missed you!" cried Feisi, pouncing on them.

"Back off! I didn't miss you!" said Hongbing.

"Little Beijing, you've come, too?" Sun Dawei said. "I dreamed of you last night – just ask Hongbing!"

"Shit, who wanted to come here?" said Little Beijing, sounding aggrieved. "Last night I took these two to the train station and got on the train to see them off, but there were too many people traveling for the Spring Festival. I was so drunk that I couldn't get out. By the time I squeezed my way to the door, we were already at the fucking Great Wall! I figured I might as well go the rest of the way with these two."

"As long as you're here safe and sound, have dinner with us and then call home. You can spend Spring Festival with us!" laughed Hongbing. He was actually very glad that Little Beijing had come.

"Sure, I'll stay. It's no fun spending Spring Festival in Beijing anyway."

Everyone ate and drank their fill. It was almost five in the afternoon by the time they left the restaurant. All the trouble of the past few months was forgotten. Although Feisi and Lisi had lost their jobs, they had expected it, and were just glad not to have their names on a warrant. After leaving the restaurant, everyone went back to Zhao Hongbing's home for more drinking and talking. Dusk had fallen by then. The cold wind howling outside the window brought snowflakes that danced in the air and adorned everything with the silvery white gloss that makes northern winters so enchanting.

Upstairs in Hongbing's cozy bedroom, twelve guys sat around a hotplate chewing the fat. Warming on the hotplate was a tea mug full of seventy-proof sorghum liquor straight from the distillery, with peanuts to help it go down. They talked about their ideals, about the future, and about their past fights.

No one could have guessed how much this bull session would influence all of those present. The conversation set the plan of action and theoretical foundation for the criminal gangs that Zhang Yue, Xiaoji, Li Wu, and Lisi subsequently established and that made these four the city's most renowned gangsters of the 1990s. It also added depth to the fighting concepts and combat readiness of all those present, with a profound and lasting effect. Little Beijing led this evening chat, with supplementary comments by Zhao Hongbing. The initial topics were war and Zen.

"Li Wu, what did you feel like the first time you chopped someone?" Little Beijing asked. Ergou eventually had many classmates and colleagues from Beijing, and he found that the city's dialect could be divided into standard Mandarin and Beijing street talk. Little Beijing spoke a street dialect that combined drawling tones with a crisp enunciation. It was very pleasing to the ear.

"The first time I chopped someone, I was so scared I couldn't even see who was in front of me. I was only aware of swinging a cleaver around," said Li Wu.

"Hm, that's the lowest level. Xiaoji, tell us how you felt the first time you cut someone with a knife," Little Beijing continued.

"I'm much stronger than Li Wu. The first time I grabbed a knife to stab someone, I knew who I was stabbing and even where to cut him, so I was able to focus on what was going on around me and if anyone was attacking me," Xiaoji said.

"When I go at someone with a knife, all I care about is killing the guy in front of me," said Zhang Yue, not waiting for Little Beijing to ask him.

"Hongbing, why don't you talk about what our company commander taught us about fighting?" Little Beijing said.

"While fighting, you need to concentrate your attention and eliminate everything else from your mind," said Hongbing with a smile, lying on his bed with a glass of liquor in his hand. "All you should focus on is where you opponent is attacking from and how you can kill him."

"Hongbing has it right. Li Wu, Xiaoji, Zhang Yue, and Hongbing – the four of you represent four different levels of fighting. Li Wu's is the lowest level; while he's fighting, his heartbeat speeds up and his hands and feet shake. He's afraid of his opponent and afraid that he'll kill someone, so he quickly becomes confused, and this gives his opponent loopholes to exploit. Zhang Yue is at the next higher level; he focuses on his opponent and pays no attention to what's going on around him. This helps him concentrate on destroying one enemy, but it leaves him vulnerable to other enemies around you. Xiaoji is at a higher level than Li Wu and Zhang Yue and can be considered a top-grade fighter; he not only targets the opponent in front of him, but also takes note of others around him. But this can easily distract him and expose him to unnecessary injury. The level Hongbing describes is the top level of fighting. The fighter dismisses all secondary concerns from his brain; his heartbeat and hands are steady.

His attention is highly focused on the various points where he might be attacked, as well as the various points for his own attack, and he doesn't let himself get distracted. This gives him a big advantage in a brawl with a lot of people. For example, when Hongbing was fighting with Little Tiger, what he focused on his fists and knees. He just had to concentrate on grabbing Little Tiger's fist and then giving him a hard kick on the knees. Meanwhile, Little Tiger was focusing on Hongbing and flailing at him without rhyme or reason. How could he be a match?"

"That makes sense. Next time we fight, we need to focus our attention," everyone agreed.

"What I described just now was the first level," said Little Beijing. Anyone who has fought to the death knows it."

"So what's the second level?"

"That's breaking through the barrier between life and death," Little Beijing said. "Hongbing, Lisi, and I have all fought hand-to-hand with the 'Nam devils. They were as skilled and fierce as we were, and anyone who fought them has effectively died once. Once someone has died, he won't take life and death as seriously any more. This gives him an incomparable mental advantage over others in his subsequent fights. Those who fear death are sure to die, while those who don't fear death usually survive," Little Beijing said.

"But there's a level even higher than this," he continued. The others listened, entranced.

"What's this highest level?"

"It's war and Zen." Little Beijing took a swallow of sorghum liquor. "Zen is divided into instant enlightenment and gradual enlightenment. In a life-or-death battle, what you need is that instant enlightenment – when your mind empties and you reach a state of unconsciousness where your hands know what to do automatically. Four hundred years ago, the Japanese swordsman Miyamoto Musashi defeated sixty-six of Japan's expert fighters, but then reached a bottleneck in his swordsmanship. The Great Zen Master Taigu helped him get past this, and Miyamoto went on to defeat Sasaki Kojiro at Ganryu-jima and became Japan's top swordsman. That is the essence of Zen."

"Fuck, man...That's too complicated for me! Is there something above that yet?"

"Yes," said Little Beijing. "Mao Zedong Thought."

The others, who had been completely absorbed in the discussion up to that point, roared with laughter. Little Beijing ignored their hooting and continued. "What I mean by Mao Zedong Thought is practical theory. Chairman Mao said that knowledge is a process of two leaps. The first is the leap from perception to rational knowledge. Once there's rational knowledge, it will guide perception and practice. Everything I've just said about fighting you have to verify through these two leaps."

"Chairman Mao's been out of fashion for years," said Sun Dawei. "What use is his stuff now?"

"It's very useful! You can solve almost anything using Mao Zedong Thought," said Little Beijing sententiously.

"Okay, so if Hongbing is half killed by a brick to the head, how are you going to solve this problem with Mao Zedong Thought?" Xiaoji asked, recalling the recent altercation.

"Didn't Hongbing tell you at the time? That was an example of Chairman Mao's 'Contradiction Theory.' Mao said contradictions are divided into those that can be reconciled and those that can't, but under certain circumstances, one type of contradiction can be turned into the other. Hongbing says this matter is finished, which means that a reconcilable contradiction was not escalated to an irreconcilable contradiction, and this was the proper way to handle it. Understand?"

"Is that really how Chairman Mao's ideas are supposed to be used?" Li Wu asked. These guys had been born two or three years before the Cultural Revolution began, and had been hearing Chairman Mao's quotations since they'd learned to talk; there wasn't much they didn't know about Mao's ideas.

"Of course it is. Next time you fight with Tiger or Railway, you should use Chairman Mao's military theories. For example, Mao said, 'Not fearing pain or death and keeping pace with each other is the way to victory.' That's the main reason we were a match for them. With Tiger, we're now in what Chairman Mao called the strategic defense phase. For example, that time at the hospital, when it was six of us against more than thirty of them, we should have run ahead and waited for them to chase us. Once we'd run a mile or so, only five or six of them would have caught up with us, and we could have taken care of them first. Then we could have run further and waited for the next few to catch up with us, and fought them. This is something Chairman Mao taught Chen Yi: divide and conquer. We attack the weak first and then go after the strong; once our weakest opponents are eliminated, the strong become weak as well."

After talking non-stop for half an hour, Little Beijing managed to convince everyone.

"Long live the invincible Mao Zedong Thought!" cheered Zhang Yue.

"Chairman Mao started off with twenty to thirty thousand soldiers and changed China. Why shouldn't we be able to pack up Tiger using the old man's theories?" said Lisi excitedly.

"I still don't buy what Little Beijing is saying," said the semi-literate Sun Dawei.

"Chairman Mao once said: Internal factors are fundamental, and external factors are circumstantial. A hen can hatch an egg into a chick, but she can't hatch a stone. You're what they call wood too rotten to carve," said Little Beijing, lacing his criticism with quotes from both Chairman Mao and Confucius.

This evening bull session bore obvious results. From then on, Zhang Yue, Lisi, and the others actually began studying Mao's thinking and military theories. Although this new generation of Chinese didn't follow Chairman Mao's theories to the letter, practical application brought outstanding results. It was more than enough to pack up the hooligan gangs.

Part Three

Fame

CHAPTER 13

The Future Is Ours

JUST ONE YEAR EARLIER, THE newly demobilized and partially disabled Zhao Hongbing had spent Spring Festival feeling depressed and discouraged. This year, he was ecstatic because he had Gao Huan. Although Gao Huan was still in school and they had to keep their romance low-profile, their love was sweet and ardent, and they were immersed in the joy of first love. Once Spring Festival ended, Hongbing launched into his new entrepreneurial role with spirit and vigor.

Little Beijing accepted Hongbing's invitation to stay in his home over Spring Festival. The elder Mr. Zhao thought highly of Little Beijing's scholarship and intelligence as well as his patriotism and good manners. Normally remote and reticent, Mr. Zhao surprised everyone by often taking Little Beijing aside to talk. Of all the young men Hongbing had brought home, it was only Little Beijing whom Mr. Zhao really liked.

"Hongbing can't handle the hotel on his own. He needs someone to share the day and night shifts with him. If you have nothing better waiting in Beijing, why don't you stay here with us and work with Hongbing?" old Mr. Zhao suggested to Little Beijing.

"That doesn't seem right. Hongbing pulled the money together for the hotel, and I haven't put anything into it."

"Hongbing is steadier than you, but you have more ideas. You're comrades-in-arms and friends for life, and you're sure to make a great team. You can contribute sweat equity instead of funding. Nowadays people talk about shareholdings. You can discuss the details with Hongbing and his brother. I'll stay out of it."

"I'll talk it over with my parents. If they agree to it, I'll be glad to."

"Tell your parents not to look down on business. Nowadays our country is letting some people prosper first. If you put it in terms of state policy, I'm sure they'll agree."

"Uncle Zhao, I'll tell my parents that I won't come back to Beijing until I'm earning 10,000 a year!"

"That's my boy!" laughed Mr. Zhao.

While Zhao Hongbing was happy, the former fugitives Lisi and Feisi were in a miserable state. Lisi's father hadn't spoken a word to him since his return, and Lisi avoided family meals. He just picked through the leftovers in the kitchen after everyone else finished. He was ashamed to be seen in public as well; losing a government job back then was a major disgrace. Feisi was even worse off. He was the fourth son in his family; his father was dead, and his three older brothers were all state cadres. As soon as he returned, his brothers gave him such a thrashing that he was left with a limp. If Zhao Hongbing and Xiaoji hadn't gone to plead on his behalf, his brothers might have run him out of the house.

Zhao Hongbing and his friends met for dinner again on the first day of the Spring Festival. But instead of the careless hedonism of the year before, they began exploring how to move ahead in the year to come.

"Hongbing, I think we should block off a good half of the first floor of the hotel and open a restaurant," said Little Beijing. "There are only a few restaurants around the train station, and the food is lousy. The hotel will always bring a set income, but with a restaurant we can earn more."

"That's worth considering," said Zhao Hongbing. He always took Little Beijing's suggestions very seriously. "Let's see how good business is and then decide. I've already borrowed a lot of money from my family. I don't want to go back to them for a handout right away. Let's earn some money and set aside some capital first."

"Okay, let's give it half a year and see how things are going," Little Beijing said.

"Hey, Hongbing. You have a hotel now, but me and Lisi don't even have a job. How are we going to manage?" Feisi said.

"What's your problem, Feisi?" said Li Wu. "Me and Dawei haven't worked since we left middle school and we're still surviving."

"We can't mooch off our parents our whole lives!" Lisi said.

"You know how my mom works at the library?" said Sun Dawei. "Well, she wants me to open a little stall downstairs to loan martial-arts novels. It's right by the No. 10 High School, the teacher's college, and the arts institute. I can lend out the books at 20 cents a day with a safety deposit of 10 *kuai.* That will make me a member of the literati," he added smugly.

"Don't make me puke," snorted Zhang Yue, who objected most strongly to Sun Dawei's lack of education. "You – a member of the literati? Can you even read the titles of those books? Last time you talked to me about *The Legend of the Condor Heroes,* you couldn't even get the chapter name right and read 'magic mendicant' as 'magic medicine'. Now you want to run a book-lending stall? You put the 'con' in 'condor'."

"Misreading 'mendicant' as 'medicine' is because I studied too hard when I was young and ended up nearsighted!" Sun Dawei said. He hated others remarking on his lack of education.

"Dawei, you're a college dodger. Go ahead and say you're the best educated of us all, but don't interrupt us," Lisi said. In the 1980s, "college dodger" was a positive term.

"Why don't you two come work at my scrap metal stall," offered Xiaoji.

"Being Lord of the Trash with you and dealing with cops coming in all the time and asking for tip-offs and bribes? Forget it!" Feisi said.

"You know why the cops come to me? It's what's called the police and military brotherhood. Go to the Western Palace, Red Flag, and Nanshan Hill police stations and see if you find anyone who doesn't know Xiaoji. I'm always telling them about fighting at Laoshan, and they respect me. They're my brothers and my friends," said Xiaoji.

"Any cop who doesn't know you shouldn't even be a cop," said Lisi caustically. "A fencing operation as big as yours is bound to have the cops checking in on a regular basis."

"Say what you like, but I have brothers at the police stations and the public security bureau! If any of you gets hauled in, just say you're my brother and they won't give you any trouble," Xiaoji boasted.

"Xiaoji, that time when you and I got into it at the No. 6 High School, you came out of the police station with a bloody nose and a black eye. Did you get that fooling around with your police brothers?" Zhao Hongbing teased.

"Shit, that night I was interrogated by some trainee baby cop. He didn't know any of the chiefs I mentioned and smacked me around on top of it. But remember, I got my ass kicked because of you trotting over to the high school in the cold dead of night to flirt with your girlfriend."

"I have to say, I think Xiaoji is doing great," Li Wu said. "He's made a lot of money by just sitting there and waiting for people to bring him scrap. If we go out and collect scrap, maybe even use a car to pick up junk from the counties and villages, we could make even more."

"Li Wu's right," said Little Beijing. "Collecting scrap from the countryside could bring in lots of money, and maybe even some antiques."

"You get antiques sometimes already, don't you, Xiaoji?" Lisi asked.

"Yeah, but I don't know much about them, so I don't take many," said Xiaoji, modest for a change.

"You don't know about antiques? That's simple!" said Li Wu. "My uncle is a history teacher at the Teacher's College. He's always appraising artifacts that have been dug up. Ask him to give you some pointers!"

"Okay, I'll ask him to take me on as his student," Xiaoji said.

"Actually, I think Xiaoji has a good idea there," said Hongbing thoughtfully. "Feisi and Lisi both know how to drive. You could take some old beater down to the countryside and collect scrap metal and make a decent living at it. You can all ask Li Wu's uncle to teach you something about antiques, too. There's got to be lots of antiques in our city. If you get a really good one, you can make decent money. In any case, neither of you has anything better to do. I think you should go for it."

"I guess I can consider it," said Lisi. "You're right; I don't have anything else to do."

"How about if I go pay respects to your uncle on the sixth day of the Spring Festival?" said Xiaoji. "Do you think he'll be available, Li Wu?"

"It shouldn't be a problem. You don't have to make a big deal of it – just buy him dinner and get to know him. That should be enough. It's not like you're a stranger," said Li Wu.

After thinking it over for a few days, Feisi and Lisi decided to start collecting scrap metal. They arranged to borrow enough money from family members to buy a small second-hand truck. With nothing better to do, Li Wu agreed to help them out. A three-man scrap team was formed.

On the sixth day of Spring Festival, Xiaoji put down money to reserve a table at the Purple Moon for an "apprenticeship dinner". The Purple Moon was the first of the large private restaurants to open in the city under the reformist economic policies. Its decor and food were top class, providing the best possible dining experience.

Ergou didn't attend that dinner, but he subsequently saw the man who taught Xiaoji and the others about antiques – Li Wu's uncle. He was a hale and imposing figure with an elegant physique. It is said that everyone who attended that meal was cowed by him. Even the relatively well-educated Little Beijing and Zhang Yue exchanged only the occasional word with him, because the elder Mr. Li was simply too learned and erudite for them. He was conversant with astronomy, geography, *fengshui*, and astrology. His references to history, metaphysics, tombs, and the dating of cultural artifacts were so wide-ranging and profound that none of them could even begin to grasp what he said; they finished the meal having learned nothing.

Amazingly, even the most garrulous of the group, Sun Dawei, spent an entire hour without uttering a word in Mr. Li's presence. Mr. Li left a few books for Xiaoji and the others to study, striding off with the comment, "Whatever you don't understand, just ask me, and don't forget to return the books when you're finished." After he left, the guys reverted to their normal hooligan behavior and wolfed down their food.

"Your uncle is really well educated," said Zhang Yue to Li Wu admiringly. "How did he get an uncultured nephew like you?"

"The Great Cultural Revolution held me back," sighed Li Wu.

"Well, Zhang Yue went through the Cultural Revolution, too, and he managed to pass the college entrance exam," said Sun Dawei disdainfully.

"The stuff Uncle Li was talking about was really interesting and mysterious," Xiaoji said. "We should try to learn it."

"You know, we don't have to buy up antiques – we could go and dig them right out of the graves!" said Feisi, always taking the most direct route.

"We can't do that. It's illegal. If they catch you, you'll go to prison!" Zhao Hongbing said.

"Hongbing, are you saying all your gang fights are legal?" Feisi asked.

"Hongbing regards that as 'driving out scoundrels and protecting the people'," said Little Beijing.

"Talking about fighting gets me steamed up. Once Tiger is discharged from the hospital, I'm going to give him a thrashing." Zhang Yue was thinking about his sole defeat.

The private rooms at the Purple Moon were simply partitioned off from the larger dining room and weren't sound-proof. When Zhang Yue said he wanted to fight, someone on the other side of the partition said, "Who wants a fight?"

"That was me. What's it to you?" Zhang Yue yelled.

The man on the other side said nothing, but there was the sound of a chair clattering. The curtain hanging in the doorway of their room was pulled aside, and a burly man strode in. He wasn't tall, but he looked tough and reeked of alcohol.

"Who was that yelling in here?" the man demanded.

"That was me. What's it to you?" Zhang Yue said again.

"You little sons of bitches. What are you bullshitting about?" demanded the foul-mouthed fellow.

"Who are you calling little sons of bitches?" demanded Zhang Yue, his temper rising.

At that point, Zhao Hongbing and the others had to restrain their laughter. They knew Zhang Yue would never let that drunk get away with his bad-mouthing. Of all the people at the Purple Moon the drunk could have insulted, he'd made the worst possible choice with Zhang Yue.

"You little sons of bitches!" The man was obviously too drunk to have heard what Zhang Yue said.

"Who are you calling little sons of bitches?!" Zhang Yue demanded again. He was definitely making progress, letting someone insult him twice without making a move and only raising his voice. That would never have happened before.

"You little sons of bitches!" said the man again, not answering Zhang Yue.

Later the others learned that Zhang Yue didn't make a move because he felt that it would be dishonorable to take advantage of the greater number on his side, as well as his opponent's obvious drunkenness.

"Brother, you're drunk. Go home and sleep it off," said Zhao Hongbing.

"You little sons of bitches! Do you know who I am? Don't you recognize me?" the man said.

"I don't know who the fuck you are, but if you don't get your ass out of here, I'm going to give it a whipping!" said Zhang Yue, running out of patience.

"I'm telling you, I'm Mighty Zhang!" said the man, gesticulating in a threatening manner, with no indication that he'd heard Zhang Yue.

The young men in the room finally understood why the drunk was so aggressive; he did have some impressive connections. Mighty Zhang had been one of the city's top gangsters before the 1983 "Strike Hard" campaign. During the campaign, he'd been named the "No. 2 criminal gang leader" of the locality and had received a suspended death sentence. He'd been paraded through the streets with a placard around his neck. When the excessively harsh sentences against some hooligans were overturned at the end of 1986, Mighty Zhang was the most prominent of those released.

"Big mighty deal! Get the fuck out of here before I beat the shit out of you!" said Zhang Yue. Even if Mighty Zhang had been a legendary swordsman, Zhang Yue wouldn't have hesitated to thrash him.

Mighty Zhang neither left nor gave any indication of having heard Zhang Yue.

"I was in my prime while you punks were still in diapers," he said.

"The future is ours!" said Zhang Yue. As he spoke, he picked up a beer bottle and brought it crashing on Mighty Zhang's head. Blood began flowing down the older man's face. Zhang Yue waved him off with the unmistakable message that if Mighty Zhang left now, he wouldn't attack him again.

Half sobered by the blow, Mighty Zhang saw the composed, grinning youth who had struck him, and finally realized that this time he had encountered a real tough guy. He knew very well that the average punk wouldn't dare raise a hand to him, but that once someone took the lead, others would gang up and beat him while he was down. But Zhang Yue was the only one among the young men before him who had lifted a hand; the others seemed to have no such intention. Mighty Zhang realized that these guys were confident that Zhang Yue could handle him on his own; perhaps they even felt that ganging up on one man was dishonorable. Under the circumstances, the partially sobered Mighty Zhang could only admit defeat.

"My young brothers, this old guy had a little too much to drink just now, and I apologize. Let's have a drink together and put this misunderstanding behind us." Mighty Zhang raised a bottle and poured a token amount for each of them and a glass for himself, which he then downed in one swallow.

Zhao Hongbing and the others made no reply, but with a symbolic gesture raised their glasses and drank their swallows of liquor. Only Zhang Yue still looked angry, glaring at Mighty Zhang without drinking. "All right then, brothers, I'll go now. If you ever need me in the future..."

Before he could finish speaking, Zhang Yue dashed the liquor in his face. "Who the fuck needs you!" he spat, disdaining to look Mighty Zhang in the eye.

Mighty Zhang looked at Zhang Yue without wiping his face. Then, he raised the curtain and left the room without a backward glance.

After Mighty Zhang left, everyone said Zhang Yue had

gone too far. Although Mighty Zhang had drunk too much and was wrong to insult them, Zhang Yue had already hit him. Mighty Zhang had apologized, and Zhang Yue should have let it go. Furthermore, the older man obviously had a short fuse, and Zhang Yue's handling of this trivial matter was bound to bring more trouble.

"Zhang Yue, you seem to think we don't have enough enemies," said Hongbing lightly. He had always been on the best terms with Zhang Yue and didn't like to blame him too much.

CHAPTER 14

No Extra Blankets

THEY SAY THAT SOON AFTER Zhao Hongbing and the others left the Purple Moon, Mighty Zhang came back for them, knife in hand. This news was of little concern to Hongbing and the others, skilled and daring fighters that they were. "When we see him, we'll thrash him," said Zhang Yue.

After the Spring Festival, Feisi, Lisi, and Li Wu bought their little truck and began going to the countryside to collect scrap metal, while Little Beijing stayed in town to help Zhao Hongbing. The hotel did a roaring business, mainly because of its location and size, and Zhao Hongbing's emphasis on cleanliness. When Ergou opened the door of a room, he felt he'd entered an army encampment; Zhao Hongbing trained his hotel attendants with military discipline, so the bedding was tidy and immaculate. Although the city had many privately-run hotels by then, most were smaller than Zhang Hongbing's, and with larger rooms and better management, Hongbing's hotel did better business than any other but the three-star Railway Hotel near the train station.

Seventy to eighty percent of Zhao Hongbing's clientele consisted of travelers passing through the city. The remainder consisted of local hooligans who rented rooms with their girlfriends, whom they referred to as "ponies". Zhao Hongbing was fed up with the latter group because they left such a mess, but over time he came to know quite a few of these punks. They were typically around twenty years old and loafed around the streets with their "big brothers", making a dreary living through pilfering, robbery, and extortion. Although Hongbing never intended to make a name in the criminal underworld, these punks were in awe of him after hearing how he and his guys had stabbed Railway, crippled Tiger, taken on Little Tiger's numerical superiority, and broken a bottle over the head of the newly-released Mighty Zhang. They always addressed him as "Big Brother Hongbing" – a moniker that spread and stuck.

Most of the ponies these punks brought to the hotel were high school drop-outs. "Pony" was a pejorative term at that time, although nowadays no one would particularly object to what these girls did. They weren't prostitutes in any sense of the word, but simply had a more casual attitude toward sex.

Ergou saw quite a few of these ponies during the time Zhao Hongbing ran the hotel. Most were still in their teens and dressed in the latest fashions. Their preference for very short skirts made them especially conspicuous in winter. For all their casual attitude toward sex, they were still girls. Most seemed quite bashful and shy, and they craved true love.

Zhao Hongbing found himself frequently pestered by these girls. Ergou's deepest impression was of a very tall girl with large eyes, milky skin, and the face of a *manga* character. Ergou was reminded of her later when he saw the character Shizuka in the Japanese animated film *Doraemon*; this girl even liked to dress in neat little skirts like Shizuka.

Hongbing's Shizuka seemed quite gentle, bashful, and innocent, and couldn't have been more than nineteen years old. She had first come to Zhao Hongbing's hotel with a tattooed punk. While paying for the room afterwards, the punk had stopped to say a few words to Big Brother Hongbing. While they were talking, one of the room attendants came over and said, "Mr. Zhao, there's blood on their sheets. Should we make them pay extra?"

"According to the rules, of course they should compensate us," said the floor captain, standing nearby, before Hongbing could reply.

Then Zhao Hongbing noticed Shizuka, her head bowed low and a deep blush suffusing her pale face as she nervously stroked the punk's arm. Hongbing could see the girl was deeply embarrassed and close to tears.

"Just toss the sheets out, Xiao Li. There's no need to charge extra," Hongbing said to the floor captain. He hated seeing girls cry. "Go on," he said to the couple. "It's all right."

He'd gotten the girl out of an awkward situation. When Shizuka reached the door, she looked back at Hongbing. Ergou believes that with Hongbing's words and that one look back, Shizuka fell in love with him, and in more than the usual way.

A few days later, Shizuka broke up with the punk and wrote a love letter to Zhao Hongbing. Ergou still remembers that the letter was sent through the mail addressed simply to "Big Brother Hongbing."

When Zhao Hongbing received the letter, he disregarded it. He didn't realize Shizuka had set her heart on him. However, a few days later, he received a glass bottle filled with a thousand origami stars that she had folded with her own hands. Fearing that Gao Huan would see it, Hongbing gave it to Zhang Yue for his twenty-third birthday a few days later, which looked very strange indeed. When Hongbing said he'd folded the stars himself, Zhang Yue tossed the bottle aside with a shudder.

From then on, a letter arrived every two days, and a present every three days. It drove him Hongbing crazy. Around this time Shizuka also wrote a letter to Gao Huan saying she intended to steal Hongbing from her. Perturbed as he was, Zhao Hongbing still didn't realize how ruthless Shizuka could be.

One spring evening in 1987, Shizuka arrived at Zhao Hongbing's hotel in a pink dress. "Hey!" Hongbing greeted her with a smile. Although he dreaded the sight of Shizuka, he never liked to hurt a girl's feelings.

"Hongbing, I got into a fight with my parents," she said. "They kicked me out"

"That's too bad," said Hongbing. "Little Beijing will give you a room on the third floor. You can stay here for a few days and eat with the staff. How does that sound?" Hongbing had broken out in a cold sweat, feeling he had no choice if he didn't want to see Shizuka wandering the streets.

"I don't want to sleep upstairs, Hongbing. I want to sleep in your bed. It's clean."

Shizuka was still a young girl, and after saying this, she blushed.

"All our beds here are clean!" said Hongbing, so shocked that the novel he was reading trembled in his hand.

"Yours is a twin bed," Shizuka insisted. "I like twin beds. That's what I sleep in at home."

"So if you sleep in Hongbing's bed, where's Hongbing supposed to sleep?" laughed Little Beijing. "You don't expect him to sleep with you, do you?"

"Er, that would be okay," said Shizuka, her head bowed as she played with her hands.

Zhao Hongbing looked ready to pass out.

Shizuka actually did sleep in the twin bed in Zhao Hongbing's room, and she stayed there for more than a week. During that week, whenever Hongbing changed clothes, Shizuka washed them immediately, and she washed his pillow cases and bedding two or three times. Every evening when it was time for bed, Shizuka made herself at home, undressing and putting on a nightgown she'd brought with her, which was pretty sexy for those days. Whenever he saw her begin to undress, Hongbing turned and left for the counter, leaving Shizuka to sleep alone. Luckily he had one of Sun Dawei's novels to read. Hongbing sat at the counter reading all night. By the time a week had passed, he was looking thin and haggard.

Every night at midnight, Shizuka would call out, "Hongbing, you need to rest! Come in and sleep!"

"I – I'm not tired yet. I'll just read for a while," Hongbing would say, not knowing whether to laugh or cry.

"Don't read! Come in and sleep!"

"The bed's too small."

"We can snuggle together."

"You go ahead and sleep!"

Gao Huan knew Zhao Hongbing wouldn't act improperly with Shizuka, but she was still jealous. Whenever she saw him, she urged him to kick Shizuka out. "If you won't do it, I will!" she said.

"She's had a fight with her parents and doesn't have any money. Where do you want her to go?"

"I'll give her 200 *yuan*, and she can go sleep anywhere she wants except in your bed. Even I haven't slept in your bed!" Gao Huan said, and blushed.

"I've told her that, but she wants to stay here and work as a room attendant."

"She wants to work here? Hongbing, you have to make her leave."

"I can't. She's just a girl. How can I throw her out on the street?"

"So what if she's a girl? So am I! Why aren't you thinking of my feelings?"

"... She's just a girl."

As far as Ergou knows, Zhao Hongbing never became involved with Shizuka. However, even after she got married and became a mother, she was still hung up on him. While he was in Reeducation Through Labor, Shizuka went to visit him every month, spending the better half of her month's earnings to buy things for him. She visited him more often than all his gang brothers put together. Shizuka is now nearing forty, but looks considerably younger. She runs a successful chain of beauty shops and is a respected member of the community. Yet whenever she knows Zhao Hongbing will appear at a function, she shows up dressed to the nines, and she calls him every three or four days. She says that at her age, she regards Hongbing as no more than a good friend, but Ergou knows that she still hopes to kindle a romance with him. As for Gao Huan, she has become numb to Shizuka's harassment after all these years, and considers it a normal part of life.

"Hongbing, why don't you just do it with her and get it over with?" said Little Beijing with a laugh every time Shizuka tried to seduce him.

"I have Gao Huan," Hongbing said.

"You don't have to tell Gao Huan, do you?"

"Even without Gao Huan, I wouldn't want her. I think she's kind of disgusting."

"Disgusting? Such a fresh young girl!"

"Leave me alone. If you like her so much, you take her!"

"She's not interested in me."

Zhao Hongbing was like that. He was never unwilling to say an unkind word to a girl, and he never guessed that Shizuka's staying with him would actually cause him trouble.

One Saturday night, after getting off from work, Zhang Yue invited everyone out. He claimed he wanted to invite his pals and Gao Huan, but everyone knew he wanted to see Li Yang. Gao Huan, Li Yang, and Sun Dawei's 'girlfriend' were inseparable. Zhao Hongbing and Little Beijing were getting bored at the hotel. When Zhang Yue invited them they immediately said they'd be there, neither of them wanting to stay behind. Zhao Hongbing had no choice but to ask his third sister to help out at the hotel while he and Little Beijing went out drinking with Zhang Yue.

Children of the same parents often look very different. Zhao Hongbing's brother had a coarser look than he did, as did his two eldest sisters, but Hongbing and his third elder sister both had movie-star looks. At that time, Third Sister was a newlywed of twenty-six, but she looked like she'd just graduated from college. She was eagerly anticipating the novel experience of managing Hongbing's hotel.

"Hey, boss lady. Do you provide extra blankets here?" asked four guys who had just come in. Back in the 1980s, this was local argot for a prostitute.

Hongbing's sister was ignorant of such disreputable matters, and taking them literally, she looked at them with her large, limpid eyes and said, "You want extra blankets at night? Sure, we can do that."

"Great! We want some rooms!" The young guys were from the provincial capital. They were pleased at the sight of this attractive hotel manager, and at learning that they could get "extra blankets". They had also noticed pretty Shizuka over in Hongbing's room. Zhao Hongbing's sister happily checked them in.

Around ten o'clock that night, Hongbing's sister had a room attendant take an extra blanket to each room. Ten minutes later, the guys all came down.

"Where are our extra blankets?"

"Didn't the room attendant just bring them to you?"

"That's not the kind of blanket we want!"

"Then what kind do you want?"

"We want girls!"

"We don't have that here!" said Hongbing's sister, finally realizing what they were after.

"Don't give us that crap! We saw the girl in the room behind the counter. She's not a room attendant!"

"She's my brother's friend."

"Your brother's friend?"

"Yes!"

"Boss lady, we actually really like you. Why don't you come up and keep us company?"

"Back off, or my brother will kill you when he gets back!"

"You give me a hard-on!"

Suddenly the hotel door burst open to reveal Zhao Hongbing and Little Beijing, both drunk.

"Hongbing, they're harassing me!" cried his sister tearfully. Ergou didn't personally witness what followed, so he won't try to describe it, but those four guys ended up on the floor.

"Hongbing, let's keep hitting them," Little Beijing said.

"They're not fighting back, so what's the point?"

"We're both precision fighters. We don't have to kill them or even hurt them badly. Let's have Feisi drive his truck over, and we'll take them to the hospital for a shot of Demerol. Once they're able to get up again, we can beat them some more." Little Beijing had lots of stupid ideas like that.

"Great idea! You go get Feisi. After they've gotten their shots, we'll beat them some more."

"Sis, you work at a hospital," Little Beijing said. "Find a doctor who'll give these guys some Demerol."

"Demerol requires a prescription. Ordinary doctors aren't authorized to write four prescriptions," said Hongbing's sister. Brought up in the home of a senior cadre, she'd never been treated like this before, and she was still angry.

"Sister, we were wrong. You're a good person. Please tell your brothers not to hit us anymore." One of the young guys, overhearing Hongbing and Little Beijing, was practically wetting himself with fear.

"Hongbing, let them go."

Seeing the shape the four young punks were in, Hongbing's sister felt obliged to help them.

"It's Third Sister who got you off tonight," said Little Beijing. "You know that, right?"

"You punks, if it weren't for my sister pleading for you, I'd cripple you or take you to the police station," Hongbing said.

The fact is that while Zhao Hongbing and Little Beijing ran the hotel, they kept it clean of prostitutes, even though almost all the other hotels near the train station offered such services.

Gao Huan had reason to be pleased with this incident, because Shizuka realized she was partly responsible and left before she could be told to go. Of course, that didn't mean she'd given up on Zhao Hongbing.

CHAPTER 15

Justifiable Homicide

FROM EARLY SPRING TO EARLY summer 1986, Zhao Hongbing and his friends had no major conflicts with others. The main reason was that they'd gained a reputation from all the tough fights they'd been in before Spring Festival, so ordinary punks didn't dare provoke them. Another reason was that after Spring Festival, they began settling into their own start-up businesses, which required too much time and effort for them to get together and cause trouble.

In these few months, the structure of the local underworld also underwent change. Prior to that Spring Festival, there were only five or six major gangs in the entire city. They were based largely in the suburbs, for instance the gangs of Rascal Zhang, Railway, and Tiger. These people had made their names after the 1983 "Strike Hard" campaign, which had rounded up the city's most prominent hooligans and cleared the way for lowlifes like Railway – who didn't even have the guts to avenge his own stabbing – to become gang leaders. From the end of 1986 to early 1987, some of the gangsters imprisoned in 1983 completed their sentences or were released early. When these genuine tough guys reemerged, several new gangs sprang up led by veteran gangsters like Old Rod Li, Liu Haizhu, Chen Wei Dong, and Mighty Zhang.

Although Zhao Hongbing and his friends didn't provoke fights, that didn't mean others would leave them alone. The main gangsters goading them were Tiger and Mighty Zhang.

Tiger came out of the hospital a cripple and with a new nickname, Limpy. He wanted to get back at Feisi, but Feisi was always in the countryside, beyond his reach.

As for Mighty Zhang, although he didn't have even the slightest sense of humor, there was something comical about him. He'd gone to prison for organizing a criminal gang and extortion, but while cruel and merciless, he hadn't committed any other major crimes. After he "transferred out", many of his old prison buddies hoped to work with him, but he'd learned a painful lesson: "I'm never going to organize a gang again," he vowed. Everyone thought this boorish thug had somehow actually been reformed by the government and was turning over a new leaf, and they praised him as the returned prodigal son. Later people realized that although Zhang had indeed forsworn gang life, he had simply set himself up as a solo operation. His main project was also unique within the hoodlum brotherhood. Other hooligans engaged in theft, robbery, and extortion, but Mighty Zhang felt all this was beneath him. He wanted to be a "battering ram" – the gangland term used back in the 1980s for a highway robber. Having just been released from prison, Mighty Zhang wasn't stupid enough to go robbing people at knifepoint. Instead, he extorted money from bus drivers who plied the routes between the urban areas and the surrounding counties, and between the counties and the villages. They say he came up with this "business plan" while still in prison.

Mighty Zhang's method was to dig ruts in dirt roads that buses and trucks were certain to use. Usually there were repairs being carried out on segments of highways that required vehicles to detour onto dirt roads. These dirt roads weren't proper highways, but roadways resulting from repeated traffic. The state had no policies or laws protecting these roads, so Mighty Zhang identified them as a business opportunity. He knew more about the area's roadways than the Director of Transport himself. Wherever there was a dirt road, there was Mighty Zhang.

He hired a couple local farmers to dig trenches in these roads. The trenches couldn't be too deep or too shallow, too wide or too narrow, but just enough to prevent a vehicle from passing over them. Coming upon these trenches, a truck or bus would stop, and the driver would see Mighty Zhang and a few humble peasants standing there.

"Brothers, why have you dug so many trenches here? We can't get past," the driver would inevitably say.

"We're digging irrigation ditches. What else can we do?" Mighty Zhang would answer, looking as if he were also in a bind.

"*Aiya.* What am I going to do with this bus full of people (or truck full of goods)? I have to get past!" the driver would say, perplexed.

"My brother, I can see you're a practical man. We can fill in this trench for you, but we can't do it for free. If you want us to fill it in for you, pay us 50 *kuai.* If you'd rather do it yourself, you can just pay us 30 *kuai,* and we'll let you borrow our spades. How would that be?" Mighty Zhang acted as if he were really trying to be helpful.

"*Ai!* Just hurry up and fill it for me, and I'll pay you."

Mighty Zhang and his guys would dig and fill in this trench a dozen times a day, and even after paying off the farmers, Zhang easily went home with 500 *kuai* in his pocket. After working one road, Zhang would switch to another in a different county to avoid having his cover blown. After a while, given the number of road repairs and detours, all the drivers of regular routes knew what Mighty Zhang was up to. There was nothing they could do about it, however, because Mighty Zhang wasn't technically breaking any law. The roads he was digging up weren't public highways; none of the drivers were any match for him, so it was easier to just pay up. Later, when Mighty Zhang talked to drivers about filling in a trench, he offered a "package deal"; since the driver had to pass by again on the way back, instead of charging him a total of 100 *kuai*, Mighty Zhang would say, "How about this. Since you have to come back anyway, and I know it's not easy for you, either, give me 80 *kuai*, and we'll fill it in for you both ways."

It seems that back in the 1980s, someone in China was already putting into practice the theory described by an American economist in the 1990s as "digging a hole and then filling it in doubles GDP" – and this man didn't even have a middle school education. If American economists had been aware of Mighty Zhang, who among them would have dared to criticize Chinese economic theories? They had plagiarized Mighty Zhang's achievements.

At the same time, no one dared to imitate Mighty Zhang. If he'd heard of anyone else digging up dirt roads, he would have creamed him with his shovel. Who would stir up trouble with a desperado like Mighty Zhang?

That's how he extorted enough money that spring, becoming a 10,000 *yuan* household in the space of two months.

With that much money in hand, Mighty Zhang didn't need to go out to the countryside as often anymore. During his free time he began thinking about getting back at Zhang Yue for splashing liquor in his face. He started carrying his striking knife on him in the hope of encountering his old adversary.

One Sunday in June 1987, the weather was already hot when Zhang Yue, Sun Dawei, and Zhang Hongbing arranged to meet Gao Huan, Li Yang, and Sun Dawei's 'girlfriend' to fly kites in Liberation Square. Most people had kites shaped like dragons, birds, or fish, but Zhao Hongbing had made one that looked like a PLA soldier. It was very eye-catching.

Right from the start they discovered that Zhang Yue didn't know a thing about flying a kite. He grabbed the string and ran like crazy for the longest time without getting it into the air. Running behind him with the kite, Sun Dawei was too fat to keep up. He sat down on the rostrum and chatted with Zhao Hongbing, Gao Huan, and the others while Zhang Yue kept running around in circles. The kite never went up, but Zhang Yue wouldn't stop trying.

Since Zhang Yue had to keep looking back at the kite while he was running, he ended up colliding with someone. He turned to apologize, only to see that the man standing in front of him was Mighty Zhang. A cold pain coursed through him as a striking knife plunged into his thigh.

Later, Zhang Yue said that in that moment he attained what Little Beijing had described as the "plane of instant enlightenment" – his mind was emptied of all concerns, he felt no pain in his thigh, and the only thing he thought about was how to grab that knife.

Before the knife even left his leg, Zhang Yue grabbed

Mighty Zhang's wrist. As he backed away, he pulled Mighty Zhang's wrist downward with a twist, causing the knife to fall with a clatter to the pavement. This move was something Little Beijing had taught him a couple weeks earlier after a few drinks. Zhang Yue had never had a chance to practice it, but in this moment of instant enlightenment on the cusp of life and death, he put it to use.

Zhang Yue picked up the knife and reflexively thrust it at Mighty Zhang.

The difference between Mighty Zhang and Zhang Yue was that Mighty Zhang aimed his knife at Zhang Yue's thigh, but Zhang Yue aimed it at Mighty Zhang's heart.

The special quality of a striking knife is that it draws blood quickly with a wound that's hard to stitch up, and it's also easy to pull out of a body. Zhang Yue sent another jab into Mighty Zhang's abdomen.

They say that Mighty Zhang didn't die right away. He kept babbling after he fell, but no one could understand what he was saying. His eyes grew large, and he didn't look so ferocious anymore.

Perhaps, lying there on the ground, Mighty Zhang saw the azure sky, the puffy white clouds, and the cheerfully winging doves. Perhaps he remembered when he was five years old and his doting grandmother sold five catties of millet to buy him a sticky rice sweet; or when he was ten and studying hard to get a red badge from his teacher; or when he was fifteen and stole ten *kuai* from the boy next door, excited by his first crime. Or maybe he was remembering when he turned twenty and left the detention center for the first time, and his parents were waiting with a nice warm rice box full of his favorite meat and vegetables, hoping he'd turn over a new leaf; or when he was twenty-five and getting thrashed by other prisoners, and the prison guards did nothing.

Now he would never have to go to prison again. They say that as people die, their lives pass before their eyes, and at this moment, Mighty Zhang must have been viewing the warm, excited and happy tableau of a wailing baby covered with blood as his family members hovered around him.

The warm breeze waned. The soldier kite drifted down on Mighty Zhang and became smeared with his blood. He had ruled the roost for a while, but now he'd died at the hands of an even fiercer man. Perhaps it really was the end of an era.

"Take him to the hospital!" Zhao Hongbing said. "Gao Huan! Call the police."

"How can we carry him?" asked Sun Dawei, flustered.

"Don't bother with him. He's dead." Zhao Hongbing, who had watched so many comrades die at his side, spoke without expression. "I mean you need to get Zhang Yue to the hospital."

The autopsy report showed that Zhang Yue's initial thrust was fatal.

Zhang Yue had no prior criminal record, and had been acting in self-defense. The man he had killed had been a notorious hoodlum, but there were multiple witnesses in Liberation Square. For that reason, he was given a token sentence of two years' Reeducation Through Labor.

The incident affected not only Zhang Yue's fate, but also that of Zhao Hongbing and Gao Huan by exposing their attachment to Gao Huan's parents.

CHAPTER 16

The Elopement

BECAUSE ZHAO HONGBING, GAO HUAN, and the others had been nearby when Zhang Yue killed Mighty Zhang, and because it was Gao Huan who called the police, the two of them had to give statements at the police station. It was late by the time they reached home. As soon as Gao Huan entered her residential area, she saw her parents standing there waiting for her.

"What have you been doing all this time?" her mother cried hoarsely.

"I was... out with some classmates," she answered in a low voice, motioning for her parents to go home where she would explain everything to them.

"Where did you go?"

"Liberation Square."

"So it really was you!" Her mother began to cry.

"Were you involved in the killing?" her father demanded.

"It was my classmate's friend who did I t," Gao Huan explained.

"Who is that holding your hand?"

"My... my friend," Gao Huan forced out the words.

"Friend? More like a boyfriend!" said her mother.

"Mom, let's not talk here. We can discuss it at home."

"We're going to clear things up right here or you're not coming home!" Her mother's voice became louder, choked with sobs.

"Mom..."

Gao Huan and her parents kept their neighbors up for more than an hour before going home. It turned out that a neighbor had been at Liberation Square and seen everything. He'd come home and told Gao Huan's parents. The family didn't sleep all that night. Gao Huan's parents simply couldn't understand how a girl who had been reserved and well-behaved all her life could have become infatuated with someone who was mixed up with a killer. In the course of one night, Gao Huan's parents descended from Heaven into Hell.

Early the next morning, they decided to go and see Gao Huan's teacher and Zhao Hongbing's father. The time for the college entrance exams was approaching, and they couldn't have their cherished daughter distracted by other matters. They had no idea that their excessive concern would be so counterproductive.

At that time, Gao Huan's father was deputy secretary-general of the municipal people's consultative conference, as well as editor-in-chief of the *City Gazette* and one of the area's most prominent men of letters. Typical of China's literati in the 1980s, he was aloof, stubborn, and lacking in interpersonal skills. He declined to go to see Gao Huan's teacher, sending his wife to the school instead. The two of them planned to see Hongbing's father that night.

Gao Huan's mother arrived at the head teacher's office at noon that day.

"Gao Huan has formed a romantic attachment, hasn't she?" she said.

"Goodness!" the teacher said. "How would such a nice girl be involved with a boy? I know nothing about it."

"He's some sort of delinquent."

"Oh! I had no idea!"

"What kind of teacher are you?"

"I'm sorry. I really had no idea. Gao Huan is such a good student. Even if she doesn't get into Tsinghua, she'll surely be admitted to Beijing University of Posts and Telecommunications, or a school of a similar standard. I haven't noticed any change at her in all!"

"I entrusted her to you, and you can't even keep track of her! You didn't even know she was involved with someone. How can you call yourself a teacher?"

"What are you saying? I can only control what Gao Huan does in school, not what she does in her free time."

Gao Huan's mother continued to argue with the head teacher for a good long while before finally slamming her hand on the desk and leaving in a huff.

Gao Huan had her head teacher for the next class period. The teacher wasted no time venting her rage in front of all the other students, using the worst language a teacher was allowed. She berated Gao Huan for twenty minutes non-stop. Gao Huan had spent her whole life being commended by her teachers and had never been subjected to such humiliating treatment. Until school let out that afternoon, she sat motionless with her head buried in her arms on her desk, her tears soaking her sleeves, her self-esteem in tatters.

That night, her parents went to see Mr. Zhao. Ergou witnessed the entire conversation.

"Director Zhao, your son and my daughter are romantically involved," said Gao Huan's father – a refined middle-aged man in horn-rimmed glasses.

"Secretary Gao, isn't it a good thing for our children to be involved?" said Mr. Zhao with a chuckle. He was less relaxed than usual. "I'm not sure why you're so indignant. My Hongbing is twenty-four years old."

"But my daughter is still young. She's still in school."

"A girl of eighteen or nineteen is not that young. I was fifteen when I married, and Hongbing's mother was only fourteen."

"Things are different now. In any case, my daughter is about to take the college entrance exam."

"It's not improper for young people to court each other. It shouldn't affect her exam results."

"This is a crucial time. I hope your son will stay away from her."

"Secretary Gao, you..."

"Director Zhao, you're a top official in the city. My family cannot aspire to such an elevated alliance."

"How can you say such a thing? Your literary talent is renowned throughout the city. If anything, it's we who are beneath you."

Silent all this time, Gao Huan's mother couldn't restrain herself any longer.

"Do you know what kind of person your son is?" she said. "Do you know what he's been doing? Are you perhaps too preoccupied with your work to keep him under control?"

"Of course I understand my son! He was given a medal for individual distinction in the army, and he sacrificed three fingers for our country. If not a hero, he's certainly no coward." Of all his five children, Mr. Zhao was fondest of Hongbing.

"But do you know what he's doing now?" Gao Huan's mother asked.

"He's running a hotel. He's not involved in any illegal dealings."

"His friend killed someone in Liberation Square yesterday!" Gao Huan's mother said.

"Hongbing told me all about it last night. First of all, he wasn't involved in the incident. After it happened, he immediately contacted the police, and he took his friend in to give himself up. Furthermore, his friend acted purely in self-defense! So what's the problem?"

"Of course you don't believe there's any problem with your son!"

"Of course there's not!"

Mr. Zhao was a headstrong man; why would he listen to Gao Huan's mother? The parents parted on bad terms, but Mr. Zhao's forbearance left a profound impression on Ergou. The things Gao Huan's mother said were very unpleasant, but Mr. Zhao was able to respond without sounding either obsequious or arrogant. Although Gao Huan's mother was exceedingly agitated, Mr. Zhao finally managed to see them to the door. "Lao Gao, we may well be in-laws in the future, so I hope you'll cool your anger and have a good talk with your child," Mr. Zhao said to Gao Huan's father as they parted. "I'll also speak with Hongbing and ask him not to see Gao Huan until she's taken her exam."

"*Ai*, Director Zhao..."

When the Gaos got home, Huan was gone. After spending the whole day crying and the entire evening questioning herself, this intensely self-respecting girl had finally written a letter to Zhao Hongbing:

> Hongbing, I want to go with you to a village that no one can find on a map, where there is none of the bustle of the city, but only flocks of sheep and cattle, and where we can live happily in a grass hut we built ourselves. All I need is your shoulder to lean on. You can play your guitar while I sing along and the birds flutter joyfully in the sky above us. In the evening we can snuggle together by the stream that runs alongside the village, my head resting on your strong chest. Hongbing, I want to go with you to a place that can't be found on a map. Perhaps our parents will not come to our wedding; it will only be the two of us, our happy faces warmed by the blazing campfire. In the morning we'll open the window to fresh air and warm rays of sunlight… We'll have a child, perhaps a little plump one, and we'll see both of our features in the baby's face. Fifty years later, when we're old and gray, we'll still be snuggling together by the pond beside that village. Hongbing, today I want to go with you to this place, this village that can't be found on a map.

The letter filled a sheet of paper, and teardrops smeared some of the words. After finishing her studies at nine-thirty, Gao Huan went to Zhao Hongbing's hotel and handed him the letter without a word and then walked into the room behind the counter. Five minutes later, the door opened and Zhao Hongbing walked in.

"Let's go," he said.

"Go where?"

"To that village that can't be found on a map."

Ten years later, when Gao Huan and Zhao Hongbing finally married after so many trials and tribulations, Gao Huan read the letter out loud.

CHAPTER 17

The No. 3 Archeological Team of the Northern China Tomb Research Institute

GAO HUAN'S MOTHER NEVER GUESSED that venting her anger on the head teacher would lead to her daughter's self-respect being so thoroughly demolished. The fragile heart of an eighteen-year-old girl bled that day. The owner of that heart didn't have the courage to face the deriding, ridiculing, and gloating gazes of her classmates, nor the parents who had always regarded her as the apple of their eyes but now considered her beyond redemption. This bleeding heart now had only one refuge: Zhao Hongbing. There was no other option.

Fearing that Gao Huan's parents would come looking for her, Zhao Hongbing took her to the Railway Hotel that night. Ergou assumes that they gave themselves to each other that night, and that both of them were virgins. However, he is unable to provide an on-the-spot report of what transpired between them.

Gao Huan's parents' excessive concern pushed her and Zhao Hongbing together. Parents typically think more about their children's futures than about their self-esteem. If her mother hadn't made such a fuss at the No. 6 High School, Gao Huan might have had a much happier life. If all parents showed a bit less concern for their children and a little more trust and understanding, might the world not be a better place?

Zhao Hongbing and Gao Huan left town the next morning, but not before Hongbing had gone to see Little Beijing.

"How much money do we have left?"

"22,500 *yuan*."

"How much do we need for revolving funds?"

"We just gave out this month's salaries, so 2,500 *yuan* should be enough."

"Give me 20,000. I have to go."

"Where?"

"I don't know."

"Are you taking Gao Huan with you?"

"Yes."

"Then go. I'll get the money. Don't worry. I'll take care of things here."

"That goes without saying, brother."

Although he was a man of many words and opinions, Little Beijing didn't make rash promises, and always kept the ones he made. He and Zhao Hongbing had faced hails of bullets together, and although they often ridiculed and teased each other, they were closer than blood brothers. Over the course of more than twenty years, they never fought or quibbled over money. Little Beijing was always the person who looked after the hotel's finances.

Before leaving, Gao Huan and Zhao Hongbing went to see Li Yang. "Tell my parents that I've left, that I'm safe, and that I'm with Hongbing," Gao Huan said.

"Where will you go?"

"I don't know."

"You're sure you won't take the college entrance exam?"

"College doesn't mean anything to me anymore."

"I had a dream last night, Gao Huan."

"About what?"

"About the kite and Zhang Yue. I'll never forget it."

Li Yang was the last person to see them that day.

Word of Zhao Hongbing and Gao Huan's elopement caused a stir throughout this medium-sized city. It was mainly due their fathers' status, but also because Hongbing and Huan were well-known among their peers. If there had been tabloid newspapers in that city, this scandal would have made headlines for at least a week. Rumors abounded, and Ergou heard several different versions of events:

"Director Zhao's son left the army and became a major hoodlum. He aimed to sleep with a hundred girls, and Gao Huan was the one-hundredth."

"Gao Huan was a pony that lots of boys at the No. 6 High School had mounted."

"Gao Huan was pregnant, and Zhao Hongbing took her away to have the baby."

Gossip can create a lot of damage. It's often the self-professed upstanding citizens who have the filthiest minds and most vivid imaginations. They embellish one X-rated story after another with vile language while taking the moral high ground. The narratives they exchange in flurries of spittle satisfy their darkest fantasies while providing mutual reinforcement of their own "morality". Although Ergou has no way of knowing whose lewd imaginations came up with the stories, he can categorically state that it took a sick mind to claim that

Zhao Hongbing had a hundred women. To this day, Zhao Hongbing has never been with any woman except Gao Huan.

Unfortunately, it was Zhao Hongbing and Gao Huan's turn in the rumor mill. But how many people knew them as well as Ergou did? They were such pure, honest young people. Previously known only in hooligan circles, Zhao Hongbing had now become the subject of after-dinner chatter for every gossip in town. As always, whatever he did increased his fame.

Within a few days, his gang had whittled down substantially. The most respected member, Hongbing, had left town. The fiercest member, Zhang Yue, had gone to jail, and it was not yet known how much time he would serve. The most agile fighter, Little Beijing, was tied up with the hotel, and the man with the shotgun, Big Mouth Sun, spent his days at his book stall. Only four core members of the gang remained active, and three of them – Lisi, Feisi, and Li Wu – were usually in the countryside collecting scrap metal. If Tiger had come to the recycling stall around that time, Xiaoji would have been out of luck. The fact is that Xiaoji overestimated Tiger and his gang. When all was said and done, Zhang Yue had just killed Mighty Zhang. Even though he was in custody, the rest of the gang continued to benefit from his reputation. Tiger and the others now knew that Zhao Hongbing's guys were capable of killing, and this discouraged any rash moves.

Even so, Xiaoji had been attacked at his recycling stall by Tiger and his gang in the past, so he still felt uneasy. On the day that Zhao Hongbing left, Xiaoji decided to take temporary leave from his stall and have Li Wu's two "little brothers" look after it, even though it meant losing some money. He started going to the countryside with Li Wu and the others to collect scrap metal, figuring he'd resume running his stall when Zhao Hongbing returned. Xiaoji had been operating his stall for a year and a half by then. Since he would take almost anything, he had quite a bit of money in hand.

Before, they'd spent their days talking and laughing and horsing around together, regarding each other as brothers without thinking much about who was the leader. Now that Zhao Hongbing was gone, Xiaoji and the others realized how important he'd been. To a certain extent, they were all psychologically dependent on him. Without him around to make decisions when something came up, the others felt somewhat at a loss.

Lisi, Feisi, and Li Wu turned to Xiaoji, who was the gang's main schemester, along with Little Beijing. Xiaoji's strength was that if he became interested in something, he could actually apply the effort necessary to learn it. After requesting the tutelage of Mr. Li during the Spring Festival, Xiaoji had acquired considerable knowledge about cultural relics, and was making extraordinary progress. Whenever Feisi and the others came across artifacts in the countryside, they had Xiaoji appraise them. Xiaoji took several of the objects to Mr. Li for evaluation, and Mr. Li was full of praise for his abilities: "I've been teaching for years. I teach more than sixty history majors every year, but not one of them has learned as well or as fast as you. You mustn't use your knowledge inappropriately, though," he said. Mr. Li was not only an intellectual, but a thoroughly upstanding man.

During his free time, Xiaoji's interest expanded from the appraisal of cultural relics to studying things like graveyard geomancy. Ergou believes that Xiaoji was genuinely curious about this mysterious subject, rather than intending from the outset to apply his knowledge to grave-robbing.

The little truck seated four people. The day after Zhao Hongbing left, Xiaoji joined Li Wu and the others on a drive down to the countryside. The acquisition of more than a dozen cultural relics in the previous months had given them great satisfaction, and they were now less interested in scrap metal than in antiques. Of course, they still accepted scrap as well, to bring in pocket money.

That day, they drove to a place called Red Flag Township, where one village had produced two relics dating from the Jin dynasty. Xiaoji had seldom joined the others on their forays to the countryside, but he wanted to come along this time to see if they could find more valuable objects. Xiaoji got out of the truck on the outskirts of the village and inspected the terrain until Feisi and the others came back from their rounds in the village.

"Did you get anything?" Xiaoji asked.

"We got a few pounds of copper wire and some broken iron tools, as well as an iron-grilled door, but that's about it," Feisi said. He was anxious to make real money. He was bored with his nickel-and-dime existence.

"What exactly were you hoping for?" Lisi asked. He took a more diligent and conscientious approach to earning money.

"Relics, of course! A ton of this scrap won't bring us as much as one decent relic," said Feisi as he started the truck.

"Relics don't grow on trees!" Xiaoji said with a laugh. "And farmers aren't so stupid nowadays."

"You know Old Rod Li? After he got out of prison, he and his brothers started dealing in cultural relics," said Li Wu, who knew a lot of street punks.

"Ha! So he's dealing antiques! Does he come to the countryside to buy them, too?" Xiaoji asked.

"He doesn't go about it honestly like we do," Li Wu said. "How many can you find, after all? He and his guys go and dig the stuff right out of the graves. You can see Old Rod and his boys are doing a lot better than we are. They're out every night drinking and whoring at Ten Thousand Cranes, the VIP Lounge, and places like that." It looked like he was envious of Old Rod Li and his gang.

"We should go dig up some graves, too!" said Feisi, slapping his hand on the steering wheel.

"Fuck that, Feisi! You go ahead if you want to, but it's too unscrupulous. Leave me the hell out of it!" Lisi was an honest man, and had kept Feisi out of a lot of illegal activity when they had skipped town.

"Don't be such a hypocrite, Lisi! Do you think the relics we've been buying haven't been snatched from under some old skeleton?"

"That doesn't mean I'm going to dig up a grave myself!"

"This village has pretty good *fengshui*. It's a perfect location for a graveyard. There might be some ancient tombs here." Xiaoji had spent more than half an hour looking around the village and evaluating it on the basis of what he'd learned from his books. In fact, his method for judging whether there were old tombs nearby was very simple and based on two points: whether they'd gotten any relics in the area before, which meant it must have been inhabited hundreds or even a thousand years ago; and whether there was a spot near the village with good enough *fengshui* for a geomancer to select it as a burial ground.

Xiaoji wasn't a professional, however. He didn't know about Luoyang spades or other tools that can dig down forty feet or so to detect traces of relics in the soil, nor was old Mr.

Li likely to teach him such things. Looking at the lofty mountain range behind the village and the stream that encircled it, Xiaoji concluded that this would be an ideal burial ground. Events proved him right. Although the village currently bore a Han Chinese name, in times past the surrounding area had been known as Boyinbula. Ergou doesn't know if this is Manchu or some other language, but apparently its meaning is "place encircled by a streamlet". People had lived there as far back as the Jin Dynasty, nearly a thousand years ago.

"Xiaoji, should we give it a try?" said Li Wu, genuinely game for it.

"Don't talk crap. If Hongbing were here, he'd never let you guys do something like that," Lisi said.

"Whoever wants to should do it," Feisi said. "Lisi, you don't have to, if you don't want to. If we dig anything up, we'll still share the money with you."

"Who cares about the money!" Lisi cried. "What you want to do is fucking illegal! If you're arrested, you'll go to prison! Zhang Yue's already inside, and now you want to join him?"

"If you're caught it's illegal; if you're not, it's not." Li Wu was also enthused with the idea.

"If we're going to do it, let's get started," said Feisi, ignoring Lisi altogether.

"How about if we give it a try tomorrow?" said Xiaoji, who was probably less interested in a quick profit than in the artifacts themselves and in testing his own judgment.

On their way back to the city, the three discussed the details. They decided to go back for a dig the following night, to see if they could find anything. Lisi refused to go. The next day he went instead to Zhao Hongbing's hotel to hang out with Little Beijing and learn the latest about Zhang Yue's case.

Meanwhile, Li Wu, Xiaoji, and Feisi gathered up the tools for their expedition. They weren't savvy enough to take proper hole-digging implements like serious grave robbers. They figured they could just poke around with spades and see what turned up.

"What if we see a ghost while were digging up a grave?" asked Feisi. Ghosts were the only thing he was afraid of.

"We'll show it who's boss," Xiaoji said.

"Why should a ghost be afraid of us?" Feisi asked.

"My dad says ghosts are afraid of guns," Li Wu said.

"But we don't have a gun," said Feisi. His desire for riches was tempered by his fear of ghouls.

"Doesn't Dawei have a shotgun? It's not that great, but a gun is still a gun," said Xiaoji, who was apparently scared as well.

"Then let's go borrow it," Feisi said.

Around three o'clock that afternoon, the three of them set off for Boyinbula in Dongfeng Township. They had a sinister encounter on the way.

It happened at twilight, when it was still possible to vaguely see a human figure. Since they were near their destination, they stopped the truck along the road about three miles from the village to have a smoke and decide where to park. Feisi got out first. Right away he noticed two people waving at him from the other side of a gully that ran along the highway. In the dim light he could just about make out that one of them was an old man. He was holding one of those long-stemmed pipes unique to the northeast.

Having lived in the south for years now, Ergou rarely sees those big gullies that are so common in the northeast. Gouged from the earth by mountain torrents, they measure thirty to a hundred yards wide and fifteen feet deep. Perhaps it's because there are fewer mountains in the south. In any case, the highway where Feisi and the others stopped the truck that evening was out in the middle of nowhere, about two hundred yards from one of these gulleys. The gully was around fifty yards wide. The two people on the opposite side were about a hundred yards from it, which meant they were about three hundred and fifty yards from Feisi and the others, with the fifteen-foot-deep gully between them. Feisi and the others looked around and saw there was no other road nearby, but a fairly precipitous path around four hundred yards east of the gully.

Feisi waved back at the old man. "Do you need a ride, old fellow?"

Back in the 1980s, people were still honest and willing to help others. Feisi always made a point of offering a ride to any old people or women with children whom he encountered while collecting scrap. Especially in such an isolated place at night, it would never have occurred to him not to help this pair across the gully.

The old man said nothing, but the way he shook his pipe indicated he wanted a ride.

"Walk east to that path and follow it here to us, pal. We'll wait for you," Feisi said accommodatingly.

The old man waved his pipe again. At that point, Lisi and Xiaoji also climbed out of the truck.

"So where should we park while we're digging?" Xiaoji asked, lighting a cigarette.

As he extended his hand to light Li Wu's cigarette as well, the three of them were startled to see that the two people – who just a moment ago had been standing more than three hundred yards away – had suddenly appeared on their side of the gully, just thirty yards away. Given that one of them was clearly an old man, how could they have covered that distance and crossed such a deep, wide gully in less than half a minute? Had they flown across?

"What the fuck?" cried Xiaoji.

He grabbed the dumb-struck Feisi and pulled him into the truck. As soon as Li Wu jumped in, they took off. All three were badly shaken. Once they got going, Li Wu – the boldest of them – looked back and saw that the two people had disappeared without a trace.

Ergou subsequently heard the three of them recount the incident in detail over and over again. No matter how they tried, they couldn't explain how the two people had reached them so quickly over such a long distance across that gully. All three had seen them, yet when they looked back, they were gone...

They'd been scared out of their wits that night.

"We've been jinxed," said Feisi. "We'd better not dig tonight. Let's go back."

"Don't be scared," Li Wu said. "Maybe we just weren't seeing clearly."

"So all our vision was blurred the same way? Fuck, man!" said Feisi, thoroughly petrified.

"It's too weird here. Let's go back. And let's take a detour." Xiaoji was also scared witless. "There's no way I'm going down that road again."

"Why are you guys so chicken?" said Li Wu, a genuinely ballsy guy. "We have a gun, don't we? You guys aren't afraid of anybody, so why are you afraid of ghosts?"

"Then I get to hold the gun," Feisi said.

"Fine," Li Wu said. "But it's too early to go digging yet.

Let's wait until after ten o'clock. We'll find someplace to have a drink first."

They drove to a little town about twenty miles from Boyinbula and drank there until ten o'clock. They felt less frightened with some liquor in them. They took the truck to a place about a half a mile from the entrance to the village. By the time they parked it was a little after eleven o'clock. Back in the 1980s, a lot of villages in the northeast still didn't have electrical cables. Those that did seldom had electricity, so by eleven o'clock at night most people were fast asleep. Since the place Xiaoji and the others had in mind was close to the village, they'd chosen this time to avoid detection.

Wielding his geomancer's compass with a knowing air, Xiaoji pointed at a corn field and said, "Let's dig here. We may find something."

Xiaoji and Li Wu grabbed their shovels and pushed their way into the corn field. Feisi kept watch with the shotgun gripped in his hands. By June the corn stalks were already very tall, and Xiaoji and Li Wu quickly vanished from sight. Only the sound of their clothing brushing against the corn stalks was detectable to Feisi. He recalled that there was no wind that night, and that the moon was very bright. After losing sight of the others, he began to feel frightened, which made him need to relieve himself. Crouching his way into the corn field, he could vaguely see Xiaoji and Li Wu about twenty yards away, bent over and digging into the earth. He could hear the sound of their shovels.

Still gripping the shotgun, Feisi pulled down his zipper and was about to loosen his trousers when he suddenly sensed someone standing behind him. The hairs stood up on the back of his neck. He turned to look. Under the moonlight he saw someone standing about five yards away –none other than the old man with the pipe whom he'd seen across the gully just a few hours earlier.

"Ghost!" Feisi yelled. His scalp was tingling as he tossed down the shotgun and ran toward Xiaoji and Li Wu. A tall, robust man, Feisi knocked down numerous corn stalks as he plunged pell-mell through the field.

"What the hell?" said Xiaoji, scared stiff by Feisi's yelling.

"Don't ask, just run!" Feisi grabbed Xiaoji, who threw down his shovel and followed him.

Dauntless as Li Wu was, this was too much even for him. He hurtled out of the field as well. The three of them reached the truck in record time. They jumped in and drove off, leaving the shotgun and two shovels behind.

Afterwards Feisi said that when they ran out of the corn field, he saw the old man again, but Xiaoji and Li Wu insisted that they didn't glimpse him. Li Wu swore up and down that there hadn't been any old man in the corn field that night and that Feisi had imagined it all. In any case, Feisi was scared for a long time afterwards.

"We should have listened to Lisi. We shouldn't be doing this kind of evil shit. I never saw a ghost in my life, but today I've seen one three times!" he said after they returned to the city.

"I'm not going to try it again, either," Xiaoji said. "Feisi scared me so bad I almost pissed myself."

"Xiaoji, do you think there really were any ancient tombs there?" Li Wu asked, still thinking about that corn field.

"How the fuck should I know? I'd only dug up two shovels of dirt when Feisi yanked me away."

"But do you think there really might be something there?" Li Wu insisted.

"Judging by the *fengshui*, there might well be a tomb somewhere around that corn field," Xiaoji said.

"If you guys aren't willing to go, I will!" Li Wu said.

"Are you crazy?" Feisi said.

"I'll dig during the day," Li Wu said. "No one sees ghosts during the day."

"But aren't you afraid someone will see *you* during the day?" Xiaoji asked.

"I have an idea," Li Wu said.

The next day, he went to one of his gang members who was a truck driver and told him what he had in mind. Before becoming a driver, this kid had been a professional thief. When Li Wu explained his idea to him, he was very interested. Li Wu turned the truck into a criminal conveyance, and on its side he stenciled the words: Northern China Tomb Research Institute No. 3 Archeological Team.

On the third day, he brought his little gang to the corn field. The shotgun and shovels were still there. Apparently the farmer was about to harvest his corn and hadn't gone to weed the field for two days. Li Wu found the farmer and paid him 500 *kuai*, telling him, "We're a state archaeological team and we want to carry out some work in your field. This 500 *kuai* is state compensation for any losses you might incur." The farmer was thrilled to accept the money and told them to dig wherever they liked. That night, Li Wu returned the shotgun to Sun Dawei.

From that day onward, Li Wu brought his three gang members every day to carry out "archaeological work" in the field, looking for graves to plunder in broad daylight. Their "official" truck was parked conspicuously along the highway, and the women and children of the village crowded around to watch. Li Wu and his gang had no luck, however. After digging deep and wide for two days, they'd found nothing but dirt. As Li Wu said after leaving prison, "If we'd dug any further, we'd have hit water." Just when they were about to give up, they ran into trouble.

That day, the county police came to the village to handle a case. When they saw villagers gathered around, the two policemen got out of their car to see what was going on. When they saw several men digging a large pit, they felt there was something fishy about it. Then they saw the truck with "Northern China Tomb Research Institute No. 3 Archeological Team" written on it. Policemen have a nose for trouble.

"Comrades, where are you from?" asked one of the officers by way of greeting.

"We're from Beijing," Li Wu said. "We came here for an archaeological dig."

"Hm... Then why do you have a northeastern accent?" the policeman asked.

"I'm originally from Changchun but I'm working in Beijing now. The accent is about the same," said Li Wu, unfazed.

"Why does your truck have a local license plate?" the policeman asked, walking toward them as he spoke.

"We came here recently to carry out archaeological digs near your city, and it was more convenient to borrow a local truck. All of our team's trucks are in Harbin right now." Li Wu left it at that, finding it increasingly difficult to answer the policeman's questions.

"I can see you're working hard, comrade," laughed the policeman. "If you run into problems, just let us know." He stood in front of Li Wu and made as if to shake his hand.

"Police officers work even harder!" said Li Wu, smiling

back and extending his hand. As their hands clasped, Li Wu felt something cool encircle his wrist. It was a handcuff.

"You're hilarious," said the policeman, leading Li Wu to the police car. "I've seen lots of archaeological digs, but this is the first time I've seen guys like you using shovels and spades. It's a real eye-opener. You've got plenty of nerve, but you're too unprofessional."

A few days later, people from the city's historical museum actually excavated a Jin Dynasty tomb just thirty yards from where Li Wu had been digging. Although it wasn't a major one, it contained a lot of artifacts, which are now displayed in the museum.

Although Li Wu was rather money-mad, he was an upstanding guy. He didn't rat on Xiaoji and the others, saying that it was all his idea to look for the old tomb. As the lead grave-robber, he was sentenced to seven years in prison.

CHAPTER 18

Little Beijing's Peace Hotel

AFTER COMING BACK FROM THE corn field, the normally audacious hoodlum Feisi was so terrified that he fell ill with a fever for several days. It seems that everyone has his Achilles' heel.

Lisi didn't believe they'd really been jinxed that day. "Feisi never saw a ghost. It was all in his head!" It wasn't clear whether he was trying to comfort Feisi or rib him.

After Li Wu was arrested, no one suggested grave-robbing again. After a week passed and Feisi and Xiaoji were sure that Li Wu hadn't ratted on them to the police, they took the truck back down to the countryside to collect scrap metal.

During this time, things had been happening at Zhao Hongbing's hotel as well. While Hongbing was running the hotel, he had become acquainted with a group of petty hoodlums who worshiped him and Little Beijing. They especially loved the "player" vibe that Little Beijing gave off.

Every afternoon between four and five o'clock, Little Beijing moved an oversized armchair into the doorway of the hotel and sat there with a glass of green tea in his left hand, a fan in his right hand, and Zhao Hongbing's guitar beside him. A group of street punks gathered around to listen to him pontificate. Every day there were more of them. Once the crowd approached one hundred, Little Beijing gave a flip of his fan, and drawled in his pure Beijing accent, "Gentlemen, I need a break. We'll talk again tomorrow". Then he tripped back into the hotel.

Ergou has known Little Beijing for more than twenty years now and admires him enormously. He especially likes his eloquence; Little Beijing's conversation has moments of brilliance that make one gasp in admiration, and his linguistic capacity is outstanding. Ergou also admires his performance ability; Little Beijing loves to gesticulate when he talks and is an excellent mimic. It's said that there are three systems for acting: the Stanislavski method, the Brecht method, and the Chinese method, but this guy melds them all together. Ergou is a fan of his agility as well; Little Beijing has fought countless times and faced all kinds of danger, but has never lost a fight. Then there's his personal loyalty and honor; he's been unfailingly loyal to Zhao Hongbing for more than twenty years, and is also willing to seek justice for people he's only just met.

One evening in June 1987, as dusk was approaching, Little Beijing moved his armchair to the doorway as usual. When he looked around, he saw no one there. This meant that he'd have to attract some attention, so he picked up Zhao Hongbing's guitar and began strumming and singing "Bloodstained Glory" – a song that was popular at that time. Zhao Hongbing had only taught him to play that one song, but he played and sang it well and movingly, dedicating it to the men he'd fought with at Laoshan.

"Brother Shen! You're out!" A street punk of around twenty years old came over and greeted him.

"Just catching some rays." Little Beijing leaned back

languidly, tossed the guitar aside, and rocked the chair upright.

"Who's tougher – the hoodlums in Beijing or our hoodlums here?"

"Each has their strengths. Ours in Beijing are called players." Little Beijing shook open his fan with a snap and began waving it in a leisurely fashion before his half-closed eyes.

"Player? What does that mean?"

"The meaning can be concrete or abstract – that's philosophy," drawled Little Beijing, taking a sip of tea.

"Can you explain it to us?" A group of half a dozen punks had gathered by then.

"In concrete terms, players are a group of young people who are unhappy with society but have no outlet," said Little Beijing. "They express their discontent in the form of attacks on the most repulsive phenomena in our society. This behavior brings them spiritual enrichment and satisfaction."

"And in the abstract?" The young rowdies were not nearly as well-read as Little Beijing, and couldn't make any sense of what he was saying.

"In abstract terms, being a player is a mentality – a sort of performance art. It's the individual pitted against the collective with resistance as its core power. It is like being a 'punk' – but there's no point in explaining further, because you won't understand."

Having finished his speech, Little Beijing waved his fan while gazing at the young hooligans with the hint of a smile on his face.

"Brother Shen, we really don't get what you're saying. What we want to know is if the street toughs in Beijing are better fighters than we are here."

"Let me correct you once more – they're called players," said Little Beijing, nodding his head for emphasis.

"Right, right. Players."

"A few of the Beijing players are pretty tough. There are tough guys among you here as well, so it's hard to compare. Wasn't Brother Zhang Yue tough when he slaughtered Mighty Zhang?"

"Brother Zhang Yue really is tough!"

"I joined the army when I was eighteen, and at nineteen I was on the Laoshan frontline. But I never did much fighting in Beijing. Even so, when I fight, I don't lose."

This was no empty boast on Little Beijing's part. In all these years, Ergou has never seen him bested in a fight.

"Brother Shen, can you tell us what it was like on the Laoshan frontline?"

"In the spring of 1985, your big brother Hongbing and I went with several others to execute our mission. The mountain was extremely precipitous…" Little Beijing rose from his armchair, stepped back a little and pointed at the hotel wall. "The cliff was at a nearly ninety-degree angle." He dropped his fan onto the armchair, signaling that he was moving from storytelling to performance mode. As he spoke, Little Beijing dashed forward and began scaling the outer wall of the hotel. The wall was made of sandstone and provided a considerable amount of traction. He was able to take three strides up the side and then grab the second-floor ledge. With a burst of strength, he propelled himself upward to sit on the ledge.

"Wah!"

The gathered street toughs and ordinary passers-by gasped in admiration, and applauded Little Beijing's agility. More and more people gathered round as he smiled down from the second-floor ledge. He beat a rhythm on it and then raised his clasped hands in a show of humble gratitude for the applause.

He then jumped lightly down.

"This is the 'cloud ladder' you read about in novels," he said as he settled back into his armchair and took a sip of tea. Leaping over walls and onto roofs was real *Kungfu*; acknowledging the applause with his clasped hands raised was pure Chinese stagecraft.

"Brother Shen! Don't stop there! After you climbed over the cliff, how did you fight the 'Nam devils?"

"The only ones in our squad who could climb to the top of the cliff were Brother Hongbing and I. The squad leader didn't let us use our guns for fear of alerting the enemy, so Brother Hongbing and I planned to wring the 'Nam devils' necks..."

Little Beijing's expressing became imposing and somber, following the Stanislavski method of "setting the scene".

His description was so vivid that the ruffians were all worried for him.

"How did you wring their necks? Did the enemy discover you?"

"Stretch your head toward me and I'll show you," said Little Beijing, motioning to one of the young hooligans. He placed one hand on the top of the youth's head and another under his chin. "I just have to turn my left hand to the left, my right to the right, apply some force, and crack!" Little Beijing's expression became savage at that moment, following the Brecht method. The audience gasped, afraid that he would actually break the young hooligan's neck, but Little Beijing gently released him.

"Did you really break the necks of those 'Nam devils?"

"I'm tired now. Come back tomorrow and I'll tell you the rest." Little Beijing squinted in the sunlight, ignoring the disappointed groans of the dozens of guys gathered around him.

"Did you wring their necks or not?"

"How can you stop in the middle like that?"

"Maybe he won't tell us the rest tomorrow, either!"

Little Beijing ignored their comments and closed his eyes with a little smile on his face, settling back in his armchair as if falling asleep.

For some time, Ergou believed that Little Beijing must have been a descendent of the street actors who performed under the Beijing Overpass – how else to explain his love for performance, his skill at it, and the clasped-hand salute so typical of professional performers? If Little Beijing had raised a monkey and put on a show in front of the hotel, he would have had a box full of money within an hour. Eventually Ergou learned that Little Beijing was simply bored. He had no one to talk to after Zhao Hongbing left. He was restless and lonely, being barely twenty-three years old.

Ergou also noticed that Little Beijing was always chatting to Zhao Hongbing's third sister. Perhaps because her husband wasn't very talkative, Third Sister didn't mind Little Beijing's prattle.

"Third Sister, I hear you're getting divorced."

"I just got married and you're jinxing me by mentioning divorce!" Hongbing's sister was a renowned beauty, attractive even when angry. When Ergou was in college, during one summer vacation he was walking around with a classmate who suddenly said, "Check out the babe!" When Ergou looked, he saw it was Hongbing's third sister. She was nearly forty at the time, but still stunning.

Little Beijing pretended to be wounded.

"I'm heartbroken that it was just a rumor," he said.

"You would be happy if I divorced?" Third Sister flashed her famously big and beautiful eyes.

"I just thought that if you divorced, I might have a chance. Sitting in the doorway every day, I've seen every girl in the city. There's no one as good-looking as you except for Gao Huan, and she's run off with Zhao Hongbing. As Hongbing's brother, I have to find a wife as good as his, which narrows my choices."

"You scamp! Hongbing is two years younger than me, and you're even younger than he is! Do you think I'm a cradle-snatcher?"

"An older bride brings good fortune, apparently. I had the blind fortune-teller at the train station check our horoscopes. He says we're particularly well matched."

"More of your teasing and I'll give you a slap!" said Third Sister.

"Slap away!" said Little Beijing, extend his face toward her with his eyes closed and his lips parted. "It would be the greatest pleasure to perish at your lovely hands."

After a moment's silence, Little Beijing felt something between his lips. He opened his eyes to find Hongbing's sister gone, and a piece of toffee in his mouth.

Little Beijing hoped every day for Hongbing's sister to come over and sit with him when she had nothing better to do, but she only came two or three times a month. After all, she had only recently married and was working as well; after work she liked to spend time with her husband at home. When Hongbing was still around, Little Beijing had been able to take time off to walk around the streets. But now that he was left alone in charge of the hotel, he had no chance to go out. He was bored to death, and he sat at the entrance of the hotel all day moaning and groaning.

One day around noon at the end of June, Pan Daqing – a young hood who was a regular customer – arrived at the hotel with a girl. Little Beijing welcomed such customers with open arms, because they not only increased the hotel's income, but stayed behind to listen to his stories after finishing their business. Although he always left people hanging with his tales, he greatly valued an appreciative audience.

That afternoon at around four o'clock, Little Beijing had just pulled his armchair up to the entrance of the hotel for a new round of story-telling when he saw four burly fellows charging over with steel pipes in their hands. They seemed to be coming for someone in the hotel.

"Hey! Brothers! What are you up to?" Little Beijing called out from his armchair.

"We're looking for someone. It's nothing to do with you."

"How is it nothing to do with me? Who are you looking for?" Little Beijing insisted. He remained in his armchair, reclining.

"Pan Daqing! Someone saw him come into your hotel with my girlfriend. That's why I'm looking for him."

"To do what? Beat him?"

"Where is he? What's his room number?"

"Don't cause trouble here. Do you know who runs this hotel?"

"Zhao Hongbing. So what? He's taken off? And even if he was here, we'd do what we wanted."

"Hey! You're going too far. I'll tell you that I know Pan Daqing. He came to our hotel today, and I'm responsible for his safety. None of you should get any ideas about laying a finger on him. But once he leaves, you can do whatever you want."

"Who the fuck are you? Some outsider who thinks he's tough shit? Do you know who our big brother is?"

"No!" said Little Beijing, sitting up straight and pretending to be terrified.

"Liu Haizhu!"

"Uh, *gesundheit*!" said Little Beijing, looking innocent.

"Motherfucker! I'll work you over, too!"

The four guys began swinging their steel pipes at Little Beijing. He flipped nimbly out of his armchair and grabbed one of the pipes as it smashed into the chair. He used his other hand to punch the pipe-wielder in his arm while kicking him hard on the kneecap. All these actions occurred in one fluid motion that grounded the guy in an instant and left Little Beijing with a pipe in his hand. It was an operation similar to the one Zhao Hongbing had carried out on Little Tiger.

The other three guys raised their pipes and aimed them willy-nilly at Little Beijing's head, but he either darted away or blocked them with his own pipe while attacking his opponents with skill and daring. He didn't aim for their heads but for their arms, knees and calves, felling each in turn without suffering a single blow himself.

"I'll take these pipes of yours to my brother's recycling stall. They should be worth at least a *kuai* or two. Now get out of here."

"Motherfucker! You haven't seen the last of us!"

"Yes, yes. I know. Let me tell you, my surname is Shen, and I'm here every day. Come back any time!"

From then on, many young hoodlums who got into

trouble and feared being chopped ran to Little Beijing's hotel to seek refuge. He never let anyone who was staying there be attacked, but he took no responsibility for what happened once they stepped outside. Of course, anyone who came in had to pay for a room. However, if someone familiar came and didn't have money on him, he could take a room on credit and pay within a week. This is how Little Beijing decided to deal with the situation.

Liu Haizhu was not so easily put off, however. A few days later he came to make trouble for Little Beijing.

Little Beijing's method was very much in line with gangland ethics. Later Ergou saw a Chow Yun-fat movie called *Peace Hotel*, which presented another version of the method. Later yet, when chatting with friends from other localities, he learned that their native places also had such people and situations in the 1980s. Now hotel management has become more standardized and processed, and there are no managers who can "deal" like Little Beijing could. Even if they have that ability, they may not want to get involved in other people's business.

But Little Beijing's method was classic gangland stuff in the 1980s.

CHAPTER 19

The Knight-errant Liu Haizhu

WHO WAS THIS LIU HAIZHU who came to make trouble for Little Beijing? Since Liu Haizhu will play an important role in the story that follows, he deserves an introduction. Quite apart from his various achievements, his appearance alone inspires admiration:

At this time, Liu was around thirty-three years old. However, he was more than a little battle-scarred and looked closer to fifty. Around five-foot-ten and weighing no more than 120 pounds fully clothed, he was almost supernaturally skinny. Ergou remembers playing the electronic game Captain Commando when he first started middle school. When he chose the knife-wielding Mummy character, a classmate beside him cried out, "Shit! Isn't that Liu Haizhu?"

He had a long, fleshless face, with a high, prominent nose, thin lips, and a pointy chin. Nobody knew what his eyebrows looked like, because all year round he wore the kind of bamboo hat that's common in southern China. In all his twenty-six years, Ergou has never seen another living person in a bamboo hat like that. It was very tall, and completely shaded his eyes and eyebrows, giving him a sinister appearance: he could look into someone's eyes, but the other person could never see his. Ergou saw a similar hat in the popular television series *The Magic Blade*, worn by the character Yan Nanfei. To this day, he has no idea where Liu Haizhu got his from, but it was the only one in the entire Northeast.

Another thing that made Liu stand out was his goatee. It may not have been meticulously groomed, but it was still very stylish. Chinese men were invariably clean-shaven back in the 1980s.

Liu always wore a pair of yellow rubber-soled shoes and blue canvas clam-diggers or pedal-pushers – a style of trouser that didn't become fashionable until the 1990s. Wearing them in the 1980s made Liu Haizhu a real trend-setter. During the summer he usually went shirtless, exposing his prominent ribs. In the winter he wore a quilted army jacket with a cape draped over it. He rode a twenty-eight-inch bicycle stripped down to its barest essentials: it had no kickstand, fenders or chain guard, and no brake. Even the pedals consisted only of posts. When he rode it, he looked as if he were suspended between two bare wheels.

Walking along and encountering Liu whizzing by on a stripped-down bike – with his bamboo hat and pedal-pushers, bare and skeletal torso, and the viewable portion of his face sporting a wispy goatee – inevitably left a lasting impression. He was by no means the most feared or famous hooligan in the city, but he was certainly the most visually distinctive. Ergou recalls in middle school, when his art teacher asked students to draw the classic image of an old man in a straw hat fishing from his boat in the winter, almost all of the students modeled their figures on Liu Haizhu. He had thoroughly imprinted himself on the minds of the city's residents.

Ergou still clearly remembers the first time he saw Liu. At that time, Zhao Hongbing had not yet eloped with Gao Huan. He still took Ergou to the movies now and then, and that day they'd gone to see *Martial Arts of Shaolin* at the Culture Cinema in the city center. The theater was fronted by a medium-sized square intended mainly for public trials and rallies, with a flagpole installed at its center.

At that time, the city boasted four lunatics and two idiots. One of the idiots, surnamed Bai, was very well known. Everyone called him Dopey Bai. This foolish and thoroughly ignorant fellow was a marvelous singer who combined the stage manner, expression, tone, and wardrobe of several of China's most popular singers. He performed with gusto and in perfect pitch. Dopey Bai was notable for his urge to sing wherever there was a crowd.

Back in the 1980s, entertainment resources were sorely lacking; few homes had even an eighteen-inch television, and few stations were available to those that did. This made a new movie a major event. When Dopey Bai heard that the Culture Cinema would be showing the Technicolor widescreen kungfu movie *Martial Arts of Shaolin,* he rushed over to deliver one of his itinerant performances. The crowd outside the cinema was as massive as the Spring Festival rush for buses and trains. The square, like all public places in the 1980s, was bedecked with flags and bunting that fluttered around a huge movie poster emblazoned with bold red print, enhancing the festive atmosphere.

"Brother Bai!" a young hooligan called out. "Sing for us!"

"Sing what?" asked Dopey Bai happily.

"The theme song from *Fearless*!"

Everyone loved that song.

"Asleep for a century…" Dopey Bai began to croon as his fans applauded. "Chinese are awakening…" He really did sing well. "If anyone tramples on our land, the sleeping lion will awake!"

Ergou had never heard a northeasterner sing Cantopop so well; the illiterate Dopey Bai wasn't distracted by the written word. He simply learned songs by listening to them, demonstrating the advantages that mentally challenged people can have over the neurotypical.

The audience continued to cheer and applaud wildly. "Brother Bai, what else can you sing?"

"*Shaolin Master Haiding* – the song about Fan Wubing."

"Great! Hey, climb up the flagpole to sing it! If you do, we'll buy you melon seeds," said several young hooligans, toying with Dopey Bai.

"Really, brother?"

"Really!"

That day Ergou learned that Dopey Bai not only sang well but could also climb like a monkey. In a flash, Bai shimmied up the flag pole and began singing. When he finished, everyone below applauded.

"Brother, please! Buy me melon seeds," Dopey Bai said to the hoodlum after climbing down. He was smacking his lips.

"Who said we'd buy you melon seeds? Not me!" said the young hoodlum shamelessly.

"You said you would!"

"Who heard me?"

At that moment, the young hoodlum heard a concussive sound and felt a burning pain on his face. Someone had given him a hard cuffing. Standing before him was Liu Haizhu.

"Brother Zhu! What's wrong?" said the young hooligan, frightened more than a little.

"Go buy Dopey Bai his melon seeds!"

Skinny as he was, Liu Haizhu could pack a wallop. The young hooligan was still seeing stars.

"I was just teasing him!" the punk said.

"The guy isn't smart to begin with, and then you tease him!" Liu Haizhu's bellowing was also pretty intimidating.

"Isn't that what idiots are for?" said the young hooligan, feeling hard-done-by.

"You motherfucker! Do you think an idiot isn't a human being? Doesn't an idiot have a mother and a father? Do you think an idiot is only here for you to play around with?" Liu Haizhu's reasoning was irrefutable.

"You're right, Brother Zhu. We were wrong."

"Hop to it and buy some melon seeds for Dopey Bai – a double portion!"

The young hooligan obeyed without delay.

"What is this bullshit? Pickpocketing, chasing ponies, and harassing lunatics and idiots. What else do you little sons of bitches get up to? If I ever hear of you picking on Dopey Bai again, I'll chop up every last one of you!"

From that day forward, Ergou worshiped Liu Haizhu. He later heard that eight out of every ten of Liu Haizhu's fights involved righting an injustice. If ever that city had a knight-errant, it was Liu Haizhu.

His sense of justice and loyalty and his defense of the wronged won Liu many followers. Back in the 1980s, the only way for a hooligan to make a name for himself was as a ruthless fighter, and in the later part of the decade, Liu Haizhu enjoyed resounding fame. Even now, many people know of him.

Liu Haizhu wasn't a professional hooligan. He didn't rob or steal, but made a living repairing bicycles. He did this fast and well. The bikes he fixed seldom needed further repairs, winning him the universal praise of his customers. On the occasions when he was detained for fighting, some of his longtime customers preferred to do without their bikes until he was released rather than have them repaired by someone else. Bicycle repair stalls always had a tire pump, and other stalls charged five *fen* to pump up tires. Liu Haizhu never charged anything.

It was this valiant fellow who was now coming to make trouble for Little Beijing.

They say that the day Liu Haizhu's brothers arrived to tune up Little Beijing was like the setting of one of those decisive battles between master fighters in the novels. A thunder storm raged with lightning, thunder, and pouring rain. By five o'clock the darkened sky reduced visibility to near zero. A flash of lightning revealed the bare-chested, bamboo-hatted Liu Haizhu standing there like the last man on earth, a razor-sharp cleaver in his hand.

"Who's Shen? Come out!"

"How can I help you, sir?" asked Little Beijing with a smile as he stepped outside.

"You beat up my brothers! Why did you beat them?" Liu Haizhu asked, always talking reason.

"They were coming after someone in my hotel."

"The guy in your hotel stole my brother's girlfriend!"

"I don't meddle in other people's affairs. But if anyone is staying in my hotel, no one can harm a hair on his head."

"What makes you such tough shit?"

"Would you want me to go to your home and beat someone up?"

"Of course not. But Pan Daqing deserves a beating. What's he doing, seducing someone else's girl?"

"If he sets one foot outside my hotel you can beat him up. Just be patient, you can wait for him here."

"All right, I'll admit you have a point. But you sent some of my brothers to the hospital. What about that?"

"They broke the rules, so I had to beat them up. If they come again I'll beat them again."

"Hm… You've got a pair, kid." As a man of reason, Liu Haizhu couldn't fault anything Little Beijing had said.

"That's my style!" Little Beijing was itching for a fight and goading Liu Haizhu to make a move.

"Alright. I'm going. When that punk Pan leaves your hotel, let me know and I'll fix him for sure! I repair bikes outside the No. 14 High School."

With that, Liu Haizhu turned and left. He wasn't afraid; he just felt that Little Beijing was right. He wasn't like the usual hooligans loitering in the streets.

"Take it easy!" Little Beijing called after him.

Recognizing each other as kindred spirits, Little Beijing and Liu Haizhu went on to become fast friends.

CHAPTER 20

Mr. Zhao's Plan

AFTER ZHAO HONGBING AND GAO Huan eloped, Huan's parents were so distraught that they didn't leave home for days. Her father became even more antisocial. He'd always considered himself above such things, and never guessed that his darling daughter would create such a scandal. Ergou's father heard that the *City Gazette*, which Gao Huan's father edited, was already close to shutting down. The last straw was a vitriolic "cops and robbers" piece that he wrote about the legendary Zhen Dongyang. Mr Gao penned a vivid depiction of a bandit chieftain who stopped at nothing, killing people like flies, snatching decent girls, looting and plundering like a cross between a vulture and the notorious collaborationist gangster Hu Chuankui. This completely distorted the Robin Hood image older people still had of Zhen Dongyang as a hero of the anti-Japanese resistance.

Gao Huan's father used his pen to pour out all his anger at Zhao Hongbing and at the person he regarded as sparking this explosive incident – Zhang Yue's grandfather. He firmly believed that without Zhang Yue, he and his wife would not have learned of their daughter's love affair. And if they hadn't learned of it, Gao Huan's mother wouldn't have gone to the school; their daughter wouldn't have been humiliated into eloping, and then this scholar – who had always held himself so aloof from the world – would not have had to face the despising, pitying, and disdainful gaze of the entire city. It never occurred to Mr Gao that he himself might be the real cause of this incident.

In Ergou's view, Gao Huan's father wasn't really so far above it all. A scholar of genuine integrity and moral principle wouldn't have used a personal grudge to smear others. He had no right to look down on Zhao Hongbing when he himself was just a narrow-minded pencil-pusher.

In any case, Gao Huan's parents were beside themselves. Her mother even showed signs of mental breakdown, constantly babbling to herself and telling everyone that she no longer had a daughter.

The elder Mr. Zhao was a few years older than Gao Huan's parents, and was more experienced and mature in his thinking. Although he also found the relentless gossip hard to take, he was relatively open-minded. Realizing that the two young people had acted in desperation, he saw no point in punishing them.

Mr. Zhao came up with an idea. He called in Zhao Hongbing's third sister. "Hongyan, has Hongbing been in touch with you?"

Mr. Zhao knew that the two youngest siblings, being nearest in age, also had the closest relationship. He also believed that Hongbing would contact his family, and that it would be his third sister whom he called.

"No, he hasn't," said Hongyan disconsolately. "I don't know where that brat has run off to."

"If he calls you, tell him that Gao Huan's mother has had a stroke and wants to see her."

Mr. Zhao had shrewdly deduced that this was the only way to get Gao Huan to come back. Once she returned, there would be room to negotiate.

"I don't think that's a good idea. If Gao Huan calls home..." Hongyan never liked to lie.

"I'll have a talk with her parents," said Mr. Zhao, who could always come up with a well-thought-out plan.

"It's such a shame for her to miss the college entrance exam when she's been such a good student all these years."

"The main reason I want them to come back is so she can take the exam. It would be a waste if she didn't."

"If she gets into college, will she still want Hongbing?" Hongyan had met Gao Huan and liked her very much, but worried that she would have no use for Hongbing once she was educated.

"We'll have to put that aside for now. The main thing is that Hongbing shouldn't get in the way of her future. Tell his friends to go along with the story."

After receiving her father's orders, Hongyan set about contacting each of Hongbing's friends.

The thunderstorm had just ended. Ergou wanted to look for rainbows, so he went out with Third Sister. When they reached the hotel, Liu Haizhu had just left. Little Beijing was holding a bird cage and teasing a little sparrow inside.

"Ah, Hongyan! How nice to see you! Have some tea!" Little Beijing's eyes gleamed when he saw her.

"I've come to tell you something. If Hongbing telephones, tell him that Gao Huan's mom had a stroke and have them come home right away," she said, avoiding Little Beijing's sparkling gaze.

"Is it true?"

"No, but how else can we get them to come back?"

"Ah, the call of society and the call of nature – which is stronger?" Little Beijing always looked at things differently.

"What do you mean?" Although Hongyan had graduated from the China Medical University, her mind was not as quick as Little Beijing's.

"Hongyan, you're a well-read person. You know what I mean. The call of nature is the desire the two of them have for food, sex, and self-preservation. Meanwhile, call of society is the demands placed on them by friendship and family obligations," said Little Beijing in his usual concise fashion.

"I still don't know what you mean."

Whenever Hongyan didn't understand something, she would open her big eyes wide and fix them on the other person, flustering anyone less imperturbable than Little Beijing.

"What I mean is that everything depends on whether sexual desire will overcome their sense of family obligation," Little Beijing said.

"Why do you have to make it sound so ugly? Can't you call it love? When Gao Huan hears her mother's ill, she's sure to come back." Although Hongyan was a married woman, Little Beijing's talk of "sexual desire" made her blush.

"Not necessarily. I think people follow their natural needs first. Social obligations come second. Love is a god-given right, and no one has the power to strip it away. Hongyan, what if it were you? Would you say that love was more important, or family obligations?" Little Beijing asked.

"Er… they're both important," said Hongyan with a thoughtful nod.

"I can tell that you put the emphasis on love and have a strong sex drive," said Little Beijing with a leer.

"I'm leaving!" Flushing scarlet, Hongyan cuffed Little Beijing on the back of the head and stalked out of the hotel. "Don't forget, if Hongbing calls, that's what you have to tell him!" she called back before she disappeared.

"All right," said Little Beijing, rubbing the spot Hongyan had slapped and watching regretfully as she departed. Although he always for her to come over and chat, he always managed to drive her off after just a few words.

When Hongyan found Sun Dawei, he was calculating the price of some books he was loaning out to some high school students. "Brother Sun, can you lower the price?" one student asked. "Why do you charge by the hour when other stalls charge by the day?"

"That's impossible. These books are too popular – I have people lining up for them every day," Sun Dawei said.

"But charging by the hour is a rip-off!" said the student.

"Look, if you borrow it for a day, I'll charge you one *kuai* as a special deal. How about that?"

It turned out that Sun Dawei's stock included a dozen soft porn novels. Back then there was no Internet, no DVDs, and no video cassettes. Students could only divert themselves by reading salacious novels, so Sun Dawei's offerings were always in high demand. Dawei displayed unusual business acumen by applying different marketing and pricing strategies to different products. Ordinary books he rented out for twenty cents a day, but for the soft porn he charged fifty cents for four hours, increasing his income while also speeding up circulation.

"Dawei, what books are you renting out at such a high price?" asked Hongyan after the students left.

"A few novels. Those students haven't been brought up right, so that's what they like to read." Sun pretended to be very proper.

"Eh? What books are that good? *Spring Dream*?" Hongyan picked up one of the volumes.

Ergou clearly remembers the title of that book, because he asked Hongyan what it meant, not knowing it was an expression for "wet dream". She told him it was simply a dream in springtime.

"Hey, go ahead and take it if you want to read it," said Sun Dawei as Hongyan flipped through it.

"Hm, I'll take it home. You can stop by my office to pick it up when you pass by the hospital, the day after tomorrow," Hongyan said. That's how Ergou learned so early on that women like porn novels, too.

"Hongyan, what did you want to talk to me about?"

"If Hongbing calls, lie to him and say that Gao Huan's mom is seriously ill. Tell them to come back right away."

"That's not right! I've never lied to Hongbing. If he knows I lied, he'll kill me when he gets back!"

"If Hongbing wants to kill you, tell him I told you to say it and have the brat come after me!"

"Um, okay."

Hongyan went from there to Xiaoji's recycling stall, but he wasn't around and no one knew where he'd gone. Finally she gave up and went back to her office to pick up some things before going home. Her work unit was a hospital under the medical school. When she got there she found Xiaoji. But he was unable to talk to her, because he was being wheeled into the operating room. He'd been stabbed again, but the person done it was less merciful than Tiger.

Part Four

Revenge

CHAPTER 21

Ten Years from Now, I'll Kill Your Whole Family

XIAOJI WAS STABBED WHEN HE returned to his recycling stall after the thunderstorm. The person who did it was Old Rod Li. The story of Xiaoji's stabbing circulates in the local underworld even today, because it ignited the countless battled that followed. The gangs of Old Rod Li and Zhao Hongbing gained fame and numbers as a result of these fights. They also prompted Hongbing's leap from part-time hooligan to full-time gangster.

Actually, Xiaoji wasn't wounded by stabbing, but by Old Rod Li hurling a knife at him. Hooligans were stabbed every day, but being injured by a hurled knife was exceptional.

Ergou clearly recalls how the incident came about. After several days of hard rain in June 1987, mountain torrents exposed several old tombs in a certain village. Nearby farmers had collected a number of burial relics. Ergou can't recall what exactly they found, but in any case, one old guy in his sixties picked up a jade carving of some kind.

There were not many relic collectors in the city, and

everyone in that small circle soon heard the news. Xiaoji and Old Rod Li both went to the village. Xiaoji went to buy relics while Old Rod went to pillage tombs.

When Xiaoji, Feisi, and Lisi arrived in the village, Rod Li hadn't been there yet. Xiaoji noticed one of the village children playing with a piece of precious jade, He wanted to swap it for a piece of candy but Lisi stopped him. Lisi's greatest merit was that he never took advantage of people.

"Son, go tell your folks there's a guy outside who wants to talk to them," he said.

"My mom and dad have gone to work in the fields," the child said. "Only my grandma is home."

"Then ask your grandma to come out."

"Madam, how are you?" Xiaoji said in his usual polite fashion when the woman emerged.

"What do you want?" asked the child's grandmother, holding a pipe.

"Madam, I'd like to buy that piece of jade your grandson is holding. I'd like to give it to my girlfriend," Xiaoji said.

"That trinket isn't worth much. What do you want to pay for it?" the old lady asked.

"You name a price," Lisi said.

"Ten *kuai* if you want it," the old woman said. It apparently took all her strength to come up with this astronomical figure.

Xiaoji was ecstatic but still felt compelled to bargain.

"Would five *kuai* be enough? Ten *kuai* is too much."

"All right. Five *kuai*!"

That's how Xiaoji spent five *kuai* for a piece of jade that was worth at least 30,000. Back in the 1980s, 30,000 *yuan* was real money.

Xiaoji's major flaw was his big mouth. After returning to

the city, he was so excited that he couldn't help relating the incident to several others in his trade. Some of these guys were members of Old Rod Li's gang. Clearly, a lower profile is always best.

The next evening, Old Rod Li and his guys went to that village to "clean" a tomb that had been washed out by the rainstorm. They didn't dig anything up, but in the neighboring village they found a piece of jade exactly like Xiaoji's. As specialists in this field, they could tell in a glance that this piece and Xiaoji's were meant to be a pair. Based on their calculations, if the pair was sold on the black market, it would bring at least 200,000 *yuan*, while each sold separately would bring only 40,000. Old Rod Li therefore hoped to buy Xiaoji's.

As previously mentioned, when Mighty Zhang was arrested in the 1983 "Strike Hard" campaign, he was the locality's No. 2 gang leader; the No. 1 gang boss was Old Rod Li. Unlike Mighty Zhang, who struck out on his own after being released from prison, Old Rod had assembled a new gang focusing on cultural relics.

It was also previously mentioned that Railway was a coward, while Tiger and Little Tiger were rural thugs, and Mighty Zhang was foolhardy. None of them was capable of becoming a renowned gangster; if Zhao Hongbing hadn't packed them up, Liu Haizhu and others would have. Old Rod Li was different. After his release, he went back to being the top man in the local underworld. As one of the area's most infamous hooligans before being put away, his nickname gave an indication of how long he'd been in the life. Before going to prison, he'd been known as Westside Boss, because he'd dominated the city's west side; even women and children knew of him. He had joined Mighty Zhang and others in operating a "black cat company", and thus managed to corporatize his gang in the early 1980s.

Bicycle thefts were a serious problem in the early 1980s. At one point, Old Rod's bicycle was pilfered. He couldn't be bothered pursuing petty thieves, so he simply went to the place where the bike had been stolen and wrote in chalk, "I am Old Rod Li. Whoever stole my bicycle needs to return it immediately." He didn't even bother with a threat like "or bear the consequences." That very night, Old Rod's bike was quietly returned, which gives an idea of his reputation back then. Most of his gang came from the western suburb. The hoodlums from that part of town were known for their ruthless cruelty.

After leaving prison, Old Rod concentrated on grave robbing and trading in cultural relics. He was the wealthiest gangster in town, reserving several tables at the city's best restaurants almost every night. No one could rival him. Liu Haizhu would have been considered Old Rod's match before the "Strike Hard" campaign. However, after leaving prison, Liu went into honest work with his own small bike repair business. Although Liu still had many followers, it was because they admired his personal qualities; all of his guys had their own small businesses, and none of them lived off him.

Lacking Liu Haizhu's chivalrous sense of justice, Old Rod Li was cruel, merciless, and treacherous. He would kill his own brother for personal gain. Ergou later learned that he even dared to kill police officers.

Old Rod Li was tall, thin, and nearsighted, wearing black horn-rimmed glasses so large that they obscured half his face. He kept his head shaved after leaving prison. Ergou saw Li many times, and always noticed a trembling in his left hand

and a twitch on the left side of his mouth that made him look even more abnormal and terrifying.

Old Rod's actions and behavior typified the germination of the formal criminal underworld. Parents who wanted to frighten their children into submission evoked Old Rod's name. Only after Zhang Yue left prison did local citizens learn that the world held a man even more ruthless and vicious than Old Rod Li.

Old Rod was counting on his reputation to "buy" the other piece of jade from Xiaoji at an extortionate price. Apparently some of his guys advised him not to approach Xiaoji himself.

"Big Brother, you just want to buy the jade from Xiaoji. Evil can handle it," said one of them. "Xiaoji wouldn't dare refuse him!" Evil Huang had his own reputation as one of Old Rod's most vicious underlings.

"That won't work," Old Rod said. "I hear Xiaoji and his pals have been involved in some rough stuff these last couple years, and if Evil gets knocked around, it'll make us look bad."

Old Rod Li went to see Xiaoji after the thunderstorm, taking only three of his gang with him. In the Northeast, a thunderstorm is often followed by a brilliant rainbow, and the air bears the fragrance of damp soil. It is indescribably lovely. The city's roadways had not yet been widened back then, and still had flower beds planted alongside them. After the rain, multicolored blooms surged upward in vibrant splendor against the setting sun.

"Boss Ji, are you busy?" Old Rod Li asked with a show of teeth as he approached.

"Heh. Big Brother Li. How did you find time to visit today? I was just locking up for the day," said Xiaoji with a smile.

"I hear you ran into some luck and thought we might grab a bite."

"Me, lucky? You must be joking. Everyone knows you have the deepest pockets in town! But of course I'd be glad to buy you dinner. Let's go. I'd like your advice on dealing in relics, since you're such an old hand."

"Let's cut the crap, Boss Ji. I have something to discuss with you. Once we settle it, dinner's on me."

"And what do you want to discuss, brother?"

"I hear you picked up a piece of jade a few days ago."

"That's right. Paid five *kuai* for it! What a deal!"

"I'm interested in it. I was wondering if you'd sell it to me."

"That's nice of you! What price did you have in mind?"

"I thought 5,000 *kuai* should make you happy."

"You're such a joker! That jade would easily sell for 30,000."

"You think I'm joking?" Old Rod Li's tone shifted radically. "You think I have time to come here and fuck around with you?"

"Brother, there's no way I can sell at that price," said Xiaoji, and quickly came up with an excuse. "I have two friends who are partners in this business. If they hear I sold the jade for only 5,000, they'll never forgive me."

"I've got two rolls of tens here – one role with fifty, and one with a hundred. Which one do you want?" Old Rod Li snarled.

"Doesn't that add up to 15,000? Brother, we run in the same circles; if you raise the price a little, I'll sell the jade to you even if I lose out. I have to split the proceeds with my brothers. They're my old war buddies, and we haven't made any money since we were demobilized. We were hoping this could be our big break." Xiaoji was afraid of Old Rod Li and hoped to patch things up with him.

"This 15,000 is in two rolls," Old Rod Li said. "You can only choose one of them."

"What do you mean?"

"If you chose the 5,000 roll, I'll take the jade and we'll still be friends. If you choose the 10,000, I'll take the jade and cut you up. The extra 5,000 will be for your hospital fees. And every time I see you from then on, I'll knock you around. So which one do you want?" Old Rod Li asked.

"What if I don't want either of them?"

Scared as he was, Xiaoji never liked to come across as a soft touch. He now knew that Old Rod Li had come to extort the jade piece from him.

"If you don't take either on, I'll cut you up and give you 5,000 for your hospital fees. Sooner or later, that jade will be mine," Old Rod Li said.

"I've spent my whole life being threatened. Just because I show you respect by calling you Big Brother doesn't mean you're anything special. Do you know how Mighty Zhang died?" Once Xiaoji's temper rose, he could be just as belligerent at Zhang Yue.

"Aren't you the big swinging dick? If your gang leader Zhao hadn't skipped town, I'd fucking cut him up too! Since he's not around, I'll have to settle for chopping you up to avenge Mighty Zhang!" Old Rod Li pulled out a knife with a wooden handle and very sharp blade that he'd clearly made himself.

"Kill me today if you have the balls!" Xiaoji, unarmed, had automatically retreated a few steps.

"Motherfucker! You're a dead man!" Old Rod Li roared as he charged forward with his knife. Fearing he would actually kill Xiaoji, his gang members grabbed his arms. But Old Rod, his eyes ablaze, was able to move his hand enough to hurl the knife at Xiaoji. Given that Xiaoji was standing only about six feet away, he had no way of dodging the knife. It hit him square in the chest. Apparently Old Rod Li spent his idle hours hurling his knife at wooden targets. At such close proximity, it did a lot of damage.

Wracked with pain, Xiaoji turned and ran off with the knife still protruding from his chest. After about one hundred yards, he collided with a bicyclist and tumbled into a flower bed, where he lay immobilized.

Afterwards people said that this was the difference between Zhang Yue and Xiaoji. If Zhang Yue had been stabbed in the chest with a knife, he would have disregarded his own survival to pull it and use it on Old Rod Li. People as cold-blooded as Zhang Yue are rare indeed.

A pedicab driver rushed Xiaoji to a nearby clinic. He was quickly patched up and then sent to the university hospital nearby. When Zhao Hongbing's third sister and Ergou saw Xiaoji, he was covered with dirt and blood. His face was deathly pale with blood loss, and he had fallen into a coma. Ergou wept with fear and asked Hongyan, "Third Aunty, is Uncle Ji going to die?"

Hongyan didn't reply.

They say that if Xiaoji hadn't been so powerfully built, he would have bled to death. Ergou doesn't know exactly how much blood Xiaoji lost, but Hongyan said, "You know the bucket we have a home for fetching our cooking oil? Your Uncle Ji must have lost at least half a bucket's worth of blood."

Eventually Xiaoji was saved. After regaining consciousness, his first words were, "Old Rod Li! Ten years from now, I'll kill your whole family!"

To this day, Ergou doesn't know why Xiaoji wanted to wait ten years instead of doing it right away. Even if he didn't go after Old Rod Li's family, Old Rod would still come for him, because Xiaoji still had that piece of jade.

On Xiaoji's third day in the hospital, one of Old Rod Li's guys brought him 5,000 *yuan* and told him, "You took the knife for your brother Zhang Yue. Brother Li has showed you plenty of respect by giving you money for your medical expenses. If you don't hand over the jade, you'll lose your life next time."

When all was said and done, Xiaoji's dealings in cultural relics were against the law; if he reported Old Rod Li, he would implicate himself as well. He could only resort to the laws of the underworld to avenge himself. "Do whatever it takes to get Hongbing back here fast," Xiaoji told Sun Dawei after Old Rod Li's man left.

CHAPTER 22

The Weary Birds Fly Home

ZHAO HONGBING CAME BACK ON July 5th 1987, just a little more than a week after Xiaoji was stabbed. Old Mr. Zhao had guessed correctly that Hongbing would eventually telephone his third sister, Hongyan. Hongbing was as unwilling as his father for Gao Huan to miss her college entrance exam. Since Gao Huan had already signed up for the exam and taken the physical before leaving home, Hongbing would have secretly brought her back to sit, even without Mr. Zhao's scheming; Li Yang already had the exam registration certificate in hand. Both Mr. Zhao and Hongbing had that essential male virtue: a sense of responsibility.

"Hongyan, I want to bring Gao Huan back to take her exam," Hongbing said over the telephone.

"Hongbing, please come back! Things have been happening here!" she said.

"What things?"

"Gao Huan's mom had a stroke because she was so upset, and your friend Xiaoji was almost stabbed to death."

"Really?"

"Just come back! Where are you?" A poor liar, Hongyan changed the subject as soon as she could.

"Don't ask. I'll be back tomorrow afternoon at three o'clock. Which hospital are they at?"

"The one where I work. Come to my office first."

Mr. Zhao had correctly surmised that Hongbing wouldn't want to face him when he came back. Even so, he was there with his driver when Zhao Hongbing pushed open the door of Hongyan's office on the afternoon of July 5th. Hongyan later said that as soon as Hongbing and Gao Huan came through the door, she felt that Hongbing had aged in those few weeks. Gao Huan couldn't even raise her head. She clutched Hongbing's arm as if death couldn't pull them apart. They looked travel-worn and had on the same clothes they'd been wearing when they eloped.

"Gao Huan, I've wronged you. I lied to you. Your mother is fine. I just wanted to get you home." Hongyan was soft-hearted. The sight of the weather-beaten couple drove her to tears.

"Don't cry, Hongyan. I knew that already." Rather than being shocked, Gao Huan tried to comfort her. It seemed that what she'd gone through had made her stronger.

"Child, I'm Hongbing's father," said old Mr. Zhao, who had been silent up until then.

"Oh… hello," said Gao Huan, her head lowered as she continued to clutch Hongbing's arm.

"It's been hard for you, child," said Mr. Zhao, walking over and stroking her hair.

Gao Huan burst out sobbing. Mr. Zhao's loving, fatherly comfort was a balm after the weeks of hardship and injustice this fragile and sensitive girl had suffered.

"Child, let me take you home. I'll come along and talk everything through with your parents. Parents can forgive their children for anything. All parents are the same that way. All right?" Mr. Zhao said gently as Gao Huan nodded and wept. "Come. Your parents are waiting for you. I'll take you home, and then tomorrow you can take your exam."

Old Mr. Zhao seemed to have a magic power to make others obey him. He spoke to his driver and then took Gao Huan by the arm. Finally she released her grip on Zhao Hongbing. As he led Gao Huan to the door, Mr. Zhao spun around and gave Hongbing a sharp kick. "We'll have no more of this!"

Although a highly-trained soldier, Hongbing staggered under the fierceness of the unexpected booting. "Dad, I was wrong," he said, head bowed.

He knew that after this kick, his father would forgive him. It was the way this father and son – two strong-willed men – communicated with each other. His father would never mention this matter again, but would also never let Hongbing repeat the mistake.

"Sister, was Xiaoji actually stabbed?" Hongbing asked anxiously after his father left.

"Yes."

"Where is he now?"

"He's out of danger and recovering in Room 205. I arranged for a private room."

Before his sister had finished, Zhao Hongbing turned and ran from the room.

"Come back here! Don't cause trouble!" Hongyan stamped her foot anxiously. She understood her brother well enough to know that he would take revenge once he saw the state Xiaoji was in.

When Hongbing found Xiaoji, he was on an intravenous

drip and connected to several tubes. Hongbing gripped his hand and murmured, "Brother, get some rest."

"Avenge me!" said Xiaoji through gritted teeth, immobilized on his bed.

Zhao Hongbing nodded and gave him a light pat. Xiaoji closed his eyes serenely and said no more. He knew even without an explicit promise that Hongbing would avenge him, and that the pat was his way of saying, "Rest assured."

Zhao Hongbing and his friends were a classic gang of the 1980s. There was no clear-cut leader, and they spent their days joking around and fighting on an equal footing. But once this serious incident occurred, everyone became aware of Zhao Hongbing's importance and knew he had to be the one to take the lead. Apparently it takes major events like these to reveal a person's significance.

It may be hard for people nowadays to understand why Zhao Hongbing felt compelled to avenge Xiaoji, but back in the 1980s, nothing could have been more natural. Now, twenty years later, people consider such chivalrous actions idiotic.

That night, the fourth "rumble summing-up meeting" was held in a most mournful and repressed atmosphere in Xiaoji's hospital room. It focused on how to deal with Old Rod Li. In the month preceding the meeting, Zhang Yue had been locked up for defending himself and had not yet gone to trial. Li Wu had been arrested for grave-robbing, and now Xiaoji lay seriously injured. The effective force of the gang had been reduced from eight to five, and this included the fight-averse Sun Dawei.

Zhao Hongbing presided over the meeting. The main topic was how to avenge Xiaoji. The content and analysis resembled the SWOT method that businesses routinely use now, evaluating their strengths and weaknesses, and the opportunities and threats in the current situation. The meeting, while brief, was highly effective. Five people did most of the talking while Xiaoji, Xiaobo, and Ergou listened. The meeting reached the following conclusions:

Strengths:

- Zhao Hongbing, Little Beijing, and Lisi had outstanding fighting skills and could take on a minimum of three to one. Although Feisi had lesser capabilities, he had outstanding courage.
- The five brothers acted with great cohesion. Unity is power, and after several fights, they'd become better coordinated.
- Old Rod Li was the instigator, so if the police eventually became involved, Hongbing and his guys would have right on their side.

Weaknesses:

- The reduction of manpower from eight to five had spread them very thinly.
- Their weapons were rather rudimentary; apart from Sun Dawei's shotgun, which had never been fired, all they had were cold weapons.
- If the police became involved, Xiaoji might also end up in prison.
- Zhao Hongbing and Little Beijing had a hotel, Xiaoji had a recycling stall, and Sun Dawei had a book stall. All were obvious and easy targets for a surprise attack by Old Rod Li.

Opportunities:

- While running the hotel, Little Beijing had attracted a following of young hooligans, some of whom might be useful as external resources.
- Li Wu and some of his guys had been arrested, but there were still others who could be pulled in. Lisi would handle this.
- Old Rod Li would definitely come for Xiaoji again, so this was the best time to go after him; no matter how badly Old Rod was beaten, he would have to suck it up.

Threats:

- Old Rod Li was cruel and ruthless; if anyone in the city was capable of killing, it was him.
- His underlings were many and fearless.
- His cousin was captain of the police crime squad.
- He was determined to seize the jade.

After analyzing the strengths, weaknesses, opportunities, and threats, the following battle plan was devised:

- Old Rod Li was bound to stage another attack. He wouldn't bring a lot of guys with him, so they should take the opportunity to launch a frontal assault.
- They should organize all available manpower in case Old Rod Li retaliated after being attacked.
- They should focus on protecting Sun Dawei's book stall and Zhao Hongbing's hotel.
- Little Beijing and Feisi formed one group, and Zhao

Hongbing and Lisi another, to watch over Xiaoji in shifts. Sun Dawei was to serve as a mobile force.

After the meeting ended, everyone was silent for a long time, no doubt aware that something big was coming up.

Zhao Hongbing and the others were expecting Old Rod Li, but it was his top lieutenant – Evil Huang – who appeared a few days later.

CHAPTER 23

Zhao Hongbing and Evil Huang

GAO HUAN TOOK THE COLLEGE entrance exam and breezed through it. No one knew where she and Zhao Hongbing had been all that time or what they had done, but it was clear that her studies hadn't suffered. One month later, her high exam score gained her admittance to her first choice, Renmin University. Her parents were able to hold their heads up high. But more about that later.

Evil Huang came to "buy" the piece of jade from Xiaoji the day after Gao Huan took her exams. Zhao Hongbing and Lisi were watching over Xiaoji at the time.

Before the television series *The Legend of the Condor Heroes* came out, Huang had gone by the nickname Weasel. However, once people began watching that series, they started calling him Evil Huang after one of the characters – because he was truly evil.

It was obvious to anyone that Evil Huang was a hoodlum just from how he shimmied along. Tall and thin, with a thief's cunning eyes, he was actually better suited to his original nickname, Weasel.

In spite of his shifty-eyed demeanor, he made a great show of refinement and elegance. He never used foul language, and spoke with soft deliberation. If you heard him without seeing him, you'd think he was a young intellectual. Apparently his air of cultivation created resentment among his gang brothers, who couldn't stomach an illiterate hoodlum playing the gentleman. A rumor circulated of the following exchange:

"Evil Huang, would it kill you to quit being such a poser?" Old Rod Li once scolded when it became too much for him.

"No," Evil Huang replied softly and firmly.

"Then what the fuck's the point?" said Old Rod, thoroughly fed up.

"It wouldn't kill me, but posing will make me live longer," Evil Huang replied with a smile.

Everyone rolled their eyes.

Ruthless as Evil Huang was, he was known to fear one man: Liu Haizhu. Soon after Evil entered the hoodlum life, Liu Haizhu picked up a cleaver and chased him for three blocks, cutting his jacket to shreds. Evil Huang finally knelt on the ground and said, "My grandfather! My living ancestor! Have mercy!" at which Liu Haizhu let him go. Even though Liu Haizhu was now semi-retired, Evil Huang still didn't dare walk by his bicycle repair stall at the No. 14 High School.

Always wanting to stand out from the crowd, Evil Huang eschewed the bayonets and double-barreled shotguns of his fellow gang members, preferring a flexible blade known as a belt sword, which he wore around his waist. China doesn't have that kind of thing anymore, but in the 1980s it was very popular. Although the belt sword was less lethal than a dagger, Evil Huang felt that carrying a gun or a knife on the street was too coarse and déclassé; it just wasn't his style. He had also dreamed of using a metal fan as a weapon, thinking it would suit his elegant bearing. However, he'd sent money three times to an address advertised in *Story Magazine* – 28 *kuai* for a metal fan, and then 78 *kuai* two other times for a boomerang-style metal fan – without the products ever being sent. Enraged, Evil Huang had traveled all the way to the address in Wenzhou, Zhejiang Province, intending to hunt down the fraudster. It turned out to be a woman, so he didn't do anything. Finally the woman refunded his 180 *kuai*, and he returned triumphant. It should be noted that his round-trip fare to Wenzhou cost more than 1,000 *kuai*.

Other hoodlums made their names through repeated victories in battle, but Evil Huang became famous for taking a beating. Whenever Huang's name came up in conversation among the city's gangsters, someone would say, "That guy is totally invincible. Even after Liu Haizhu stabbed him more than thirty times and he was covered in blood, he still kept running." Or maybe, "At the entrance to Red Flag Park, a couple of dozen guys went at him with steel pipes and clubs for at least five minutes, but he still made it to the hospital on his own two feet."

In short, Evil Huang had become famous for a physique that could take a lot of punishment. However, he didn't become truly vicious until he began following Old Rod Li. When he joined up with Old Rod, he didn't yet have his belt sword and was using nunchucks for fighting. When he went with some gang brothers to help Old Rod settle a matter, the people he knocked around ended up in the hospital for two or three months. Among Old Rod Li's top lieutenants, Quint and Tudou were the toughest, but while far from the most daring or able, Evil Huang was definitely the most famous.

Evil Huang arrived at the hospital that day wearing a pair of flip-flops, red velvet pants and an untucked white shirt with a bright red tie. He was accompanied by three young gangsters carrying cans of fruit and malted milk powder as he swaggered into Xiaoji's room with his hands in his pockets.

"Greetings, Brother Xiaoji," said Evil Huang urbanely.

"Eh – who are you?" Xiaoji asked. Although Hongbing and his friends had been in several fights by then, they still had limited contacts in gangland circles.

"My surname is Huang, but you can call me Xiaohuang like everyone else," said Evil Huang, who apparently wasn't too fond of his nickname.

"Brother Xiaohuang, we seem to have met before," said Xiaoji, having no idea that Evil was one of Old Rod Li's guys.

"Within the four seas, all men are brothers," quoted Evil Huang, putting on his usual airs with an old saying from his stock repertoire.

"Well, thanks for coming!" said Xiaoji. "I see you've brought me a lot of stuff."

"No need to thank me! Just thank Brother Li," said Evil Huang, coming to the point of his visit.

"Oh..." Xiaoji didn't reply, but turned to look at Zhao Hongbing and Lisi, who had quickly caught the drift of the conversation.

"Brother Li asked me to come and make amends on his behalf. He acted impulsively, and there's no reason we can't all be friends," said Evil Huang in a deeply sincere tone.

"Make amends?" Xiaoji asked.

"Yes, and Brother Li says he hopes to continue doing business with you. If you'll make the jade available, the price can be discussed." It was now clear what Evil Huang had come for.

"How much is he willing to pay?" asked Xiaoji with some effort.

"What would you say to 8,000 *kuai*? If that's acceptable, I've brought the money with me."

"No sale," said Xiaoji, closing his eyes.

"Brother Xiaoji, don't reject the face we're giving you." Even when angry, Evil Huang spoke softly.

"Xiaoji is tired and needs to rest. You can discuss the jade with us," said Zhao Hongbing, standing. "Let's go out in the hallway so we don't disturb him."

"Why should I bother with you?" asked Evil Huang, looking askance at Hongbing.

"You'll know that by the time we finish." Hongbing showed no reaction to the provocation.

"I don't have time to waste, so just cool it over there," said Evil Huang.

"The jade's with me," said Hongbing with a smile. "So let's step outside."

Without waiting for Evil Huang's reply, Zhao Hongbing and Lisi walked out of the hospital room, certain that Huang would follow. Indeed, he came out with his companions.

"If you don't have that jade with you, I'll twist your head off," purred Evil Huang.

"I have the jade, but I'm not going to sell it to you." Hongbing and Lisi grinned at Evil Huang. Neither of them liked to start a fight, but today they wanted to get him fired up and then "fairly and reasonably" give him a thrashing on Xiaoji's behalf.

"Perhaps you haven't heard of me. I'm not known for my good temper," said Evil Huang, his anger building.

"Aiya, I'm so sorry, Brother Huang. My brother's temper

is even nastier. He's mentally unbalanced besides, so you shouldn't mess with him," said Zhao Hongbing, pointing at Lisi with a show of concern. "They don't impose capital punishment on the mentally ill, and it's been quite a while since he killed someone. He was just saying to me that he'd love to knock off a couple, so you should be careful."

"Ha! You're the one who's mentally ill!" laughed Lisi, giving Zhao Hongbing a push. Evil Huang finally realized that they were merely distracting him.

"I'll fix you!" Evil Huang stepped back and groped at his waist where his belt sword lay concealed beneath his shirt.

His action startled Hongbing and Lisi, who thought he had a gun there. The two of them lunged toward his hand. This was the reflexive action of army scouts. Lisi, being closer, reached Evil first. Taking a long stride forward, he pushed down on Evil's hand while striking him hard in the chin with the elbow of his other arm and knocking him to the floor. Twisting Evil's arm to the side, Lisi discovered that all he had concealed at his waist was the belt sword.

One of Evil Huang's guys came charging out, and Zhao Hongbing sent him sprawling with a single kick. Ergou thinks martial arts novels are unrealistic when they describe a hundred rounds of fighting; in an actual battle, well-trained fighters usually fell petty hoodlums in one or two moves. That's all it took Lisi and Zhao Hongbing against these punks. Their moves were very simple – none of those spin kicks or other fancy footwork; just a simple grab and kick or an elbow and a knockout punch. Within two minutes, Evil Huang and his three companions lay groaning on the floor. After flaunting his strength for quite a while, the ruffian Huang had once again tasted a real beating. He never guessed that anyone would dare to rough him up after he joined Old Rod Li's gang. He'd apparently forgotten that he'd asked for it.

The thought of Xiaoji lying in a hospital bed after being stabbed for no reason made Zhao Hongbing burn with anger. "You! Huang! If you're a man, stand up and leave this hospital the way you came!" Evil Huang lay on the floor and waved his hand; it appeared he was genuinely incapacitated. "Okay. If you won't go, I'll drag you out!"

Zhao Hongbing grabbed Evil Huang by the hair and started to haul him away. Hongbing's principle was to never make the first move, but if he did, he would always subdue his opponent to the point where he'd never trouble him again. He had dragged Evil Huang just a few steps when he saw his sister Hongyan limping toward him. It turned out that Hongbing was causing too much of a commotion. The duty nurse, afraid to intervene, had gone to fetch Hongyan. In her hurry, she had tripped on her high heels and twisted her ankle.

Hongyan had never seen Hongbing in such a temper. He dragged Evil Huang across the terrazzo floor as if he were carrying a briefcase.

"Hongbing, stop! You'll kill him!"

"They've gone too far!" said Hongbing, loosening his grip on Evil Huang's hair.

"Take him to the outpatient clinic right away!"

"All right," said Hongbing reluctantly, grabbing Evil Huang's hair again to drag him the rest of the way.

"Let go of his hair! You and Lisi need to carry him there!"

In Hongbing's eyes, Evil Huang was a vicious hooligan who had been blackmailing his old comrade-in-arms. Yet to a medical professional like Hongyan, Evil Huang was a pitiful patient who required treatment.

Lisi and Zhao Hongbing reluctantly propped up Evil Huang and carried him downstairs with Hongyan leading the way. It was summer then, and Hongyan hadn't put the usual white medical coat over her thin skirt. After carrying him a few steps, Hongbing and Lisi noticed Evil Huang staring lasciviously at Hongyan's curvaceous figure. Even in that condition, he was in the mood to gawk at women.

"Don't you dare look at my sister!" said Hongbing, tossing Evil Huang on the floor and kicking him savagely.

"I – I didn't!" stammered Huang.

"Hongbing!" cried his sister, stopping him again.

That evening, Hongbing and the others held another informal meeting. They concluded that Old Rod Li was not prepared to let things go. They would have to remain on the lookout and pull together all available resources.

CHAPTER 24

Kindred Spirits

EVIL HUANG WAS BEATEN BADLY enough to be admitted to the hospital. Old Rod Li put out the word that Zhao Hongbing and the others could bounce around a few more days before he and Evil came by to settle scores with them.

Evil Huang reportedly spent his recovery wallowing in self-pity over the devastation of his flower-like visage by Zhao Hongbing and Lisi's boots. He contemplated the destruction of his reputation at Hongbing's hands as he sat in his courtyard on a summer evening. He surveyed the starry vastness of the firmament with chin in hands, the summer breeze ruffling his neatly coifed hair and troubling his heart. That night he composed an untitled poem, which Little Beijing subsequently read out for everyone's enjoyment. Zhao Hongbing suspected that Evil had a ghostwriter, since even such sloppy doggerel seemed beyond his capabilities:

> I, the west side's Evil Huang, lie beaten half
> dead by my foe,
> Awaiting the day when I will rise up and
> bloody him head to toe.

Reciting this poem calmed Evil Huang; he would wreak his revenge. When Old Rod Li went to visit him, Evil was sitting atop the enclosing wall of the courtyard of his home. He was gazing at a bed of sunflowers in full bloom.

"What's up, Evil?" Old Rod Li asked.

"I'm enjoying the flowers," Evil Huang replied softly without turning his head.

"This is what happens to posers!" Old Rod Li scolded. Indeed, if being a poseur were a crime, Evil Huang would have been sentenced to a hundred million years in prison, and no number of appeals would have won him a sentence reduction. "When will you be up and around again?" Old Rod asked.

"In two or three weeks," said Evil Huang, still gazing calmly at the flowers.

"I found out that the guy who beat you up is named Zhao Hongbing, and he runs a hotel by the train station. You and Quint should take some guys and guns and wreck his hotel, then trash him," Old Rod Li said.

"I will avenge myself," said Evil Huang.

While Old Rod Li and Evil Huang were preparing their revenge, Zhao Hongbing and his friends were also making arrangements. The eight members of Hongbing's gang had varying degrees of intimacy and could be divided into three sub-groups.

The first group consisted of Zhao Hongbing, Xiaoji, Feisi, and Lisi. They had been friends for years, and even though they hadn't served in the same Army unit, they'd all fought on the Laoshan frontline; they shared a common language and had stuck together since their demobilization.

The second group consisted of Zhao Hongbing and Little

Beijing. After facing life-and-death struggles together, the two had become almost like a single person. It was not a question of one following the other. Rather, Little Beijing listened to Zhao Hongbing on fighting, and Hongbing listened to Little Beijing on business matters. Because Little Beijing had strong personal loyalty toward Zhao Hongbing, he was also loyal to the rest of Hongbing's brothers; these brothers liked and admired Little Beijing for his conduct and his wisdom.

The third group consisted of Zhang Yue, Sun Dawei, and Li Wu. These three had grown up together, and Sun Dawei and Li Wu had been in awe of Zhang Yue from their youth. In his turn, Zhang Yue greatly admired Zhao Hongbing, and also Little Beijing in many ways. Zhang Yue was also on very good terms with Xiaoji and the others. Sun Dawei was a decent man with no ulterior motives, always joking around. While a timid fighter, he was well liked by the others. Li Wu was an outlier in that he hadn't known the others before joining the gang, and was always involved in shady dealings. Zhao Hongbing and Little Beijing looked down on him, but since he was Zhang Yue's "brother", they didn't show it.

In short, Zhao Hongbing was the nucleus, and the gang was generally tight. Although the others didn't think much of Li Wu, he showed them proper consideration, so they didn't give him any trouble.

Lisi was a skilled fighter. Loyal and honest, he as a typical northeastern man. After Li Wu was arrested and Xiaoji was wounded, the young hooligans who followed Li Wu began to follow Lisi instead. Li Wu's band of little brothers was always out pilfering, and Lisi didn't like it. Since he'd earned quite a bit from the recycling business, he decided to buy some billiard tables to set up along the street and pay each of the young guys 100 *yuan* a month to look after them. This would bring him some additional income while keeping his gang out of trouble. The young guys were very excited at the idea: "It's a way for us to make a living!" "Who wants to steal stuff!" These young brothers continued to follow Lisi over the next two decades and became core members of his underworld gang. When Zhao Hongbing began pulling together "available resources", they were naturally included.

After being scared out of his wits while grave robbing, Feisi had gone over to mysticism, absorbing beliefs from Buddhism, Taoism, Lamaism, and Christianity. Back then, he could be seen with a Crucifix around his neck, Buddhist prayer beads around his wrist, and a little peachwood sword amulet in his pocket. He appeared ready to confront a whole convention of ghouls, secure in the knowledge that the Buddha, the Jade Emperor, and Jesus Christ would come to his aid. Of course, Feisi was only nominally devout. He still indulged freely in drinking, meat-eating, and brawling.

Little Beijing and Zhao Hongbing continued obsessing over their limited manpower and how they could take revenge on Old Rod Li and his men. "Even with Lisi's little brothers, how can we go up against Old Rod Li?" Little Beijing asked.

"Of course we can't," Zhao Hongbing agreed. "But, wait – haven't you pulled in a lot of followers with all your blabbing and boasting at the hotel?"

"Sure, but not many of them are real fighters," said Little Beijing. "Why don't we invite them for dinner one of these days?"

"Sure, we can invite them for a meal and bring them over our side," Zhao Hongbing said. "But none of them looks like much in terms of fighting material."

"Hah! If you're worried about fighting skills, why don't you just call in some other scouts from our army unit? You know they're combat ready," said Little Beijing.

"Sounds like you're planning an overthrow! Do you know any street hoods?"

"You grew up here, and you don't know any. Why ask me?"

"When would I have had any contact with those bullies and loafers? I'd just as soon punch them out as look at them," said Zhao Hongbing.

"Maybe we need to start thinking about using them instead of smacking them around," said Little Beijing. "If you'd talked things out with Railway and Tiger, maybe you'd be friends with them. They could be helping us right now."

"I'd rather be beaten to death by Old Rod Li than be friends with those low-lives," grinned Zhao Hongbing.

"I actually know a major hoodlum who's a decent guy. I'm not very familiar with him. We only met once."

"Who is it?"

"Liu Haizhu."

"You know him? Why didn't you say so? That guy isn't like those other punks. He has a real sense of justice. A while back I saw him beat up some hooligans who were harassing Dopey Bai in front of the movie theater."

"Let's take some time to get to know him better. He told me he has a bike repair stall by the entrance of the No. 14 High School."

"I know where you mean. We should go over one of these days and look him up."

"Not one of these days! Today!" said Little Beijing.

When they went, Liu Haizhu was fixing a young girl's bicycle.

"Are you busy?" Little Beijing asked him as they approached.

"Have you brought someone here to give me trouble?" asked Liu, grabbing a big wrench and standing up. They couldn't see his expression under his bamboo hat. Now it was Zhao Hongbing's turn to be surprised: Was this Little Beijing's idea of knowing someone – when he was ready to attack them at first glance?

"Heh! Calm down!" laughed Little Beijing. "We came to see if you can help us with something."

"What would you need me for? You beat up my four brothers all by yourself," said Liu Haizhu, squatting down again to work on the bicycle. It looked like he still bore a grudge against Little Beijing.

"Could we buy you a drink when you're free?"

"Buy me a drink? I don't know you well enough."

Liu Haizhu focused his attention on the bicycle and didn't even raise his head.

"Why bother with such a bullheaded guy? Let's go," Zhao Hongbing muttered. He had a strong sense of pride; he had thought Little Beijing knew Liu Haizhu better, and had only wanted to ask for his help for lack of a better choice. But being treated in this dismissive way got his dander up, and now all he wanted was to leave.

"If you have something to discuss with me, come out with it. I don't need you to buy me dinner or a drink." Liu Haizhu was standing now, having finished with the bicycle.

"We beat up Evil Huang, and now Old Rod Li wants to pack us up," Little Beijing said. "We'd actually like to take on Old Rod Li, but we don't feel we have enough manpower."

"Evil Huang and Old Rod Li are thugs," Zhao Hongbing jumped in. "They're trying to force our friend to sell them a piece of jade."

"Fuck – Old Rod Li? We shared a cell back in the day, and he was always picking on people. I'm not afraid of that fucker."

"Yeah, we want to take care of him once and for all. That's why we came looking for you," said Little Beijing.

"Normally I wouldn't be interested in helping out. You beat up my brothers, Shen. I already gave you plenty of face by not calling you to account – not to mention the fact that I hardly know you. But coming here to ask for my help shows that you respect me, and I also consider you a decent guy. If you're really afraid, you can hide out at my place. See if they'd dare come there!" said Liu Haizhu as he began cleaning up to go home.

"What are you saying? Do you think we'd go into hiding? We want to fix Old Rod Li for good, and we want your help. But if you don't want to, that's all right. As for hiding, we'll never do that." Zhao Hongbing talked steadily, calmly, and firmly.

Liu Haizhu gave a short laugh. "You two really have guts! Who else in this city is willing to take on Old Rod Li?" It was dawning on him that Little Beijing and Zhao Hongbing were kindred spirits.

"When someone picks on my comrade-in-arms, I'm going to give him a beating. Shen and I aren't afraid of death. We already died once on the battlefield," Zhao Hongbing said.

"You served in the Army? So did I! Let's go have a drink. It's on me." Having packed up his tools, Liu Haizhu left them with the entrance guard at the school and grabbed his old stripped-down bike.

CHAPTER 25

Unassailable

THE SMALL TAVERN LIU HAIZHU took them to was clearly a regular haunt; everyone greeted him at the door.

"So how'd you get on the wrong side of Old Rod Li?" he asked once they'd sat down.

"My old army buddy bought a piece of jade," said Zhao Hongbing. "And Old Rod Li is trying to force him to sell it to him cheap."

"That's how Old Rod Li makes his money. He's such a fucking loser," said Liu Haizhu, sipping his liquor. He was still wearing his bamboo hat.

"The other day, Old Rod sent Evil Huang to blackmail my friend, so another army buddy and I gave him a beating," Zhao Hongbing continued.

"Ha! Well done! Evil Huang deserves a beating. Sounds like you're a decent fighter. Little Brother Shen is also pretty good, taking on my four brothers all by himself. What branch of the army did you serve in?" Liu asked.

"We were scouts."

"I was a soldier in the 1970s. Transport corps. After

demobilization I was sent to a glass foundry, but I lost my job when I beat up our leader."

The three were delighted to discover their common background and temperament.

"Why do you always wear that bamboo hat?" Little Beijing asked Liu.

"During a fight back in 1981, my head got split open with a pickax, so I started wearing it to protect the wound when I went out. After a while, I got used to it and didn't want to take it off anymore. In any case, being outside all the time in the sun and rain repairing bicycles, I'm glad to have it."

"Guys like Old Rod Li who were as famous as you back then are all rich now," Zhao Hongbing said. "Why do you make your living repairing bikes?"

"I won't get involved in things that go against my conscience. Old Rod Li will get payback for what he's done, and didn't Mighty Zhang wind up stabbed to death on a sports field? That's payback, too! After I got out, I borrowed 100 *kuai* from my sister and bought some tools to repair bicycles. Bike repair is skilled labor. In the army I learned how to repair motor vehicles, and I'd like to open a shop eventually. I don't have enough capital just yet, so I've been saving up my earnings from my bicycle repair stall. I quickly gained a lot of customers, and I earn more than other bike repair stalls – even more than the average job. I figure it'll only take a few more years to save enough for an auto repair shop. The bicycle I use now – I put it together from parts of other bikes that people threw out, but it's a good bike."

Despite his unique appearance, Liu Haizhu was clearly a good man with a practical approach to life.

He continued saving money a nickel and dime at a time. By 1990 he was finally able to open an automotive repair shop with an auto parts shop next door. He prospered through his skill and hard efforts, and eventually even the mayor's driver became a regular customer. They say that Liu could tell what was wrong with a car just by listening to it start. He was the first of the city's residents to own a Mercedes Benz. Few people ever guessed that the driver of that car was the same man who used to ride around on a stripped-down bike. Every dime he earned was through his own hard work. Eventually he exchanged his bamboo hat for a fedora, becoming the only man in the city who wore a hat year-round. During the time Liu Haizhu was repairing cars, the taxi business was at its worst. If someone brought in their cab and said, "Brother Liu, I don't have the money right now, but I'll pay you in a few months," Liu would fix the car without a word, even if expensive parts were required. It's been a long time now since Liu, now in his fifties, had worked in the shop himself. However, if Zhao Hongbing or any other old friend has car trouble, Liu will strip down and climb under it. He still fights chivalrously for victims of injustice, but his body isn't what it used to be. Given his earlier fame and his relations with Zhao Hongbing, Xiaoji, Lisi, and other top gangsters, Liu doesn't have to worry about any hoodlums giving him trouble. If they did, Ergou is certain that Liu would jump out of his Benz with a cleaver and chase them down. He reportedly now runs a "4-S" automotive shop offering sales, spare parts, servicing, and surveys for China-made vehicles. It seems it really is possible to earn a decent living from hard work and honesty.

Little Beijing asked, "Brother Liu, how does a man like you run a bike repair stall and not feel..."

"Fuck off! What's embarrassing about earning a living from my skills?" When he got agitated, Liu Haizhu's goatee became drenched in liquor.

"You're right, Brother Liu. We salute you!" said Zhao Hongbing with genuine admiration.

"If Old Rod Li gives you guys any more trouble, you come straight to me," said Liu Haizhu.

That day, the three of them went through five bottles of liquor and got so drunk that only Little Beijing still had his wits about him. He had to practically carry Zhao Hongbing home. Liu Haizhu got on his bike and rode only about fifteen feet before plunging into a roadside flower bed. Little Beijing dropped Zhao Hongbing and went to pull Liu out.

"Are you all right? Better just lie here and sleep it off. I'll stay with you until you wake up."

But Liu Haizhu waved him off from the flower bed.

That was twenty years ago, and Zhao Hongbing, Little Beijing, and Liu Haizhu are still tight. They all remember that first time they went drinking together. It was the start of a lifelong friendship.

After recovering from his hangover the next day, Zhao Hongbing said two things, sighing with each. The first was, "Shen, don't ever tell me you 'know' someone you've only met once in your life. When I saw Brother Liu pick up his wrench, I thought he was going to use it on you!" The second was, "Brother Liu is a good guy to know."

As the saying goes, man proposes but God disposes. That afternoon, Evil Huang and Quint led their gang to Zhao Hongbing's hotel armed with shotguns and bayonets. At the time, only Little Beijing and Sun Dawei were there.

Apparently Sun Dawei had just closed his book stall and

had come to the hotel to deliver some martial arts novels to Little Beijing and Zhao Hongbing. When he arrived, Little Beijing was talking animatedly with two female staff about a time in the army when he had caught Zhao Hongbing masturbating. He described the episode so amusingly that the two women couldn't stop listening, even while blushing to their ears.

"Little Beijing, you and your rotten mouth! No one comes out well the way you talk. Who knows if you're not just making it all up!" laughed Sun Dawei.

"It's just because I'm bored," said Little Beijing.

"If you're bored, then drag your armchair out and bore other people with your stories."

"It's not time yet. I don't go out until the sun drops behind the hills. Why don't you go strum some tunes? I'll join you after I finish Hongbing's stroking story."

"Okay, I haven't performed in a long time!"

Sun Dawei dragged the armchair to the doorway. Coddling his guitar, he began singing "A Fire in Winter." Ergou couldn't stand it when Sun Dawei sang this song, mainly because the expression on his face was like one of those Japanese porn stars in the throes of ecstasy. It was disgusting.

Just as Sun Dawei was hitting his climax, Evil Huang and Quint arrived with seven or eight tough guys, each holding a weapon and ready to fight.

"Get outta my way, you fat fuck," said Quint, landing a kick that sent Sun Dawei and the armchair tumbling down the hotel stairs. Old Rod Li's underling was infamously brutal. They'd come to trash the hotel and beat up its owners.

Hearing the commotion outside, Little Beijing went to the door. He found his way blocked by Quint and Evil Huang.

"Which one is Zhao Hongbing?" Quint asked with the dim look of a perfect lunkhead.

"He isn't here. What's your business?"

"Who are you?"

"I'm his friend. You can call me Prince Shen."

"Start smashing the place up, brothers! These are Zhao Hongbing's friends!" said Evil Huang, raising his bayonet and thrusting it at Little Beijing's head.

Huang seemed to have sacrificed style for the sake of revenge, carrying a super-lethal weapon like a bayonet. It was common knowledge that for all his street cred, he didn't really have what it took. He hacked at Little Beijing rather than trying to stab him, making his bayonet less effective than a cleaver.

"Let's see you try!" said Little Beijing, nimbly evading the blow and grabbing Evil Huang by the wrist.

"Stop right there, fucker!" yelled Quint, taking out his shotgun and advancing on Little Beijing with the muzzle aimed at his brow.

"Okay, I stopped," said Little Beijing nonchalantly.

"Cut him up, brothers!" Quint hollered.

Quint made three incorrect judgment calls. He watched too much TV and thought pointed a gun at someone's head would make him stay put; in TV shows, people carry handguns, but he'd brought a long-muzzled shotgun; the guy he was dealing with had survived hails of bullets and wasn't the least bit afraid of a shotgun.

Little Beijing surprised Quint by thrusting his head forward and then grabbing the muzzle with both hands and pulling it sharply backward.

Boom. The shotgun blasted but hit no one. However, Little

Beijing had used a little too much force. When the gun went off, both he and Quint fell to the floor. Seeing this, Evil Huang jabbed his bayonet at Little Beijing, who wasn't able to dodge it in time and took a stab to the arm. Infuriated, Little Beijing grabbed Evil Huang's wrist again and twisted while kicking him, grabbing the bayonet as Huang went flying. Still enraged, Little Beijing wheeled around and stabbed Quint in the thigh and then thrust the bayonet into Evil Huang's leg as well. Both blows were solid.

"Let's see who dares to make another move," said Little Beijing, aiming the bayonet with the blood of three men dripping from its blade. None of his opponents moved, even though one of them was still holding a shotgun.

Sun Dawei recalled Little Beijing looking like the famous Communist soldier Dong Cunrui – indomitable and fierce, subduing others with his manner alone. Little Beijing later said that his rage was fueled by pain. He'd kept his cool enough to only stab Quint and Evil Huang in the thigh, but if they'd attacked again, he would have killed them. Little Beijing had the quality of mercy; his Party and army training distinguished him from a desperado like Zhang Yue.

"Dawei, get in there and close the door!"

Injured by his tumble down the stairs, Sun Dawei limped into the hotel and closed the door. The guys outside helped Evil Huang and Quint stagger away.

Watching them go, Little Beijing began howling with pain through gritted teeth. The left half of his shirt was covered with blood. It was one of the very few times that he was wounded in action.

Two hours later, Zhao Hongbing arrived at the hospital. Seeing Little Beijing with his arm in a bandage, he bared his teeth and hissed, "This isn't over, Old Rod Li..."

CHAPTER 26

Shizuka as Peony Messenger

LITTLE BEIJING HAD BEEN SERIOUSLY injured. He went around with his bandaged arm, sniveling constantly. Zhao Hongbing couldn't resist a sarcastic comment: "Shen, have you switched from story-telling to singing? Your tune is pretty monotonous, though. What do you call it? The 'Woe-is-me Song'?"

"Just remember, I've never been stabbed before," said Little Beijing, aggrieved. "Maybe I should have jabbed them a few more times when I had the chance."

"I'm sure they'd like to return the favor!" Hongbing said. "I hear Old Rod Li plans to come for us in the next few days."

"Fine. If they bring out their knives and guns again, I'll be obliged to butcher a few of them. Isn't Zhang Yue about to go to trial? Third Sister says he'll get three years at most. His case is considered self-defense. I'll do some self-defense, too, and go keep Zhang Yue company." Little Beijing was itching for the chance to repay Old Rod Li and his gang for his rare humiliation.

"Don't follow Zhang Yue's example," said Zhao Hongbing. He didn't like the idea of taking a life. "That was a close call the other day. If Quint had shot you, I'd be at the hospital plucking pellets out of you now."

"I guess it doesn't matter if I'm disfigured. Since your sister refuses to get a divorce, my good looks get me nowhere," grumbled Little Beijing.

"If you keep chasing my her, I'm going to castrate you."

"You have Gao Huan. Of course you don't know how I suffer."

"Gao Huan is going off to Beijing to study. She's leaving tonight."

"So you'll have to look after yourself? You've already raised calluses down there, so there can't be much feeling left. Say, I'll call my parents and have them invite Gao Huan to dinner on the weekends."

"Leave that for now. We need to figure out how to deal with Old Rod Li," Zhao Hongbing said.

"Brother Liu is a good guy. Let's go take him out. Last time he took us drinking even though he didn't know us very well. We owe him one, especially since we have our own business and can afford to return the favor."

There weren't many people Little Beijing respected, but Liu Haizhu was one of them.

"Sure, we can have Brother Liu bring some of his brothers around to meet us. You can invite some of your little brothers, and Lisi can come with his gang. We'll pull together three or four tables and have a good time. Let's reserve a table at the VIP Lounge and get Dawei to order the food. I'll go see Brother Liu."

Zhao Hongbing was also interested in getting to know Liu Haizhu's band of brothers.

Sure enough, that evening Hongbing reserved three tables on the second floor of the VIP Lounge and arranged a dinner for thirty guests. Everyone turned up except for Liu Haizhu. They started to worry.

"I'll go down and look for him," said Zhao Hongbing.

It turned out that Liu had arrived a while ago, but the maître d' downstairs had taken one look at his slovenly get-up and said he couldn't come in. As a result, he'd had gotten into a fight with three or four waiters. In spite of their numerical advantage, the waiters were no match for Liu Haizhu. Hongbing went down just in time to see him brandishing a chair.

"Stop! He's my friend!" Hongbing cried out.

"Mr. Zhao! He's a friend of yours?" the restaurant owner asked.

"He's my elder brother. Do you always beat people up like this?" Zhao Hongbing was angry.

"My apologies. I'm really sorry." The owner didn't know Liu Haizhu, but he was intimidated by Zhao Hongbing.

"You guys need to apologize too," Hongbing said to the waiters. Although still peeved, he was handling the matter better than Little Beijing, who would have started fighting right along with Liu Haizhu. Liu just gave a laugh and walked up the stairs.

Half a minute later, Liu Haizhu joined the others with his bamboo hat, pedal pushers, yellow flip-flops, and bare, sweaty, grease-streaked arms. Everyone rose from their seats.

More than thirty guys went home drunk that night. Zhao Hongbing had managed to bring together Liu Haizhu, Lisi, and Little Beijing's gangs to form a rudimentary underworld organization. Everyone agreed that Zhao Hongbing and Liu Haizhu would be the leaders of this gang. Someday they'd join up against their common enemy and take out Old Rod Li.

Someone took a picture of the group, with Zhao Hongbing in the center, Liu Haizhu standing behind him, and everyone smiling happily. There were a lot more people in this photo than in the one taken the year before, but Zhang Yue, Li Wu and Xiaoji were missing.

That night, when Little Beijing returned to the hotel alone he found Shizuka waiting.

"Is it true that Gao Huan is going off to college in Beijing?" she asked bashfully.

"Yeah, she's leaving tomorrow," Little Beijing slurred.

"Do you think Hongbing will start to like me once Gao Huan's gone?"

Shizuka hadn't pestered Zhao Hongbing for a long time after that previous incident.

"That depends on your strategy and methods," said Little Beijing, who managed to sound philosophical even when drunk.

"What kind of strategy and methods can I use?" asked Shizuka, bewildered.

"You need me to teach you? In any case, every man has his own likes and dislikes." Little Beijing sank into his armchair.

"Please teach me. What kinds of things do guys like?" Shizuka asked.

"Well, for example, Hongbing likes a girl to be pure, while I like a more mature woman."

"Oh, I'm sure Hongbing thinks I'm not pure enough... What can I do?" Shizuka regretted giving herself so rashly to those young hooligans.

"The chasm you have to leap over isn't Hongbing. It's Gao Huan. If you want to win over Hongbing, you have to defeat her."

It was another of Little Beijing's lousy ideas.

"How can I defeat Gao Huan?" Shizuka wondered.

"Four hundred years ago, before the decisive battle between the Japanese swordsmen Miyamoto Musashi and Yagyu,

Yagyu cut some peonies and presented them to Miyamoto to convince him to withdraw. Do you know this Zen move?"

Miyamoto Musashi was Little Beijing's spiritual teacher.

"No, I don't understand," said Shizuka, perplexed.

"The point was to make him see the difficulty and cause him to withdraw." Little Beijing didn't want to waste his words when Shizuka wouldn't understand anyway.

"Mm," said Shizuka, trying to look like she knew what he meant.

"Do you see your advantage?" Little Beijing settled back into his armchair.

Shizuka nursed that thought as Little Beijing drifted off to sleep.

Ten days later, she came to see him again.

"Brother Shen, can you tell me Gao Huan's address?"

"Sure," said Little Beijing, and told her.

"Thanks."

"Why do you ask?"

"I understand the Zen move you told me about."

According to Little Beijing, two weeks after starting classes, Gao Huan received a package from Shizuka. It was an extra-large brassiere – size 36F. Apparently the flat-chested Gao Huan thought Shizuka was trying to bury the hatchet. She actually tried it on, but when it didn't fit, she tossed it aside.

When Little Beijing heard about this, he banged his head against the wall and groaned.

"Shizuka, can you stop pretending to understand when you don't? Maybe I should send Hongyan's husband a jumbo-sized condom."

Little Beijing began thinking of Zhao Hongbing's sister again. Those killer eyes really cast a spell.

CHAPTER 27

'Til Death Do Us Part

ZHAO HONGBING AND LITTLE BEIJING were aching for Old Rod Li to come for them. They spent all of September 1987 anticipating a ferocious battle. Little Beijing stopped telling stories at the hotel's entrance and paced back and forth in front of the reception counter, covering that space a thousand times as he stared at the doorway.

Back then, Ergou didn't understand why these two men – who had already died once on the battlefield – were so restless about this fight.

"Shen, can you stop pacing? It's getting on my nerves." Zhao Hongbing might also have been on pins and needles, but he never showed it.

"It's been almost a month, Hongbing. Why hasn't Old Rod Li come for us yet?" Little Beijing made another circuit.

"I'm not Old Rod Li, so how would I know?" said Hongbing with a grim laugh. Even when uneasy, he gave the impression that he had some secret knowledge.

"Hongbing, back during the war we wrote out our wills. Remember? When the company commander gave the order, we charged, and we could have died at any minute. We were calm enough then, so why am I so nervous now?" asked Little Beijing as he paced.

"Back then we were facing the 'Nam devils. We wanted to kill as many as possible. But this time it's our own countrymen. Are you afraid you'll hesitate?" Hongbing gave a teasing laugh.

"Old Rod Li doesn't qualify as a countryman. He's less human than any 'Nam devil!" said Little Beijing, finally pausing. Zhao Hongbing was his best tranquilizer.

Ergou now understands why the skillful and fearless Zhao Hongbing and Little Beijing were so uneasy. Years ago, when they charged up the hillsides of the Laoshan frontline, their dauntlessness came from knowing they had the one billion people of the People's Republic behind them; convinced of the righteousness of their cause, they faced death unflinchingly.

They cherished that nameless hill on the southern border where their comrades-in-arms had spilled their blood and gradually melded into the lush, green mountainside. Now they faced a notorious old hoodlum, and they could have killed him just like the 'Nam devils back then. But instead of the Republic's one billion citizens behind them, they had police officers carrying handcuffs. They still loved their country, and passing from the side of justice to a life of crime caused them tremendous inner conflict.

"Shen, you're starting to act like Zhang Yue. That's not like you," Zhao Hongbing said.

It was true. Little Beijing had been in a very bad temper over the past few days. Although he'd gained street cred in the fight with Evil Huang and the others, he'd still taken a hit – a loss he'd never suffered in the hail of bullets on the southern border.

"Hongbing, is it possible Old Rod Li won't come for us? And if he doesn't, how can we avenge Xiaoji?"

"Then we'll go for him." Zhao Hongbing was gazing out the doorway.

Years later, Ergou read a story about a family in the United States. It was a traditional American family, consisting of a loving father and mother and their teenage daughter. They lived in perfect happiness along the coast, but their tranquility was destroyed when a newly commissioned detachment of soldiers was stationed nearby. The soldiers were tall, handsome, and gallant. The parents lived in a state of constant anxiety that one of them would seduce their adolescent daughter. One day the girl's mother rushed home weeping and told her husband, "Our daughter is pregnant!" To her surprise, the father gave a sigh of relief and said, "Finally we can stop worrying!"

It's better for the inevitable to come sooner rather than later. Endless waiting can be torture.

On National Day – October 1st – Zhao Hongbing once again invited Liu Haizhu and the others to dinner. The main topic of the evening was how to mount a challenge against Old Rod Li. As well as Zhao Hongbing and his six gang brothers, Lisi had brought along five guys, Liu Haizhu seven, and Little Beijing seven more, making a total of twenty-six. They were spread across three tables.

That night, the "fifth enlarged rumble meeting" was held in the VIP room. It was an "enlarged meeting", in Party parlance, because the main participants were the former soldiers Zhao Hongbing, Little Beijing, Liu Haizhu, Xiaoji, Feisi, and Lisi. The others merely listened. The main topic was to analyze Old Rod Li's gang so they would know their enemy and have a better chance of beating him. The larger scale of Old

Rod Li's gang, its economic interests, and its protective umbrella gave it the characteristics of an underworld criminal syndicate. Zhao Hongbing and the others carried out their analysis on seven interrelated aspects:

Style: Old Rod Li's management of Evil Huang and the others could be described as carrot-and-stick. Old Rod's subordinates all feared the notorious old gangster, while also depending on him for their livelihoods.

Structure: Old Rod Li's subordinates – Evil Huang, Tudou, and Quint – each had ten or so "little brothers", making a total of around forty gang members. Those below submitted to those above in a cohesive vertical management model.

Members: All were vicious and ruthless types, most having served time in either "labor reform" or "reeducation through labor". Each carried a bayonet, striking knife, shotgun, or some other lethal weapon. Their dealings in tomb artifacts gave them a sinister aura.

System: Proceeds were distributed according to the profit produced by each gang member. There were substantial rewards for meritorious service in the form of grave-robbing, delivering merchandise, extortion, and fighting. Families of imprisoned gang members were paid an allowance, and medical expenses were covered. Gang members didn't receive a regular salary, but all had fairly stable incomes.

Special skills: All were uneducated and unskilled, but that was what made them so fierce.

Strategy: Old Rod Li's gang members were the city's biggest hoodlums. They expected to profit from their reputation.

Shared values: to enrich themselves by any means, and to gain street cred.

Liu Haizhu's brothers provided the source material for

the above points, with Zhao Hongbing, Little Beijing, and Xiaoji carrying out the analysis. They arrived at the following conclusion and plan:

Step 1. Engage the enemy: If Old Rod Li was challenged to a fight, he was sure to step up; he couldn't afford to lose his status in the underworld. The best location for the contest would be the sparsely-inhabited riverfront west of the city.

Step 2. The fight: Old Rod Li's subordinates were cruel and ruthless and armed with lethal weapons, and his reward system ensured that most would be daring and top-notch fighters. The fight would be set one week after Zhao Hongbing's side had made their preparations, giving the other side little time to prepare. Today was October 1st, so the date for the fight was set for the 8th.

Step 3. After the fight: If anyone on their side was wounded and hospitalized, the other guys would protect them from Old Rod Li at the hospital. At the same time, they would find out where Old Rod Li's guys were being treated. If the opportunity presented itself, Hongbing's group would go there for a last hit.

At the end of the hour-long meeting, Liu Haizhu and the others praised the superb analytical skills of Zhao Hongbing, Little Beijing, and Xiaoji and thoroughly endorsed their battle plan. If Liu Haizhu, Little Beijing, and Zhao Hongbing were united by the spirit of chivalry, Zhao Hongbing's cool-headed and deliberate thinking during this analytical discussion made Liu Haizhu appreciate his friendship even more.

Just as everyone raised their glasses in a final toast, two voices could be heard arguing downstairs. It sounded like a tussle between the love rivals Pan Daqing and Gourdy.

Little Beijing should never have brought Pan Daqing along, given that he was the kid who had sought refuge in the hotel after stealing the girlfriend of one of Liu Haizhu's guys.

Pan was a pretty boy but fairly cowardly when it came to fighting. He'd spent two weeks in the hotel rather than face Liu Haizhu's brothers. Even so, he knew he owed Little Beijing, and insisted on attending the meeting so he could help him take revenge. Little Beijing hadn't wanted to bring in such a week-kneed fighter, but had been unable to dissuade him.

After years of bachelorhood, Liu Haizhu didn't think it was such a big deal that Pan Daqing had stolen Gourdy's girl. He'd made the two shake hands before dinner, and sat them at the same table so they could talk it out. Constrained by his need to give face to Liu Haizhu, Gourdy had initially kept his language in line. However, after a few drinks, with his eyes bleary and ears aflame, he became increasingly offensive. "Liu Ge's pretty good in bed, isn't she? I know that for a fact," Gourdy said, dredging up the old matter.

"Brother, I think you've had one too many," said Pan Daqing in a low voice.

"I'm not drunk. I popped her cherry when she was seventeen, so I should know," said Gourdy.

"She's my girlfriend now. Don't insult her, okay?" said Pan Daqing, stung by his words.

"Girlfriend? She's just a pony, isn't she? I'm done with that bitch."

This wasn't necessarily true, of course, but after going after Pan Daqing and getting beaten up by Little Beijing, Gourdy had been aching to let off steam. While he didn't dare mess with Little Beijing, Dutch courage made him vent at Pan.

"Have another drink. I have to hit the head."

Pan Daqing hoped to take refuge in the washroom, but Gourdy followed him downstairs, hot on his heels.

While Pan was in the washroom, Gourdy grabbed a cleaver

from the kitchen. He was standing in front of Pan before he had a chance to zip his trousers.

"So I take it you didn't like what I said just now?" said Gourdy provokingly, his hands clasped behind his back.

"Say what you want about me, but don't insult Liu Ge."

"Who's insulting Liu Ge? She's nothing but a tart. A pretty boy like you is hardly worth the bother."

"Watch your mouth!"

"How about if I watch your pretty face get cut up instead?"

Gourdy suddenly slashed the cleaver at Pan Daqing's face. "Fuck your mother!" Ignited, he pounced on Pan. They both went tumbling into the urinal. Although Gourdy was holding a knife, proximity kept him from using it to full advantage. However, he did manage to cut Pan a few times.

"Enough, damn it!" roared Liu Haizhu as he arrived on the scene.

The two men stopped fighting as Zhao Hongbing and the others rushed down.

"Who started this?" demanded Liu Haizhu. His goatee was trembling with anger.

"I did, Brother Zhuzi," said Gourdy, head bowed.

"I should have known," said Liu Haizhu, seething with rage. Expecting the two to make peace out of respect for him, he never thought they'd come to blows in a public toilet.

"Brother Zhuzi…"

Gourdy had followed Liu Haizhu long enough to know that once Liu lost his temper he might use the knife himself. And indeed, Liu Haizhu's next words were, "Give me that knife."

Head still bowed, Gourdy handed the cleaver to Liu Haizhu.

"Gourdy, you need to remember that I'm brothers with Shen and Hongbing. Their brothers are my brothers. Tonight I made you two sit down and drink together, and that makes you brothers. Attacking your brother is completely out of line," said Liu Haizhu harshly.

"I was wrong."

"Now I'm going to cut you the way you cut your little brother," said Liu Haizhu, raising the knife.

Little Beijing and Lisi reached out simultaneously and grabbed Liu Haizhu by the waist and arms. "Brother Liu, Pan is also to blame. Let's end the matter here," said Zhao Hongbing softly, patting Liu Haizhu and drawing him out of the restroom. Liu Haizhu left it at that.

Ergou has always wondered if Zhao Hongbing had some power of hypnosis. How is it that even a cold-blooded bastard like Zhang Yue and a powder keg like Liu Haizhu could be subdued with just a few of his words? Apparently there's no limit to the influence a steady person can exert to make a good situation better or a bad situation less horrendous.

After this, they took Pan Daqing to a nearby hospital. Pan's girlfriend – the Liu Ge whom Gourdy had described as a slut – arrived soon afterwards.

"Doctor, will Daqing be all right?" asked Liu Ge, overcome with weeping.

"His life's not in danger, but... "

"But what?"

"He's likely to be disfigured."

"That doesn't matter."

"It doesn't?" The doctor looked perplexed.

Ergou had the opportunity to witness Pan Daqing's subsequent conversation with Liu Ge, because Zhao Hongbing's third sister had brought him to the hospital for a bath. Ergou's grandmother was also there. Something she said left a deep impression on Ergou.

"I did this to you. If it wasn't for me, you wouldn't have been slashed," said Liu Ge, clinging to Pan Daqing.

"I'd do anything for you, Liu Ge."

"You've been so good to me. It's only since meeting you that I've known a man could treat a woman so well. I won't leave you, even if Gourdy kills me. Even if you come out looking like a monster, I won't leave you."

"Same here."

"You weren't my first man, but I want you to be my last."

On the way home, Ergou asked his grandmother and Zhao Hongbing's sister what the couple had been talking about. "'Til death do us part," said Ergou's grandmother in her thick Tianjin accent. And that's all she said.

More than ten years later, Ergou finally understands what this phrase means in the context of romantic relationships. It's an emotional yearning completely removed from physical desire. It means courage before rumor and slander, and giving without calculation of return – a noble sentiment that transcends worldly and material concerns. And this sentiment exists not only among nobles and poets, but also between what the world regards as a hooligan and a slut.

"It's a good thing Brother Liu's guy cut Pan Daqing rather than vice versa," said Zhao Hongbing to Little Beijing after they returned to the hotel.

"Yeah...If it had gone the other way, we'd never have a chance at Old Rod Li."

As it was, Zhao Hongbing faced a long road ahead trying

to keep three dozen guys in line and handling the conflicts between them.

On October 9th 1987, Old Rod Li received a verbal message from Zhao Hongbing:

"Tomorrow night, seven o'clock, beneath the big bridge along the west side waterfront. Let's settle this."

"All right," said Old Rod Li.

Part Five

The Battle

CHAPTER 28

Tell Third Sister I Love Her

OCTOBER 10TH 1987 WAS A clear day. The setting sun cast a rosy tint on the shimmering waters of a river that had nurtured generations of people for a thousand years without resentment or regret. A flock of south-bound wild geese passed over two solitary figures seated along the riverbank.

"Hongbing, sunsets in the northeast are really beautiful – much nicer than in Beijing."

"Are you homesick?"

"This is my home."

"Heh."

"Hongbing, what do you live for?"

"To practice Communism and liberate the toiling masses of the world."

"Can you be a little more realistic?"

"For my loved one, Gao Huan, and for love of this rolling river and purple mountain majesty."

"Hongbing, you already have Gao Huan, and you've drunk the river's water and hiked on the mountain. What else do you live for?"

"To have all this for as long as I live."

"You're a happy man. I know what I live for, but I'll never get it."

"And what is it you live for, Prince Shen?"

"... I don't want to say."

"Are you afraid to die?"

"Yes."

"Why?"

"Because I've never gone to bed with your sister."

Zhao Hongbing kicked Little Beijing into the river.

A minute later, Little Beijing, soaked to the skin, crawled silently to the riverbank but didn't climb ashore. "Hongbing, if I'm killed today, tell Third Sister I love her," he said in a low voice.

Zhao Hongbing shot him a glance, then picked up a stone and flung it into the river, where it skipped three times. After a long silence he said, "All right, I'll tell her."

Zhao Hongbing and Little Beijing were brothers in life and death. Neither of them spoke after that.

Five minutes later, they heard voices behind them singing a military song, 'Returning from Target Practice', and recognized the loudest singer as the recently recovered Xiaoji. Turning, they saw Xiaoji advancing with a shotgun and accompanied by Lisi, Feisi, and the dozen or so young street hoods from Lisi and Little Beijing's gangs. Each was carrying a triangular blade, bayonet, or other weapon they'd managed to pull together over the last few days, and were singing in chorus: "The sun sets scarlet in the west, soldiers return to their lair, medals shining on their chests, joyful singing fills the air..."

"Xiaoji, if Chairman Mao saw you carrying a lousy old musket like that to a fight, I don't know if he'd be infuriated or delighted."

Having gotten what he had to say off his chest, Little Beijing returned to his usual cynical 'player' mode.

"Hey, why did you and Hongbing come empty-handed? Wouldn't that infuriate Chairman Mao? What would he say? 'Fight no battle unprepared, or that you're not sure of winning'." Xiaoji loved taunting Little Beijing.

"Hongbing and I despise weapons. 'Doing a good job requires preparing one's tools.' Hongbing and I honed our weapons years ago. Our weapons are our wills," said Little Beijing, ever ready with a come-back.

"Hey, Prince Shen, how did you get so wet? Did you just finish honing your will?"

"I was hot and jumped in to cool off."

"When Old Rod Li gets here, I'll blast him." Sun Dawei was full of bluster before every fight, and he backed the others today, as always, with his never-fired shotgun.

"Will you ever shoot that thing, Dawei? Try to keep your hands from shaking." Little Beijing would never give Sun Dawei a break.

"Dawei, be sure to aim at Old Rod Li's crotch. They say he's violated a lot of girls," said the ever-vindictive Lisi.

"Hey, Brother Liu and his guys are here. Check him out!" said Little Beijing as Liu Haizhu approached.

Liu Haizhu was extra stylish that day. He wore his usual yellow flip-flops, pedal pushers and bamboo hat, but his bare chest was covered with a black cape reportedly made of curtains from the slideshow room of the No. 14 High School. In his hand he carried a long chopper; a chivalrous type like Liu Haizhu would never use an insidious weapon like a triangular blade. Seven years later, while watching the movie *Swordsmen in Double Flag Town*, Ergou saw a character fitted out just like Liu Haizhu.

The most distinctive characteristic of the seven gang brothers Liu Haizhu brought with him was that they'd tied their weapons to their hands with medical bandages. A warrior is a warrior and a ruffian is a ruffian, and there was something to be said for experience. With their weapons sealed to their hands with bandages, their opponents wouldn't be able to snatch them away without cutting their hands off.

"Old Rod Li isn't here yet?" Liu Haizhu was ready for the kill.

"I'm sure he'll be here soon," chuckled Zhao Hongbing, looking completely relaxed.

"He'd better hurry up. I have bicycles that need fixing." Not only did Liu Haizhu have a model work ethic, he also never doubted he'd be back at his stall after the fight.

"Here they are," said Zhao Hongbing slowly, staring at the bridge about five hundred yards away.

The slope running down from the bridge was steep. Hongbing saw Old Rod Li and his guys park their vehicle on the bridge and then walk down the slope. Hongbing tossed his cigarette aside, and the others gathered around him. By then darkness was falling.

Zhao Hongbing, Little Beijing, and Lisi walked in front, their tread steady and powerful. Facing a formidable enemy, those accustomed to major situations took the lead with the others close behind. No one said a word.

Old Rod Li had more than thirty guys with him, and weapons gleamed as the two sides drew closer. Then suddenly, the sound of a siren shattered their ears, and they saw a police van speed across the bridge and stop along the slope.

"Retreat! Run!" Little Beijing shouted, and they all turned and sped off.

"Toss your tools in the river!" shouted Zhao Hongbing.

Everyone hurled their blades and bayonets into the river so they wouldn't be caught carrying weapons. Sun Dawei was so scared that he forgot to toss his shotgun and just ran for his life. Worst off were Liu Haizhu's brothers, who had fastened their weapons so securely to their hands that there was no hope of untying them as they ran.

"Split up!" Little Beijing shouted.

Everyone ran off in different directions and disappeared under the curtain of night.

An hour later, Little Beijing and Xiaoji returned to the hotel.

"Did any of us get caught?" Little Beijing asked.

"I didn't look behind me. Man, you run fast!" Xiaoji was still gasping.

"You think I'm fast? I saw Lisi and Feisi running even faster."

"Ha – the fastest runner was Dawei. That fat bastard is in better shape than he looks." Zhao Hongbing stood smiling in the doorway.

"Hongbing! You got away, too!"

"Brother Liu and I didn't run too far. After a few minutes we looked back. The cops hadn't even gotten out of their van, so we just strolled the rest of the way back. It was fun watching you guys run for your lives."

"No one got out? They just blew their siren and sat there?" Xiaoji asked.

"I'm surprised, too. It looks like they didn't bother once they saw us run."

"So Old Rod Li's guys didn't get arrested, either?"

"We ran along the river, and Old Rod Li's guys ran into

the little woods on the west side of the river," Zhao Hongbing said. "If the police were sitting in their van, how could they catch anyone?"

"Shit. If I'd known the police weren't after us, I wouldn't have tossed my shotgun into the river. Now I'll have to borrow another one," Xiaoji said.

"What about Lisi and Feisi? I saw them running in front of us, but where are they? They wouldn't have skipped town again would they?" Little Beijing wondered.

"You're the one who ran off!" Feisi, Lisi, Sun Dawei, and their dozen gang brothers appeared at the door of the hotel. Everyone had made it back.

"The gang's all here," grinned Little Beijing. "What about Brother Liu?"

"He went back to his stall to fix some bikes. I told them to meet us at the Purple Moon in half an hour. Even though we didn't get to fight, after what we've been through, I think we could all use a drink and something to eat," Zhao Hongbing said.

Although the battle was aborted, word of it spread throughout the local underworld – not because of the ferocious fight that followed, but because no one could understand how the police arrived just in the nick of time and why they just sat there. No one ever got to the bottom of it, but everyone arrived at the same conjecture: Old Rod Li must have tipped off the cops.

Since Zhao Hongbing and the others had challenged Old Rod Li to take revenge according to their code of personal loyalty, there's no way they would have called the police. It was different for Old Rod Li. He had no code of honor; all he cared about was money. He had little to gain from a showdown with Zhao Hongbing, and could even have ended up inside again. This fight presented too many risks and no benefits, but if he didn't show up, he would lose all his street cred. In the 1980s, a hoodlum only had to do this once and he'd be finished.

By showing up for the fight but calling in the police to break it up, Old Rod Li could save face and avoid a nasty battle. This was completely consistent with his underhanded nature. Of course, all this was pure speculation, and with Old Rod Li long turned to dust, there's no way to verify it. What was subsequently determined, however, was that one of the cops who showed up that day was Old Rod Li's cousin.

But Old Rod Li and Zhao Hongbing were destined for a face-off that day. When Hongbing and the others arrived at the Purple Moon a little after eight o'clock that night, they found Evil Huang ordering food at the first-floor bar.

CHAPTER 29

My Blood Wasn't Spilled for the Republic

EVIL HUANG'S FATE SEEMED TO be in the hands of Zhao Hongbing, Little Beijing, and Liu Haizhu. Following his rise to fame, all his beatings were at the hands of one of those three. Each beat him more than once. Evil Huang was a notorious tough guy who injured countless people from the late 1980s until the early 1990s, but when he saw any of these three guys, his legs turned to jelly. In the year since Zhao Hongbing and Lisi had nearly made him a vegetable in July 1987, he was never out of the hospital for more than ten days before one of the three sent him back again.

As Zhao Hongbing and Little Beijing went into the Purple Moon, Evil Huang turned his head. Two tiny, shifty eyes met four large, bright, and piercing ones. Two of his three archfoes had descended upon him at once. They say that when Zhao Hongbing and Little Beijing saw Evil Huang turn toward them, both of them smiled, thinking, "We looked all over and couldn't find you, but here you are. Let's see where you can run off to!" Seeing the two of them smiling at him, Evil Huang bared his teeth in a forced grin, no doubt scared speechless.

"Hongbing, why is his smile so hideous?" wondered Little Beijing as they advanced toward Evil Huang with Lisi and the others grinning behind them.

"It's what's called a pasted-on smile," said Zhao Hongbing as they closed in on Evil Huang.

This time Little Beijing and Zhao Hongbing didn't hit Evil Huang right away. They just grabbed his hair. Whether they were too fast or Evil was too scared to react, he offered no resistance. They hauled him out of the restaurant like a sack of grain. Evil Huang was like a docile puppy, bent over at the waist and not uttering a sound.

After years of fighting without being wounded, Little Beijing had never expected to be stabbed by a rat like Evil Huang. His arm wasn't yet completely healed and he was still extremely angry. He wasn't about to let Evil off this time.

Once Evil Huang was outside the restaurant, Little Beijing swung him by the hair and sent him tumbling to the ground. Little Beijing had changed into his army boots after Zhao Hongbing had kicked him into the river. Once Evil Huang was on the ground, he stomped on his body and head. After being stamped on at least thirty times, Evil Huang was curled up like a dried shrimp, his arms covering his head.

Zhao Hongbing and Lisi stood to the side and let Little Beijing vent his wrath. More than ten years later, Evil Huang – whose nickname had by then changed to Floozy Huang because of his pimping activities – recalled this assault by Little Beijing with lingering terror: "At first, every time he stomped on me I felt like I was being hit by a car; then the stomping became harder and felt like I was being hit by a train. I couldn't even draw a breath and hoped he'd just pull a knife and end it once and for all. Finally he stomped on my temple and I passed out, and he finally let up on me." He added, "He stomped on my face, too, and broke my nose. I used to be a lot better looking." Even with the passage of time and change of nicknames, Evil Huang was still a poseur.

During a fight, Little Beijing liked to overcome his enemy through intimidation. There's probably no better way to break down an opponent's mental defenses than to stomp on him, and this method was particularly appropriate against a depraved hoodlum like Evil Huang.

"That's Evil Huang being beaten up!"

"That guy is Zhao Hongbing!"

Little Beijing heard the shouting just as he knocked out Evil Huang. Under the dim streetlamps he saw about three dozen guys running toward them, led by Old Rod Li. It turned out that Evil Huang hadn't gone to the river that evening because he was still recovering from being stabbed in the leg during the earlier fight with Little Beijing. Instead, he'd come to the restaurant to reserve a table and order food for Old Rod Li and his gang, never expecting such a disastrous encounter.

"Which one is Old Rod Li?" Zhao Hongbing said, advancing toward the group with Lisi and the others close behind.

"I am." The speaker was a sinister-looking fellow with horn-rimmed glasses covering half his face.

"I'm Zhao Hongbing. I've been looking for you," he said evenly.

"We let you off, down by the river, but now I'm going to trash you," said Old Rod Li, pulling out a triangular blade as the gangsters behind him brandished their weapons.

When Zhao Hongbing and the others saw that their opponents were all armed, their first thought was, "We're sunk!" After dumping their weapons in the river, they were all empty-handed and didn't have a chance against this band of ruffians.

Ergou recalls going home for the Spring Festival in 2007, and his father saying he wanted to raise a Tibetan Mastiff. When Ergou went on the Internet to find material on this type of dog, he stumbled onto Baidu's "Tiger" message board and tumbled into the bottomless pit of the "Tiger and Lion – Which is Mightier?" thread, which had at least 10,000 postings dating back for years. While sighing over how much free time Chinese people seem to have, Ergou also couldn't help wondering which of these beasts actually was mightier. The next day was the first day of the Lunar New Year, and Zhao Hongbing arrived early in the morning to pay his respects to Ergou's family. Ergou asked, "Uncle, which is mightier, the lion or the tiger?" Zhao Hongbing said off the top of his head, "I don't know. But the one way to find out is to put them in a pit and let them go hungry for three days, then drop a goat in there and see whether the lion or the tiger survives. No argument is as accurate as an actual experiment."

This is how Zhao Hongbing thought things out and solved problems. He never engaged in useless arguments but proved his point through actual practice. Today it's obvious whether Zhao Hongbing or Old Rod Li was tougher, but back then it was an unfair fight, because the tiger – Zhao Hongbing – had his teeth pulled out when his brothers dumped their weapons in the river.

"Old Rod Li, I'm going to butcher you today!" roared Xiaoji, his usual affable manner vanishing at the sight of the man who had stabbed him.

"Motherfucker! I'll nail you!" One of the guys behind Old Rod Li raised his shotgun and aimed it at Xiaoji. This turned out to be Tudou, the most ruthless of Old Rod Li's subordinates.

"You have a gun, asshole?" Feisi stepped forward with Sun Dawei's shotgun in his hands and aimed it at Tudou. Having failed to toss his weapon two hours earlier, Sun Dawei was finally putting his shotgun to use. It was the only weapon Zhao Hongbing and his guys had just then.

The two gangs were standing about ten feet apart at the time. A shotgun was unlikely to kill anyone further away than that. However, its threat couldn't be underestimated, because it fired scores of pellets in one shot, and some might be impossible to remove.

"Give it a try, why don't you?" Feisi yelled again.

"Don't push me, motherfucker!"

Feisi opened his eyes wide and gritted his teeth. Zhao Hongbing knew from the look on his face that he would fire that gun. It was hardly beyond a man who could grab someone's army knife with his bare hands. Zhao Hongbing and Lisi launched themselves at Tudou's gun barrel just as Feisi and Tudou both fired. Feisi fired first, hitting Tudou in the face and neck. Tudou's gun went off a split second later. Most of its pellets hit Zhao Hongbing in his damaged right hand as he reached for the gun. Leading the assault, Zhao Hongbing then suffered a stab to his lower abdomen. His left hand gripped his assailant's hand while he delivered a kick to the guy's privates. At the same time, Zhao Hongbing's thigh took a thrust from Old Rod Li's triangular blade. Little Beijing kicked Old Rod Li away, and the two began fighting.

All of Old Rod Li's guys had knives. Seeing the odds stacked against them, many on Zhao Hongbing's side turned tail and ran. Little Beijing, Lisi, and Feisi couldn't run, however, because Zhao Hongbing was too badly injured. If they ran off without him, Hongbing would certainly be stabbed to death by Old Rod Li.

Apart from the knife Lisi had managed to snatch, the others were empty-handed. Within half a minute, Xiaoji had sustained cuts to his legs and arms. If things continued this way, all of them would be dead within three minutes. It was just at this moment that a stripped-down bicycle plowed into the mêlée. The man on the bike wore a bamboo hat, yellow flip-flops, and a black cape. He was carrying a big chopper.

Liu Haizhu and his brothers had arrived for dinner. Every one of them was carrying the weapons they'd brought to the riverside, bound to their hands. Dropping his bicycle, Liu Haizhu aimed the first blow of his chopper at Old Rod Li's head. Unable to dodge it in time, Old Rod could only raise his left hand to ward off the blow. Liu Haizhu brought his chopper down again, this time hitting Old Rod Li on the back as he turned. Unlike a lightweight melon knife or cleaver, a chopper can inflict a fatal blow.

"Hold it, fuckers! Whoever moves gets blasted!" Gourdy burst in with an assault rifle, which was much more powerful than a shotgun. No one moved.

Ergou later learned that after the atomic bomb was invented there were fewer large-scale wars, making this most deadly of all weapons the savior of the world. At that moment, the assault rifle in Gourdy's hands was like an atomic bomb. Unlike Feisi, Gourdy wouldn't rashly fire the gun; he only used it to shock and awe.

Seeing Zhao Hongbing lying on the ground, Liu Haizhu yelled, "Get Hongbing and Xiaoji to the hospital, quick!" Turning to Old Rod Li's gang, he said, "Get the hell out of here!" The sight of Zhao Hongbing so badly injured left Liu Haizhu in no mood to fight.

Little Beijing waylaid a taxi and carried Zhao Hongbing into it. Months later, Little Beijing and Zhao Hongbing had this conversation:

"When you pulled me in, I was conscious enough to notice that the taxi was blue, but I don't remember anything after that," Zhao Hongbing said.

"After we got in, the tape deck played 'Fifteen Moons' and 'Bloodstained Glory'. The taxi driver wanted to turn it off, but I wouldn't let him," Little Beijing said.

"Why?" Hongbing asked.

"I thought that if you heard those songs, you wouldn't die, because even if you were unconscious, hearing them would make you think of the Laoshan front. When it came to the line in the song that says, 'The banner of the Republic is graced with your blood,' I said, 'Hongbing, remember, the squad leader told us to stay alive.'"

"But my blood wasn't spilled for the Republic that day," Zhao Hongbing said lightly.

Little Beijing said nothing more. He took a deep drag of his cigarette.

Lisi, who was with them in the taxi that night, said he saw Little Beijing cry for the first and only time. It was not a pretty sight. Little Beijing muffled his sobs, but he was shaking too hard to wipe his streaming nose and eyes.

CHAPTER 30

Porcelain and Jade

THE STREET FIGHT – WHICH resulted in gunfire and left both Zhao Hongbing and Old Rod Li seriously injured – caused quite a stir. For Old Rod Li, a genuine challenger had emerged. This inevitably flustered him, and compelled him to retaliate against the threat to his income and gangland status.

Apart from Old Rod Li being chopped by Liu Haizhu, Tudou had been shot in the face and neck by Feisi. While the injury wasn't fatal, it had left him badly disfigured. In addition, Evil Huang had suffered multiple fractures all over his body at the hands of Little Beijing. As for the guy Zhao Hongbing kicked in the groin, he went to work at the brewery a few years later; his colleagues said he couldn't get it up anymore because Hongbing had smashed his testicles.

They say that the minute Old Rod Li checked into the hospital, he began planning how to finish off the similarly laid-up Zhao Hongbing.

From the late 1980s until the early 1990s, whoever was the top man in the city's underworld passed his days uneasily. Too many others wanted this title, even though it was meaningless and potentially deadly. No one had ever held this position for two years running. It was the equivalent of a suspended death sentence. After Old Rod Li, it was the same for Zhang Yue, Lisi, Li Wu, Little Tiger, Loony Gou, and Geezer. Only Zhao Hongbing has survived until today, by maintaining a low profile and involving himself as little as possible in gangland matters.

These gangland leaders came to two possible ends: death or imprisonment. Being merely crippled or imprisoned was considered lucky. Ergou used to wonder how Zhao Hongbing managed to survive and even live happily.

"Uncle," he said. "Back then, Lisi and Zhang Yue rose to fame at the same time you did, and now they're gone. They considered you their big brother. You were even more famous than them, so why have you had such a good life?"

"Ergou, I raised you since you were a boy. You should know that I live by two principles: don't get involved in unscrupulous activity – in all my forty years, I've never gotten involved in really evil doings, and not many who take this road can say the same; and don't get destroyed by dirtbags. These two principles are why I'm alive today."

"I understand the first one, but not the second. How can you decide whether or not you'll be destroyed by dirtbags?"

"I'm jade, so I don't mix with porcelain. Anyone I deal with also has to be jade. If porcelain keeps trying to mix with me and I can't avoid it, I'll find another piece of porcelain to deal with it."

"But I don't understand why, back when I was seven or eight, you spent two years fighting with Old Rod Li. Weren't you afraid of becoming broken jade?"

"At that time, I was porcelain and Old Rod Li was jade," said Zhao Hongbing, smiling and tossing Ergou an apple.

"So, you were porcelain back then, but Jingdezhen porcelain," said Ergou, laughingly referring to the porcelain capital of China.

Over the past few years, Ergou hasn't been able to spend much time with Hongbing, but whenever they're together, their conversations invariably yield insights on philosophy and life.

"I wouldn't lay claim to Jingdezhen – more like the local chinaware they used to sell for 20 cents in the shops here. After fighting with Old Rod Li for two years, I turned into jade. Of course, when your Uncle Lisi and Uncle Shen and I were fighting with Old Rod Li, we weren't thinking of making a name for ourselves. We just couldn't stand that lowlife." Hongbing gave another laugh.

After hearing this, Ergou understood what made someone a gangland big brother, and why Zhao Hongbing hasn't been involved in fights for ten years. He also knew why Hongbing's businesses had no relationships with underworld organizations, and why, when the city's underworld gathers, Hongbing is always seated in the middle. He understood why the top gang leaders always offered toasts and light cigarettes for 'Big Brother Hongbing'. It wasn't just because Zhao Hongbing had never engaged in any really heinous activities; clearly, his philosophy of life had served him well.

Old Rod Li lacked Zhao Hongbing's intelligence. Back then he was jade, but after the rumble outside the Purple Moon, he was constantly thinking about how he was going to mix with Zhao Hongbing's porcelain.

Zhao Hongbing underwent an emergency operation at the city's No. 1 Hospital. By the next day he was out of danger, and was recovering in a private room on the fourth floor that the elder Mr. Zhao had arranged for him. Xiaoji was less compromised by his injury, but he still had to be admitted for treatment and was in a ward on the second floor. This was the third time Xiaoji had been admitted in less than a year. After so much time in the hospital, he'd gained a good understanding of external injuries, and was able to discuss treatment options with the doctors.

Little Beijing worried that Old Rod Li would come to the hospital for a last hit. So, he borrowed the assault rifle captured from Gourdy and guarded Zhao Hongbing's bedside day and night. When Ergou went to visit Hongbing on his third day in the hospital, he found that Hongbing's forehead was burning hot. Little Beijing looked wan and thin, and was taciturn compared with his usual exuberance.

"If Old Rod Li comes, I'll kill him!" Little Beijing said more than once at Hongbing's bedside.

"Shen, we'll get our revenge for sure, but it'll depend on the circumstances," Lisi advised him.

"If he doesn't come here, we'll wait until Hongbing has recovered and let him deal with it himself," said Little Beijing.

"Go back to the hotel, Shen. No one's been there for days. It's a complete mess," Lisi said. "I'll keep an eye on things here. How about that? Can you trust me?" Lisi was just as good a fighter as Little Beijing.

"But what about your business?" Little Beijing asked.

"I don't have much to do right now," Lisi said. "It's too cold to put the pool tables out, and Feisi can deal with the recycling stall on his own."

Among the eight gang brothers, Lisi's character was most like Zhao Hongbing's. Both were steady, fair-minded men of few words, who valued the code of brotherhood. But Lisi was a dirtier fighter than Hongbing, and more vengeful. The fact that he waited outside Tiger's door all night in freezing weather was a testament to his ruthless forbearance. In the 1990s, there was a saying in the underworld that it was better to offend Big Brother Hongbing than Brother Lisi. The greatest similarity between the two men was that apart from fighting, they refused to engage in any illegal activity. Xiaoji, Feisi, and Sun Dawei, on the other hand, would do anything as long as it wasn't outrageously evil. When Xiaoji and the others went grave-digging, Lisi would rather offend them than go along.

Old Rod Li's guys came to the hospital less than an hour after Little Beijing and Ergou left. They didn't go for Hongbing first, but rather for Xiaoji on the second floor.

Somehow they'd learned which hospital Hongbing and Xiaoji had been admitted to, but not which floor they were on, nor that they weren't together. They finally found Xiaoji after asking a duty nurse on the second floor.

Four of them came to the hospital led by Quint, who was still limping after being stabbed by Little Beijing. Quint was carrying an assault rifle, and one of the brothers with him was armed with a shotgun, while the two others carried triangular blades. Although fully armed, they didn't come to kill Hongbing. They only wanted to stab him a few times to avenge Old Rod Li. The guns were just there for intimidation, and would only be fired if absolutely necessary.

They say that when Quint and the others entered the ward, Xiaoji was playing a game of chess with another patient. None of the others were protecting him; he hadn't been badly injured, and everyone expected Old Rod Li to target Zhao Hongbing.

"Which one is Ji Donghai?" Quint asked.

Xiaoji didn't even raise his head. He could tell from the voice that someone had come for a last hit.

"Ji Donghai's next door," said Xiaoji, pointing left as he continued to play chess.

"Thanks, brother." Quint hadn't been at the fight outside the Purple Moon and didn't know what Xiaoji looked like, so he went where he pointed.

As soon as the door closed, Xiaoji gritted his teeth against the pain, then ran to the window and jumped out. Although it was a fairly hard fall from the second floor, he managed not to break a leg, and rolled into a standing position.

"Hongbing! Old Rod Li's guys are here!" Xiaoji yelled as he began running toward the infectious disease ward behind the hospital's inpatient department. He knew the lie of the land; a few steps would take him to the hospital's rear exit, where no one could catch up with him.

Although the semi-conscious Zhao Hongbing couldn't hear Xiaoji yelling, Quint could.

"Shit! We got tricked!" he said furiously.

Bursting into Xiaoji's hospital room, he pushed open the window and fired his assault rifle in the direction of Xiaoji's voice. The darkness prevented him from hitting his target.

Up in Hongbing's hospital room, Lisi clearly heard the gun's report. While most people might have mistaken the sound for a firecracker, the veteran soldier recognized it immediately. Grabbing the rifle that Little Beijing had left behind, he ran out of the hospital room toward the second floor, knowing that Xiaoji must be in trouble.

"Go to the third floor! Zhao Hongbing must be there," said Quint as he led his gang up the stairs.

Lisi had just reached the third floor when he heard

hurried footsteps. He immediately knew it was them. They were coming for Zhao Hongbing. There was no way he could get Hongbing out in time; worse still, there was no place for them to go. He would just have to fight it out. Taking the initiative would give him the upper hand.

To Lisi's surprise, the men didn't continue to the fourth floor. Instead they went to the third-floor duty nurse and asked for a patient named Zhao Hongbing. When he saw them go to the desk, Lisi decided to wait for them in the stairwell. This provided him with a wall for cover as well as an escape route – a location from which he could attack, defend, and retreat. The men would certainly take this staircase to the fourth floor. Indeed, a minute later, the men left the duty nurse's desk and began walking toward the staircase. "Zhao Hongbing must be on the fourth floor," Lisi heard one of them say.

It looked like a bunch of rural thugs who couldn't even hit a rabbit were going to have a shoot-out with a discharged PLA veteran.

Lisi listened to the sound of their footsteps. When he judged that they were about fifteen yards from the stairway entrance, he leveled his gun and poked his head around the corner. He knew that a hunting rifle was not the same as a military rifle. Its accuracy couldn't be relied on beyond twenty yards, no matter how well he aimed. In any case, Lisi didn't want to kill anyone unless absolutely necessary, and certainly not because of bad aim.

Bang! Quint and the others were taken completely by surprise by the sound. Lisi's bullet hit the leg of the guy next to Quint, and caused him to drop the shotgun he was carrying. From a distance of fifteen yards, Lisi could pick them off one by one.

"Fuck! We're ambushed!" yelled Quint. He dragged his wounded brother into the hospital room on the right, which held only one elderly man. Lisi later joked that Quint's yelling made him feel like he was in the middle of the TV series *Wiping Out the Bandits on Wulong Mountain.*

Gripping his gun, Lisi crouched down and ran toward the room where Quint and his guys had taken refuge. Standing next to the doorway, he calmly listened for footsteps inside so he could determine where to shoot. About five seconds later, Lisi fired through the door, aiming low to avoid a fatal wound. Lisi's aim and hearing were both accurate. He hit his target, which turned out to be Quint's calf.

Someone inside also fired a shot through the door, but had no hope of hitting Lisi, who was pressed against the wall. Lisi fired again into the room, but this time it was a wild shot intended merely to cause panic.

Afterwards, Little Beijing and Zhao Hongbing had nothing but praise for how Lisi had run down from the fourth floor and bunked down in the third-floor stairwell. He had launched a surprise attack, advanced rapidly toward the enemy, and fired through the door. "If I'd been there, I may have been able to chase them off, but I wouldn't have managed it as nicely as Lisi," said the normally arrogant Little Beijing.

And indeed, Lisi's last shot sent Quint and his guys leaping from the window. Xiaoji had only jumped from the second floor. However, while Quint and others leaped from the third floor, they were lucky enough to have their fall broken by the roof of a bicycle shed.

This showdown was a great boost to Lisi's reputation.

After confirming that his opponents had fled, Lisi hid the gun in his shirt and went to Xiaoji's room on the second floor.

"Where's Xiaoji?" Lisi asked with a smile, as if nothing had happened.

"He just jumped out the window!" said Xiaoji's roommate.

"Is he all right?"

"He's fine. Even with a wounded leg, that kid can run faster than most!"

"All right, better go."

Lisi sauntered calmly out of the room and then ran like crazy. He knew that with so many shots fired in a hospital, the police must be on their way.

CHAPTER 31

Lowlife Hood

AN HOUR AFTER LISI FLED, the police came to question Zhao Hongbing. A third-floor duty nurse had reported the altercation.

The questions the policemen asked indicated that the nurse must have said something like this:

"First, four men came in here and asked if there was a patient named Zhao Hongbing on the third floor. I checked our records and saw there was no such person, so they turned and walked away. Less than half a minute later I heard gunfire. When I went out to look, I saw a man with a gun rushing toward Room 308. He fired into the room, and I was so scared that I jumped back. I didn't see his face, but he was very agile and looked even more professional than what you see on TV. You could tell he was trained."

"What's your name?" the police asked Zhao Hongbing.

Hongbing told them. He was still groggy, and looked like he might pass out at any moment.

"There was a shoot-out downstairs just now. Do you know anything about it?"

"No."

"How did you get injured? The doctor says you were stabbed twice, and also shot."

"I was attacked."

"Who attacked you?"

"I don't know."

"Do you know why you were attacked?"

"No."

"Don't keep saying you don't know. We're responsible for your safety."

"I really don't know." Zhao Hongbing spoke with great effort.

"Don't think saying you don't know will keep us from cracking the case."

"I really don't know."

The police couldn't keep questioning a man who was so badly injured. As their frustration mounted, an even more infuriating person appeared – Little Beijing. Upon returning to the hotel, he'd found a letter from Gao Huan. In spite of his weariness, he'd decided to cheer Hongbing up by bringing it to the hospital.

"Hey! Hello there, officers!" he said, giving a salute.

"Who are you?"

"I'm an old war buddy of Zhao Hongbing's."

"You don't sound like a local."

"I'm from Beijing."

"Why are you in town?"

"I'm in business with Zhao Hongbing here. We run a hotel next to the train station, don't you know? We don't have prostitutes, but we can tell you who does," said Little Beijing, smiling and sitting down at Hongbing's side.

"We're with the criminal squad. We're investigating a

shootout that just happened here. Whether you're involved in prostitution or not is no concern of ours."

"Come on, now. If I were a hooker, who would want me?" Little Beijing was startled to hear there'd been a gunfight, but he maintained his composure.

"Okay, enough of that. You said you're an old war buddy of Zhao Hongbing's. Were you in the army?"

"Yes. I enlisted in 1982 and was demobilized in 1985. Were you in the Army?"

"Yes."

On hearing Little Beijing's reply, the policeman asking the question nodded at the officer beside him.

"Zhao Hongbing and I were both scouts. How about you?" Little Beijing always enjoyed sucking up to people.

"Same as you. Scouts. Do you have any other old comrades-in-arms around here?"

"Sadly, no. Several in our squad gave their lives and some are still in the army; only Zhao Hongbing and I were demobilized." Cynical as Little Beijing was, he was uncomfortable talking about his sacrificed comrades.

"Did you know there was a shoot-out on the third floor?"

"There was a shoot-out? I had no idea! What happened? Did anyone die? Have the culprits been arrested? Do you want me to help catch them?" Behind Little Beijing's garrulousness was a genuine desire to find out exactly what happened. He was sure that Lisi must have fought with Old Rod Li.

"No, thanks. We'll manage. But from what we've learned, some of them came here looking for Zhao Hongbing."

"Oh, really? Then officers, you have to protect Zhao Hongbing."

"Mm. We suspect that another person involved is an associate of yours. How did Zhao Hongbing get injured?"

"You suspect us? That's just wrong! I went back to the hotel and was bringing this letter to Zhao Hongbing. You can ask the attendant at our hotel. Don't make false accusations!" Little Beijing looked dreadfully affronted.

"I didn't say it was you. I was asking you how Zhao Hongbing got injured."

"Some bad guys attacked him. You have to catch them!"

From what the policemen said, Little Beijing could tell they hadn't caught Lisi. This relieved him greatly.

"Who attacked him and put him in this condition?"

"I don't know." While Little Beijing's impersonation of a model citizen might have duped the average person, these eagle-eyed policemen weren't fooled.

"Why didn't you report it to the police?"

"Oh, I completely forgot about that part! Zhao Hongbing's only just gotten out of danger, and I was planning to report it one of these days. How about if I go down to the station first thing tomorrow morning? Last time when a guest at our hotel misplaced some money, I reported it. Your officers came and questioned me for two hours, then wrote up a report and took fingerprints, but you never did catch the thief, did you? There was another time when a guest in our hotel misplaced a wristwatch, and I reported it and..."

"That's enough. We'll come back in a few days when Zhao Hongbing has further recovered. But you come to the station tomorrow morning and file a report. We don't want to disturb the rest of a sick man."

"Hey, are you leaving already? That watch my guest lost..." Little Beijing looked as if he wanted to keep going.

"That's not our case. Don't forget to come to the station tomorrow!"

"Goodbye, officers!"

"And that's enough shoe-shining," said the cop, perturbed by Little Beijing's smarm.

Right after the policemen left, Zhao Hongbing's sister arrived.

"Hongyan, you're here! I was just talking to Hongbing about you, I was saying..." Little Beijing began rambling again.

"You brat! Were you giving those policemen a hard time?"

"Were you eavesdropping?"

"Who has time for that! When I came in just now, I heard the policemen saying, 'That kid doesn't know how to shut up!' So I knew it had to be you."

"Those policemen ran into some trouble and they wanted to ask my advice, and I naturally wanted to help them crack the case. We know it's a tough job being a cop."

"Then why don't you try giving them less work? I'm begging you...Don't get into any more trouble, please! This is too much!" Hongyan had started looking very fragile lately.

"Yes, I promise. But under one condition."

"What?"

"Let me kiss you, just once." Little Beijing was always mesmerized by the sight of Hongyan's peach-like complexion.

"If you really want a kiss, I'll buy you a nice old sow and you can kiss her all you want."

"But you're so much prettier than an old sow," said Little Beijing with complete sincerity.

"What on earth are you saying?" Hongyan was growing peeved.

"Sorry, I mean..." said Little Beijing, giving himself a smack in the mouth. "I mean you're not as pretty as an old sow."

"You...!"

The next day, Little Beijing went to the police crime squad to "report" the attack on Zhao Hongbing. Inevitably, he talked a lot of rubbish and wasted a great many police hours. The police found no victim. Since no one had died in the shoot-out and there was inadequate evidence to connect it to Zhao Hongbing, the matter finally faded away.

The letter Gao Huan wrote to Zhao Hongbing was in the form of a chain of paper hearts, and reading it caused Hongbing considerable vexation. Before, while his right hand was missing three fingertips, he could still fold paper without difficulty. However, after being wounded again by the shotgun, he could only use his other hand, and even opening a letter was impossible. Hongbing saved every letter that Gao Huan wrote to him. The paper hearts were simple in form, but unfolding them was much more complicated; he was afraid he would tear them. After repeated failed attempts, he finally asked Little Beijing to open the letter for him the next evening. Ergou was present at the time. After opening the chain of hearts, Little Beijing read out the letter expressively:

"'It's been a month since we parted, and how I miss you! Yesterday I walked in the Fragrant Hills. Watching the wild geese fly south in the autumn wind, I wondered if you were also watching them. In these Fragrant Hills, so far from home, the wind, rain, trees and flowers were rich with the scent of autumn. At least you and I can gaze at the same autumn moon...'" Pausing in his emotive reading, Little Beijing groaned, "How disgusting!" Zhao Hongbing flushed scarlet with embarrassment, yet had no choice but to let Little Beijing keep reading.

After receiving the letter, Zhao Hongbing began to worry. Now that he was effectively one-handed, how could he send a chain of hearts back to Gao Huan? He certainly couldn't tell her that he'd been injured. Hongbing had Little Beijing fold a chain of hearts for him. But as clever as Little Beijing was, he was hopeless at paper folding. It took him a week to come up with something approaching Gao Huan's creation. Even then, the middle section was too narrow.

"Now that I've learned how to make a chain of hearts, I'll write a letter to Hongyan," said Little Beijing excitedly.

"With your sloppy penmanship, don't bother," said Zhao Hongbing from his hospital bed, still stinging from Little Beijing's earlier ridicule.

"I can practice a few times and then rewrite it. I want to write to her about national events and philosophy."

"Oh, get lost!" Hongbing scoffed.

Ergou never found out whether Little Beijing actually wrote to Hongyan, but he knows that he really did buy a copy book and practiced his penmanship. Now his calligraphy is bold and flowing, and almost professional.

After the shootout, all of Old Rod Li's top lieutenants were injured, and he couldn't organize the manpower to launch a new counterattack against Zhao Hongbing. Hongbing himself was still confined to a hospital bed and powerless to take revenge. This enforced truce lasted a month.

A month later, Old Rod Li's underling Quint shattered not only the peace, but also the rules and customs of the underworld. They say Quint was taking revenge on his own behalf rather than for Old Rod Li.

Sometime around the summer of 1994, Zhao Hongbing's third sister took Ergou to a new outdoor swimming pool that had been opened by the municipal sports committee. On that day, Hongyan wore a black bikini. Few women in the city dared to wear such revealing swimwear, but Hongyan was always on top of current fashions and international trends. She had bought a bikini that she'd seen a girl wearing in a calendar photo. As soon as she arrived at the swimming pool, she attracted the gaze of nearly every man there. But five minutes later, no one was looking at her anymore, because Quint had arrived.

Already very much down on his luck by 1994, Quint made a living driving a pedicab, and he had snuck into the pool without paying. Stripping down to a faded pair of briefs, he leaped into the water with a splash. Everyone was amazed to see him carrying a washcloth. As they watched in mute horror, he used the washcloth to scour little rolls of filth from his body. The pool cleared out in a matter of minutes, leaving Quint there alone to use it as his bathtub. He showed not the least anxiety or embarrassment as he continued to scrub himself.

Zhao Hongyan never went to that pool again.

This incident shows that Quint was not only crude and ignorant, but lacked even the most basic decency. How could anyone else swim in the pool once he'd washed himself in it?

Evil Huang was nothing great, but at least the guy could strike a pose; Quint didn't even try. It was no surprise that someone like him would break the underworld code, but he's sure to have regretted it afterward.

In the month after the shootout, the only slightly wounded Quint asked around and learned that the guy who had shot at him was Lisi. Although intimidated by Lisi's shooting skills, he craved revenge, so what could he do? He came up with the underhanded method of going after Lisi's family. Before this, local hoodlums had never gone after the families of their antagonists; that was considered despicable behavior. But Quint didn't care.

When Quint went to Lisi's home, only Lisi's elder brother was there. It was noon, and the brother had come home from work to eat lunch. He had just finished cooking when he heard glass breaking.

"Who's that?" Thinking it must be a naughty neighbor kid, Lisi's brother walked to the courtyard and opened the door.

"It was me!" Quint glared at him with fearless stupidity. Four street punks were standing behind him.

"What are you doing smashing my window?"

"Smashing your window? I'll smash you! How are you related to Lisi?"

"I'm his big brother."

"Well, I'm going to smash Lisi's big brother."

Quint walked up and cuffed him around the ear. He didn't take it lying down, and cuffed Quint right back. The gangsters surrounded him and attacked. Lisi's brother wasn't a skilled fighter like Lisi, and he was soon flat on the ground with his front tooth knocked out.

Lisi found out about it that afternoon. He gazed silently at his injured brother and then went off to the hospital to see Zhao Hongbing.

"Quint went to my home and beat up my brother," he said, eyes blazing.

"What's he playing at? Is he a man? That's about as low as it gets!" said Hongbing, likewise enraged.

"I've never seen the likes of it."

"When I get out of the hospital, we'll go after him together." Zhao Hongbing had almost fully recovered, but he still needed more bed rest.

"No. I have to take care of this myself. I just wanted to let you know."

"Don't be rash. Wait till I get out, and we'll fix him for good."

"No can do," Lisi sad, then left.

"Be careful!" Seeing the mood Lisi was in, Zhao Hongbing knew Quint was in for it.

"I know how far to go!" Lisi called back to him.

Quint may not have known that he'd crossed Lisi's red line. If it was Lisi himself he had beaten, the consequences may have been less serious. But going after his brother was intolerable. Everyone has his bottom line. Once it's crossed, anything can happen.

CHAPTER 32

A Tooth for a Tooth

LISI DIDN'T ASK ANYONE FOR help. He felt he could handle the matter himself. Feisi insisted on going with him, but Lisi absolutely refused. Feisi knew Lisi's ferocious character, and probably worried that once he started fighting, even more trouble would ensue. The gang brothers who looked after Lisi's pool tables were also outraged on his behalf and shouted that they would go with Lisi to take revenge, but Lisi refused them all. What he asked was for them to track Quint down. Lisi wanted to avenge his brother with his own hands.

Lisi was the most patient and most vengeful person Ergou had ever met. For the sake of revenge, he could tolerate more than almost anyone else. His planning was deliberate and nearly flawless.

If the matter had been left to Zhang Yue, he would have taken care of Quint with a single stab of his knife. Feisi would have gone straight to Quint's home and had it out with him, while Zhao Hongbing would have openly challenged him to a fight. Sun Dawei would have wept and wailed and gotten others to take revenge for him, while Li Wu would have resorted to an underhanded scheme. As for Xiaoji and Little Beijing...

Ergou doesn't know what kind of lousy ideas those two would come up with, but he's sure that no one would have waited patiently for several days the way Lisi did, just for the opportunity to launch a surprise attack on Quint.

One week later, one of Lisi's young gang brothers told him that Quint had been frequenting a guest house with a prostitute over the last few days. Lisi nodded and said nothing.

Ergou firmly believes in the saying "A barking dog never bites, and a dog that bites doesn't bark". A dog that really wants to bite someone focuses all his attention on that and doesn't waste time barking. As a young boy, Ergou saw lots of hoodlums threaten and flaunt their strength, but when push came to shove they were the most useless, like Evil Huang and Railway. People like Zhang Yue, Lisi, and Feisi didn't say much – if anything – before a fight. They never threatened anyone, but once they moved, they struck terror to the heart.

Lisi was confident that he could beat Quint and his band of street punks, but he didn't want to take unnecessary risks. He wanted to catch Quint off guard, when he could be sure of taking him down. They used to say in the underworld back then, "Brother Lisi likes a sneak attack". Later, some wondered if Lisi had made a rash move as a scout on the frontline that had entailed loss, and had been criticized by his senior officer; perhaps the lasting shadow this cast over him had made him a patient man.

Lisi had some misgivings about the assault rifle Quint carried with him, so he had to launch a rear attack.

That day, Lisi confirmed that Quint and the prostitute had gone to the guest house. The next morning at seven o'clock, Lisi took up a position near the doorway of a little restaurant across the street from the guest house, ordering some cold dishes; he knew that Quint would come out, but he didn't know when, and hot food was sure to get cold. After ordering, he called for a bottle of sorghum liquor and then asked for the bill.

The restaurant proprietor had never seen such an odd customer – he'd ordered cold dishes and liquor first thing in the morning, and then paid before he finished eating.

Lisi sat there chain smoking and sipping his liquor, his eyes never leaving the door of the guest house. By the time Quint and the prostitute came out, it was three o'clock in the afternoon; the heavy-drinking Lisi had only drunk about three ounces of liquor.

He jumped up and grabbed the extra-large and very thick glass ashtray that he'd noticed on the table. "Boss, I'm just going to borrow this for a minute," he said as he ran out of the door.

"Sure, go ahead!" said the proprietor with a wondering shake of his head. It never occurred to him that Lisi would use the ashtray to knock someone's teeth out.

Quint's prostitute headed north, apparently to get something to eat. Lisi quickly came up behind Quint and brought the ashtray down hard on the nape of his neck while kicking him in the ankle and sending him tumbling to the ground.

Later Ergou asked Lisi, "Why do you always hit people at the nape of neck?"

"Back when I was a solder, our instructor told us that this is where a person's nervous system is most concentrated. If you want to subdue someone without killing him, that's the best place to aim a blow."

"And why do you like to kick people in the knee and ankle?"

"The purpose of fighting isn't to show off but to seriously injure or immobilize your opponent. The knee and ankle are the weakest of the human body's resistance points, so they're the best choices."

After felling Quint, Lisi quickly pinned down his left shoulder with his knee. With a snap, he twisted both of Quint's arms out of joint, quickly depriving him of all power to resist. "Do you know who I am?" Lisi asked, jerking Quint's head up by the hair.

"No," said Quint stubbornly.

"Then let me tell you that it's Lisi who's knocking your teeth out. Today it's your teeth, but next time it'll be your life!"

Lisi said no more. He raised the ashtray and brought it down on Quint's mouth.

Afterwards it was learned that Quint's lower jaw was broken, his nose was smashed, and he lost nine teeth.

Lisi beat Quint into submission. However stupid and fearless Quint may have been in the past, he was thoroughly cowed after the beating. From then on, Quint seldom took part in any street fights. He gradually withdrew from Old Rod Li's gang.

In a way, Lisi saved Quint. If he'd continued on his trajectory, likely as not, the only way to see him now would be to visit the Nanshan Hill Public Cemetery.

After the incident, Lisi became even more famous – second only to Zhao Hongbing in their gang. When anyone mentioned Hongbing and his friends, it was as "Zhao Hongbing and Lisi's gang".

While Hongbing was recovering from his injuries, Zhang Yue was sentenced to two years in prison. Soon after Lisi beat up Quint, Gao Huan's classmate Li Yang went to see Zhao Hongbing in the hospital.

"Have you been in touch with Gao Huan?" she asked. She was one of the girls who had been at the school athletic field that day – the only one who hadn't gone on to college.

"Yes," Zhao Hongbing said. "She's doing great."

"I've also been in touch with her. Did you know that Zhang Yue was sentenced?" Li Yang had only gone out to dinner once with Zhang Yue, but she had become so fond of him that she was determined to marry no one else.

"I heard. But it's just two years, and he's already served half a year in detention. He'll be out in just over a year."

"I went to see him at the No. 6 Detention Center a few days ago. He seems to be doing well."

"I'll go visit him once I'm discharged. I really miss him. I was the one who made him turn himself in. I still don't know if it was the right thing to do."

"No, it was."

"Well, I'll go see him as soon as I'm out."

Ten days later, when Zhao Hongbing was discharged from the hospital, the first thing he did was visit Zhang Yue.

Zhang Yue had always been fair skinned, but in jail he'd become paler. Almost bloodless. But he seemed to have been treated well enough.

"Great to see you!" he said when Hongbing arrived.

"How are you doing?" Hongbing asked with a grin.

"A few days ago Li Yang came to see me and said you've had some problems. Just wait 'til I get out!"

"My situation is pretty much taken care of. How are things for you in here? Has anyone been picking on you?"

"Picking on me?" Zhang Yue laughed.

Zhao Hongbing laughed along with him, knowing that anyone who picked on Zhang Yue was unlikely to come out alive.

"Don't get in trouble. Reform yourself," Zhao Hongbing advised him.

Hongbing wasn't that easygoing himself, but he was much more rational than Zhang Yue, and was always trying to keep him out of trouble through gentle nagging.

"I'm staying out of trouble and completely submitting to the education of the Party and the government," said Zhang Yue ironically. "I may be promoted to head of a brigade pretty soon."

"Good luck!"

After this visit, Zhao Hongbing said to Little Beijing, "I wonder why Zhang Yue's eyes looked so crafty and malicious this time."

"You mean they didn't look crafty and malicious before?" asked Little Beijing. He was practicing his calligraphy and didn't even bother to raise his head.

Part Six

Negotiation

CHAPTER 33

Ceasefire

Apparently, Quint was admitted to the hospital just as Evil Huang was having his cast removed. They looked at each other in mute sorrow.

"If things keep on this way, someone's going to end up dead," said Old Rod Li from Quint's bedside.

"Then what should we do, Big Brother?" Evil Huang had been beaten into submission and hoped a truce could be called as soon as possible.

"I'll talk with them about calling it quits. Neither side is getting anywhere this way, and the PSB's going to start coming around."

Old Rod Li still had a killer's nerve, but he only killed for money and had nothing to gain from fighting Zhao Hongbing and his gang. Since the shoot-out at the hospital, Old Rod Li had decided that Zhao Hongbing's crew was too hard to handle. Seeing Quint in this state truly gave him pause.

"Yeah, that seems best," sighed Evil Huang.

"Set up a time to talk with them, all right?"

"Me?" Evil Huang's legs trembled at the very thought of seeing Zhao Hongbing and Little Beijing again.

"You have more culture than anyone else in our crew. If you don't go, who will?" said Old Rod Li, salving Evil's fear with flattery.

"Oh, come on..." said Evil Huang, but he was clearly pleased.

"It's true. You're the most cultured."

"Well, I do have some culture... All right, I'll go."

Evil Huang loved to hear people say he was cultured, and flattery prevailed over his fear of Little Beijing and Zhao Hongbing.

Zhao Hongbing was delighted to hear that Old Rod Li wanted to negotiate with him. When all was said and done, he'd spent the past half year on tenterhooks, and it wasn't a great feeling. Besides that, they'd gained the advantage through their series of fights, having revenged themselves and given a licking to those who deserved it. A ceasefire was just what Zhao Hongbing wanted right then.

That evening, the "sixth rumble discussion meeting" was held in a jubilant atmosphere. By the standards of the 1980s, Zhao Hongbing and his friends were definitely well off. Business was booming at the hotel, and the recycling stall was flourishing. Even Sun Dawei's book stall was pulling in a reasonable income. So when they went out to eat, it was at the best restaurant in town.

The main purpose of the meeting was to discuss what was referred to as the "current situation of the enemy and us" in political parlance. They would also choose their negotiator and establish the general orientation, while summing up their battle with Old Rod Li. It was decided that Liu Haizhu, Gourdy, and the others would also be invited and allowed to speak at the meeting.

As for the current situation, Old Rod Li's gang had sustained heavy injuries: Tudou had been sent to the provincial capital for treatment, Evil Huang was still going around on crutches and Quint had been admitted to the hospital a short time ago. Although Old Rod Li himself had largely recovered from his wounds, too many of his lieutenants were incapacitated for him to organize the manpower for a counterattack any time soon.

Old Rod Li's gang was physically and mentally exhausted. After so many fights in less than half a year, Old Rod had probably had enough of living in a state of high anxiety, and his underlings Evil Huang and Quint had been beaten into complete submission.

Zhao Hongbing's side had sustained injuries too. However, Hongbing and Xiaoji had basically recovered from the fight outside the Purple Moon. If another fight came up, everyone would be able to take part. As for their morale, Lisi's blocking action at the hospital and his surprise attack on Quint outside the guesthouse had greatly bolstered spirits. In general, the current situation was very much in their favor, and even though they'd started out at a distinct disadvantage, Brother Liu Haizhu's support of their battle strategy had put them in a windward position.

As for electing a negotiator, the requirements were to be articulate and thick-skinned. Candidates must not have experienced any conflicts with the other party, so as to avoid a clash during the negotiation. The negotiating principles were absolutely no compensation for the other side's medical fees, and Old Rod Li had to apologize to Xiaoji. After discussion, everyone agreed that Sun Dawei was the most appropriate choice. "Of all of us, you're the best talker," Zhao Hongbing said to him.

"Hey, I'm all right, but Prince Shen is even better!" said Sun Dawei modestly.

"But Shen already beat up Evil Huang and stabbed Quint," Lisi said. "So he's not a good choice."

"Yeah, I see what you mean. Okay, I'll go." In fact, Sun Dawei loved doing this sort of thing; his modesty was just for show.

The negotiation was set for the evening of the Winter Solstice. Sun Dawei arranged to meet Evil Huang at a dumpling restaurant. They say that on the night of the negotiation, fate arranged for a heavy snowfall that lent a desolate atmosphere to this memorable contest.

A solitary figure headed toward the shabby dumpling restaurant through the snow. Streetlamps revealed the vague image of a sturdy figure in army boots and the kind of tobacco brown overcoat popular in the 1980s. From behind, Sun Dawei could have been mistaken for Xu Wenqiang, the character played by Chow Yun-fat in *The Bund*.

A squeal of brakes signaled the arrival of a taxi. The door opened and a walking stick poked out. Huang had arrived.

"Evil Huang?"

"Yeah. Who are you?"

"Sun Dawei."

A brainwave passed between the two poseurs. They smiled at each other and walked into the restaurant together. Sun Dawei's shoulders were covered with snow. He blew lightly at it, relieved that it wasn't blood.

CHAPTER 34

Burying the Hatchet

OUTSIDE THE WINDOW, THE SNOW stopped falling but the north wind continued to moan. The old dumpling restaurant was warmed by its roaring stove.

"How's it going?" said Evil Huang, smiling at Sun Dawei with narrowed eyes as he brushed the snow from his coat.

"So we meet at last." Sun smiled back. He'd memorized a couple of opening lines for this occasion, but unable to recall them, he fell back on platitudes.

"You guys want garlic sauce?" the waiter asked.

"No," they answered simultaneously.

"Major halitosis," remarked Evil Huang.

"You said it!" smirked Sun Dawei.

"What are you drinking?" the waiter asked.

"Single malt pulp liquor from the brewery."

"Good choice! You're a man who knows his liquor."

In 1987, anyone who wanted to look like a big shot went for 70 proof liquor.

"It's good booze, but I don't know how much I can handle." Evil Huang appeared lost in thought as he gazed at the tumbler of viscous spirits.

"I have a classical allusion for you. May I?"

"Please!"

"A pony carrying a sack of table salt to the market came to a river. The pony asked an old water buffalo along the river bank how deep the water was. The buffalo said the stream was shallow – less than knee deep. The pony took his word for it and was about to cross the river when a rat stopped him. The rat told the pony the river was very deep, and one of his friends had drowned in it just a few days before. Now the pony didn't know who to believe, so he decided to go home and ask his mother. When he got home, the pony told his mother of his experience at the river. His mother said, 'Child, if you want to know how deep the water is, shouldn't you test it yourself?' The pony trusted his mother and returned to the river. He no longer heeded the buffalo's reassurance or the rat's warning, and proceeded to cross, step by careful step. He found that the river was neither as shallow as the buffalo claimed, nor as deep as the rat had said."

With a smile, Sun Dawei concluded his story, which in fact was "The Pony Crosses the River" from his elementary school text book.

"Good story," said Evil with a short laugh. "Sounds familiar somehow. You're right, I shouldn't listen to other people. I'll just have to decide for myself how much I can drink."

Sun Dawei smiled and nodded silently.

"I'm a friend of Old Rod Li's. I hope to become friends with you, too."

"A new friend is like a new path."

"How right you are. Your story reminds me of another tale: A crow was thirsty and went looking for water. He saw a bottle that had water in it, but the neck was too long and narrow for him to reach it. What could he do? The crow saw a lot of pebbles nearby, and he thought of a way. He dropped the pebbles one by one into the bottle, until the water inside rose high enough for him to drink it."

Evil Huang had apparently also mastered his first-grade lessons. His tale was Aesop's "The Crow and the Pitcher".

"What does it mean?" Dawei asked.

"When the crow couldn't get to the water, he thought of pebbles. If you were a crow, one more friend would be one more pebble." The allusion was somewhat strained, but Evil Huang's flexible application worked.

"Haha! I see."

"There've been some misunderstandings between us, but we can still be friends. Right?"

"Right. We should put the past behind us. But your brother started it by stabbing Xiaoji..."

"Tudou is in a hospital in Beijing as we speak. Quint's got a smashed jaw, and Brother Rod got slashed twice. As you can see, I'm still using a cane. Wouldn't you say you guys have pretty much evened the score?"

"Brother Huang, every grievance starts somewhere. Brother Rod stabbed Xiaoji first, and all he got was payback."

"And by that you mean...?"

"Okay, let me tell you another story: A little goat made friends with a chick, who invited him to eat bugs. The little goat said, 'Thank you, but I don't eat bugs'. The little goat made friends with a kitten, who invited him to eat minnows. The little goat said, 'Thank you, but I don't eat minnows'. The little goat made friends with a puppy, who invited him to eat bones. The little goat said, 'Thank you, but I don't eat bones'. The little goat made friends with a calf, who invited him to eat grass. The little goat said, 'Thank you!' And the two of them ate grass together."

It was obvious that Sun Dawei had been a better student than Evil Huang in first grade.

"What's your point, Dawei?"

"You may not know what we want. We want to eat grass, but you're giving us bugs, minnows, and bones."

"So what exactly do you want?"

"Get Brother Rod to apologize to Xiaoji. If we're going to be friends, an apology shouldn't be a big deal."

"That's..."

"If he doesn't want to apologize to Xiaoji, that's also all right."

"How do you mean?"

"Then we'll just keep fighting," said Sun Dawei with a smile.

"Well... I'll have to go back and discuss it with Big Brother Li."

"If I may offer a bit of advice, also in the form of a literary allusion: A kitten and an old cat went to the riverside to catch fish. The kitten was half-hearted about it, and kept running off to chase dragonflies and butterflies. He didn't end up catching anything. The old cat told him, 'You have to be wholehearted in what you do, or you'll never catch fish'. So the kitten set his mind to it, and sure enough he caught one. This tells us that you should focus on your antiques business and not waste your time on stuff like fighting, otherwise you won't get anywhere!"

Sun Dawei was good at this.

Both guys were largely illiterate. However, Sun Dawei was able to recite three classic tales, while Evil Huang could only muster up 'The Crow and the Pitcher'. That was the difference.

Sun Dawei left with a smile on his face. However, the street was mostly empty, and under the pale yellow street lamps, a feeling of desolation welled up inside him. A master is always lonely.

A week after Sun Dawei and Evil Huang held their negotiation, Old Rod Li went to the recycling stall and apologized to Xiaoji.

For the sake of a single sentence – "I'm sorry, brother. I acted on impulse" – nine people on both sides paid the price of serious injury. Was it worth it?

After this matter passed, everyone was able to relax and go back to business. A year after the hotel made its turn for the better, Zhao Hongbing and Little Beijing had more than 80,000 *yuan* put away. They needed to renew their contract to run the hotel. Zhao Hongbing had already mentioned to the director that he was planning to convert the first floor into a restaurant. Little Beijing had started making arrangements for the renovation, and construction could begin as soon as the new contract was signed.

One day just before the New Year, Lisi came to the hotel.

"Everything's finally been taken care of, and we can concentrate on business," he said.

"That's right," said Hongbing, smiling more than speaking, as usual.

"Are you planning to fit up a restaurant here?"

"Yeah. Shen's been making all the arrangements these last few days. We'll be able have our meals at home from now on."

"You guys have done really well here," Lisi said.

"You're doing all right, too, with your pool tables and the recycling stall."

"Yeah, but I haven't been able to put the pool tables out since winter started. They only make money in the summer."

"Why don't you open a pool hall? There aren't many in town right now."

"I'd like to, but I don't have the cash. Dawei asked his mom, and there's a big hall downstairs from the library that we could rent for 20,000 a year, but I don't have that much money."

"That's a good location," Zhao Hongbing said. "The rent's very reasonable."

"But where can I get the money?"

"You really want to open a pool hall there?"

"Of course! It's sure to make money. At fifty cents a cue, one table should bring in at least 30 *kuai* a day. If I have eight tables, I'll make real money." Lisi had a real head for business.

"How about this: When Shen gets back in a little while, I'll ask him how much money we'll have left after paying for the new lease and the restaurant outfitting. If there's enough left over, we can lend it to you. We should be able to come up with 20,000."

Zhao Hongbing's greatest shortcoming was his poor money sense. He never knew how much he had, and it was fortunate that the more detail-oriented Little Beijing held the purse strings.

"How about if you and Little Beijing become shareholders in the business? You could have shares in the pool hall."

"Sure. Why not? As long as you can keep the business going, Shen and I can get by on our income here."

"Let's settle it then. You and Shen will become shareholders." Lisi preferred this to borrowing such a large sum from Hongbing.

"If that's what you want!" laughed Zhao Hongbing.

After Spring Festival in 1988, Lisi finally had his own "wharf" – a pool hall.

On the third day of business, an old enemy turned up – Tiger.

CHAPTER 35

Medical Expenses

THE EIGHTH DAY OF THE Lunar New Year in 1988 was Gao Huan's birthday. Since she'd been with Zhao Hongbing throughout her winter vacation, it went without saying that they'd spend this day together as well. Zhao Hongbing invited Lisi, Sun Dawei, and the others to his restaurant to celebrate. In the northeast, during Spring Festival most people eat two meals a day – one at ten o'clock in the morning and the other at three o'clock in the afternoon. That afternoon, everyone had more than enough to drink.

Not long after Lisi left that afternoon, a young hooligan came to his pool hall demanding a game with a "table boss". Back in the 1980s, it was normal for friends to come to a pool hall and play against each other, but occasionally someone wouldn't be able to find anyone to go with. Since it wasn't much fun to play alone, pool hall proprietors usually had one or two guys hanging around who would play with unaccompanied customers. Since these guys were usually skillful players, they were known as "table bosses". The table boss at Lisi's establishment was a young brother named Wang Yu. He also took charge of the till when Lisi was away. At that time, Wang

Yu was known as one of the city's best pool players and could take even the toughest shots.

While the young hooligan was playing pool with Wang Yu, he kept swearing and cursing. It wasn't clear whether he was swearing at the ball or at Wang Yu. Wang Yu had quite a temper, but this was Big Brother Lisi's business, so he held it in. The two of them played five rounds, and Wang Yu won every time. When Wang Yu hit the winning eight-ball into the pocket, the young hooligan spoke up.

"That black eight ball is mine. What are you doing hitting it?"

"The eight ball is yours? Don't you know how to play?" Wang Yu had had enough. He could tell the kid was just a troublemaker.

"What the fuck are you talking about?" demanded the hooligan, gripping his cue and advancing toward Wang Yu.

"Do you know who owns this pool hall?" Wang Yu asked, keeping his cool. If he beat up anyone in the pool hall, Lisi would scold him when he got back.

"I don't care who owns it! You hit my eight ball into the hole, so I'm not paying. I'm outta here!" The young hooligan turned to leave.

"Stop right there! You think you can play for free?" said Wang Yu angrily.

"Fuck your mother!" The young hooligan suddenly jabbed his pool cue at Wang Yu. Wang Yu wasn't able to duck in time, and the cue split his lip open. It wasn't a serious injury, but it looked nasty. Infuriated, he swung his pool cue and brought it down hard on the young punk's head.

Wang Yu was as skilled with his fists as with a cue. He hadn't actually learned kungfu, but he was fast and fierce, and the average person was no match for him. Knowing that a long pool cue was little use at close range, he grabbed a billiard ball and smashed it against the young punk's cheek, making him see stars. Then he grabbed the punk by the hair and whacked him a few more times with the ball until his face was covered with blood.

"Now fuck off!" Wang Yu said.

"Just you wait, motherfucker!" said the punk, running off with his hands covering his face.

"Sure, I'll wait. Let's see what you do."

Two hours later, as dusk was falling, Tiger arrived with six or seven guys. Now better known as Limpy, he was unshaven and was wearing an old army coat. His hands were tucked into his sleeves as he hobbled in. He looked like he was on the skids but still had a gleam in his eye. Wang Yu realized that Tiger had sent the young punk to make trouble.

"That's him, Brother Tiger," said the punk, pointing at Wang Yu.

"He's the one who smashed you in the face with the billiard ball, is he?" Tiger asked the punk.

"That's right."

"All right, so what you do is you pick up a billiard ball and smash his face. If he fights back, I'll trash him."

The young hooligan picked up a billiard ball and advanced toward Wang Yu.

Wang Yu showed no sign of backing down. With Lisi behind him, he had no fear of Tiger. He picked up a billiard ball and watched the punk draw closer. When the two were about three feet apart, they began swinging at each other. Again, Wang Yu was faster. His billiard ball caught the punk in the eye while a nimble sidestep deflected the punk's ball to his shoulder. The young hooligan howled with pain.

"Get him!" snarled Tiger. The gangsters behind him leaped into action.

Hopelessly outnumbered, Wang Yu was soon on the ground. He wrapped his arms around his head and curled up as Lisi had taught him, covering his head with his arms and burying his face between his legs like a baby in the womb. That was how you ensured the least injuries in a fight.

"Stop right there!" Just back from dinner at Zhao Hongbing's restaurant, Lisi stood in the doorway of the pool hall. He was smart enough to see that it didn't make sense to get into a fight when the odds were against him.

"Do you remember me?" asked Tiger, his cigarette hanging from his lip as he squinted at Lisi.

"Limpy! How's that Achilles tendon?" Lisi said.

"Do you know why I came here today?" asked Tiger slowly, his hands still jammed in his sleeves.

"Looks like you came to make trouble."

"No, I came here for my medical expenses."

"Medical expenses?"

"After what you guys did to me and my brother, I didn't call the cops, and that was pretty decent of me, right?"

"Uh, sure."

"I spent half a year in bed, and now my leg is permanently disabled. Isn't it reasonable for me to come and ask for medical expenses?"

"If you want to ask for medical expenses, that's one thing, but why beat up my brother?"

"If you don't pay my medical fees, my brothers are going to play pool here every day until my expenses are paid off."

"But what if I don't pay your medical expenses, and also don't let your brothers play pool?"

"Brothers, rip up these tables for me!" As Tiger spoke, the gangsters behind him pulled out daggers and made as if to rip open the felt on the pool tables.

"Wait! Limpy, how much do you need?"

"Fifty thousand. I hear business is good these days, so you shouldn't have trouble coming up with that much. Once you hand over the medical expenses, I'll consider our account settled."

"Fifty thousand?"

"And not a penny less."

"How about if you leave and let me think about it."

"Sure, I'll give you a few days to pull the money together. I'll come back in a week to collect it."

"Okay." Lisi kept a smile on his face, but he was so angry that his teeth itched.

After Tiger left, he went back to the hotel to talk with Zhao Hongbing. Little Beijing and Gao Huan were with him, but he had drunk too much and was fast asleep in bed.

"Shen, Limpy just came to see me."

"Who's Limpy?"

"Remember that time we went to view the lanterns on National Day? You kicked that guy to the ground, and then Feisi and I trashed him later on?"

"Wasn't he called Tiger?"

"That was before Feisi trashed his leg. Now he's called Limpy."

"What does he want from you?"

"He says he wants medical expenses. The truth is, he's noticed that I'm making money, so he's blackmailing me."

"Is that guy blind? Why is he still asking for trouble? If he comes back, we'll have to pack him up again."

"That's what I was thinking. Let's get Hongbing up."

Little Beijing went outside and broke off a big icicle, then stuffed it under Zhao Hongbing's quilt. "Here's a hot water bottle for you," he said.

Hongbing gave a yell. The ice quickly sobered him up. Gao Huan broke out in laughter beside him.

"Hongbing, Tiger came today to demand medical expenses from me, and he beat up Wang Yu, too."

"Medical expenses are one thing, but why beat someone up?" said Hongbing, now wide awake.

"He says if I don't pay him, he's going to come to the pool hall every day and make trouble. If he does, how can I keep doing business?"

"It's reasonable enough for him to ask for medical expenses when you trashed him and he didn't call the police."

"Sure, but the way he's going about it is so slimy – it's pure extortion. Not only that, but he wants fifty thousand. Where will we get that kind of money?"

"We can't give him that much," Hongbing agreed. "If he'd discussed it properly with us, it would be normal for us to pay some of his medical expenses. But if we pay him off this way, we're sunk."

"So, what do you think we should do?"

"No matter how much influence he has in the eastern suburb, if he comes back, we'll fight him again," said Zhao Hongbing lightly as he stretched.

Lisi was hoping Zhao Hongbing would say this. It was as Lisi had said – paying medical expenses was reasonable, but Tiger's way of demanding it was unacceptable. Tiger didn't know Zhao Hongbing and his crew well enough. Maybe he thought everyone in business only cared about money and liked to keep trouble to a minimum; if he kept showing up, Lisi would eventually pay him off. But Zhao Hongbing, Lisi, and the others valued reputation and face above life itself. How would they give in to a lowlife like Tiger?

"I think they were carrying guns today," Lisi said.

"What is it that Chairman Mao said?" Little Beijing said. "It's not one or two advanced weapons that decided the outcome of a war. During the Korean War, didn't the 'American imperialists' have the atomic bomb? And did they win? That's why I say all reactionaries are paper tigers!"

"When is he coming back?" Hongbing asked.

"He said he'd be back in a week – the fifteenth day of the New Year."

"So we'll have to go after him before then. We'll tell him to round up some money for medical fees, because he's going back to the hospital," Hongbing said.

"Are you going out fighting again?" Gao Huan didn't look very pleased.

"It's not because we want to. Someone's picking on us," said Little Beijing with a laugh.

"Who would pick on you, Brother Shen? I always see you picking on others."

"That's not quite right. I've been in a lot of fights, but I never pick on anyone," said Little Beijing.

"It's getting late," Zhao Hongbing said to Gao Huan. "I'll take you home."

It was a snowy night. On the wide, empty thoroughfare, snowflakes danced under the pale-yellow street lights. The occasional rattle of firecrackers broke through the wailing of a north wind that cut their faces like a knife. The two of them huddled together as they trudged forward. Their footsteps creaked in the snow.

"Hongbing, is this fight really necessary?" Gao Huan asked softly.

"Yes, it's necessary, because the whole thing started with me." Zhao Hongbing didn't speak loudly, but his tone was very firm.

"Do you fight to fulfill your spiritual life, or to enrich your material life? I really don't see what you hope to get out of it."

"I've never really thought about getting anything out of fighting."

"You all held respectable jobs at one point, but then you neglected your work and lost them," Gao Huan said, worried that Zhao Hongbing was headed for disaster.

"We're doing well enough now," Hongbing chuckled.

"You've been fighting since the day I met you, and you're still fighting now, even after your hand has been damaged so badly. I want you to tell me when this is going to stop."

Hongbing laughed. "When I'm dead."

"Maybe you really will be killed someday, and I'll be left a widow."

"In my heart, the ties of brotherhood are as important as love."

"In my heart, only love matters."

"A lot of girls like money as well."

"You don't understand women, Hongbing. Every girl hopes for genuine love, and to spend the rest of her life with the man of her dreams. She will give up anything for love, even her own wellbeing. And the man she loves doesn't have to be rich. He can even be down and out. True love is the biggest dream in every girl's heart. It's only when she can't get it that she settles for material things. A girl who pursues love is happy. However, a girl who pursues material things is miserable, because it's just her way of venting frustration over the love she can never have."

"Maybe."

"I have love, and I'm happy. A girl who has love is the happiest person in the world. True love may only come once. Hongbing, promise me you'll be careful. I'm so worried about you. I don't want to lose my happiness."

"Nothing will happen to me," said Hongbing lightly.

A blast of wind hit them. They huddled closer together.

CHAPTER 36

Rustic Hoods

BACK IN THE 1980S, SPRING Festival was an exciting and convivial time in the northeast. Most businesses were closed until the fifteenth day of the Lunar New Year. During those two weeks of imposed leisure, everyone relaxed, and friends and relatives got together to eat, drink, and chat.

On the ninth day of the New Year, Zhao Hongbing's gang gathered at Lisi's pool hall to discuss how to deal with Tiger. They planned to go out for a drink after the discussion, so Ergou and Xiaobo tagged along. A dozen or so guys were playing pool at Lisi's place, and the gang had gathered around the cash counter to talk.

"We spent all of last year fighting. I didn't think we'd have to keep fighting this year, too," grumbled Xiaoji, who'd been wounded twice during the previous year.

"As the saying goes, 'the trees desire stillness, but the wind keeps blowing'," said Little Beijing, smiling from his perch on Lisi's counter.

"There's no point going on about it. This fight is going to happen," said Zhao Hongbing.

Ergou never understood why Hongbing and Little Beijing

got along so well, when one never wasted words and the other did almost nothing but.

"It's only Tiger anyway," said Feisi, scorning an opponent he'd already defeated.

"Tiger is definitely afraid of you, Fei. Because you're a 'tiger' too," Xiaoji said.

In the northeastern dialect, 'tiger' is used as an adjective to express impetuousness, fearlessness, and rashness. It can be used in a commendatory or derogatory sense, but when combined with the slang term 'dick' it takes on the meaning of 'dickhead, and implies that a person, while brave and fierce, is also somewhat brainless.

"Yeah. Ever since Zhang Yue went inside, Feisi is our number one tiger," teased Sun Dawei.

"You can bullshit all you want, but I'll trash him for sure," said Feisi, big-eyed and glaring.

Zhao Hongbing once said that the only things that ever scared him were when Zhang Yue glared and bared his teeth, and when Feisi glared and huffed, because then they were beyond his control.

"We're wasting time," Hongbing said. "We need to go eat. Let's talk about why Tiger waited until today to demand his medical expenses."

Everyone was puzzled about this. As soon as Hongbing mentioned it, they became lost in thought. After a while, Little Beijing spoke.

"I think there are five reasons."

Realizing they were in for a long speech, the others listened quietly and didn't interrupt.

"First, after Tiger was trashed by Feisi, he spent half a year in the hospital. He couldn't take his revenge during that time.

By the time he got out of the hospital, we'd already started battling Old Rod Li, so he was happy to sit out the fight and reap the spoils.

"Second, the guy who helped him most was his brother, Little Tiger, who also ended up in the hospital. This left Tiger in no position to fight us.

"Third, he's just a thug who makes a living from extortion. Now that we have some money in hand and he can use the pretext of medical expenses, why wouldn't he try blackmailing us?

"Fourth, right now Lisi's status is different from a year ago. Back then, you were just a kid who could fight. But after those battles with Old Rod Li, you've made a name for yourself. Tiger could lose to a kid, but not to a genuine rival. If he loses to a kid, he can call it bad luck, but if he loses to another big brother, he loses status. While Lisi was making a name, Tiger was adjusting his mentality. So basically, he's reverting to his old habits but also trying to gain back his street cred.

"And there's a fifth point, which is most important of all. Lisi runs his pool hall like a law-abiding citizen. If Tiger keeps sending guys there to cause trouble, Lisi won't be able to keep going. Businessmen want to make money. Tiger knows that this is Lisi's soft spot, and that's why he has the nerve to blackmail him. When we put these five reasons together, we can work out why Tiger waited more than a year to come after us."

"Brilliant!" said Lisi with admiration.

"So now we have to let Tiger see whether we're afraid of him now that we're in business." Xiaoji was still looking for a chance to pay Tiger back for stabbing him.

"Send someone to tell Tiger to come to your pool hall tomorrow night," said Zhao Hongbing, lighting a cigarette.

"Should we ask Brother Zhuzi to come along?" ventured Sun Dawei, a little timorously.

"No. We'll deal with it ourselves," Zhao Hongbing said. "Brother Liu has already helped us enough. We should leave him to run his own business."

"Let's go have a drink!" said Little Beijing.

Lisi sent one of his little brothers to tell Tiger to come the next evening to "collect his money", and then the friends sauntered out for some dinner. Zhao Hongbing drank too much, and Little Beijing and Xiaoji had to take turns carrying him to the hotel on their backs while Feisi and Lisi took Ergou and Xiaobo back to the pool hall to watch the fireworks. Sun Dawei arrived soon after that, saying he thought he'd forgotten to lock up his book stall.

Ergou was an eyewitness to the bloody battle that followed. Twenty years later, he still remembers every detail. He also remembers that during the battle, the sky was lit up by a beautiful firework display. He only remembers the visuals, not the sound. His recollection is like an old silent film – soundless slaughter; fresh blood flowing. Every scene would have scared the average person out of their wits. That day, on the bustling avenue in front of the library, no one stopped to watch this gang war. No one dared.

When Lisi returned to the pool hall, he took a bunch of 'sky rockets' and asked Wang Yu – who had his whole head encased in bandages – to take Ergou and Xiaobo out to set them off. When Xiaobo set off the first one, it burned the space between his eyes and the bridge of his nose. Xiaobo was a tough little kid and didn't shed a tear, but the incident scared the wits out of Lisi and the others. How could they face Zhao Hongbing if they took his nephew out and got him hurt?

"That's bad luck during the New Year. There will be blood," joked Sun Dawei.

But in fact, Dawei got it right. He was the Nostradamus of China. He'd hardly finished speaking when Wang Yu dashed in and said, "Tiger and his gang are here! Two cars full."

Ergou ran out to look. Indeed, there were two vehicles full of men.

Tangled together like an acrobatic troupe on one farming pedicab, at least twenty guys hopped down one by one. The other vehicle was the kind of motorized pedicab common in the northeast, fitted with a motor in the front and pulling a little shed that opens from the back. Usually three or four people can sit inside, but when the rear door of this pedicab opened, one man after another kept jumping out – at least nine guys, as Ergou remembers it. Heaven only knows how they all squeezed inside. Whenever Ergou recalls the men jumping out of that motorized pedicab, he thinks of the electronic game Captain Commando, when an endless stream of little soldiers pours from a dark passageway at the sixth level.

Suburban hoodlum gangs combine urban and rural characteristics. Their conveyances are more rural, and the weapons they use – apart from bayonets and pipes – include sickles, pickaxes, and other farming tools. That day, Tiger and his gang didn't bring guns, but only cold weapons, perhaps intending to intimidate rather than kill.

Soon enough, Tiger and his guys were standing in the doorway. The men who had climbed out of the motorized pedicab were shaking their arms and legs like crazy, probably to get the blood flowing again.

"Do you guys have a death wish?" said Feisi.

Never one to waste words, he lunged at them with a shovel

as he howled. That shovel was the only weapon Sun Dawei, Lisi, Feisi, and Wang Yu had that day. By plunging into the pack of men and swinging his shovel without rhyme or reason, Feisi took Tiger and his gang completely by surprise. Lisi and the others followed right behind the shovel, their intention being to run rather than be trapped inside the pool hall. Feisi's shovel struck Tiger on the shoulder. Tiger grabbed the handle with both hands and pulled with all his might. Behind Feisi, Lisi raised his foot and kicked Tiger in the chest. Already lame, Tiger released his grip. Feisi raised the shovel again, and Ergou could see him brandishing it like a madman at whoever was in front of him, friend or foe. He even struck Sun Dawei and Wang Yu several times. They were badly outnumbered, and their opponents were armed; there was no way they could break through.

The first to be stabbed was Sun Dawei, bringing up the rear. He was felled by a prong and then surrounded and savagely kicked. Unable to regain his footing, he covered his head with his arms. Ergou guessed that the one who was kicking the hardest was a peasant, because his posture looked less like a fighter than like a farmer digging in a field. Seeing Sun Dawei fall, Lisi turned to help him and left Feisi on his own. The formation they'd been maintaining so well fell apart.

Lisi grabbed someone's prong and swung and jabbed it until he drove away the people encircling Sun Dawei. He reached out to pull Dawei's arm, but it felt soft and unresponsive. It turned out that Dawei's arm had been fractured in several places by steel pipes. Lisi grabbed Dawei around the waist with one arm and retreated into the pool hall.

"Get back in!"

After pushing Sun Dawei inside, Lisi closed the door,

taking a fierce stab to the shoulder from a bayonet in the process.

The badly injured Lisi continued to fight. Meanwhile Feisi, having lost Lisi's protection, smacked down several men with his shovel but then finally had it torn from his hands. He fell with four knife wounds. The shovel he'd used on others was now being swung at him. Besieged by seven or eight guys with knives and prongs, he was unable to regain his footing. Wang Yu managed to grab a sickle. Closing his eyes, he swung it crazily, cutting a bloody swath through the mob and gaining his freedom. He was the only one of the four who got out that day. A minute later, Lisi fell, covering his head with his hands and curling up like a dried prawn. After two minutes of mayhem, Tiger and his gang finally stopped. On the ground lay Lisi and Feisi, the two who had trashed Tiger.

That day, the snow was packed deep. The light from the pool hall was glowing on the pure white snow, revealing a dozen big black splotches: blood – some from Feisi, some from Lisi, and some from Tiger's gang. Ergou now thinks that the reason he can't remember the sounds from back then was that the noise was so horrific that he expunged it from his memory. He wished even more to forget the sight of all that gore, but the scene proved indelible. It had imprinted itself deeply in his memory. The more a person tries to forget, the more entrenched the memory becomes.

In half an hour, Lisi and Feisi were in the hospital. Zhao Hongbing and the others arrived an hour later.

"I remember where Tiger lives. I'll go to Gourdy and borrow his shotgun." That was the first thing the newly sobered Zhao Hongbing said.

No one could figure out where Sun Dawei had gone;

Ergou and Xiaobo looked all over the library but didn't find him. The next day, Dawei came staggering into the hospital, his arm dangling. It turned out that he'd hidden all night in the women's restroom on the third floor of the library, too afraid to come out. When he saw Lisi lying in the hospital bed, he began sobbing and couldn't speak.

The next day, Zhao Hongbing said gently to Sun Dawei, "I know you follow the code of brotherhood, but from now on, you shouldn't fight along with us."

Sun Dawei said nothing but bowed his head. His eyes filled with tears.

CHAPTER 37

Boys Don't Cry

ZHAO HONGBING WAS GUILT-STRICKEN. IF he hadn't fought with Tiger and the others at the lantern show that night, Lisi and Feisi wouldn't have become Tiger's enemies and might still be respectably employed. If Hongbing hadn't insisted on fighting instead of paying Tiger's medical fees, Tiger might not have launched his attack on Lisi and the others. Seeing the semi-comatose Lisi, who not long before had risked his life to save him, Zhao Hongbing was heartbroken.

The more serious the situation, the more taciturn Hongbing became. At the hospital he uttered just one sentence, stood quietly there for about half an hour, and then turned and left. Little Beijing followed close behind, knowing what Hongbing had in mind.

Zhao Hongbing and Little Beijing were joined at the hip. Later someone joked that the only time they were apart was when each was sleeping with his own wife; they even went to the bathroom together. That's been the case for more than twenty years.

After leaving the hospital, Zhao Hongbing and Little Beijing went borrow Gourdy's shotgun while Xiaoji stayed at the hospital to watch over Lisi and the others.

At this point, Zhao Hongbing's gang had been reduced to its lowest possible fighting capacity. Of the original eight brothers, two were in prison and three seriously injured, leaving only Hongbing, Little Beijing and Xiaoji. They couldn't possibly muster the manpower for a counterattack. Neither could they take this incident lying down, so what were they to do? The only option was an ambush.

"Hongbing, why do you want the shotgun? Don't tell me you're going to fight again!" Gourdy said as he fetched the gun for its hiding place in the coal pile in his home. Ever since Lisi had used it in the shootout at the hospital several months ago, Gourdy had been in a state of constant anxiety that the police would eventually trace it to him.

"It's not for a fight. We're going to hunt some wild game on Nanshan Hill tomorrow. Our restaurant has been serving a lot of pheasant and rabbit, and I can't find that kind of meat at the market," said Little Beijing, knowing Zhao Hongbing was a hopeless liar.

"Shooting rabbits is fine, but don't go shooting any people with it. I'd rather give it to you outright than get dragged into anything, now that I know you guys are so trigger-happy!" Gourdy had owned the gun for years without firing it once, while Hongbing and his friends had already fired it several times.

"You'll give it to me?" grinned Little Beijing. "Then I'll kindly accept it. I'll send a guy over tomorrow to pay you for it. I've always wanted a gun. That's why I joined the Army!" He always had a line to spin.

"Yeah, well…Just don't go shooting someone with it, or I'll pay you to take it from me."

Like his big brother, Liu Haizhu, Gourdy was ruled by

emotion. Although Little Beijing had given him a beating, once they'd had a drink together, Gourdy had put it all behind him and treated Zhao Hongbing and his guys like his own brothers. He knew very well that Zhao Hongbing and his gang were capable of anything.

"Thanks, Gourdy. See you later," said Little Beijing with an evasive titter.

From Gourdy's house, Little Beijing and Zhao Hongbing took a taxi straight to the woolen mill residential compound in the eastern suburb. Hongbing clearly recalled where Tiger lived, and they arrived at around ten o'clock.

More than a year ago, seven people had stood outside this door. They'd all been high-spirited and vigorous. Most had still been respectably employed, regarding a fight as just something to spice up their lives. They ended up suffering their first setback outside this door. Since then they'd fought countless times, spending their days in a state of constant anxiety as fighting became a way of life. As of today, only Zhao Hongbing and Xiaoji were still standing; even still, they had nearly lost their lives in the gunfight outside the Purple Moon.

Zhao Hongbing took a deep breath. Win or lose, he would never knock on Tiger's door again after tonight. He gave a signaling glance to Little Beijing, and then the two of them simultaneously leaped six feet to the roof of Tiger's gatehouse.

Ergou had heard Little Beijing spinning his yarns in front of the hotel, claiming that he and Hongbing had been the most agile in their squad, and that only the two of them had been capable of carrying out the mission by surmounting a ninety-degree precipice. This had been no empty boast; even with a crippled hand, Hongbing was able to execute the series of grabs and kicks that rapidly propelled him to the roof.

Tiger's home was typical of dwellings in the northeast in the 1980s. In front was a squat little storehouse, known as the 'gatehouse'. Behind it were the residential quarters where the occupants ate and slept. Between the gatehouse and the residential quarters lay a courtyard less than twenty yards long, where bicycles and other such items were kept. Tiger's home was in a seven-household compound with pointed, tiled roofs and walls separating each family's quarters.

Zhao Hongbing and Little Beijing climbed up on the roof of the gatehouse so they could see how many people were inside the house. If it was like last time, with a dozen or so guys inside with three guns, they wouldn't take action that night. After careful inspection, they found a light on in only one of the house's three rooms. However, the window was covered with plastic material, so they couldn't see how many were inside.

Little Beijing made a hand signal and then followed the wall toward the house, with Zhao Hongbing close behind. The wall was only around six inches wide, but they darted quickly across it in a crouched position. In two or three seconds they had leaped onto the roof of the main house. They were so light-footed that they didn't even rouse the neighbors' dogs.

Zhao Hongbing and Little Beijing had been waiting on the roof for less than five minutes when the light inside the house went out, but no one came out. They decided the television programming must have ended for the night. Apparently Tiger and his guys weren't there, because there was no way they would go to bed so early.

In order to confirm their conclusion, Little Beijing pulled a tile from the roof, broke it over his knee and then flung a piece at the iron door of Tiger's home. The tile banged against door, and a neighbor's dog started barking. Little Beijing tossed another piece, and all the nearby dogs began to bark as well.

"Who's there?" an elderly voice called from inside.

Naturally there was no reply from outside. Little Beijing broke another tile and threw two more pieces against the metal door.

"Who's there?"

This time the voice was accompanied by a light turning on in the darkened room, and then the door light was turned on as well. The door light, located right over the door by the eaves, had a large, 200-watt light bulb, and Zhao Hongbing and Little Beijing leaned directly over it. They knew that the bright light created a blind spot. Looking towards it required a person's eyes to get used to the intensity; looking into the darkness behind the light required another period of adjustment. This would give them time to aim and fire.

The front door opened to reveal a stooped figure clad in woolen underwear and an army coat. This was clearly Tiger's father. Zhao Hongbing and Little Beijing had no interest in attacking him.

"Who's there? Who's knocking at my door so late?"

The stooped figure began walking toward the main entrance at the gatehouse. As he neared it, Zhao Hongbing and Little Beijing jumped the ten feet down from the roof and slipped into the house through the curtained doorway. Hongbing went first with Little Beijing behind him.

By now they'd reached a preliminary conclusion about the house. The lack of reaction to the tiles thrown at the door indicated that Tiger had made no preparations at his home that night. Also, Tiger's room was most likely on the west side of the house, because the eastern room where the light had turned on seemed to belong to his father.

Zhao Hongbing burst into the door of a western room while rolling to the front of the brick bed. Little Beijing followed, turning on the light. He knelt down and aimed his gun, finger on the trigger. Their motions were fluid, orchestrated, and perfectly executed. But there was no one on the brick bed.

They then did the same thing in the second western room, and again found no one in bed. The entire process of establishing that both rooms were empty took less than ten seconds.

Later, Little Beijing said that Zhao Hongbing rolled over to the brick bed so he could immediately subdue anyone who sat up when the light went on, and Little Beijing knelt down with his gun aimed in case there was more than one person in the bed. Even if five or six people had been in that bed, Hongbing and Little Beijing would have overcome them.

Zhao Hongbing and Little Beijing then dashed into the eastern room where the light had gone on. There they found an old, white-haired woman sitting half-way up in the bed, staring mutely at them. With a wave of Little Beijing's hand, the two left the room and went into the courtyard. They now knew that Tiger had not come home that night. From the moment they had reached the door of the house, the two of them had not exchanged a single word, communicating purely from glances and hand signals.

Inside the courtyard they came face-to-face with Tiger's father tottering along. "Who are you?" the old man asked, drawing the bolt of the door.

"City police," said Little Beijing calmly.

"Why have you come to my home?"

"That's quite a son you have!"

After saying this, Little Beijing and Zhao Hongbing opened the door and sauntered out, leaving Tiger's father standing dumbstruck in the courtyard. The old man had no trouble believing that Zhao Hongbing and Little Beijing were policemen; he knew very well what his three sons were up to, and Tiger was the only one not currently in jail.

Later someone ridiculed Zhao Hongbing and Little Beijing for the misfire at Tiger's home:

"You guys are usually so cool-headed. Why didn't you scope things out before striking? Didn't that warn him off?"

"I was still too hung over to think clearly, and too impatient to wait," Zhao Hongbing said.

"An ambush requires the element of surprise," said Little Beijing complacently. "And besides, even though we didn't nab Tiger, we gave him a mental shock. We let him know that if we wanted to get him at home, it would be like stealing candy from a baby."

After leaving Tiger's home, they politely shut the metal door behind them. This was the difference between PLA veterans and rural hoodlums.

"Lisi and Feisi wounded some of Tiger's brothers, so they're sure to be in the hospital. We should look for Tiger there. If we don't find him tonight, it'll be harder later," Zhao Hongbing said.

He and Little Beijing were preparing to hail a taxi about thirty yards from the entrance to the *hutong* when a motorized pedicab with glaring headlights careened toward them.

"Dim your lights, asshole!" Little Beijing scolded as the pedicab passed.

"Shen, look!" Zhao Hongbing said in a low voice. They

watched as the pedicab stopped at the entrance to Tiger's *hutong*. The door opened, and two people stepped out. One was limping, and they were sure it was Tiger.

Zhao Hongbing and Little Beijing advanced toward the pedicab, stopping about fifteen yards away. This brought them within range of the gun Little Beijing was carrying. However, if they came too close and Tiger and his crony were armed, Little Beijing wouldn't enjoy the advantage of his marksmanship.

"Tiger!" Zhao Hongbing shouted, not to warn him, but to make sure the limping man really was him. Little Beijing had already aimed his gun, awaiting the reply.

"Yeah? Who is it?" Tiger said, turning.

At almost the same instant, Little Beijing's gun fired with a low 'boom'. Tiger yelped as a bullet tore through his thigh.

"Brother! Get in!" The gangster with Tiger pulled him toward the back door of the pedicab. Tiger had been lame to start with, but now that he was shot, it was even harder for him to run. Even so, they were less than ten feet from the pedicab and reached it in just a few steps. The gang brother jumped in first and began pulling Tiger in with all his might.

"Boom!"

The gun fired again, this time hitting Tiger in the buttocks.

The gang brother pulled him into the pedicab and yanked the door shut. The driver gunned the motor and sped off into the distance.

Little Beijing and Zhao Hongbing didn't chase after it. In fact, neither had moved throughout the process, apart from Little Beijing's leisurely pulling of his trigger. The second shot, when Tiger and his man were scrambling for cover, came much later than the first. The cooler Zhao Hongbing and Little Beijing were, the more frantic Tiger and his man became. No one could beat Little Beijing when it came to psychological warfare.

When the pedicab was about ten yards away, Little Beijing smirked and fired another careless shot into the air. It was the last shot he fired that night; like the third shot Lisi had fired at the hospital the year before, it was meant purely to intimidate. It raised another yelp of alarm from the speeding pedicab, whose passengers had every reason to expect this bullet to meet its mark as well. It was too dark for the pedicab's passengers to see how many people were outside, and how many guns they had.

"Tiger won't go to the police," Zhao Hongbing said on the way home. "He did worse to Feisi than we did to him. If we go in, we'll take him with us."

"He wouldn't dare," Little Beijing agreed, ever confident.

At around midnight, Little Beijing and Zhao Hongbing went back to the hospital. Feisi was in worse shape, having just gone through surgery under general anesthetic. Although his life wasn't in danger, his mind was still foggy. Lisi's condition was better, and he was already in a bed on the ward.

"Shen took care of things for you," Zhao Hongbing whispered in Lisi's ear as he gripped his hand.

Lisi's jaws had been wired shut. He couldn't speak. He gripped Zhao Hongbing's left hand tightly, looking at him with his huge eyes. A tear trickled down his cheek. His lips and face were twitching.

This is how it goes for men and heroes. The tears they shed are only for their brothers.

CHAPTER 38

The Investiture of the Gods

ON THE 15TH DAY OF the Lunar New Year, Zhao Hongbing learned that Tiger had not gone to the police, or even to one of the city's hospitals, fearing that Hongbing would attempt a last hit. After a quick patching up at a nearby clinic, he was sent to the provincial capital for long-term treatment. Zhao Hongbing knew that this time Tiger was truly and thoroughly vanquished.

One month later, Hongbing had a visit from Liu Haizhu.

"Yesterday a friend of Tiger's looked me up. He has two friends who were buddies of mine 'inside'. He knows you and me are friends, so he asked me to help negotiate a truce with you," Liu chuckled.

"A truce?" Zhao Hongbing hadn't expected this from Tiger.

"Yeah, and he asked me to give you 30,000 to cover hospital fees for Feisi and the others."

"If that's what you say, I'm happy to let the matter end here," said Zhao Hongbing, who always respected Liu Haizhu.

"You don't have to listen to me. If you want to keep fighting, you go right ahead and pretend I never came here. If you think the hospital expenses aren't enough, I'll ask them for more," said Liu Haizhu firmly.

"No more fighting. At this point, if we keep going, someone will end up dead," Zhao Hongbing said. In any case, he'd gotten his revenge, and he was weary of the fighting and anxiety.

"Take the money then."

"Okay."

What should have been a tragedy turned into a comedy. Two of the three wounded men, along with Xiaoji – who stayed with them the whole time – ended up finding their better halves during the months they spent in the hospital.

The first to nab a nurse was Xiaoji.

His great advantage was that he was bright and studious, and not too proud to learn from others. His request for Mr. Li's tutelage in archeology showed his love of learning, and on top of that he was actually very smart. Over the past year, he'd learned a lot about cultural artifacts. Also, as a result of repeated hospital stays and contact with many hospital patients and prominent surgeons, he'd gained such an in-depth understanding of trauma treatment that he was half-way to becoming a doctor himself. His knowledge was even greater than that of most young nurses, who had graduated from nursing school or nursing courses at medical school.

With nothing better to do while keeping his friends company in the hospital, Xiaoji liked to chat up pretty nurses and discuss trauma treatments with them. His ability to talk theory and generally bamboozle was very convincing, and one very pretty young nurse in particular admired him immensely. Not yet twenty years old, her name was Binbin and she was adorable. After scoping out the situation, Xiaoji homed in on her. He asked one of Lisi's little brothers to run his recycling stall while he spent all day at the hospital. After spending the first half month looking after Lisi and the others, his objective shifted to chatting up Binbin. By mid-March, he had managed to take her out for dinner, and the two had established a romantic relationship.

"Xiaoji, why are you spending all day at the hospital?" Little Beijing asked when he figured out what was going on.

"Me? I'm looking after the guys," said Xiaoji innocently.

"How can you look after them when you spend the whole time at the nurses' station?" Little Beijing asked with a wicked smile.

"Just showing one of the nurses my bedside manner," said Xiaoji with a lewd grin.

"In bed already! Maybe I should try," said Little Beijing enviously.

"Well, not yet, but soon enough. I want to seal the deal pretty soon so she'll marry me for sure. If you want to show off your bedside manner, stick with Lisi and the other guys!"

"Lisi's not my type. But I'm all for you nabbing that nurse."

"Why?"

"You're such a lousy fighter. You're bound to take a beating next time around. This way you can get your treatment at home instead of at the hospital."

"How thoughtful! Maybe I should get Binbin to set you up with one of her colleagues," Xiaoji said.

"I prefer a doctor."

"A doctor? Which doctor?"

"Hongbing's sister! She's a doctor, isn't she – a pediatrician?" At the mention of Zhao Hongyan, Little Beijing's eyes glowed.

"Cut the crap. She's married!"

"I can pretend she's divorced."

"The marriage is solid."

"I'm a patient man. Right now I'm 24 and Hongyan is 28. Check out my palm – my life line is extra long; I should live until at least 90. I've had a look at Hongyan's husband's palm, and he's got 70 years at best. I'll just wait for him to drop dead and then I can marry her."

"Yeah, you'll live to at least a thousand years, like one of those old tortoises."

It looked like Little Beijing would marry no one but Hongyan.

The second of the gang to nab himself a nurse was Sun Dawei. While Xiaoji used his encyclopedic mind and glib tongue to conquer Binbin, Sun Dawei relied on his "adorable cowardice" to attract another young nurse. Dawei's high school crush had broken off all contact with him since going off to college. She hadn't even looked him up over Spring Festival, leaving him broken-hearted. Love can arrive in many different ways, and Sun Dawei's was particularly unusual.

This is how it came about:

Fractured in several places, Sun Dawei's arm hadn't set properly the first time around, a fact that was not discovered until x-rays were taken more than two months later. The doctor proposed removing the pin and rebreaking the misaligned bone to reset it. Horrific as this solution sounded, Sun Dawei felt he had no choice but to accept it.

They say that when Dawei was put on the operating table and saw the doctor with a pair of scissors and hammer in hand, he fainted dead away. However, Dawei himself denied this, saying he actually heard his bone being broken.

The morning after this second operation, a still-woozy Sun Dawei saw a smiling young nurse approaching him with a tray in her hands. As he opened his eyes wide, the nurse drew closer while lifting a pair of scissors identical to the ones the doctor had used on him the day before.

Dawei gave a blood-curdling scream and fainted all over again.

When he came to a minute later, the first object that met his eyes was that pair of scissors.

"Aaah!" he yelled again, and fainted.

Sun Dawei had developed a phobia of scissors and hammers. To this day he locks those tools away where he doesn't have to look at them.

This young nurse thought Sun Dawei's faint-heartedness was extremely cute and funny. From then on, she came to chat with him whenever she had a free moment. Dawei was a smooth talker and enjoyed striking a pose, and things quickly progressed to the hot and heavy stage. Before long they were making wedding plans.

"When posers encounter love, love becomes a pose," Little Beijing remarked.

The woman Lisi fell in love with was Feisi's younger sister. She was very beautiful, and shared her brother's large eyes. Unfortunately, she also shared his violent temper. Since Lisi had a more sedate character, the two complemented each other. Feisi's sister admired Lisi's upright and courageous character and even pursued him to a certain degree, so they quickly became a couple.

"Aren't you a sneaky devil, Lisi!" Little Beijing said. "It seems a bit incestuous, though."

"Aren't you always after Hongyan?" Lisi said.

"Yes, but I haven't actually done anything."

"Even if you tried, do you think she'd let you?" Lisi grinned.

"Let's not talk about it," sighed Little Beijing, disconsolate at the very mention of Hongyan's name.

Usually the friends were busy with their businesses and spent their free time drinking together, so they'd had little opportunity to meet women. Being badly injured and confined to hospital beds for an extended period presented them with a golden opportunity. In Ergou's opinion, they owed a debt of gratitude to Tiger.

By the time the guys were discharged from the hospital, they found they'd suddenly become respected figures in the gangland world through their fight with Tiger. Everyone in gang circles now knew that Zhao Hongbing's gang knew how to fight and also how to use a gun.

As the spring of 1988 turned to summer, some people with nothing better to do labeled the city's most powerful gangs based on the "Five Greats" in *The Legend of the Condor Heroes*. Ergou recalls that it went "Tiger in the East, Old Rod in the West, Loony in the South, Wei Dong in the North, and Hongbing in the Center," but another version put Lisi in the east in place of Tiger. Zhao Hongbing lived in the middle of the city, which is why he was assigned that turf. This ranking shows how famous Hongbing and his gang had become. People's impression of "Hongbing in the Center" was that he was the most formidable, just as the "Central Divine" was the most powerful and skilled of the Five Greats.

Liu Haizhu wasn't included in this ranking because he seldom involved himself in gangland affairs, and was known for striking out on his own. His gangland status at that time was something like Qiu Qianren, leader of the Iron Palm Sect, who retained his formidable reputation without taking part in the Huashan swordfight.

CHAPTER 39

A Quiet Half Year

FOR THE ENTIRE FIRST HALF of 1988, Zhao Hongbing and his friends had no conflicts with other gangs. They were able to enjoy some rest after nearly two years of fighting. Ergou believes there were several reasons for this:

Feisi and Lisi – the guys most prone to stirring things up – were confined to the hospital for much of that time, and Xiaoji also spent most of his time there. Zhao Hongbing and Little Beijing were busy running their restaurant and hotel, both of which were plying a roaring trade with customers from all over. They had no time for fighting.

Meanwhile, Zhao Hongbing and his gang had already made a name for themselves. An ordinary street punk would have to be exceptionally daring to provoke them. The stronger gangs of Old Rod Li and Tiger were now thoroughly cowed after intense conflicts with Hongbing's indomitable army veterans. Old Rod and Tiger were petty hooligans rather than proper underworld gangsters.

Zhao Hongbing and his gang didn't fight for a living but in retaliation against bullying. In any case, there was no money to be made through fighting back then. Rather, it was costly in terms of money and even human life. The code of brotherhood and chivalry was what sustained them when they fought.

Zhao Hongbing never put himself out for anyone but his brothers and Liu Haizhu. Once Hongbing became famous, it was common for a hoodlum who was being picked on to ask Hongbing to wreak revenge. Under these circumstances, Zhao Hongbing would help mediate the matter, but nothing more than that. His philosophy was never to pick on others or to raise his hand against anyone with whom he had no personal conflict.

Most importantly, Zhao Hongbing never started anything.

Although the hotel restaurant wasn't a large establishment, Little Beijing was an able manager and the food was first-rate. It soon became the most popular eatery in the vicinity of the railway station. While not yet up to the standard of the major downtown restaurants, it was highly profitable.

Zhao Hongbing didn't have a lot of friends. Apart from his gang brothers, it was only Liu Haizhu who was reasonably close to him. Having little better to do while so many of his brothers were bedridden, Hongbing was always itching for a drink with Liu Haizhu. Ergou thinks there were several reasons why Zhao Hongbing was inclined to drink at this time. Firstly, Little Beijing was so capable that he took on a lot of the work that Hongbing should have been doing. Secondly, Gao Huan wasn't around. Finally, after reading the martial arts novel *Sword of Justice* that Sun Dawei had lent him, Hongbing felt that he resembled the book's protagonist, Yu Peiyu. He became a big fan of the author, Gu Long. In Gu's novels, the heroes were usually heavy drinkers, so Zhao Hongbing started emulating them.

Drinking habits usually reflect character. While both Zhao

Hongbing and Liu Haizhu had trouble holding their liquor, they appreciated good booze and gained Dutch courage from it. When together, they inevitably over-imbibed, leaving poor Little Beijing to deal with their drunkenness. Zhao Hongbing's greatest flaw was that once he started drinking, he always got drunk. Drinking didn't make him go out looking for trouble, but it inclined him toward three bad habits. The first was that when drunk, he liked to show off his awesome jumping ability; the second was that he would fall asleep almost anywhere; the third was that he would start secretly trailing some burly fellow in the street, although he never went further than that.

Everyone suffers some ill effect from drinking; some cry, some laugh, some sing, some get rowdy, some fall asleep. But the effect it had on Zhao Hongbing was something Ergou seldom saw in others. The first two were understandable, but the third was really inexplicable and kind of creepy. If you were out walking in the street in the middle of the night and suddenly realized that someone was following you, wouldn't you be scared? Of course, Zhao Hongbing seldom recalled engaging in the third activity. He remembered only three instances.

Ergou observed the first two behaviors practically every weekend, especially during the late 1980s, when Zhao Hongbing was drinking most heavily. He vaguely recalls an afternoon when Zhao Hongbing took him to the No. 2 High School near the railway station to watch a basketball game. They were watching rather than playing, because Hongbing's injured right hand meant that he couldn't dribble anymore. He had played very well in high school, and still loved the game so much that he liked to watch even if he couldn't play. On this occasion, he was already so drunk that Ergou had to lead him to the basketball court. Half of the court was being used by six high school students, and they were pretty lousy players. Zhao Hongbing pulled a stool up and smirked with a bleary-eyed squint at the students.

"What's so funny, asshole?" said one of the students irritably. "Why don't you try?"

Of course, he had no idea that the person sitting there was Zhao Hongbing.

"Give it here!"

Ignoring the student's foul language, Hongbing reached out his left hand for the ball. Playing one-handed, he ran right up under the basket and used his momentum to leap up and make a slam dunk with one arm. The students stood there with their mouths hanging open. Zhao Hongbing was only about five-foot ten, but still, it was unlikely that any student of his height was capable of a dunk shot.

They had an even bigger surprise coming. They heard a snapping sound. Zhao Hongbing's lack of self-control under the influence of alcohol, coupled with the inferior quality of the basketball stand, resulted in his pulling the net and stand down with him. The students gaped with admiration.

A few minutes later, another student asked, "Who did that to the basketball stand?"

"Him. The guy asleep on the stool."

"How does he sleep like that?"

Zhao Hongbing had already dropped off. The image he'd just created of himself as a basketball star was immediately demolished by his unsightly slumping.

Ergou remembers another summer evening when Zhao Hongbing had too much to drink with Liu Haizhu. Little Beijing wanted to get Hongbing up to the hotel's third floor to sleep it off, but when he turned around, Hongbing had vanished. Ten minutes later, he appeared out of nowhere on the third-floor roof.

"Brother Liu! Watch me jump to the second floor!"

Drunk as a lord, Zhao Hongbing was grinning down at Liu Haizhu, who was just walking out of the restaurant. Liu turned and saw a gap of at least fifteen yards between the third-floor roof and the second-floor roof across from it, which even the world long-jump champion couldn't possibly cover.

Frightened half sober by the prospect of Hongbing either killing or crippling himself, Liu called up, "I know you can make it, but wait for me to get Shen so he can watch, too!"

"Hurry up, then!"

Liu Haizhu dashed into the restaurant. "Get up to the third-floor roof and grab Hongbing. He's about to jump!"

Little Beijing turned and ran upstairs.

When Liu Haizhu walked back out and raised his eyes to the third-floor roof, he couldn't see Zhao Hongbing anymore. Half a minute later, he saw Little Beijing standing on the roof, huffing and puffing.

"Where's Hongbing?" Liu Haizhu was panicking.

"He fell asleep on the roof," said Little Beijing with exasperation.

"Hongbing, next time you get drunk, I'm going to tie you up. Sooner or later you're going to scare the life out of me." Every time Zhao Hongbing awoke from one of his drunken stupors, Little Beijing was always furious.

"I won't do it again," Hongbing promised with a contrite grin. Normally so steady, he blushed scarlet whenever someone mentioned his drunken antics. Ergou thinks it may have been because Hongbing was normally so staid and immovable that he became so hyperactive when he drank.

Although his other habit of following people when he was drunk occurred much less often, it once resulted in someone calling the police. Zhao Hongbing had scared a burly fellow half to death by stalking him. When the police traced him to his home, he was not yet sober. They interrogated him after he'd dried out in the drunk tank.

"Why are you stalking people?"

"I'm an army scout!" Hongbing wasn't completely sober.

"You were discharged years ago. How can you be a scout?"

"Even ordinary citizens have a duty to defend their country!"

"What does that have to do with stalking people?"

"He might be a secret agent."

"A secret agent? For whom? Do we even have secret agents nowadays? What makes you think that? If there really is a secret agent, we should take you to the State Security Bureau!"

"I don't know. Anyway, I heard a telegraph, and right after that I saw him, so I followed him."

"A telegraph?"

"Yeah, the sound of a telegraph. I heard it."

Zhao Hongbing was released that night; the police decided he'd hallucinated in his drunkenness. When Little Beijing came to bail him out, Hongbing was largely sober, but still insisted he'd heard a telegraph. "How would I get that wrong?"

"Yeah... Of course you wouldn't get it wrong. Hurry home and get some sleep!" Frustrated, Little Beijing didn't know what else to say.

Two other times that Zhao Hongbing followed people also occurred in the first half of 1988. Both times he said he heard a telegraph, but he couldn't see where it was coming from so he just followed the first suspicious person he saw. In both cases, after he'd sobered up, he still insisted he'd heard it.

Overall, the first half of 1988 was the easiest half year in Zhao Hongbing's career. He was in a nominal truce with his two main opponents. With no need to worry about people plotting against him, he spent his time drinking and partying and waiting for Gao Huan to come home for her summer break. If only life could have gone on like that forever.

Part Seven

Prison

CHAPTER 40

Chen Wei Dong and Zhao Shanhe

WHILE ZHAO HONGBING WAS PASSING the first half of 1988 in a drunken haze, Chen Wei Dong's gang was expanding rapidly in the north of the city. Back then, the gang's main business was the underground sex industry. There was a children's rhyme that went, "In 1988, I learned Labyrinth Boxing, conquered the master fighter Huo Yuanjia, and stole the lovely Zhao Qiannan…" which shows that people were no longer as conservative about male-female relationships as they had been in the past.

Chen Wei Dong was an old hoodlum. Prior to the 1983 "Strike Hard" campaign he'd been on an equal footing with Old Rod Li, Liu Haizhu, and Mighty Zhang. He was tiny and nasty-looking, with a belly full of evil. However, he always thought of himself as a pretty boy – the handsomest thug in the city. It was said that the hideous Chen Wei Dong modeled himself on the comely prodigal Yan Qing in *The Water Margin*, even copying Yan Qing's tattoos on his own torso. Ergou saw the tattoos once: snarling dragons, execrably drawn and unevenly colored, obviously the work of a rustic amateur.

If Zhao Hongbing and Liu Haizhu adhered to the code of chivalry, Chen Wei Dong was an out-and-out scumbag. In 1988, Chen was around thirty-five years old but already hunch-backed, earning himself the nickname 'Archy'. He was said to suffer from a pox along with all his gang members, as a result of cross-infection.

Chen Wei Dong left prison in 1987 around the same time as Liu Haizhu, Old Rod Li, and Mighty Zhang. They'd gotten to know each other in the cells, but were in no way friends. They say that Liu Haizhu regularly tuned up Chen Wei Dong, who came to fear Liu more than anyone. After leaving prison, Liu Haizhu began fixing bicycles, Old Rod Li plundered graves and peddled antiques, and Mighty Zhang was a highway robber until Zhang Yue stabbed him to death. The three of them had distanced themselves from civilian life, for good or for ill. But Chen Wei Dong was notorious because his trade was organized prostitution. In the 1980s, pimps were thoroughly despised in that locality; even street punks looked down on them. So how did Chen Wei Dong establish a gangland reputation? Ergou believes there were three reasons:

Firstly, Chen Wei Dong had already made a name for himself before 1983 and was a bona fide gangland veteran. He had fought some tough battles and gained a measure of fame. Secondly, although engaging in the sex trade was a badge of infamy, Chen made good money at it, and money makes everything a little easier. Last but not least, he had a cousin who ran away from home after watching *Shaolin Temple,* purportedly to become a monk at the Shaolin Monastery. Although he certainly never made it there, he did acquire some martial arts skills. He was known as the top solo fighter in the city, and quite a few young fellows had joined his gang. This cousin always came to help Chen out in gang fights.

The cousin was not yet twenty years old, and only became truly famous after Chen Wei Dong died in around 1996. At that time, the Hong Kong film *Young and Dangerous*, based on the comic book *Wiseguy*, was all the rage. Chen Wei Dong's cousin resembled the character Shanji in both appearance and style. He was known as Zhao Shanhe.

The relationship between Chen Wei Dong and Zhao Shanhe was like that of a wolf and a jackal. Of the two, the jackal is the most genuinely evil, bracing its short forelegs on the wolf's back and feeding evil schemes into his ear. Who can win against the ferociousness of the wolf combined with the treachery of the jackal? Chen Wei Dong was the jackal, and Zhao Shanhe was the wolf. Although the wolf is fiercer and crueler, he listens to the jackal. The jackal Chen Wei Dong was at least fifteen years older than the wolf Zhao Shanhe.

Chen's restaurant was near the steel window-frame factory in the city's northern district. It had around twenty tables, and the prostitutes who worked there were waitresses as well. When the restaurant first opened, business was poor, mainly because neighborhood people didn't know it was an underground brothel. Chen Wei Dong quickly thought of a romantic way to attract customers. When the prostitutes served food to customers, they made a point of exposing themselves just a little. At lunchtime or in the afternoon, when business was slow, he had them take turns standing outside the restaurant. Again, they always found some pretext to expose themselves.

While injurious to public morals, this method of attracting customers was very successful. The restaurant was soon doing a roaring trade. Its name was Spring Deer. A doggerel indicative of the restaurant's corrupting influence soon spread throughout the city – "If your wife gives you a sneer / Head north for the Spring Deer".

One afternoon in June 1988, Gourdy and two of his friends, who had drunk quite a bit over lunch, passed Chen Wei Dong's restaurant and noticed several girls posing coquettishly around the doorway.

"Little sister, go boldly, go boldly ahead..." One of Gourdy's friends sang the theme song to the then-popular film *Red Sorghum*, exhaling boozy vapors at the prostitutes.

"Blow, wind! Blow her skirt up!" cried Gourdy.

Although Gourdy and his friends usually hung out with Liu Haizhu, they didn't share his ascetic lifestyle; they were great lovers of women, wine, and song and took liberties whenever they could.

"Brother Dong, do you see that bunch of jerks out there?" one of the prostitutes asked Chen Wei Dong, who was sitting at a table near the entrance.

Chen laid down the small mirror and wooden comb he was holding and stood up. He never went anywhere without that mirror and comb. Something of a narcissist, he was always looking in the mirror and singing a song made popular by the Chinese-American singer Fei Xiang: "Reading you a thousand times and never bored." Whenever he reached that line while gazing in the mirror, his voice became low and resonant.

"Brothers, will you come in for some lunch?" Chen Wei Dong asked the men.

"Nah. Can't you tell we've had enough already?" Gourdy like to stir up trouble after drinking, as demonstrated by his legendary brawl with Pan Daqing in the restaurant bathroom.

"So why are you harassing our waitresses?" Chen Wei Dong asked.

"Waitresses?" Gourdy snickered. "You mean your hookers?"

"Watch your tongue, brother," Chen Wei Dong said. He was alone in the restaurant that day and didn't want to take on three guys at once.

"Who are you telling to watch it? Who the hell are you?" Gourdy didn't know Chen, and he was itching for a fight.

"My name is Chen Wei Dong. Go ask around. Everyone here knows who I am." Chen was vain not only about his looks, but also about his reputation.

"I'm Gourdy, and if you ask around downtown, everyone knows who I am," he said, imitating Chen.

"Okay, you've given me your name. Someday I'll come and look you up."

"If you don't come looking for me, you're a fucking pussy," Gourdy said aggressively.

"You said it," said Chen Wei Dong, happy to put off the encounter until the odds improved.

Gourdy and his friends sauntered off, with Gourdy yelling back one more time, "If you don't come looking for me, you're a pussy." He probably thought Chen Wei Dong would never dare.

The minute Gourdy left, Chen Wei Dong told one of the waitresses, "Go get Zhao Shanhe."

CHAPTER 41

The Supreme Ultimate Plum Blossom Mantis Fist

THAT NIGHT, ZHAO SHANHE BEGAN trolling the city's main entertainment venues with the intention of giving Gourdy a beating, to vent the fury of his cousin, Chen Wei Dong.

As far as Chen was concerned, no one got away with violating the rights of the call girls under his car. This was his basic interest. Anyone could come and hire a prostitute, but no one could take liberties with her. If anyone infringed on his basic interests, he would have to engage in violent suppression; Gourdy couldn't be allowed to set an unhealthy precedent.

Ergou vaguely recalls that at that time, Zhao Shanhe wore a buzz cut hairstyle – trimmed very short all around his head in apparent imitation of the Chinese-American FBI phone jockey Bill Kim in the second season of *Prison Break.* Apart from setting hairstyle trends for local hoodlums, Zhao Shanhe was also their fashion guru, invariably sporting bell-bottomed trousers and a kind of black button-up jacket that no one else in the city was wearing yet. Zhao Shanhe's style was totally rock-and-roll. However, his fashion sense wasn't the main reason for his fame; that still rested on his superb fighting skills. In solo combat, he had no rival in the entire city. There were confirmed reports that in the years Zhao Shanhe had spent roaming around and studying under master practitioners, he learned a fighting method called the Supreme Ultimate Plum Blossom Mantis Fist.

Zhao Hongbing and Little Beijing once said that Zhao Shanhe's fighting method combined the greatest achievements of Chinese martial arts, just as its name implied. The boxing style was the quintessence of mantis boxing, which emphasized thought over form and employed the *taichi* method of using the opponent's strength against him. The plum blossom referred to keeping fists and feet in constant motion to render the opponent defenseless. The phrase Zhao Shanhe always spoke before he began fighting was: "One-on-one or gang fight?" He was confident enough of his own fighting skills to give his adversary the choice. They say that once, when Zhao Shanhe got into a fight with three local hooligans, he couldn't resist asking his usual question: "One-on-one or gang fight?" The punks figured they'd have to be idiots to fight him one-on-one when they could combine their strength to take him down. "Why the fuck should we fight you one-on-one? Get him!" The young hoods looked set to surround and annihilate him, but the result was just the opposite: Zhao Shanhe single-handedly wiped out the three young hooligans. Although he had politely given them a choice, they didn't have a cat in hell's chance either way.

Back then, anyone who learned martial arts considered himself a warrior who followed the code of chivalry. Zhao Shanhe also followed this code, but only toward Chen Wei Dong.

That evening, Zhao Shanhe found Gourdy playing pool at the Railway Workers' Cultural Palace. Accompanied by three other guys, he strode in, trailed by a gust of wind.

"Which one is Gourdy?"

Gourdy set down his pool cue. "That's me."

"Do you know who I am?" Zhao Shanhe barked belligerently. "Do you know who you offended?"

"Why should I care?" snorted Gourdy.

"I'm telling you. My name is Zhao Shanhe, and Chen Wei Dong is my cousin. Do you know why I've come here looking for you?"

"Whatever it is, just tell me and cut the fucking bullshit!"

"Your smart mouth is going to get you hurt."

"Listen, you little shit. You came looking for me, so don't waste any more of my time!" said Gourdy, striding forward. While not particularly skillful, he never avoided a fight.

"One-on-one or gang fight?" Zhao Shanhe courteously asked his usual question.

"Here's one!" said Gourdy, sending his foot sailing toward Zhao Shanhe.

Zhao Shanhe stepped back lightly. He grabbed Gourdy's ankle, flipped it backward, and sent him sprawling. He then began kicking Gourdy hard all over, apparently intent on putting him in the hospital for several months. The three gang brothers who followed Zhao Shanhe everywhere were also decent fighters, and Gourdy's gang didn't come close to matching them. In the space of two minutes, the pool hall was a shambles. Gourdy and his gang brothers lay moaning on the floor.

"Remember! Beating you up is kid stuff for me. Unless you have money in your pocket, keep your jerk's ass away from my cousin's place," Zhao Shanhe said, and stalked off.

Around nine o'clock that night, a battered Gourdy turned up at Zhao Hongbing's restaurant looking for Liu Haizhu. Liu and Hongbing had drunk too much again and were sound asleep on the third floor. Little Beijing was relatively sober.

"What happened to you?" he asked.

"While I was walking around by the steel window frame factory, I got into an argument with Chen Wei Dong, and he sent his cousin after me."

"Chen Wei Dong.... You mean the guy who runs the Spring Deer?" Little Beijing was still fairly tipsy.

"That's him."

"What makes him such tough shit?" asked Little Beijing, always thinking of himself as the top dog.

"Let's get brother Zhuzi up."

"Forget it. Do you think either of them can get up right now? I'll go."

As far as Ergou can remember, this was the only time Little Beijing ever put himself out for someone besides Zhao Hongbing. Little Beijing looked down on all street punks, and to this day he has never admitted to being a hooligan. Although an excellent fighter, he never considered mixing with the underworld, and only fought to ensure that no one took advantage of him or Zhao Hongbing. He helped Gourdy this time mainly out of gratitude. When all was said and done, in the big fight with Old Rod Li, Gourdy had joined Liu Haizhu and the others in coming to their aid without a word. He'd also taken the risk of lending them his gun in the fight with Tiger. If Little Beijing allowed Gourdy to be beaten into this condition without doing anything, he didn't deserve to be called "Prince Shen" – a name he enjoyed hearing, even in jest.

"I'll have the cook whip you up some food," he said. "You guys sit here and take your time eating. I'll be back in a minute."

"Are you going? We'll go with you."

"No. Have something to eat first," said Little Beijing, grabbing his motorcycle helmet on the way out.

A month or so before this fight, Little Beijing and Zhao Hongbing had bought a red Xingfu motorcycle. It was a noisy machine with a heavy frame and high horsepower, and out on the road it drew everyone's eyes. Little Beijing loved speeding around on it. He drove it around the city every day to create a spectacle. Often, when someone heard the roaring of the motorcycle, by the time he turned to look, all he would see was a puff of smoke coming from the back of the bike. That's how fast Little Beijing drove.

The only one who dared to ride Little Beijing's motorbike was Zhao Hongbing. He didn't go as fast, but could ride along without batting an eye. He had full confidence in Little Beijing's conduct and motorbiking skills, born of the incomparable mutual trust that had developed from the countless times each had put his life in the other's hands. It's possible that Zhao Hongbing had more faith in Little Beijing's driving skills than Little Beijing did himself.

The day that Little Beijing and Zhao Hongbing brought the motorbike back to the hotel, Hongbing's sister was there. Little Beijing offered her a ride home, revving the motor thunderously. Hongyan had ridden in cars since she was young, but she had never ridden a motorcycle. She climbed eagerly on. Needless to say, they drove at lightning speed. By the time Little Beijing dropped her home, she was so terrified that she just sat on the bike stupefied before breaking into hysterical sobs. The elder Mr. Zhao gave Little Beijing a harsh scolding for that. In fact, this was not only the first time Hongyan had ridden a motorcycle, but also the first time that Little Beijing had ever driven one. Just before setting off, he'd read the instruction manual to learn how to apply the clutch and gas and how to shift gears.

"You're going to drive that thing into a tree sooner or later!" said Hongyan the next day when she'd calmed down. "Don't drive so fast!"

"How can I die before I've married you?" said Little Beijing, gazing into her almond eyes."

"It's a quick way to go, at least," smiled Zhao Hongbing appraisingly.

According to statistics from the local transport department, by the year 2000, out of 900 consumers who bought motorcycles in the 1990s, fewer than 200 were still alive and physically unimpaired. Of course, Little Beijing was one of the lucky few.

When Little Beijing sped off, Chen Wei Dong's restaurant was still doing a roaring business. After all, the joint was not like most others, which had already closed for the night by the time he was just getting started. Arriving at the Spring Deer, Little Beijing took off his helmet and hung it on the motorcycle's handlebar. He didn't turn off the ignition. "Is the boss around?" he smiled to a waiter as he entered.

"Yes, he is. And you are?" Hearing Little Beijing's accent, the waiter thought he must be a business associate of Chen Wei Dong's.

"I'm a friend of his. I need to talk with him for a minute. Could I trouble you to call him over?"

The waiter responded to the famous Beijing courtesy by saying, "All right, just wait a moment."

A few minutes later, the unsightly Chen Wei Dong walked over. He was glancing around. "Who's asking for me?"

"Mr. Chen! How are you? I'm the one asking for you," said Little Beijing politely, approaching him with his hand extended as if to shake.

"And you are?" Chen Wei Dong had put his hand out as well, but had a suspicious look on his face.

"Heh. Don't you recognize me?" said Little Beijing as he drew closer.

Just as the two were about to shake hands, Little Beijing swung his fist and punched Chen Wei Dong in the gut, then grabbed his hair and punched him in the face. Before Chen could figure out what was happening, Little Beijing had knocked him to the floor. When Little Beijing heard Gourdy say that Zhao Shanhe knew *kungfu*, he thought Chen Wei Dong also had some martial arts skills. That's why he camouflaged his murderous intent with smiles, to catch Chen unawares.

Little Beijing grabbed a bottle of liquor. Gripping Chen Wei Dong by the hair, he began clubbing him fiercely with it. Little Beijing's way of gripping people was different from most people's – after grabbing the hair, he twisted his fingers ninety degrees and then pulled hard to tighten his hold. Chen Wei Dong had been a local overlord for so many years that he hadn't needed to fight for a long time. This time he was not only beaten, but had his hair pulled as well. He'd never been in such a humiliating situation, taken by surprise and helpless.

Little Beijing later said that although he liked to pull hair in fights with local bullies and punks, it wasn't a good idea when facing someone with martial arts skills. This rudimentary tactic had too many weak points and could be defeated by at least seven methods. The reason he grabbed Chen Wei

Dong's hair and then beat and kicked him was that he was skilled and bold enough to keep Chen under his control.

"Gourdy is my friend and Liu Haizhu's brother, so if you pick on him again, I'll trash you!" Little Beijing shouted at Chen Wei Dong, who was lying on the floor, face covered with blood. Then, Little Beijing turned and quickly left.

Just at that moment, Zhao Shanhe appeared in the doorway of the restaurant. He'd apparently drunk too much and had gone out to vomit, returning just in time to see Little Beijing finish off Chen Wei Dong and turn to leave.

"Stop him!" Chen shouted to Zhao Shanhe as he staggered to his feet.

"One-on-one or gang fight?" demanded Zhao Shanhe, still woozy from drinking.

"One-on-one," said Little Beijing, squinting his eyes and sneering at Zhao Shanhe, his voice loud and clear.

CHAPTER 42

The Celestial Maiden Scattering Blossoms

ZHAO SHANHE DIDN'T WANT TO smash up the restaurant.

"Let's go out and fight!"

"Let's go!" said Little Beijing, planning to escape once they were outside.

Little Beijing was by no means afraid to take on Zhao Shanhe. Although Zhao was an outstanding fighter, he was at most only Little Beijing's equal, and less smart. Even so, Little Beijing was afraid of the three wolves standing behind Zhao Shanhe; they were sure to leap into action once Little Beijing beat him. With the restaurant's waiters added in, Little Beijing would end up lying in the doorway for sure. Having survived hails of bullets without a scratch, was he really going to fall at the hands of these thugs?

When good fighters trade blows, one or two are usually enough to decide who will win. Of these two men, one was a young fellow who practiced martial arts diligently every day and was well versed in the Supreme Ultimate Plum Blossom Mantis Fist. The other was a demobilized army scout who regularly pondered war and Zen. The crowd outside the restaurant fell silent, hardly daring to breathe.

Zhao Shanhe stooped and arched his back, one foot slightly raised as he focused his attack. Little Beijing subsequently recalled that his many years of sizing people up led him to sense his opponent's rich vitality and outstanding fighting skills immediately. He came up with his best idea: the Eight Trigram Swimming Palms stance.

This startled Zhao Shanhe and everyone else. They were all thinking, "What's this – a movie set?" Hooligans fought all the time back then, but they just lunged right in rather than giving a preview of their martial arts moves; even Zhao Shanhe's Supreme Ultimate Plum Blossom Mantis Fist had no set moves. At that time, *kungfu* movies were very popular, and people regarded China's traditional martial arts with almost blind devotion. When Zhao Shanhe saw Little Beijing's palm force, calm bearing, and credible (though bogus) footwork, he was momentarily at a loss.

In fact, Ergou is aware that Little Beijing knew nothing whatsoever about any Eight Trigram Swimming Palms stance. All he had learned in the army was life-and-death fighting; none of this fancy footwork. He could only demonstrate the swimming palms stance because he'd read an article about it in *Martial Arts World*. Now, at this critical juncture, he was putting it to use.

Zhuangzi once said, "If water does not accumulate to a sufficient depth, it will not have strength to support a large boat. Upset a cup of water in a hollow, and a mustard seed will float on it as if it were a boat..." Little Beijing could put on this pose and startle his opponent because he was agile, well-trained and unflinching. If Ergou had tried to strike such a pose, everyone would have died laughing.

As its name implies, the Eight Trigram Swimming Palms has motion as its essence. Taking advantage of the distraction of Zhao Shanhe and the others, Little Beijing made his palms and feet swim off in the direction of his motorcycle. The tension was suffocating.

Little Beijing suddenly grabbed the helmet hanging on his handlebar and hurled it with all his strength at Zhao Shanhe's head, just six feet away.

Zhao Shanhe and the others never expected the grandmasterly Little Beijing to suddenly attack with this hidden weapon. The highly-focused Zhao Shanhe was immediately thrown into confusion. On impulse he reached out to ward off the flying helmet, opening the door for escape. Little Beijing took advantage the interruption to aim a kick at Zhao Shanhe's lower abdomen. It was actually more of a stomp than a kick; Little Beijing knew that a kick wouldn't be enough to fell a seasoned fighter like Zhao Shanhe. His "stomp" was unlikely to inflict real injury, but could knock Zhao over.

In fact, the kick sent Zhao Shanhe flying a couple of yards, at which point Little Beijing grabbed his motorcycle and began running. After a few steps he jumped onto the motorcycle, gunned the engine, and sped off with a roar. It was in anticipation of this kind of trouble that Little Beijing had left the motorcycle running.

Now, the only people left in front of the restaurant were Zhao Shanhe – who was gripping his stomach, Chen Wei Dong – nursing a battered face, and Zhao Shanhe's three gang brothers, still too dumbstruck to have realized what happened. By the time they came to their senses, all they saw was a puff of exhaust from Little Beijing's motorcycle.

Afterwards someone teased Little Beijing: "Prince Shen, it's not like you to give someone a kick and then run off!"

"When we agreed to a one-on-one, we didn't specify what constituted winning or losing, nor whether other weapons could be used. I sent him flying with a kick, which meant I won. Once I'd won, of course I left."

In the time it took for Little Beijing to speed back to the hotel, the cook hadn't even finished preparing Gourdy's meal. It had taken Little Beijing just fifteen minutes to drive out to the Spring Deer and back, including eight minutes on the road and seven minutes fighting.

The next day, after recovering from their hangovers, Zhao Hongbing and Liu Haizhu learned what had happened the night before.

"I don't think Chen Wei Dong and the others will let things go at that," said Zhao Hongbing. "He may not know who Shen is, but he definitely knows that Gourdy is your little brother.

"Yeah, I guess this fight will continue for a while," said Liu Haizhu. "But it's nothing to do with you guys. I'll tidy up Chen Wei Dong."

"Your business is our business, brother Liu," said Little Beijing sincerely.

"When I was inside, I was always tuning up Chen Wei Dong. No one scares him more than I do," said Liu, cool as ever.

"Regardless, that was before. Gourdy says Chen Wei Dong's cousin has a bunch of hooligans following him, and they're always fighting for Chen. You have to watch out."

"How am I supposed to do that? Does that mean I can't put out my bicycle repair stall? That I can't plant my crops when I hear the locusts buzz?" Liu Haizhu was surly with everyone, but Zhao Hongbing and the others knew the warm heart under that gruff exterior.

"That's not what I meant. Anyway, if something happens, be sure to let us know," Hongbing said.

Liu Haizhu didn't speak. He gave Hongbing a pat on the shoulder as he left, the barest hint of a smile showing under his goatee. That smile revealed his true feelings of brotherliness and loyalty toward Zhao Hongbing and Little Beijing.

Liu was right; Chen Wei Dong was truly afraid of him. But there was someone who didn't fear him, and that was Zhao Shanhe. At that stage, Zhao Shanhe and his gang were like Zhao Hongbing and his friends had been two or three years earlier: too green to know fear, like birds of prey testing their wings.

The difference between Zhao Shanhe and Zhao Hongbing was that Hongbing became famous by accident through defying the bullying of other punks. Zhao Shanhe had a burning desire to annihilate all of the city's major gangsters and establish his name in the underworld. The two of them had very different points of departure.

They say that several days after Little Beijing visited the Spring Deer, Zhao Shanhe had the following conversation with Chen Wei Dong:

"Brother, can you find out who kicked me that night? I have to get my revenge."

"I don't know who he was, but for sure he was a gang brother or friend of Liu Haizhu's," said Chen Wei Dong."

"So let's go look for Liu Haizhu!" said Zhao Shanhe with the boldness of ignorance.

"Steady there. Anyone who's been in the life for a while knows Liu Haizhu is famous for being a tough fighter."

"So what if he's tough? We're tough, too. Why should we be afraid of him?"

"Brother, when Liu Haizhu began mixing in the streets, you were just a kid; you don't know anything about what he did back then."

"You make him sound like hot shit, but all he does now is fix bicycles. If he was really so tough, would he be doing that?"

"What do you have in mind?"

"Let's go find him and tune him up! How can we keep up our street cred if we don't? I know I can beat him!" Zhao Shanhe was determined.

"Of course you can beat him," said the streetwise Chen Wei Dong. "But some things can't be settled by fighting."

"I was always being bullied at school. You were inside, so you couldn't take revenge for me. Why have I spent so much time and energy learning martial arts if I can't make a name for myself?"

"Make a name for yourself? And then what? You think you can handle it?"

"You made a name for yourself long ago, and aren't you living well?"

"If I'd spent all my time fighting like you do, I'd be long dead."

"Brother, don't forget, when he came to our restaurant that night, the first person he hit was you."

"So what is it you want to do?"

"Go find Liu Haizhu and knock him around!"

"And after that?"

"That's it. What else would happen?"

"You think it would end there just because you say so? You think Liu Haizhu has spent ten-plus years on the streets for nothing? He has a pretty big gang of his own, and he's also very friendly with Zhao Hongbing and his lot. Hongbing and his guys are the kind who'll take a gun to you."

"Who the fuck is Zhao Hongbing? Tell him to come over and try aiming a gun at me."

"I'm wasting my breath. Do what you want."

"I have to get Liu Haizhu!"

"I told you, do what you want. I'm out of it."

There was an obvious generation gap between Chen Wei Dong and his cousin. Back then, a lot of people would have had trouble understanding what Zhao Shanhe was thinking and saying, and why he would risk his life to make a name for himself in the gang world. People need ideals, but some ideals become seriously distorted. Zhao Shanhe's ideals took shape before he gained a proper understanding of right and wrong. All he cared about was fame, and he didn't have the slightest sense of chivalry. Gangsters eventually stopped following the classic mold and became obsessed with fame and wealth. But in the 1980s, the era of the classic gangster had not yet ended.

CHAPTER 43

Round-heels

THEY SAY THAT IF ZHAO Shanhe's beloved hadn't stood in his way, he would have gone the next day to settle the score with Liu Haizhu. Zhao Shanhe's lady was named Mao Qin, and she was a woman with a past. Beautiful and voluptuous, she was always casting sidelong glances with her bewitching eyes. If a man responded with a lustful gaze, she would duck her head bashfully, bringing him completely under her spell. Mao Qin understood all too well that men had an aversion to bold and unrestrained women, but couldn't resist one who looked pure and reserved but was a tiger in bed. She was a brilliant seductress – a fox fairy who could see into men's hearts.

Rumor had it that Chen Wei Dong had pulled Mao Qin into a sorghum field outside the city and had his way with her when she was just seventeen. Chen was her first man, and one of only two she'd truly loved. Chen Wei Dong got her hooked on the joy and glory of sex, and she had slept with just about every major gangster in the city except for Zhao Hongbing and his friends. Ergou knows that back when she was still young and innocent, Mao Qin had her eye on the handsome Zhao Hongbing, but Hongbing never gave her a chance.

Mao Qin came to Zhao Hongbing's hotel on many occasions with other men, a different one each time. Ergou clearly remembers one occasion when she attempted to seduce Zhao Hongbing. She came to the restaurant for a meal, and seemed to have had a bit too much to drink.

"Boss Zhao, where's that pretty girlfriend or yours?" she asked. Her lips curled into a smile and her phoenix eyes fixed on Hongbing behind the bar.

"She's at school in Beijing."

Zhao Hongbing could be bashful at times. Whenever a woman looked at him, he would drop his head – an action that naturally tantalized Mao Qin, who knew it as a flirting tactic.

"When's she getting back?" she asked, still directing her sardonic smile at Zhao Hongbing.

"During her summer break in July." Out of courtesy, Hongbing raised his face long enough to answer, but on meeting her gaze he quickly averted his eyes again in a pretense of looking through his accounts.

"Ha. I'm surprised you don't have a temporary girlfriend while she's away," said Mao Qin teasingly, gazing at Zhao Hongbing.

"I... I can't find one." One of Hongbing's weaknesses was his inability to handle flirtation. He was gentlemanly by nature, and was never willing to speak rudely to a woman.

"I can't believe there isn't a single girl who wouldn't go for lively young fellow like you." Mao Qin looked like she could eat him alive.

"It's true. I can't find one." Zhao Hongbing was clearly finding Mao Qin a nuisance, but still he played along.

"How about me? Would I be good enough for you?" With

Hongbing refusing to take the bait, Mao Qin was becoming desperate. She was unaccustomed to such a tough seduction.

"I'm not good enough for you." In spite of being completely fed up, Hongbing managed to say it with a polite smile.

"You're definitely my type," said Mao Qin, resorting to undisguised provocation.

Hongbing was flummoxed.

"Boss Zhao, don't tell me you're a virgin?" Mao said with a lascivious smile.

At this Hongbing became truly offended. Instead of replying, he buried his face in his accounts again.

Little Beijing piped up with:

"I'm a virgin!"

He smiled and raised his hand.

"Are you really? Shall I give you a try?"

"I don't dare!" said Little Beijing with a look of feigned regret.

"Why not?"

"I'm afraid of getting sick."

"What sickness are you afraid of?"

"STDs."

"You..." Speechless, Mao Qin turned and stalked out.

"That was a bit much," said Hongbing, even though he was glad to be rid of her. "She was only teasing us. Why offend her like that?"

"If I hadn't done something, she would have ended up raping you. I was coming to your rescue!" Little Beijing was gleeful.

"You should think about how that mouth of yours offends every woman you know. Can you think of anyone you haven't antagonized?" Hongbing knew Little Beijing couldn't change his ways.

"I haven't offended Hongyan. She still likes me."

"Get lost!"

Mao Qin never managed to seduce Zhao Hongbing.

She had only ever loved two men: Chen Wei Dong and Zhao Shanhe. Although she had been with countless men and continued her unconventional ways after meeting Zhao Shanhe, this didn't affect the burning love between them. It's possible that the vigorous and youthful Zhao Shanhe brought her the greatest physical satisfaction. Their relationship was one of teacher and student, friends and family members. At first, Mao Qin was introduced to Zhao Shanhe as Chen Wei Dong's intimate friend and effectively family. Later, after going to bed with Zhao Shanhe, she became his teacher in the ways of love. Usually, however, they were good friends who kept nothing from each other, even as Mao Qin maintained her long-term relationship with Chen Wei Dong. In short, things were complicated.

When Mao Qin and her "comrade-in-arms" finished their passionate encounter that night, Zhao Shanhe brought up his intention to fight Liu Haizhu.

"I'm going to pack him up tomorrow for sure!" he said.

"Liu Haizhu? Do you know who he is? You know Old Rod Li, right? Liu Haizhu chopped him twice in the back, and Old Rod hasn't dared go after him since."

"That's just because Old Rod Li has no balls."

"No balls? Tell me anyone in the city who's willing to go up against his gang!"

"Anyway, Liu Haizhu is famous, right? And I'm a famous fighter."

"You need to talk to your cousin about this. Don't be impulsive."

"I already discussed it with him. He's doesn't have balls, either. I don't know why I ever respected him."

"I've known Wei Dong for ten years now, and you've known him for twenty. Are you suggesting he's a coward?"

"Not usually, but this time he is."

"It's not your cousin. It's Liu Haizhu. He's notoriously fearless. Years ago he picked off basically every hoodlum in the city, large or small. You were just a kid then, so you don't know."

"Then what do you think I should do?"

"I just mentioned that he's at odds with Old Rod Li. Why don't you see if Old Rod is willing to help you out?"

"I need help tuning up a bike repairman?"

"Liu Haizhu has a lot of followers and a lot of friends. Have you heard of Zhao Hongbing and his gang? They're tight with him. If you go to Zhao Hongbing's restaurant, you'll always see them drinking together."

"That's what my cousin said, too. How about if you go see Old Rod Li tomorrow and feel him out?"

"Your cousin's in business now, and there's some things he's not in a position to help you with. If you really want to make something out of this, I'll talk with some people in our circles."

Although Mao Qin had slept with Zhao Shanhe countless time, she still acted like a big sister to him.

"If this thing really blows up, I know my cousin will help me."

"Of course."

Mao Qin loved Zhao Shanhe so much that she'd sleep with a man she wasn't attracted to if that's what it took to help him. That's how she ended up in bed with Evil Huang the following night, after meeting him when she went to see Old

Rod Li. Ergou is pretty sure that a man like Evil Huang had trouble attracting women. Of course, it's always possible that Mao Qin had unusual taste in men. Based on what followed, and on what Ergou knows of Evil Huang and Mao Qin, he guesses that the two of them had a conversation something like this after their night of passion:

"My little brother is going after Liu Haizhu," Mao Qin said.

"Liu Haizhu?" Evil Huang practically wet himself at the mention of that name, remembering all too well the time Liu had chased him with a cleaver.

"What, are you scared of him? And here I thought you were a big man," said Mao Qin, somewhat disdainfully.

"Who said I was scared?" Evil Huang took a drag off his cigarette and blew a smoke ring with studied casualness. "I've been wanting to go after him for ages."

Evil Huang wasn't much of a fighter, but he knew how to strike a pose. Mao Qin, with her vast experience, had picked the right man.

CHAPTER 44

Reckless Love

EVIL HUANG'S SMOKE RING SLOWLY rose and dispersed into the surrounding air. Only Great Production brand cigarettes, at 2.5 *yuan* a pack, produced smoke dense enough for such satisfying rings. Evil Huang adored that brand, and loved blowing smoke rings with them. He believed that the choking fumes carried a hint of debased nobility that ordinary people couldn't detect, which suited his personal style. He believed that in a former life he'd been the Qing poet Nalan Xingde – a Manchu nobleman who'd made his name in the south for being melancholy, lithe, and delicate, with expressive eyes. Now that Huang had to fight Liu Haizhu – a reincarnation of General Zhang Fei – could his frail physique again withstand that flailing cleaver? Evil Huang shook his head lightly. He decided that this qualified as reckless waste.

Huang gently pushed Mao Qin from his embrace. His mind was as muddled as his unraveling smoke rings. When all was said and done, plenty of people had died while striking a pose.

"You can count on me," Evil Huang said softly.

Mao Qin heaved a worshipful sigh.

Evil Huang pulled on his army pants and combat boots and strode out the door. He had his own rather unconventional style. At a time when blue jeans were becoming the fashion for men and women alike, Huang had gone retro. The early morning air was filled with the characteristic flavor of summer mornings in those parts back in the 1980s – a heady mix of coal smoke billowing from chimneys and the perfume of summer flowers blooming along the road. As he stepped outside, Evil Huang took a deep breath. A sensitive man, he detected a faint sadness in the air – a note of farewell. He turned and looked back at the door he'd just closed, behind which lay a beautiful woman among fragrant quilts still warm from his presence.

Evil Huang realized that he'd fallen in love with the vixenish Mao Qin.

The first person he thought of who could help dispel his terror of Liu Haizhu was Tudou, the young hoodlum whose face had been ruined by Feisi. After repairs to his disfigurement, Tudou was more irrational and ruthless than ever. He was one of Old Rod Li's three top lieutenants, along with Quint and Evil Huang. But Quint had basically withdrawn from gang circles after Lisi knocked his teeth out, and this had put Tudou in a stronger position. Although Old Rod Li was opposed to making further trouble, Tudou was absolutely determined to take revenge on Liu Haizhu for chopping Old Rod.

Friendships are often forged through a common enemy. Zhao Shanhe, Evil Huang and Tudou had a mutual foe in Liu Haizhu.

They say it was Evil Huang and Tudou who approached Zhao Shanhe. The tactic they decided on was that if Liu

Haizhu was alone or with only one or two others, Zhao Shanhe and his guys would take care of him. If the situation became more serious and Liu Haizhu called in reinforcements, then Evil Huang and Tudou would put in an appearance.

As it happened, the rise of Zhao Hongbing and his gang was as inevitable as it was fortuitous; they were on an entirely different intellectual level than people like Evil Huang. In anticipating future developments, Evil Huang and Zhao Shanhe indulged in wishful thinking that matters wouldn't escalate, forgetting what kind of person Liu Haizhu was, and what kind of friends he had.

One midday in July 1988 – one of those typical blazing northeastern summer days when the asphalt actually melts in the heat – Zhao Shanhe and his gang arrived at the entrance to the No. 14 High School. They were looking for Liu Haizhu, who was absorbed in repairing a bicycle with his wrench.

It was the first time in years that Evil Huang had set foot on that street; his fear of Liu Haizhu always propelled him to an alternate route. Today, his rage was fueled by Mao Qin. Tudou and Evil Huang hung back about fifty yards, watching Zhao Shanhe approach Liu Haizhu.

"Are you Liu Haizhu?" Zhao Shanhe radiated malevolence with his three wolves behind him.

"What's your business?" Liu Haizhu kept working on the bike, not even bothering to raise his head.

"I'm Chen Wei Dong's younger brother."

"I asked you what's your business," said Liu Haizhu, still not raising his head. This was the difference between a young upstart and a battle-scarred veteran – it was no easy matter to remain so calm and steady in the face of such a belligerent invader.

"Your friend beat up my brother and gave me a kick." Fighting a mental as much as a physical contest, Zhao Shanhe was no match for Liu Haizhu. Liu asked his questions without even raising his head, while Zhao Shanhe felt compelled to answer, sapping his momentum.

"You still haven't stated your business," said Liu Haizhu a third time.

"Your friend started it, so now you have to hand him over," said Zhao Shanhe, restoking his energy.

Gangsters regularly used the term "hand him over" to refer to a situation in which a member of Gang A offended someone in Gang B. The head of Gang B would demand that the leader of Gang A hand over his gang member. Making such a demand usually required Gang B to be in the stronger position.

"Hand him over?" Liu Haizhu finally put his work aside and stood up, gripping his wrench. Zhao Shanhe still couldn't see his eyes, only his goatee.

"Yeah. The guy had a Beijing accent. If you hand him over, we can talk; otherwise we'll find him ourselves, and then he'll be in for it!"

"You want me to hand him over?" Liu Haizhu seemed bewildered by the demand.

"Are you going to, or not?" Zhao Shanhe was getting nastier by the minute.

"Your big brother Archy is a lot smarter than you. Hasn't he taught you anything?" In Liu Haizhu's eyes, Zhao Shanhe was still a milky-breathed kid.

"Are you handing him over or not?" shouted Zhao Shanhe.

"In all my years on the streets, I've never handed anyone over!" Drained of all his patience, Liu Haizhu lunged at Zhao Shanhe with his wrench.

Zhao must have sensed the inevitability of a tussle with this wrathful and strange-looking man.

"One-on-one or gang fight?" he demanded.

"One-on-one with your mother!" roared Liu Haizhu as he swung his wrench at Zhao Shanhe.

Zhao darted to one side to evade it, and at the same time punched Liu Haizhu in the nose, which immediately began bleeding.

Ten years before, Liu Haizhu had been the city's top solo fighter; now that honor belonged to Zhao Shanhe.

The older fighter had never been properly trained in martial arts. However, he'd fought countless battles, and his experience of actual combat was hard to match. The younger fighter honed his skills on a daily basis and rarely fumbled; his lack of experience was compensated by his physical prowess.

Liu Haizhu was a smart guy, and he recognized from Zhao Shanhe's agile moves that his opponent was a skilled martial artist. What was the best way to deal with such a person? Close hand-to-hand fighting; wrestling would deprive Zhao Shanhe of the advantages of his training.

Liu Haizhu was also extremely fast, and after being punched in the nose, he grabbed Zhao Shanhe's collar with lightning speed and tripped him. Stumbling, Zhao Shanhe reached out and pulled Lu Haizhu's arm. Liu pushed in the same direction, sending the two of them tumbling onto the sun-softened asphalt. As they wrestled, the hand of one kept a death grip on that of the other, so that each had only one hand and two knees to use against the other.

Liu Haizhu swung his wrench at Zhao Shanhe, while Zhao's rained punches on Liu's face and body. After a couple of minutes, both were panting and bloodied.

Standing in the background, Zhao Shanhe's three wolves didn't move, either out of fear for Liu Haizhu's reputation, or because they believed Zhao was sure to win.

The two kept fighting for seven or eight minutes. Liu Haizhu fought like a tiger, but even so, that tiger was a good thirty-five years old; Zhao Shanhe, more than ten years younger, was at the height of his strength, like the scorching noonday sun.

Liu Haizhu was finally overcome by the broiling heat and could fight no more. By then, Zhao Shanhe was also dizzy from Liu's blows, and his punches no longer packed their previous strength.

They stopped fighting. Zhao Shanhe, seeing stars, rose unsteadily to his feet and wiped the blood from his mouth. Liu Haizhu's gaunt form remained curled and immobile under the blazing sun.

"You hand that guy over or don't bother coming back here again!" Zhao Shanhe spat.

"Fuck you!" Liu Haizhu retorted coldly as he sat up and adjusted his bamboo hat.

Zhao Shanhe didn't even bother to reply. He flicked his hand and stalked off with his three wolves.

CHAPTER 45

'Fight and Die', or 'Death Destroying Death'

ACHING FROM HEAD TO TOE, Liu Haizhu lowered himself gingerly to the curb. The corner of his left eye was split open, blurring his vision with blood.

"Brother Zhuzi, are you okay? Rinse your mouth out with some watermelon." A melon hawker next to Liu's bicycle stall passed him a slice. The hawker had just set up his stall that summer, and the respect he showed on such short acquaintance was a measure of Liu Haizhu's reputation.

A bite of melon revived Liu somewhat. He was in bad shape, but his wounds were all superficial.

"I'm all right," he muttered.

"Brother Zhuzi, when I saw the two of you rolling around on the ground just now, I really wanted to stab that punk with my melon knife. But I was afraid that if I made a move, the guys behind him would jump in. Let me take you to the hospital."

"Wait a minute." Although hurting all over, Liu hadn't uttered so much as a groan. He wanted to rest before going to the hospital; his head was still spinning.

"Then at least come into my stall and cool down."

"Okay."

It was while Liu was resting that Evil Huang arrived. Evil and Tudou and their guys had been watching the epic battle from a distance with their hearts in their mouths. It was only when Zhao Shanhe stumbled over to them that they came to their senses and rushed him to the hospital. Halfway there, Evil Huang realized that something important had been left undone. Something very important – he hadn't yet had a chance to strike a pose. How could he show his face in public if he left the scene of such a major rumble without flexing his muscles?

Life only gives a man so many chances to shine. If he missed this golden opportunity, he might never again have a chance to kick the ass of the famous Liu Haizhu – the equivalent of a sure goal in the World Cup. He would be cheating not only himself, but also Mao Qin, whose irresistible allure stoked his posturing.

Evil Huang decided to turn back for a face-off with Liu Haizhu. Only then would he be able to claim bragging rights before Mao Qin and his gangland brothers.

"Tudou, you guys get Zhao Shanhe to the hospital," Evil said, stopping in his tracks.

"Why? What's up?"

"There's something I need to do," he said with a smile. What he meant was, "There's some ass I need to kick."

"Okay. Go ahead."

Evil Huang turned back toward Liu Haizhu's bicycle stand. After all his years of acting the big man, he failed to realize that he'd met his match this time. Today would bring the most painful lesson of his life.

"Hey, do you remember me?" A cocksure Evil Huang strode over to the melon stall and planted himself in front of Liu Haizhu.

"Weasel Huang!" Liu said with disgust. "Get the fuck out of here!"

"Big talk for someone who just got the shit beat out of him!" Huang was even brasher than usual that day.

"Fuck off!" If it hadn't been for his arm and leg shooting pain through his entire body, Liu would have cold-cocked Evil Huang already.

In his puffed-up state, Evil couldn't resist asking Liu: "You know why I'm here today?"

"You haven't been smacked around enough yet?" Liu sneered.

"Listen, Zhao Shanhe is my little brother." This was a claim that Zhao Shanhe himself might have disagreed with. "If you get my drift, hurry up and turn the guy over. I know who did it – it was that guy Shen, right?"

"It was your dick!" spat Liu. He could put up with Evil Huang, but he couldn't stand him threatening Little Beijing.

"Still a fucking blowhard!" said Evil Huang, ever the pot calling the kettle black.

Before he'd finished speaking, he suddenly felt his scalp go numb. Liu Haizhu's iron fingers gripped him by the hair while his other hand swept the melon knife from the table in front of him. Evil squealed like a stuck pig as the knife stabbed his shoulder and the back of his head. He grabbed the wrist that gripped his hair and jerked up his head as he kicked at Liu Haizhu's stomach. The pain of the blow caused Liu to loosen his grip.

Evil Huang spun around and ran. He'd always had a

phobia of Liu Haizhu, and had only been emboldened by seeing him so badly injured. He'd never guessed that the he would rise up so fiercely. He was scared out of his wits. He ran for his life. Liu Haizhu, enraged by Evil's kick, forgot his pain and set off in hot pursuit.

Years later, people still recalled the scene of a blood-drenched man running desperately and squealing in terror as he was chased by a bare-chested guy in a bamboo hat clutching a melon knife.

They say that Liu Haizhu chased Evil Huang more than a mile that day, and stabbed him twenty-nine times. It's also said that Evil was a strong sprinter who could run a respectable hundred-yard dash, but wasn't a long-distance runner. Liu Haizhu was just the opposite – not much of a sprinter, but with amazing endurance. After about three hundred yards, Liu caught up with Evil Huang and stabbed him in the back. Evil screamed and shot forward, widening the gap between them, but after another seventy yards or so, Liu caught up and stabbed him again. In this way, Liu Haizhu managed to stab Evil Huang more than twenty times before letting up. By this time, Evil's back was hacked to ribbons, and his flowered Aloha shirt was reduced to scarlet strips like head bands.

It was impossible not to admire Evil's resistance. Anyone else would either have collapsed from his wounds or fainted at the sight of his own blood. It was also impossible not to admire Liu Haizhu. Who else would have had the persistence and stamina to chase a terrified opponent for a mile?

Afterwards, Little Beijing wrote a poem parodying Evil Huang's style:

Evil Huang charges down the gangland path,
full of derring-do;
He lost his reputation twice, being chased by
Liu Haizhu.

That afternoon, Gourdy learned that Liu Haizhu had been injured because of him. He grabbed his automatic and went to Zhao Hongbing's hotel. Gourdy had followed Liu Haizhu for years, and was fiercely loyal to the man he considered his brother. To have this happen because of him, and to have it result in such serious injury to Liu Haizhu, called for revenge. Although Gourdy was a lady's man and liked to rumble after drinking, he was still a stand-up guy. That's why a righteous gangster like Liu Haizhu had associated with him for so long. Gourdy wanted to borrow Zhao Hongbing's motorcycle so he could chase down Zhao Shanhe and trash him. He had never fired his automatic before, but this time he was determined to use it.

"Shanhe beat up Brother Zhuzi today," Gourdy said to Hongbing.

"Really? Brother Liu's been hurt?" The normally imperturbable Zhao Hongbing was agitated.

"He'll be all right."

Hongbing sprang to his feet. "Let's get Zhao Shanhe!"

"Not today," said Gourdy. "Later."

"Later?"

"Yeah. Let's plan things out before we go. Right now, I just want to borrow your motorcycle so I can buy some ointment for Brother Zhuzi."

"Which hospital is he at?" asked Zhao Hongbing, wheeling out his motorcycle.

"They didn't admit him. He was just treated and discharged."

"When Shen gets back, we'll go and visit Brother Liu. He can decide when to go after Zhao Shanhe."

"Great. I gotta go, but I'll see you tonight at Brother Zhuzi's place."

"Sure."

Gourdy turned and left. That was the last Zhao Hongbing ever saw of him.

Little Beijing arrived just as Gourdy was leaving. "What was he here for?" he asked Hongbing.

"Gourdy? He wanted to borrow the motorcycle to buy some ointment. Brother Liu got roughed up in a fight with Zhao Shanhe."

"Why does he need a gun to buy medicine?" The detail-oriented Little Beijing had noticed the clear impression of a gun in the fiber bag slung over the motorcycle's bumper when he passed by.

"He was carrying a gun?"

"Yeah!"

"Shit! That means he's gone to hunt down Zhao Shanhe himself! We need to catch him right away."

But by the time Zhao Hongbing and Little Beijing had run out of the hotel, Gourdy was long gone.

He took the motorcycle straight to the Spring Dear, certain that Zhao Shanhe would go there. He never guessed that he would run into Tudou, who was at the restaurant to ask Chen Wei Dong for money to pay Evil Huang and Zhao Shanhe's hospital bills. More badly injured than Liu Haizhu, Zhao Shanhe needed to be admitted. He'd sent Tudou to his cousin for some money. Chen Wei Dong hadn't come in yet, and Tudou was waiting impatiently for him.

Gourdy didn't follow Little Beijing's example of keeping the ignition on when he parked the motorcycle in front of the restaurant. This was his downfall.

He grabbed his bag with the automatic weapon in it and hooked his finger around the trigger as he entered the Spring Dear.

"Where's Zhao Shanhe?" he yelled.

Seated at the bar, Tudou turned. His eyes met Gourdy's. They recognized each other from the bloody battle outside the Purple Moon the year before.

Tudou jumped up and grabbed his shotgun, aiming it at Gourdy. He knew Gourdy was here on a mission, and that if he was slow on the draw he'd be a goner. Although Gourdy hadn't taken his gun out of the bag, Tudou knew it was in there. At the same time, Gourdy aimed the gun in his bag at Tudou. The two men approached each other with their guns raised until they were only about three feet apart, their weapons aimed at each other's heads.

"Recognize me, motherfucker?" Tudou snarled. They say he'd been wanting to take revenge on Zhao Hongbing, Feisi, and the others, but Old Rod Li had been holding him back. Now, face to face with his enemy, his eyes blazed.

"Back off, dickhead," Gourdy said. "This is nothing to do with you."

"Carrying that shitty gun gives you balls, eh? Well I've got one, too!" Since his face was ruined, Tudou had lost his relish for living.

"Keep talking and I'll blast you!" Gourdy said.

"I'll count to three and we'll both shoot. Do you have the guts?" Tudou thought this might scare his opponent off.

"You think I'm some kid? Count away!" retorted Gourdy.

Sweat coated both men's palms as they stared each other down, their breathing hoarse. A dose of cowardice would have saved them both. Unfortunately, neither was a chicken. The truth is that sometimes being a chicken is the wiser choice.

"One!" Tudou's throat constricted around the word. Gourdy gulped as well.

"Two!" Beads of sweat rolled down both men's faces; their nerves were at breaking point.

"Three!"

Only one gun fired, and it was Gourdy's. Tudou never managed a shot. He fell to the ground with a bullet in his head.

CHAPTER 46

Thank You for Finally Arresting Me

TIME STOPPED AT THAT MOMENT.

Tudou was dead. The look on his face was dreadful. They say he died with a startled expression, still gripping the shotgun he'd never managed to fire. Only seconds earlier he'd been alive, and yelling for a duel with Gourdy. Now he was reduced to a rigid husk enmeshed in a web he'd spun for himself.

Still gripping his rifle, Gourdy wore an expression as shocked as Tudou's. He'd come here to trash Zhao Shanhe. But now he'd killed Tudou, a man he had nothing against. He'd killed someone! Gourdy's hands trembled. In all the years he'd held this gun, that was the first time he'd ever fired it. And with just one shot, he'd killed somebody.

Perhaps both had considered themselves big men, capable of earth-shaking deeds. But for the next twenty years, any hoodlum who mentioned this showdown typically appraised them as a couple of tiger dicks.

According to Ergou, the term "tiger dick" refers to

someone who does things without considering the consequences. However, it can also have the positive connotation of brotherhood and daring. The term "big man" is somewhat different, referring to a sense of brotherhood, honor, and responsibility, but also an appropriate capacity for forbearance. A tiger dick with patience and common sense becomes a big man. With a little more patience Gourdy would have killed Zhao Shanhe or Chen Wei Dong rather than Tudou, and then he would have ended up a big man instead of a tiger dick.

After standing there gaping for a few seconds, Gourdy finally grabbed his gun and ran out of the restaurant, knowing that was all he could do. When he went to start the motorcycle, he found that in his panic he'd managed to drop the key. Abandoning it, he took off on foot and soon vanished down the far end of the street. And so began his period of exile.

The motorcycle outside the Spring Deer became the first clue for the PSB in solving this case. The registered owner was Zhao Hongbing.

They say that while on the run, Gourdy spent several days on Changbai Mountain eating wild herbs and tree roots. He even ventured into the Greater Khingan mountain range and lived like a wild man before crossing over into the Hulun Buir steppes of Inner Mongolia. There, he herded goats and cut hay, always on the brink of starvation and experiencing all the greatest torments of human existence. He was finally arrested two years later while working as a casual laborer at the Huolinhe Coal Mine. As the police officer slapped the handcuffs on his wrists, Gourdy gave a long sigh and a smile that expressed greater relief than he'd known in a very long time.

"Thank you for finally arresting me," he said to the policemen, his eyes revealing the depths of his gratitude. He'd had enough of this life. To him, the green-clad police officers were like the goddess Guanyin of the South China Sea, saving the needy and relieving the distressed. For Gourdy, death had become preferable to life. In all of the 3.75 million square miles of the People's Republic, there'd been no place for him to take shelter or get a peaceful night's rest. He probably wished he'd died in Tudou's place at the Spring Deer.

On the night of the shooting, the police came and took Zhao Hongbing away. They gave two reasons. Firstly, the motorcycle parked in front of the restaurant was his; secondly, Hongbing had been involved in the earlier shooting at the hospital. Who else would the police come for if not him?

Several days later, the crime squad identified the perpetrator and established that Zhao Hongbing had nothing to do with the killing. He was released. The next day, a woman arrived at Hongbing's restaurant. It was Gao Huan's mother.

"Welcome, Auntie!" said Hongbing, flustered. "Shen, boil some tea."

But Gao Huan's mother walked straight over to Zhao Hongbing, fell to her knees, and gripped his legs.

"I beg you! Please let my daughter go," she pled, face streaming with tears.

"What are you doing?" cried Zhao Hongbing as he quickly pulled the woman to her feet.

"I beg you! Please let my daughter go," the woman went on, sobbing uncontrollably. "I don't want to see her become a widow."

"What do you mean? Everything's fine with Gao Huan and me," said Zhao Hongbing, still at a loss.

"I know the reputation you have outside, and I know that you're involved in a killing. If you keep on like this, my daughter is sure to end up a widow! I beg of you, let her go!" The woman fell to her knees again as she spoke.

Zhao Hongbing now realized that she knew what he was mixed up in, and wanted to force him to break up with Gao Huan.

"Everything's fine with Huan and me," he assured her. It was true, as far as he was concerned. He'd never even thought of leaving Gao Huan, and expected to grow old with her.

"Don't you know that if you keep on this way, you'll be the death of my daughter?" the woman wailed.

"So what do you want me to do?"

"I want you to break up with my daughter and never have anything to do with her again."

"Why don't you ask Gao Huan how she feels about this? You can go and persuade her."

"She won't listen to me. If you don't break up with her, I will die here and now." The woman was hysterical.

"Calm down! Please! Just rest for a minute," said Hongbing, visibly moved. He understood that she was doing this out of genuine love for her daughter.

"I'm begging you..." she sobbed, unable to say anything else.

"I'll talk with Gao Huan tonight about breaking up. Please don't worry," Zhao Hongbing said softly, after long consideration. By then he was very upset; he couldn't give up Gao Huan, but he couldn't help pitying the desperate mother before him.

"Thank you," she said, kneeling again.

Zhao Hongbing lifted her up and said, "Don't worry. I'll telephone Gao Huan tonight."

"Thank you..." The woman was trembling from head to toe.

Zhao Hongbing and Little Beijing took her home. She was beside herself. To her, it seemed Hongbing was the devil incarnate.

"Do you really want to break up with Gao Huan?" Little Beijing asked lightly on the way back.

"Hm..."

"Could you really do it?" Little Beijing's voice became urgent.

"Maybe it would actually be good for her," said Zhao Hongbing after a while. "Maybe her mother is right."

Little Beijing didn't say anything more. He passed Zhao Hongbing a cigarette.

Later that day, Hongbing telephoned Gao Huan at her dormitory. "When does your summer break start?" he asked with feigned casualness

"In a week. I'll be seeing you soon!" Gao Huan was in high spirits.

"Uh... There's something I want to tell you."

"Oh?"

Summoning all his courage, Zhao Hongbing said, "I think we should break up."

"What kind of joke is this?" Gao Huan laughed and tried to sound lighthearted, but she sensed something in Zhao Hongbing's voice. Her own voice trembled.

"I'm not joking," said Zhao Hongbing after steeling himself again. "I mean it."

"Why? Tell me why," said Gao Huan softly. She was the kind of girl who acted calmer the more upset she was.

"I've fallen in love with someone else."

"That's impossible!"

"We're breaking up. I don't love you anymore." Zhao

Hongbing forced back the tears swimming in his eyes and did his best to keep his voice from shaking.

"I don't believe you. What you said just now was just a joke, right?" Gao Huan's voice was trembling.

"No. I don't love you. We shouldn't see each other after you get back."

"You..."

Zhao Hongbing hung up before Gao Huan could finish. He was afraid that if he heard her say anything more, he'd change his mind.

He was heartbroken. That night, he and Little Beijing drank four bottles of liquor. It was the first time that Little Beijing had ever gotten drunk. Zhao Hongbing was taken to the hospital with bleeding in his stomach caused by too much alcohol.

The next time Zhao Hongbing saw Gao Huan was six years later. By then, she was a mother.

After being discharged from the hospital a few days later, Hongbing returned to the restaurant. A letter was waiting there in Gao Huan's elegant handwriting. He put the letter away unopened. He didn't dare to read it.

This was a man who dared to do anything, but he couldn't bear to witness the pain of the woman he loved. He knew that his letter was Gao Huan's broken heart.

CHAPTER 47

A Soldier Disgraced

AFTER ZHAO HONGBING WAS RELEASED, the first thing he heard was that Old Rod Li had gone after Liu Haizhu.

Over the past year, three of Old Rod's top lieutenants – Quint, Tudou and Evil Huang – had been picked off one by one. They'd either been forced into retirement, badly wounded, or killed by Zhao Hongbing and Liu Haizhu and their guys. Old Rod's gang was on the verge of collapse. Old Rod couldn't sit still any longer. He knew that if he didn't make a move, he would lose his place in gangland circles, and his avenues of profit would be cut off.

Old Rod Li had no choice but to stake all the prestige he'd accumulated over more than a decade in a fight to the death with Liu Haizhu. If Old Rod emerged victorious, he would continue to enjoy preeminent fame in the criminal underworld.

Old Rod Li went to find Liu Haizhu at his bicycle repair stand outside the No. 14 High School, where the ever-diligent Liu had returned even before his injuries had fully healed.

"Are you busy, Zhuzi?" Old Rod Li stood with his hands in

his pockets. His eyes were gleaming behind his glasses, but he showed no intention of picking a fight.

"Yeah, what's up?" Liu Haizhu put down his tools and stood.

"We've known each other for more than ten years, and we've had our differences. But regardless, we were once comrades-in-arms in the same cell. That time outside the Purple Moon, you gave me a couple of chops, but did I come after you? I've always respected you as a big man. If it had been anyone else, I'd have ransacked his home ages ago. But it was you who stabbed me, and what's done is done. In all these years, have you heard of anyone stabbing me and getting away with it? Only you." Old Rod Li sounded completely sincere.

But Liu Haizhu knew he hadn't come to talk about the past.

"Say what you've come to say. Stop wasting time."

Old Rod considered this mild rebuke as a serious loss of face.

"In all these years, that fucking temper of yours hasn't changed a bit," he snapped. "Can't you even let a guy finish?"

"All I said is for you to say your piece. Whatever it is you've come for, just get it out!"

"I'm sure you know that Gourdy killed Tudou."

"I know. So what? Do you want to kill me in return?"

"Tudou's mom keeps coming to see me. She only had the one son, and Gourdy killed him. What's she supposed to do? Now Gourdy's run off, who should I come talk to?"

"If Gourdy killed someone, that's for the police to sort out. Why are you talking to me?"

"Oh, cut the crap. Gourdy was your gang brother. Everyone knows it."

"So what the fuck is your point? Get to it and don't waste half my day beating around the bush!"

"My point is that you're doing well in your little business here. You've made a little money, and so have your gang brothers. You should pull together 50,000 for Tudou's mom. We both know how things are done in the street, you even better than me."

"So you've come to stick me for some cash, is that it?" Liu Haizhu's temper was flaring.

"Don't you think that's how this should be handled?"

"And what if I don't want to pay?"

"Then you'll have to pay for Tudou's life with your own!" Old Rod Li continued to speak in an even tone of voice, but it was clear that he was getting angry as well.

"You come here asking for 50,000 *yuan*. How the fuck's a guy supposed to live?" Liu Haizhu felt that he should pay some compensation to Tudou's mother, but there was no way he would meet Old Rod Li's extortionate demand. Liu always responded better to persuasion than to threats.

"It's 50,000 and not a penny less. I'll be at the hospital visiting Evil Huang tomorrow. Bring the money over and say a few words to Evil while you're at it. After all, look at the shape you left him in. When you beat a dog, you'd better mind who his master is!" In other words, while delivering the money, Liu Haizhu would have to apologize to Evil Huang as well.

The mention of Evil had Liu steaming with anger.

"Get the hell out of my sight!"

"Think it over," said Old Rod Li as he turned and walked away.

"Piss off!"

The next morning, Zhao Hongbing went to see Liu Haizhu while Little Beijing kept an eye on the hotel.

"I hear Old Rod Li came to see you, brother Liu."

"Yeah. He came to stick me for some money."

"What did he say?"

"He wants me to deliver the cash to him at the hospital this afternoon."

"What do you plan to do?"

"I have some money in hand, just about enough to start my auto repair business. But why should I give in to Old Rod Li's extortion?" Liu Haizhu had built up considerable savings through his years of hard effort.

"Did he say what would happen if you don't pay?"

"He said I'll pay with my life."

"That's interesting! What's his room number?"

"309."

"Okay, got it."

Zhao Hongbing turned and walked away, surprising Liu Haizhu, who expected him to stick around and accompany him to the hospital.

Hongbing normally spent his nights at the hotel, but that day he went straight home instead. Groping under his bed, he pulled out the bayonet he'd snatched during the battle with Little Tiger at the hospital. He'd kept it hidden away even when they were preparing for the showdown with Old Rod Li's gang by the river. Now he was taking it out. As an army veteran, Zhao Hongbing knew very well that this was one of the most lethal weapons ever made. If he was determined to kill someone, it would do the job. Under the right circumstances, it was even more effective than a handgun.

Zhao Hongbing never carried weapons in a fight, so why

was he taking the bayonet now? Ergou thinks that he had given up on life. Hongbing's greatest flaw was that he kept everything bottled up inside and never talked to anyone. His internal life was very complicated. It seemed that no one really understood him. Hongbing didn't even confide in Little Beijing, especially if it might lead someone else to suffer on his behalf. He had never dared imagine what it would be like to live without Gao Huan, and his frustration required an outlet.

But Ergou thinks that venting was actually a secondary matter. The most important thing was that Zhao Hongbing was a Mohist – a follower of the philosophy of Mozi, as practiced during the Warring States period. In the 1980s, the chivalrous spirit of the outlaws of *The Water Margin* still inspired people like Zhao Hongbing, Little Beijing, Lisi, and Liu Haizhu, who could all be considered modern Mohists. But by the 1990s, the world belonged to gangland big brothers like Zhang Yue and Li Wu, who were bona fide hoodlums.

The essence of Mohism is the defeat of tyranny through violence. Old Rod Li was scum, and would remain an irritant until he was eliminated. One of the basic standpoints of Mohism is to "rid the world of harm".

People like Zhao Hongbing and Liu Haizhu didn't follow the Confucian ideal of "relationships between gentlemen being as flavorless as water"; rather, their brotherhood had the fiery intensity of the 70 degree sorghum liquor produced in the northeast in the 1980s – burning, spicy, but deeply warming. This was Mohism, and the friendships among Mohists.

The motto "Never turn back, no matter how great the suffering" encapsulates the Mohist spirit. People like Zhao Hongbing emphasized righteousness and loyalty over matters of life and death. "Use Mozi to govern a world of chaos; use

Mengzi to rule a flourishing world". Mohism was the essential philosophy of the chaotic local underworld of the 1980s.

Zhao Hongbing knew that Liu Haizhu was in crisis. The flower he'd painstakingly grown with the sweat of his brow was on the verge of being snatched away by Old Rod Li. As Liu's friend, Zhao Hongbing couldn't stand watching from the sidelines. No less, he had contributed to the antagonism between Liu Haizhu and Old Rod Li.

With only two usable fingers on his right hand since being shot by Tudou, Zhao Hongbing concealed the dagger in the left sleeve of the black shirt he was wearing. Northeastern summer days tend to be oppressively hot, but that day some relief came in the form of an all-day drizzle. Zhao Hongbing strolled down the noonday street inhaling the freshness brought by the summer rain. Gazing at the city where he'd been born and raised, every brick and tile familiar to him, his face was expressionless and his pace slow and deliberate as he approached the hospital where his third sister worked.

Perhaps in his heart he could no longer distinguish between his thoughts about Gao Huan and Liu Haizhu.

Hongbing reached the third floor of the hospital at twelve-thirty. It had taken him more than an hour to walk the mile from his home.

They say Old Rod Li had summoned seven or eight of his gang brothers for the showdown with Liu Haizhu. But Old Rod was expecting Liu Haizhu in the afternoon, and Zhao Hongbing arrived at noon. When Hongbing arrived, the only people in the hospital room were Old Rod Li, Evil Huang, and one gang brother. Apparently Old Rod Li was less familiar than Zhao Hongbing with the battle strategy of "attacking before the enemy has fully assembled". Zhao Hongbing knocked at the door of Room 309 with the two remaining fingers of his right hand.

"Who's there?"

No one answered. Evil Huang's gang brother went over and opened the door. The moment it opened, a rust-streaked dagger was at the gangster's throat. The wielder of the knife was a handsome man with a tired, pale and expressionless face. He gripped the knife in his left hand.

"Are you with Old Rod Li?"

"Yes."

"Good."

"Ow!" The gangster cried as Zhao Hongbing stabbed him in the leg.

Old Rod Li responded by lunging with a shiny army dagger in his hand.

"Ow!" He also took a stab to the leg. This was followed by a thumping sound as Evil Huang pulled out his IV tube and leaped from the window.

Realizing that he was no match for his assailant and might well end up dead, Old Rod Li also ran to the window ledge. Zhao Hongbing caught up with him and stabbed him in the thigh from behind. With a rush of pain, Old Rod Li leaped to the ground. By then the other stabbed gangster was on another window ledge trying to muster the courage to jump.

"You don't have to jump. I won't kill you," said Zhao Hongbing, his face still expressionless. Then he turned and left, his hand still gripping the bayonet, which was now dripping with blood. It was later learned that Old Rod Li broke both legs and a wrist, while the eccentric Evil Huang managed his descent without injury.

Half an hour later, sirens were heard as the police arrived

at the scene. They say it was a nurse who called the police. This nurse knew Zhao Hongbing and his sister. In the 1980s, there were too many cases of gangsters going to hospitals for a last hit; they'd become major venues for gang fights. The director of this hospital had ordered nurses to call the police as soon as a gang fight erupted, and to tell them everything they knew, or be subject to discipline. An hour later, the police went to Zhao Hongbing's home and to his hotel, but they didn't find him.

At that moment, Hongbing was sitting on the roof of what was then the city's tallest structure – the fourteen-story municipal guesthouse – mutely watching the police cars passing below. Raising his head, he took a deep breath and look out on the verdant peak of the distant Nanshan Hill and the great river that surged alongside it. Zhao Hongbing no longer had a place in this vast land; soon he would be arrested. Hongbing had once said that he lived for his family and for Gao Huan, and for his love of that hill and river. Now he no longer had Gao Huan, and could no longer enjoy his beloved scenery. In the space of less than a week, he'd lost everything.

CHAPTER 48

Seek Refuge in Buddha and Dispel the Evil from Your Heart

UNLIKE GOURDY, ZHAO HONGBING DIDN'T run for the hills. After leaving the city, he went straight to an old temple about ten miles away. He knew it would take a while for the police to find him there. Before the founding of the New China, this old temple had been heavily frequented, its halls filled with incense. But it had been ravaged during the "Smash the Four Olds" campaign. Although it had undergone repairs after the Cultural Revolution, by the 1980s few Buddhists were left in the city, and the site was now largely deserted. Hongbing went there not to become a monk, but to achieve a measure of tranquility.

Striding into the temple's main hall, he immediately caught sight of the majestic statue of the Buddha. On impulse he bowed before it, kneeling for a while on a cushion made of bulrushes.

"*Namo Amitabha* – I seek refuge in Buddha."

They say Zhao Hongbing recited this sentence with tears streaming down his face. He himself later said that the last time he had cried was when his mother died. From then on, he never shed another tear.

At this moment, thoughts poured through his mind, one scene after another since his discharge from the Army. That winter day, more than two years before, returning home a hero with a medal on his chest. Then, a few months later, in a moment of rashness, losing his job; after that, gaining fame for his fights with Tiger, Little Tiger, and Railway over petty and worthless matters; meeting Gao Huan and eloping with her; fighting Old Rod Li on behalf of his comrade Xiaoji and establishing his position in the gang world… All in the space of just over two years.

Now he was going to be arrested.

Had he always been so irrational and ruthless? The army had trained him to defeat the enemy, but had that turned him into a brawler? Had he betrayed the medal on his chest and the patient teaching of his father? Had he lived up to the ultimate sacrifice that three of his comrades had made at Laoshan, giving their lives for the safety and happiness of their fellow citizens? Of course, Zhao Hongbing had once been just like them. But now the bayonet, still familiar in his hand, was no longer pointed at the enemy on the battlefield. Was this the same Zhao Hongbing who'd been willing to lay down his life on the Laoshan frontline?

"Turn yourself in!" a voice shouted in Zhao Hongbing's heart.

He kowtowed before the Buddha three times and then turned and left the temple. He later said that he resolved to start his life afresh that day.

That night, when Hongbing's third sister reached her residential complex, she saw a familiar form beckoning to her from a dark corner. Tears poured down her face. She understood Hongbing, and she knew that her brother was a brave man who would face reality. Taking flight would only lead him further down the path of crime.

"Hongyan…"

She was sobbing too hard to respond.

"Sister, I'm going to turn myself in."

Still speechless, Hongyan stroked his face.

"Is Dad all right?"

"He's fine. Go home, and he'll take you to the police station," said Hongyan, sobbing as she looked into his eyes.

"I'll go tomorrow night. There's something I still need to do tomorrow."

"Hurry and turn yourself in. What's left for you to do?" Hongyan insisted, managing to control her emotions.

"Gao Huan's on summer break. She should get home tomorrow. I want to see her one last time."

"Go, Hongbing. I asked your brother-in-law, and he says that with your military service and lack of a criminal record, you should get a lighter sentence. Besides, Old Rod Li is hardly an upstanding citizen."

"Even if I get a heavy sentence, I have to turn myself in. I have to bear the consequences of what I did. Sister, promise me something."

"What?"

"If Gao Huan comes and asks you, tell her I don't love her any more. And tell Shen and Dawei to tell her the same if she asks."

"Are you breaking up with her?"

"Should I ask her to wait for me to get out of prison? Ask a college graduate to marry a criminal?"

"You're a good boy, not a criminal," said Hongyan tearfully as she stroked Hongbing's face.

"Promise me, Sister. I have to go." He turned and disappearing into the darkness.

Hongyan stood there motionless for a long time, finding it impossible to accept that her brother was about to go to jail. Just three years ago, he'd been her pride and joy – the pride and joy of their whole family.

Early the next morning, Zhao Hongbing appeared under a tree about thirty yards from Gao Huan's home, wearing a straw hat that concealed his face. He just wanted to see her one last time. He expected her to be on the train that arrived from Beijing early that morning.

Finally, he saw her in the distance. The usually high-spirited young woman looked wan and thin as she disembarked from the No. 7 bus and trudged home with her backpack on her shoulders. While delicate, she had always walked with her head held high. Now, though, she looked at the ground and kicked a pebble along, apparently lost in thought. Her name spun through Zhao Hongbing's throat countless times but never reached his lips. He thought, "If I call out just once, it could destroy her prospects of a happy life." He hoped Gao Huan would forget him and even hate him; only then could she be happy. Eventually, she knocked on the door of her home and went in, leaving Zhao Hongbing alone in the street. He later said that he would never forget the sight of her back, and that he recalled it countless times over the next five years.

After that, he went home. His whole family was waiting for him – his father, elder brother, and third sister had been up all night waiting for him. As soon as he walked through the door, his brother went over and cuffed him in the ear, smacking him seven or eight times until Hongyan pulled him away.

"I'm sorry, Brother," said Zhao Hongbing softly.

Hongbing's brother wept. His tears mingled with the stubble on his face.

"Hongbing, come with me." The elder Mr. Zhao, who had been sitting quietly in a chair, finally spoke. His voice was hoarse.

Dry-eyed, Zhao Hongbing went with his father and brother to the Public Security Bureau. He discovered that his father had become a limping old man. Hongbing had always thought of his father as a tough, resilient fellow in the prime of life, but that day, he saw this was no longer true.

Zhao Hongbing later recalled that on the way to the police station that day, he heard a radio broadcasting the song "The Clouds of My Old Home":

Clouds on the horizon of my hometown
Constantly beckon to me;
A breeze blows gently
As a voice calls my name:
Come home, come home,
You wandering soul;
Come home, come home,
Drift no more.
My footsteps are heavy,
The road is so long.
The breeze blows gently
With the fragrance of my hometown's soil.
Come home, come home,

You wandering soul;
Come home, come home.
I'm weary of drifting,
Too tired to go on,
My eyes are full of tears.
That breeze, those clouds of my hometown
Erase my scars.
I went out to take on the world,
But return with my knapsack empty.
That breeze, those clouds of my hometown
Are balm to my wounds.

Years later, after a few drinks Zhao Hongbing often alluded to that song. He said that at the time, he was thinking of the wind and looking at the clouds of his hometown, and when he heard the words, "Come home, come home," it made him even more determined to return to "the side of the Party and the people". Everyone reached the same conclusion: Hongbing didn't think like other people, and that's why he became a gangland Big Brother.

The next year, Zhao Hongbing was sentenced to four years and six months in prison. Ergou recalls that after he went to prison, the elder Mr. Zhao went to visit him once and brought him a book, the *Classic of the Way and Virtue.* Perhaps Mr. Zhao hoped that this book might help Hongbing overcome his impetuousness. They say father and son sat together for fifteen minutes and only exchanged two sentences the whole time.

"Hongbing, you need to rely on yourself."

Mr. Zhao had been diagnosed with lung cancer, but Hongbing didn't know it.

"Dad, when you go back, ask Ergou to loosen up the strings on my guitar so it doesn't warp."

Zhao Hongbing was trying to create a relaxed atmosphere. Mr. Zhao smiled without replying. He understood the meaning behind his son's words. He understood that Hongbing was telling him, "Dad, when I come out, I'll be a good man. I love life, and I want a good life."

Zhao Hongbing benefited from *The Classic of the Way and Virtue* for the rest of his life; it helped him weather every storm he encountered in the gangland world from then on. The legendary sssgeneral Guan Yu had his volume of the *Spring and Autumn Annals*, and Zhao Hongbing had his *Classic of the Way.*

On the opening day of the Asian Games in Beijing in 1990, the elder Mr. Zhao passed away. He had a grand funeral, but Zhao Hongbing wasn't there. Word went around that he was to blame for his father's death.

At this point, the era of the old-style underworld came to an end. You could say this was a glorious period, or that it was a blood-soaked age, but in any case you'd be compelled to admit that it was worth remembering.

Too many of the good things from those times no longer exist.

Few people remember those doyens of 1988 – Zhao Hongbing, Little Beijing, Liu Haizhu, Lisi, Gourdy, Evil Huang, Old Rod Li, Chen Wei Dong, Zhao Shanhe, and Tiger.

They are long forgotten. Ergou has written this book in memory of a world that has faded from public memory – a very different world of twenty years ago.

Printed in Dunstable, United Kingdom

77222695R00255